TACTILE THERAPY

Volume 1

DURELL ARRINGTON

Thank you, Brent! I hope you enjoy thoroughly!

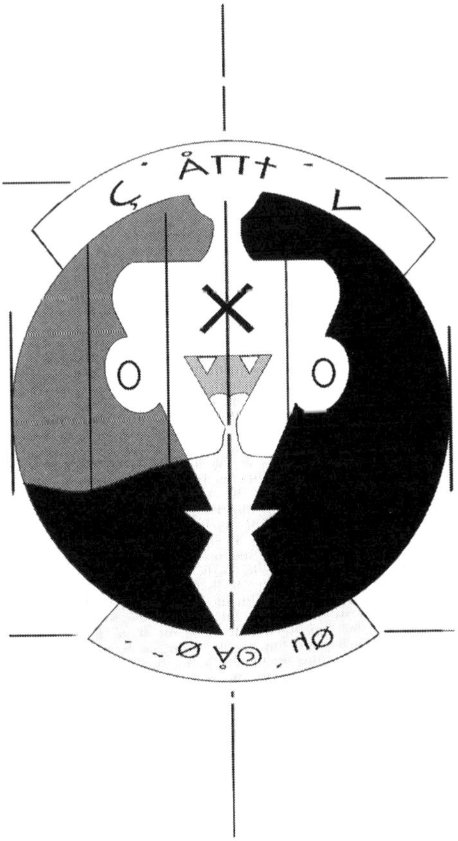

Cover art by eBook Launch.

My thanks extend far and wide to the constructs that exist, both living and inanimate, that disallows me from ever growing up. Whatever force there is that is responsible for why we are all unique, I am thankful that it continues to allow us to be. To my mother, whose voice I've long since forgotten but pretend I haven't. To my siblings whose traits and zest I continue to borrow without permission, I thank you. And finally, to science—I thank you, eternally. For the infinite, and the infinitesimal.

CONTENTS

PROLOGUE

"Congratulations! It's a girl!"

Her last push was the strongest one yet, and after six grueling hours of intense labor, she finally gets to cradle her beautiful daughter in her very own arms for the first time—the last remaining person of the Atespa name.

"What will you name her?"

"Eta," she answers after careful consideration. "He would've liked Eta."

"It's perfect."

"It is ... and so is she," she can't help but to dolefully admit, even as she remains wholly consumed by this new unbounded joy she's experiencing for the first time.

This is the most Eta's mother can manage to utter as she finally submits to the overbearing might of emotion she's been trying to fight for the past six hours. This same fight that she thought would've, at the very least, eradicated the tears that she has been shedding for the past hour. A natural conclusion considering all of the energy and hydration robbed from her during the strenuous delivery. This was the same fight that she would now continue to seek strength from to carry on, regardless of all the countless obstacles she's come to face up until now, and over the past nine months.

Irrespective of her commendable fortitude to keep it together under the given circumstances, crystal droplets continue to coagulate within the concave wells in her eyes as she cradles her daughter. Perhaps, it is the sound of the incessant wailing from her newborn that lends to this struggle, considering that she too, also, continues to cry even while in the comfort of her mother's arms.

It seems as if both this mother and child are destined to trade their bodily fluids, even after the birth, for all eternity. Only this time, the medium in which they exchange them is not some internal biological appendage, but within the air around them. It continues to allow both of their respective tears to meet, greet, shimmer, fuse and even dance under.

It isn't long, however, that baby Eta begins to acclimate to her mother's placid atmosphere. Understandably so, considering that the soft humming, cradling, and rocking now emanating from her mother is much too serene for even this child to resist.

"I'll leave you two to be, and I'll be back in a little while," her best friend tells her before leaving the room.

"Thank you ... for everything," the brand-new mother responds to the one who made it possible for her to finally meet Eta—her *new* best friend.

It doesn't take long after her arrival and subsequent adaptation to her new environment, for baby Eta to finally open her eyes to stare at her alluring progenitor. It is here where her mother sees for the first time the beautiful, brilliant colors that makes up the spectrum of visible light, better than any rainbow she's ever come across, present within her daughter's very own eyes. Even the roundness of her irises appears as perfect to her as discovering the last digit to the ratio of a circle's circumference to its diameter. And yet, all this overwhelming cascade of emotion she's currently experiencing from holding her new best friend for the first time, takes a back seat to the astonishing synchronization that these two shared before it was lost for an instant so they can officially meet. And now that it's returned, it has restored these two temporarily separated organisms back into one single perfect entity.

Not even the heat from the lights in the room, those of which slowly grow unsustainable for a mother and child to continue to thrive under, is enough for these two to take their eyes from off one another. How pleasant is it then, that it is each other that these two see, as the last thing they'll ever see again?

It is strongly believed that had this inseparable unit been given the choice, they would've still opted for this ineluctable karma—this time and every time. For if it were at all different in any way, then so would Eta's sunrise and her mother's sunset.

Chapter One

THE CHESHIRE

April 13th. 2:19 A.M. (PDT)

BEATTY, Nevada. An intriguing but common argument is currently taking place between a disgruntled employee and an unsatisfied customer.

A man and a woman shout at each other as they continue to engage in an argument in the parking lot of a motel. Even without hearing the content of their heated exchange, it isn't beyond any patron to naturally assume that the woman is apoplectic over the lack of payment for the service(s) she delivered to this client. Her off-seasonal short skirt, corresponding high-heels, and cheap, out-of-place, fur coat, are the elements that help profile the type of women that are known for visiting this motel around this time of day. People who are either awakened, entertained, or concerned by the commotion happening outside, begin to open their curtains and crack their motel doors to get a peek at some of the action unfolding on the other side of their rooms.

Even on the eastern side of the second floor of this two-story establishment, every single occupant either opens their door or gaze through their windows to watch the feud unfold between the couple—all except for room twelve. The occupant inside of room twelve is currently preoccupied with some activity of his own.

Inside room twelve, a single man lies in a twin-sized bed with his eyes closed and his shirt removed. An involuntary smirk compliments the face of this overtly attractive gentleman. He rhythmically sways his head side to side ever so gently, while his foot automatically taps in sync. Every now and again, a few strands of his long, dark-brown hair lands on his face; a nuisance that at any other time would warrant his attention. However, at this very moment, there is little in the world that can bother a man who has just finished exploiting an unfortunate accident, several towns over from where he is currently located, involving the collision of a Greyhound bus and an unsuspecting armored car on a highway off-ramp.

It isn't a hundred percent clear whether or not this man, simply known as Surii, would go out of his way to witness the public discord unfolding outside of his window, had he not just scored a small fortune. What is clear however, is that at the moment, he's currently unaware of anything unfolding anywhere around him at all. This is simply because he has his 2007-generation iPod cranked up to a decibel level that rivals that of an outdoor rock concert, and he is blasting John Lennon's unfitting but nonetheless popular, "War is Over." Back in 2007, no consumer-electronics company had created a device that can output a volume of that caliber, but nowadays, all it takes is a quick software download and some very specific headphones to get the job done.

Suddenly, an almost imperceptible wind gently shakes the entire establishment. With only three of his five main senses currently available for use, Surii's body can't help but to feel the wave of a soft vibration permeate first through the air around him, then along the bed frame and mattress he rests upon, and finally on his own skin. To the average man under the same circumstance, feeling the soft vibration of a large explosion from about a town over wouldn't be possible, especially if he's in the same euphoric state Surii is currently in while his favorite song blasts inside of his eardrums. However, Surii is just about *everything* in the world except average.

The gentle boom that courses through every single room at the Lily Inn Motel, and every other motel in a mile-wide radius for that matter, is only picked up on by Surii and perhaps any seismographs that may be nearby. The time it takes for Surii to show some sort of response to this seemingly random occurrence is somehow directly proportional to the imminent threat level that that occurrence readily proposes to him. In other words, worst things have happened to him, which is why he barely budges. Nevertheless, he finally opens his eyes, grabs his iPod from off his bare chest, and lowers his music to assess the disturbance in the air. A furtive silence hovers around him, as if some unknown entity surreptitiously stole the sounds of the world. There is no faint hum emanating from the bathroom light, no slight creaking coming from the wooden ceiling, and even the pesky squabbling coming from the pair outside seems to have vanished. Maybe it's all in his imagination. Impossible.

"SHIT!"

In the moment it takes for a person to blink, Surii has already sprung up and reached for the left edge of his mattress. Quickly, he firmly grips the lining of the bed and yanks the entire mattress over his entire body, encasing himself inside of its protective haven like a turtle retracting into its shell from a threat. He bends the mattress in a way that even the mattress didn't know was possible, and braces himself.

A full second later, an explosion with the force like that fired from a tank cannon, hits room twelve and sends Surii and his mattress flying across the room. Anticipating the blast, Surii uses his makeshift shield of cotton and fabric to absorb the brunt of the blast, which surprisingly does a great job at doing so. This does not however, prevent Surii from flying through the air, speeding towards the wall opposite from where he once comfortably rested. With him and his mattress in tow approaching the wall at a rapid one-hundred and fifty feet per second, he boasts his elegant, acrobatic dexterity by using the momentum from the blast to turn himself around in mid-air, so that it's the mattress that slams into the wall in front of him, and not his face. His efforts are successful, and the bottom side of the mattress smacks into the opposite wall, cushioning his collision, and saving him from needing hours of facial reconstructive surgery.

A second still hasn't passed since the explosion sprung him across the room, and still within that tiny frame of time, all the contents of everything that wasn't nailed to the floor go flying together, including the bed frame. This frame, which was once synonymous with themes of stability and support, is now replaced with peril and death. It, too, also comes flying across the room, heading directly at an off-balanced Surii. Without even making eye contact with it, Surii delivers a powerful, frontal kick directly at the spine of the bed frame that was about to smash into him. It splits into two mangled, pieces of wood and ricochets violently off of the wall behind him. Metal springs, shards of glass, and pieces of wood and debris of all kinds, crash and shatter all around him then rain down onto the floor all in a single instant.

Of everything that had just occurred in the past three seconds or so, perhaps the most remarkable of it all was the undeniable fact that his iPod headphones never once fell out of his ears. Surii's right leg remains extended in front of him for a while, as he takes a couple of moments to collect himself and process the damage.

Every single piece of furniture that complimented the room is now spread across the floor asunder. Even the serendipitous bag of hundred dollar bills that Surii was fortunate enough to stumble upon, is no longer stacked neatly in their distributive, compact formation. In fact, a great deal of the money is scattered across the room, with many large stacks of bills burnt or torn beyond use. The mirror and ceiling fan are now pieces of their former selves. They lay together in a way that many may rightfully mistaken for modern art. One of his boots are in the bathroom, while the other lays up against a wall. Even his tough leather/denim combo-jacket that he's come to appreciate many a cold, lonely nights on the road, now only boasts half a sleeve on one side and three-fourths a sleeve on the other.

Of all that was destroyed in this blast, only three things remain unscathed: A three-pack of Hanes V-neck, white T-shirts, his apparent blast-resistant iPod, and some sort of metallic, cylindrical apparatus that looks like something a boat will need in order for its engine to properly function. Of those things, his attention is focused on this cylinder, which happened to conveniently land an arm's length away from him on the edge of his nigh-unrecognizable mattress.

With his right leg still extended like some sort of overzealous yoga practitioner, every part of Surii remains motionless, with the exception of his eyes. He now stares at the unidentified, cylindrical, resting object with a look that makes it seem like if the object had eyes it would look back at him with the same endearing gaze of two brothers who just survived a month long zombie incursion. Surii finally breaks his physical silence by grabbing the object, getting up, and walking towards the motel room door. With him and his trusty Unidentified Resting Object, or U.R.O., in hand, he finally exits the room to face whatever it was that nearly destroyed his iPod.

Surii exits from the room that now looks like the destroyed exit ramp from the armored car he exploited not too long ago, and steps outside onto the veranda of the motel to finally witness the calamity that disturbed his nap. After a much-needed yawn and stretch, he casually rubs his eyes to clarify the madness that is unfolding below him, around him, and perhaps most interestingly, above him.

The area in the parking lot where the odd couple from earlier were fighting, is now a thirty-three-foot-wide crater. The most refined team of crime scene investigators would have trouble figuring out if any testimony they received from nearby witnesses—that a man and a woman once stood where this crater now is—is true, because not a shred of either of them remains anywhere in sight. Whatever caused this crater would've absolutely obliterated anything composed of bones, muscle, and flesh in an instant.

The sight of this crater is intriguing enough to force Surii to take his pink headphones out of his ears. While he does so, he continues to look around the establishment only to witness an assortment of bodies doing an assortment of things all around him: some are screaming, some are running, some are crying, some are hugging, and some are just dangling. The few rooms to the left of him all have windows and doors blown out just like his. Unlike his however, it's safe to assume none of those other rooms have a single survivor inside of them.

After assessing the bedlam presented in front of him, he finally turns his gaze upward to the sky above him and watches the beauty of countless streaks of fire slice through the night sky, as hellfire rains down all around him for as far as the eye can see. A battalion of meteoric, orange balls of flames that shoot down all around him, annihilates anything unfortunate enough to be in their landing zones. If a grain of sand falling at eleven miles a second contains enough power to leave a foot-wide hole in anything that isn't at least as dense as steel, then the rock that left that crater in the parking lot that totaled every single vehicle in the surrounding area had to be only about the size of a basketball.

As Surii processes this information, another meteor decides to make a beeline towards the motel; only this one is the size of a house.

As the humongous rock closes in to finish off what's left of this once auspicious motel, a nearby survivor—a father—who is tightly hugging his daughter for what could be his last time, also notices the giant boulder that now lights up the night sky. Surii looks at the man and the brave, bruised, and bloodied father stares back with a look of acceptance in his eyes. The man nods at Surii before covering his daughter entirely with his body, tucking both of their heads down. As Surii watches him do this, he squints and nods back at the man and takes one final look at the huge, encroaching brimstone.

With only seconds remaining before the rock smacks into them, Surii spreads his legs, plants his feet, squats, and contorts his torso and arms over his waist in some deliberate but unfamiliar pose. Once he attains his desired position, he LAUNCHES himself into the air like a shot from a cannon, and speeds directly towards the center of the meteor. He shoots up at inhuman speeds and reaches a height of around two hundred and fifty feet from where he stood in less than a second.

Once he reaches this altitude, he begins to flip around and around, faster and faster, and then he takes his U.R.O. and throws it with unbelievable strength and accuracy another three thousand feet higher towards the heart of the meteor. The apparatus travels upward of speeds that will make any major league pitcher's fastball seem like a toddler tossing his first Whiffle Ball to his dad.

The device spins violently onward and onward towards the rock, until it finally meets up with the killer meteor. Before it makes contact, two small nozzles rise up out of the head of the cylinder for some unknown reason. The apparatus continues to spin with twice the RPM as the tires on professional drag cars screaming down a raceway, and before it reaches within ten feet of the rock, the rock itself begins to split entirely down its center. The hyper-spinning apparatus passes through the solid metals, ore, and rock effortlessly, like a laser-edged scythe slicing through a giant jellyfish. Once it fully cuts through the meteor, it arcs around at a speed twenty times faster than a rifle bullet, and boomerangs back towards the now right-half side of the split rock. The U.R.O. continues its blinding evisceration and follows up with a horizontal passage that completely slices through both halves of the rock, subsequently turning the house-sized meteor into four individual car-sized boulders.

After basically doing to the enclosing meteor what a master chef does to a raw steak with a boning knife, Surii finally lands back on the ground below, right next to the distraught man from earlier. The man looks at him in disbelief, then looks up at the now four quarter-sized rocks that are about to land in four different areas around the motel.

"You might want to get down," Surii calmly commands as he places his body on top of him, while the man continues to protects his daughter with his own.

Four gigantic booms erupt in rapid succession around the trio, causing a shockwave that sends glass, metal, and wood flying in every direction. Luckily, the outer walls of the Lily Inn Motel prove sufficient in protecting these three from meeting an early demise; even if it will never serve to house a guest ever again.

Chapter Two

JOELLE GRACE

April 14th. 10:03 A.M. (CDT)

AN UNKNOWN CREATURE, who narrowly escaped the hellish gunfire laid upon it from a platoon of soldiers several hours ago, has finally stumbled across something that closely resembles something it's a little familiar with: a house.

After walking for several miles, this creature has crossed through acre after acre of every type of terrain—stepping on, shuffling by, and just downright pushing through droves of vegetation and crops that it has never seen before in its life.

As if doing such a task wasn't arduous enough, it doesn't help that the creature is also completely nude. Unbeknownst to it, its appearance has yet shifted again from when the soldiers first laid eyes on it, causing the creature to now resemble a woman more so than it ever has before. Resemble and only resemble, because though it now stands at the height, weight and frame of the average human female—its voluptuous curves now more apparent than ever—the foreign creature still lacks a few of a woman's more highly desirable features. Besides being completely hairless from head to toe, it also lacks a set of nipples and no apparent reproductive genitalia. In addition, distinct, solid black lines resembling detailed tattooed symbols, have appeared. They are akin to the type those from an ancient civilization who isolated themselves from the rest of society would have proudly worn, and are vastly present along every curve and arc on its body from head to toe.

The naked creature approaches the warm-looking, but obviously weathered, house with caution. Though it doesn't yet realize that walking around naked isn't exactly common around these parts, it does its best to stay out of sight, because apparently people on this planet like to shoot first and ask questions never. Also, the blue sky that it sees for the first time ever, illuminates the new world. Chances are that those soldiers, who needed flashlights to see the creature a few hours ago, must also be able to see better in this new starlight. This is a disconcerting thought that makes the creature feel uneasy. The creature finally reaches the side entrance of the house and before entering, does a little surveying of the area first to make sure no one sees it go inside.

The house it enters is starkly different on the inside than on the out. For one, inside of the kitchen, a bit dishes are all very neatly stacked on the counter near the sink. It appears as if someone had washed them but had to leave in a hurry before they could be put away. When the creature notices this, it suddenly freezes for a moment. With very little warning, an entire storm of information about basic human living conditions comes flashing into the creature's head all at once. The creature feels as if it's about to collapse, so it leans on the nearest counter top and shuts its eyes tightly due to the influx of data erupting inside of its skull. It tries its best to stay conscious while it does what it can to interpret what it is currently seeing inside of its head. The creature opens its eyes and looks at the set of dishes once again, and now it somehow knows that a group of people reside inside of this ... home. The group of people, a family.

The creature takes a moment to gather itself, and while doing so, takes a few extra seconds to this time, *carefully* inspect more of its surroundings, lest it wishes to experience another seizure. When it agrees that all is well, the creature starts walking again and proceeds towards the living room.

Thanks to that recent seizure, the creature is now somehow realizing that it is amongst a species where it isn't proper decorum to barge into the home of someone you don't know personally, especially while naked. The creature doesn't really know how it knows this, and it doesn't really know the subtle details of it, either. All it knows is that there may be a group of individuals somewhere inside of this home at the same time it's in here, so it may be in its best interest to leave before things get worst like it did last night. However, the creature is compelled to stay.

As painful as the mini-seizure it just suffered, the knowledge it gained from it was incomparably satisfying. It now has the creature desperately yearning to see what else it can learn about the environment around it. So, it continues on, looking and scanning, focusing on every single object it can, in an effort to trigger another epileptic episode.

A complete thorough scanning of the living room yields no results for the creature, so it makes its way to the staircase to the right, where an access point fraught with a wealth of information exists solely for its consumption. Apropos, it heads for the staircase and starts to walk upstairs.

The first thing it sees at the top of the second level, is the bathroom located directly in front of it, followed by two bedrooms, one to the right and one to the left. Like a squirrel inspecting an auspicious location it has never visited, the creature pokes its head in and out of the bathroom a couple of times before fully stepping inside. It stares at the toilet with a look not of confusion or curiosity, but more appreciation. It slowly approaches it, and like any human being in the history of human beings who have ever walked past a mirror, the creature immediately stops in its tracks to get its first look at the very thing that forced those soldiers last night to try with all their might to efface. Because it's in a sense seeing itself for the first time, the creature stares at the person in the mirror with conflicting expression, like a mother who's forced to confront her daughter after years of neglect and vile mistreatment. The creature acknowledges what it sees, but whether it accepts it or not cannot be determined at this point.

It proceeds to look over the innumerable, almost glyphic, cryptic, black markings etched across its body and head, and specifically focuses on the two lines that run from directly under its right eye down towards its jawline and neck. It gingerly runs its fingers across them. They feel as natural and smooth as its own skin does, with no noticeable or discernible groove between the two. Suddenly, the creature takes the hand it used to touch the black markings and reaches out towards the reflection and touches the area on the mirror where the markings on its face also appear. The creature holds its hand there and for a while nothing happens. Then after a couple of minutes, it brings its hand back, and begins to touch itself all over, as if running a diagnostic on its body to make sure everything is where it should be. The creature does this for a few minutes longer, taking its time inspecting each of its assets, before finally turning and exiting the bathroom, never once inspecting the toilet that originally drew it inside.

With two bedrooms left at its disposal practically begging for the creature to insert itself into, the creature decides to make a right first and head to the bedroom at the end. This time it doesn't peek in first before entering, in fact, it doesn't enter at all. That's because the creature is currently frozen as it stands in the doorway outside of the bedroom—and so is the old man who stares at it from his bed—granting the creature its first glimpse of an unarmed, seemingly non-threatening, human being.

They both stare at each other for a while, both still frozen. The old man for a myriad of reasons, the most important being that he doesn't want to wake up his wife, whose soft snoring is loud enough to be heard by the creature. The creature, because it just finished having another rush of memories flash through its head upon seeing the elderly couple in bed. This seizure, thankfully, not as severe as the last one.

The old man continues to stare at the unfamiliar being for quite some time—the only difference is that now thanks to the seizure, the creature knows, or at the very least, it can understand why. Though it is now aware of what the sight of the naked female body does to an older gentleman, both mentally and physically, it still doesn't attempt to move away. In fact, the creature stands there longer than it would've before it realized what gifts it's currently sharing with the man. For the first time since it woke up in some ditch somewhere, the creature is relaxed, not exactly comfortable yet, but relaxed, and more importantly, understanding. Slowly now, the creature starts to turn away and walks out of the doorway, the old man's glare following it the entire way. Neither one of them attempts to utter a single word about what just occurred, and chances are neither one of them will probably ever do so for as long as they live.

The rapidly acclimating foreigner now makes its way to the other side of the hallway, this time to the other bedroom. The door is slightly opened, but something about the look of it tells the creature that there's no one inside. It walks into what appears to be the room of a young woman that used to live here. It isn't a hundred percent sure of this, but the creature's instincts tell it that whoever occupied this room has been gone for quite a long time.

It steps fully inside and takes a good look at the setting of the cozy room. A bed that looks like someone hasn't slept on in months remains perfectly made and still near the east window of the room. As it continues to look around, the creature notices something unique about the previous dweller of this space. It discovers two more things it's never before seen in its life; one of them being a photograph. A young woman with skin much like the creature's, stands on the left side of the old man and lady currently resting in the other bedroom. The dark-haired girl in the photograph boasts a haircut that resembles a bob with bangs, except one side of the bob is much longer than the other—the left side. The curious creature picks up the photograph to get a better look at it. It can tell that similar pictures like this were taken in the past with these three people, the only difference is that the girl was much smaller in those previous photos. It isn't sure if this is factual or not, but the creature's instincts or memories, maybe, compels it to believe this to be the case.

The creature continues to stare at the photo for a little while longer, almost as if its decrypting some sort of hidden code that only it can see. It then puts down the picture, takes a full step back, and begins to vehemently whip its head back and forth. When the creature does this, copious amount of hair of the same exact variant as the woman in the photograph, begins to rapidly grow out of its bald scalp. After a few more seconds of shaking its head, the creature's hair color, texture, style and length, exactly matches the same style that the girl in the photograph has; its dark hair resembles a bob with bangs, except one side of the bob is much longer than the other—the right side. In addition, the black markings on the creature's face and presumably all over its body, have completely disappeared. Curious about the new hair that has grown, the creature slowly raises its hand to touch its head, the result causing the creature to experience its first smile as an Earthling.

The creature is now all jittery and excited to try more and learn more things, so it starts looking around the room again, and notices two wooden doors covering a space. The creature walks up to them and pulls the doors open, and reveals a closet full of clothes all hanging next to each other in pristine condition and order. The creature begins to sift through the clothing until it finds something very close to what the girl in the photograph is wearing, which was a dark-gray, hooded sweatshirt with the letters OPIA emblazoned across the front of it. Instead, it finds a light-gray, non-hooded sweatshirt, with sectional-sleeves that can be adjusted at various points in length via drawstrings that are designed to alter the style of the shirt at will. The creature lays the sweatshirt on the bed, front facing up, and looks back at the picture.

After sifting through the clothes in the closest for the second time, it pulls out a stretchy, all-black leotard that extends all the way down to its toes, and inspects it with a hint of the same reverence that all women have for the clothes they're about to put on. While the creature holds the leotard by the hanger, it puts the neck of the linen to its own neck and lets the rest of it fall along the shape of its body. Once it agrees that it'll appropriately fit, the creature removes the garment from its hanger and puts it on. Naturally, the garment fits like a glove and after looking over itself a couple of times, the creature seems to be fairly satisfied with its new look.

It then puts the sweater on, before bending down to open a box on the floor that has the letters VANS plastered across on it. The creature takes the string-less shoes out and slips them on. When it goes to take a step, it realizes there's a little bit of room inside of the shoe from where the top of its toes are, which tells it that the previous owner had larger feet than its own. Maybe here, clothes must be custom-made to fit each person differently. The creature inspects the picture for one last check and sees it's missing a pair of shorts that apparently goes over and around its thighs. It remembers not seeing anything resembling shorts in the closet. It opens the bureau where the framed picture sits, and pulls out a pair of light-blue, denim jeans with all sorts of holes all over them. The creature mistakes the stylish, destroyed jeans for completely damaged, unusable pants, and begins rigorously tearing the legs of the jeans off, leaving a shorter-than-desired pair of torn, denim-shorts. Though not a hundred percent satisfied with its tailoring job, the creature puts the shorts on anyway and smiles at the final result.

Feeling complete, the creature closes the drawer and restores the room back to the original state it was in before it entered. It then opens the door and exits out. The creature enters the hallway and finds itself unable to remove the smile that was generated from the experience. In addition, it also finds itself unable to move thanks to the soft-snoring woman from earlier who's now standing in front of her, obstructing her path. The elderly woman is using what looks like half of her strength to point a rather anachronistic version of the same thing those soldiers were all pointing at the creature, just before the sun was visible, directly at it.

It isn't long before the shabby shotgun drops out of the woman's hand and collides hard against the aged-wooden floor. Her free hand now able to cover up her own gaping mouth, covering it in disbelief, as she does what she can to make sense of what she's currently staring at.

"J-Joelle Grace?" the old woman whimpers when she looks into the eyes of the creature.

Tears begin to well up in the elderly woman's eyes right after she calls out that name. Though the creature hears her clearly, it does nothing in response—and neither does the old man. Silently, they all continue to stare at one another and a tear eventually finds its way out of the old woman's eye. As if he heard the molecules themselves accumulating inside of her tear ducts, the old man shuffles his way from the background to come console his flustered wife. When he arrives, she rests her head on her husband's accommodating chest, taking her eyes off Joelle. She begins to silently weep, and her husband comforts her almost as if he's rehearsed this a million times before. They both look down, and slowly shuffle their way back to their bedroom and close their door, leaving Joelle alone once more. The creature, now unobstructed, proceeds down the staircase and this time perhaps for a different reason, stares at the dishes on the counter before walking out of the home.

Chapter Three

WHO'S WORLD IS THIS?

April 14th. 11:52 A.M. (EDT)

"LADIES AND GENTLEMEN, the President of the United States."

The White House Press Secretary announces the leader of the Free World to the stage to a room full of rabid reporters. President Allen O. Lamarch promptly walks in after he's introduced and stands at the awaiting podium. Upon his emergence, the large room, which just a second ago was emitting a noise level that can compete with a college football stadium, has now been rendered completely quiet. It is as if every single reporter and photographer have suddenly been robbed of their ability to speak. Before he speaks, he lets the room know that he acknowledges them, by sweeping his eyes over the crowd filled with media representatives and photographers from various outlets. This entire transaction is eerily reminiscent of something one may see from some advanced other-worldly being mentally subduing a less-advanced race in some science-fiction movie.

"Approximately around 3:30 A.M. early on Friday morning, the asteroid known as Apophis entered into Earth's atmosphere," he paused as the room buzzed and the Press Secretary attempted to calm the reporters. "Despite a joint-mission collaborative effort between the United States and Russia to safely redirect Apophis away from Earth, the overwhelming gravitational pull of our planet and our moon caused

Apophis to continue its path towards us." More reporters started to clamor over each other. The President cleared his throat. "As a last-minute resort, we decided to launch one of our advanced nuclear anti-satellites towards the asteroid to prevent it from colliding directly with our planet. It brings me great joy to announce that the attack on Apophis was a success and—"

Before he can finish his statement to the country, the audience inside of the Press Briefing Room where he is currently delivering his speech, erupts in applause.

"—the asteroid has been completely destroyed," he concludes over the loud clapping, the last words of that sentence causing the thunderous applause to triple in intensity.

"I know many of you have questions, so I will now—" he continues as he attempts another statement that is cut off shortly from the amount of hands that go up and shouts of *Mr. President!* that follow.

"Yes," the President says, as he points at one of the many reporters in the room with their hand up.

"There's been multiple reports of meteors crash landing in many areas all over the country. Some of these meteors reportedly causing irreparable damage wherever they happen to land. Are these meteors anything to be concerned about?" the reporter asks.

"There are, and will continue to be many after effects from an event of this magnitude. Much like an earthquake that just hit a city, the destruction of such a large threat is bound to have some relatively minor aftershocks. Because this particular earthquake happened to have occurred in our sky and not way down below in the ground, we are bound to see some minimum after effects from the shock wave that occurred when we blew it up."

"Mr. President, Mr. President!!"

Hands again, fly up all over the room and the President points to another reporter.

"Can you comment on Russia's recent war declaration?" the second reporter asks.

"As we speak, our Secretary of State, Patricia Cooke, is already en route to Moscow to discuss our current crisis with our joint ally. Next question," the president says as he again scans the sea of reporters and photographers. "Yes, Debra?"

"Is it true that Russia made this declaration as a direct response to the missile you launched that killed two Russian astronauts aboard the International Space Station?"

The room grows silent and the President stares at Debra for a while, puzzled at the fact that she knows such a thing. He clears his throat before he answers her.

"The fate of those aboard the I.S.S hasn't been confirmed yet. We can neither confirm nor deny any rumors regarding anyone on board at the time. Secretary Cooke is flying there now to try to learn all she can about the I.S.S. and the brave astronauts on board at the time of the event," he replies.

President Lamarch almost doesn't make it through his response, as all he can think of while he does so, is wonder who in the hell told her about the Russian astronauts. Nevertheless, he somehow manages to point at another reporter, signaling another question.

"You said you launched a nuclear missile at the asteroid. Isn't the radiation from such an explosion something that can compromise the ozone layer?"

"The *anti-satellite* weapon we launched at Apophis was launched early enough to connect with and destroy the asteroid before it reached anywhere near Earth or its atmosphere. Thanks to the swift and expeditious actions from my team and I, any and all damage that occurred anywhere was only to the asteroid. You can continue to work on your tan this summer without worry," he chuckled.

"Mr. President, Mr. President!" another reporter shouts and is subsequently pointed at.

"Yes, Bill?"

"If that's true, then that means the debris from the asteroid exploding would've spread out before reaching our planet. Does that mean there are meteors coming down all over the planet and not just here in the U.S.?"

"Good question. The anti-satellite weapon that was launched earlier this morning is unlike any we've ever developed; the asteroid was only hit with one part of a dual-rocket system. When the first part of it hit Apophis, it neutralized the main threat Apophis posed by turning the large asteroid into a series of smaller, manageable rocks. The second part destroyed those smaller rocks and took care of any residual debris thereafter. This is why you haven't heard any reports from anywhere else in the world about there being any meteor sightings or collisions. Because our nation possesses the most diverse catalog to countering any threat in the entire world, we took special care and made it our sole responsibility to make certain that not just here in our borders, but that humankind everywhere was protected from this potential catastrophic event. America is the strongest nation on Earth, and because of that, we must often be the sword that destroys whatever threat comes our way, whether domestic or foreign. More importantly, we must act as the shield, and take a hit, no matter how big or small, in order to make certain that the rest of the planet and our species is completely safe from harm."

"Mr. President, Mr. President!"

He held up his hand. "That's all the questions I can take for now, thank you all very much. God bless the world, and the United States."

The president walks from the stage as quickly as he entered it. He ignores the storm of voices yelling out his prestigious handle. He knows they just want one more question answered, even though time after time again, they are reminded that once the president walks away from the podium, it's fruitless to try to get him to continue to answer any more questions.

Not a moment after he leaves the room, does he turn to his Vice President, Reed Wise, who is wearing a scowl that the audience on the other side of the partitioned wall will never ever see. The face on Wise is evident that he also noticed the blunder that almost turned that press coverage into the New York Times' next front-page article.

"How the hell did she know about the astronauts?" President Lamarch screams in a whisper to his V.P. as they stride intensely down the hall.

"I have no idea, sir. Maybe someone from Gusarov's camp contacted her," Wise aptly replies.

"Gusarov? He will never allow such a thing to get out, it will ruin his ability to put us at a disadvantage. No, it had to be someone from our side. Maybe one of the staff?" the president deduces.

"Harold?" Wise proposes, hoping to bring more attention to a man that the president tends to overlook most of the time.

"Harold? No, no the good general can be a downright barnacle at times, but he isn't corruptible. He would never conspire to something like this."

"He's the only one I can see that would be capable of leaking something like this, this quick," Wise says, reaffirming his commitment to shed more light on the general's actions.

"Reed, I'm not about to have speculation floating around that General Clemens is leaking classified information to the media. It's outlandish and unsubstantiated. Someone else in that Situation Room had more of a reason to have such a thing be known to the media, especially to Debra Levine of all people."

The president stops in his steps and so does Reed. "Yes, you're the Vice President, but you were once my chief of staff, so do me a favor, and implore some of your trademark, tenacious tactics and find out who in that room would have benefited from her knowing such a thing," he says to Wise, with a sternness and agitation that he's known to show only when he's completely blindsided.

The President continues to walk down the hall, only this time without the vice president next to him.

1:01 P.M. (EDT)

With a vessel like the Almagest always flying so high above the Earth's surface—always in constant motion, moving as fast as it's known to—it's a wonder how anyone is ever able to board or de-board the airship at all. The truth is, most people who board the ship usually stay on it for weeks or even months at a time. Though no one is a hundred percent certain, this is presumably due to craft's highly efficient engine system that allows the ship to sustain itself in the air for long periods of time. And when it does finally decide to land, it's usually in the Arctic—somewhere where no one will find it—and where nobody on board the craft in their right mind will ever choose to de-board at.

PHADSYN however, being the elite tactical unit they're known to be, are probably the only members on the airship who are able to travel to and fro from the craft at their leisure; at least when compared to most of the other occupants aboard. Much of their thanks for this capability goes out to their engineering and development facility in Kenopsia—Newform Industries. They who continue to outperform and outclass any competition in the military industrial complex with their production of top-of-the-line, future-proof vehicles, gadgetry, and weaponry, consistently allows the members of PHADSYN to continue to stay one peg above the rest of the world on the evolutionary ladder of modern technology.

It didn't take long for Newform to develop a multitude of ways for PHADSYN to disembark the airship at any time they may need to. Getting back on the ship once it's airborne, however, continues to bedevil the group.

As technologically adept as PHADSYN and Newform have come to be over the years with their joint, technical achievements, certain feats still escape their grasp, including being able to return the team back to the Almagest after completing a mission, while the ship shrieks across the stratosphere at a staggering 75,000 feet, for example. In the past, especially during the time when PHADSYN were just starting to test prototypes of surface-to-air deployment vehicles, the Almagest would have to lower its altitude and speed by over fifty percent in order for the team to return to the craft successfully. The good news is that when the craft reached that precise altitude and velocity, the members of PHADSYN were able to very quickly access the aircraft via a compact, commuter rocket that transferred them to the exact location of the airship. The trip was so fast and efficient that once upon a time, it was unanimously agreed that this would be the de facto way to get members of PHADSYN, or any other officials that had been dispatched from the ship, back onto it without a problem.

However, this decision didn't last very long, considering that every time the Almagest accessed these particular vectors, they placed themselves in very vulnerable, compromising positions. It even got to the point to where the airship was almost destroyed in an attack during one of these approaches. It is the culmination of all of these factors that gives the answer to why, at this moment, four of the five members of PHADSYN are currently huddled together in one of their numerous secret bases that are sprinkled throughout the sub-terrain below United States soil, and not on-board the aircraft like they usually are. After completing a mission as vital as the one they just completed, normally, PHADSYN would waste no time reporting back to the Almagest. This time however, for some reason, they spend quite a while debating over what exactly they should tell Odem, their altruistic leader, about how their mission went.

"Make the call."

Lay Mis gives the command to Curl to contact Odem to give him a status update on the mission. Considering everything that has transpired in the last few hours, Curl, who currently has a series of bandages wrapped around his face—in fact they all have bandages wrapped around their faces and then some, with Lay Mis showcasing the least of the team's collective bruises—stares at his superior officer before sucking his teeth and doing what she says.

"Fine," he says after a long pause, and pushes a button on the large console in front of him. No sooner than he presses a button, than does someone pop up on the screen in front of them. The person not Odem, but instead, his younger sister, Seren.

"PHADSYN, report. What's the status of the target?" Seren says the moment she enters the video feed.

"Oh. Hello, Seren," Curl says, taking extra care to warmly greet her, much of this having to do with the fact that he naturally fears her. "I was trying to contact Odem, I think I might've dialed the wrong num ..."

"Curl, *report*. What is the status of the *target?*" she says again, this time much more emphatically. Her directness quickly reminds Curl of his familiar fear.

"Oh—uh, who the target ... oh, the target's fine, man. Man, you ain't even got to ask about the target. The target's fine," he says aloud before trailing off in a mumble. "Uh hey, is it possible that you can put your brother on ..."

"Fine? What do you mean, *fine?*" she snaps as she cuts him off.

"... so that I can speak to him? I wanna ask him if—" he continues, ignoring her question.

"He's busy right now," she spats, again cutting him off. "Curl, what do you mean by *fine?*" she presses on, trying to pry as much information about the mission out of him as quickly as possible.

"Seren, who is that? That you're talking to on the phone right there? Is that Caleb?"

Odem's voice can now be heard coming from Seren's background. Seren, who doesn't immediately answer him, continues to glare at Curl as she waits for an answer. "Seren? Is that Caleb? What docs hc want?" Odem pesters again. After several more seconds of this, she finally turns and addresses her brother.

"Yes, it's PHADSYN. They were just reporting in on the Obelisk operation," she says to him.

"Oh yes, I forgot about that. How d'it go?"

"I'm trying to find out right—" she begins to answer him in an effort to shut him up, but of course to no avail.

"Seren, I wanna speak to Caleb, put Caleb on. Let me speak to Caleb," he incessantly prattles to his tense, younger sister. She stares at Curl for a bit longer with a wide-eyed glare, hoping that her eyes would demand from him what her words failed at, then takes a sharp breath before exiting the screen. Odem now pops up.

"Ah! Hello, Caleb," Odem says to his loyal subject.

"H-Hello, sir," Curl nervously replies.

"I'm not your 'sir' Caleb—oh my ... oh my, Caleb," Odem says, his tone suddenly one of dramatic concern. "What happened to your face? Who else is there witchu I see? Is that ... is that Layla back there I see?"

Odem moves his face closer to the device that transmits his video feed to them, so now he appears as a large head who is squinting and turning his head in a superfluous effort to see who else is behind Curl right now, on their screen. "Layla? You there? Is it ... is that Layla back there I see, Seren? I can't tell."

"Yes, Odem, it's me—we are all here," Lay Mis says out loud from behind Curl.

"Oh, yes, now I can hear you, Layla. Well say something back there, I couldn't see you," he says.

Lay Mis responds by stepping closer to the monitor.

"Okay, there you go! Oh my, Layla my dear, you too? Look at your face. What happened to all you guys, huh? Seren, what happened to them?" he says, turning around to ask his sister. An exasperated Seren rolls her eyes, shakes her head, and slightly shrugs her shoulders somehow all at the same time.

"We were ambushed, sir," Lay Mis reveals to her master.

"Ambushed?" he exclaims.

"Yes, ambushed. As a result, we lost the target," she states.

"Seren, you hear that? They lost Burt. Well, are you guys alright at least? You need me to come out there? I mean I'm a little busy right now, but I'll come out there if you need me to. I love y'all. All of y'all. Y'all know that, right? I'm just a little busy," he says to his beloved team. At this point, Seren is now also in the feed.

"Where is the Obelisk?" she says in a much louder tone. "Where is he?"

"He was taken," Lay Mis responds to her, trying her best to keep her cool while doing so.

"Taken? By who?" Seren fires back, spittle flying from her mouth, each answer causing her to grow more upset.

"The Cheshire ..." Lay Mis tells her after a brief pause.

Both sides of the video are now completely silent. After a few seconds, Odem laughs in the background. He is watching a security feed of many officers of his organization running through the Almagest the other day, competing with each other to deliver an important document to him. "Seren, you didn't tell me they did all *this!* Ahaha!" he says out loud, laughing hysterically.

"Odem ..." Seren says calmly, without turning around. "Surii is alive."

"*What!?*" Odem suddenly exclaims. Lay Mis lowers her head and Ridge, one of the four members of PHADSYN currently present, simply shakes his. "Well, where's Burt?"

"Surii took him! This is why I told you to send me!" Seren says as she explodes on her older brother, reaching a boiling point.

"Well, I didn't know he was alive!" he snaps back at her.

"You never listen to me!" Seren says to him before turning back to the team. "Where's Serota?" she beams to Curl, Lay Mis, Ridge and Deck—referring to the fifth member of PHADSYN, who's currently missing.

"Well, how did I know they were going to be ambushed?" Odem continues to project to her from the background. Seren temporarily ignores him as she waits for one of them to answer her.

"He went after the Tyrant," Curl eventually responds.

"He did *what? That* wasn't the *mission!*" she yells as her frustration reaches a fever pitch and her brother continues to bicker at her from the background. In addition to absolving himself of any fault for the failed mission, he continues to drone on about how much he loves his team, and will love to aid them in their time of need, but unfortunately, he's a little busy right now.

"He's got this!" Lay Mis suddenly fires back at Seren in Serota's defense. She quickly notices herself informally emoting and immediately calms down. "He has this new weapon in his arsenal. I've never seen anything like it. One capable of destroying the Tyrant once and for all."

"You idiots. You think some *gadget* is going to kill the Tyrant? Serota will be lucky if he even lands a hit on him. And you know that ... but you let him go anyway," Seren affronts as she thoroughly scolds Lay Mis and the rest of the tactical espionage team for their incompetence. "You failed to capture the Obelisk. You let the Cheshire get between you and your mission, and your director went after the Tyrant. You wanna do something right for once—since you all can't seem to handle one simple operation? Then you better hurry and get to your director's side ... before his arrogance gets himself killed."

Before the video feed is disconnected, her and Odem go back and forth for a bit, and are cut off mid sibling fight.

Chapter Four

SPEAKING OF THE TYRANT

April 14th. 1:53 P.M. (EDT)

"AAH-CHOO!!"

Olpha, Laharin, and Ori Lorraine Chambers are taking their time walking through downtown Monachopsis, which is surprisingly populated, considering the asteroid event that just took place the night before. The streets are filled with just as many people as it would have, had Apophis not ever threatened it.

"Bless you, Daddy."

On the street level, Ori, who's perched high up on her father's shoulders, is just about the only person who can see more than a few feet before looking at the back of someone's head. From her vantage point, she avoids bumping into any other citizen as her father and mother below her surely does about every two and a half seconds.

"Thank you, Princess. I can't believe how packed it is down here. Leave it to these Choppies to use the day after the world was supposed to end to shop their asses off," Olpha whines to his fiancée after wiping his nose with the tissue his daughter handed to him from atop his shoulders.

"That's how you're supposed to live. Hey, you ain't a Choppy if you ain't turning up after a natural disaster," Olpha's fiancée, Laharin, quips back.

"These people are afraid of nothing. It's amazing. I see where Ori gets it from now."

Olpha continues to convey his thoughts as they continue to push through the hordes of citizens that flood the sidewalk.

"Yup," Laharin replies. "You sound surprised; you know this city better than anyone. In fact, you can thank yourself for all this. It's because of the Tyrant that most of these people walk around like nothing can happen to them. What you thought was gonna happen to a whole city that has a monster that protects them at night?" she rhetorically throws back to him.

"Yeah, but I'm hardly here anymore, I'm in Vesto Melvin most of the time. I actually prefer it there now. It's like here, they don't even need me anymore," Olpha continues to pout as they continue walking down the bustling street.

"I'm a Choppy and *I* need you, Daddy," Ori reminds him from atop his shoulders.

"And it's not that I'm surprised, it's the fact that nothing stops these people from spending their money. Absolutely nothing. Not even the threat of the world ending. I'm the one that has to save everyone when something goes down. Can you imagine if Apophis would've actually hit? It would have to be me who has to answer to the president if there were, for instance, a massive loss of life or something. These people don't make it easy for me at all."

"They're just appreciating their new lease on life. They feelin' blessed," Laharin reminds him.

"Heh, blessed. *A blessing is but a misspelled lesson.* That's what they say in this city, right? Y'know, it should've hit—I mean these people are already walking around like they're pretty much dead anyway. Why not give them life again ...?"

"I don't think I've ever heard you complain this much," Laharin responds to Olpha's bemoaning.

"You know to be honest, it's been awhile since I've even seen Mona from the streets like this. I hardly even recognize it. Look at this," Olpha says as he nods his head in the direction of a group of teenagers all dressed alike. "Young boys with skirts on—"

"It's not a skirt, it's a kilt," Laharin corrects.

"Right—kilt," he says with a chuckle. "Young girls with shaved heads, and all of them got those sound tattoos all over their bodies and wearing those silly SHED glasses looking like a bunch of old people. It's like everyone switched roles. *Ah-choo!* Even the air down here sucks," he continues to vent to Laharin.

"You're starting to *sound* like a bunch of old people. And it's Sound*tats* and SHED *frames*— wait, what's wrong with wearing your hair short?" she responds.

"Well, I like *your* hair short. Not so much my daughter."

"Well, it's part of the 'No Hair, I Care' challenge. Shave all your hair off for an entire year to support independence from unnatural hair —what's wrong with that?" she chips.

"And that's another thing ... all these damn challenges. Every day there's a new challenge: 'No Hair, I Care' challenge, the 'Black Fire' challenge—" he says mockingly.

"Oh, I love that one. That might be my favourite."

"The 'Fly-by' challenge, the 'Group' challenge. They don't stop."

"Whatchu talkin' bout, you loved that challenge!" she says while laughing.

"Really? See who can make a video with the most fake celebrities in it? Really, Laharin?"

"Well, I absolutely love the culture of today."

"I guess. It looks like the only thing these people are doing is the 'Being Mentally Challenged' challenge."

"Womp-womp," Laharin responds to Olpha's corny clap-back.

"And plus, your legs can't handle all of this stopping and going. How are your legs feeling anyway, they good?"

"Ah, so *that's* what's really troubling my King. Yes babe, my legs are fine, see?" she says as she hikes her thigh up and slaps it hard with her hand. Olpha's eyes widen with fright when she does so, which makes her laugh out loud.

"Oh my gawd!" she says as she continues to laugh. "*RE-LAX*. The Greenground is right around the corner. We'll be able to sit in a second. Sheesh, boy."

"Well, let's hurry up and get there. I don't feel like carrying your big ass home later."

"You gon' carry my *big ass* home whether I can or can't walk. Shoot," she promises as she slaps herself on the buttocks.

"I'll carry you, Mommy. Don't worry," Ori says to her comically coltish mother.

"I know you will, baby," she says to Ori before side-eyeing Olpha. "Glad *someone* wants to hold me."

"By the way, what's does the percentage on your Vi-app say?"

Olpha refers to the application on the SHED band that monitors their overall health. Anyone who has the Vi-app can personalize their own app to monitor very specific things about their bodies in any way they want. A person, if they so wish, can record simple things like how many breaths they take or how many times they blink, to very complex things like how long until their body requires a certain level of protein intake or how much cholesterol is absorbed into their body after eating a particular meal, and tracking the flow of it through their body. Laharin currently has her Vi-app specifically set to tell her how many steps she can take before the transplanted, synthetic muscles and bones inside of her legs begin to break down.

"It's at ninety percent, Olpha. Take it eeee-zzzzz, chief."

"Ninety percent?? We *just* got out of the car!" he exclaims.

"Sorry we all can't '*bio-kinetically control the dormant energy inside of our bodies to enhance any anatomical function we desire,*" she teases while attempting to mimic his likeness.

"Oh, that's supposed to be me?" he quips back at her, not finding her mimicry necessarily funny, but entertaining nonetheless.

"Tee-heheheeee!" Ori giggles as she can't help but to laugh at her mother's version of her father's voice. "She sounds just like you, Daddy."

"Mm-hmm. Well, just monitor it for me, please honey? Ori, can you watch Mommy's percentage for me?"

"You get on my damn nerves—move. Come on, get down, Ori ,we're here," Laharin says to him as she grabs Ori off of his shoulders.

"YAAAAYYYYYYYYY!"

2:40 P.M. (EDT)

"Daddy, are you watching?" Ori yells out to her father as she swings higher and higher on a swing set much too big for her size. Even without the aid of her father, who was pushing her a little while ago, Ori is very adept at swinging and is overall a very skilled acrobat for a child her age, especially considering that she isn't and never has been enrolled in any formal gymnastic school. This is largely thanks in part to her mother, who consistently forces Olpha to train her, particularly in her gross and fine motor skills. The results have been much better than Laharin or Olpha ever anticipated. When not directly training her, Laharin has made sure that Olpha continues to allow Ori to at least watch him when he goes to his warehouse to workout. Amazingly, most of what Ori has learned has been just from watching her father alone, and though she's no skilled fighter by a long shot, the fact that she can backflip from off a swing set and land perfectly on her feet each time at only five-years-old, is beyond remarkable even to her father. Perhaps a little bit of it has to do with all those nightly swings across Monachopsis' skyline that Olpha's been taking her on since she could first walk. Her mother has even made a cute little costume for her that she can wear for the next time he gives her a tour of the grand city.

Normally, Olpha wouldn't allow his daughter to perform these kind of moves outside in the open like this, but the park is relatively empty this afternoon, despite the city being as dense as it is. So, Olpha sits on a nearby park bench next to Laharin inside of the Greenground—a playground that sits inside of an air-conditioned glass house—as they watch their daughter perform the same stunt for the 900th time, getting better each and every time she does it.

"She trains more than you, you know," Laharin says to her fiancé as they sit together on a park bench holding hands.

"Who are you telling, this is all your idea anyway. You know I'm not the biggest fan of having my five-year-old daughter doing double back-handsprings out in the open like this but you know I'll be the last one to go against your orders," he responds.

"Orders, huh?" Laharin chuckles. "You're just paranoid. Besides, I'm not the one you have to report to and I don't think we could stop her at this point if we wanted to. Speaking of orders, how has work been going, lately? You don't talk about it nearly as much as you used to."

"That's because there really hasn't been anything to talk about. Work is work, babe. As long as I get to come home to you and Ori every night, I'm straight," he responds.

"I know ... I don't know, I guess I just worry about you sometimes. Every night you go out there, all that stuff you're exposed to ... it has to have some effect on you."

"Baby, anything going on in these streets stands no chance against me. You've seen the headlines, *Crime down sixty-five percent!* This 'job' is a cakewalk," he boasts.

"It's not your body I worry about, Olpha. Nobody's coming home night after night after doing what you do, and not bringing some of that stress home with them. Even when I was in the Air Force, I had to find ways to cope with things."

"Yeah, and you're strong, so you should understand better than anyone how important it is not to bring your job home with you."

"Exactly, I do know. And I also know how hard it is to do that."

"Laharin, this is *Opia*, not Greenland. I beat up burglars and gang-bangers, not soldiers on the frontline or international Black-Op agents."

"I know. Do you ever miss it? Being a part of Chapter Five?" she asks him.

"Miss it?" he says to her, chuckling. "That's funny."

"I'm serious ..." she says back to him, which makes him look at her. "Being in Greenland—the fighting, the battles, the sense of purpose. Do you miss it?"

He looks at her for a while with a smile on his face before looking back at his daughter on the swing set.

"Sense of purpose? No. I get all of that right here," he says to her before putting his hand around her shoulder, dangerously low to her right breast. "And then some ..."

The conspicuous grope causes Laharin to lightly bite her bottom lip and they look in each other's eyes, then at the same time, both lean in for a seductive kiss. Before their lips can meet, her SHED band beeps and she looks down at her arm. The meter that gauges how many more steps she can take before she has to rest starts to blink, warning her that she's almost used up all of her steps.

"Why is it going off now?" she says as she looks at it. "These things are so unreliable."

"I guess that's our cue, imma go get Ori," he says as he removes his arm from around her shoulder and starts to get up. "ORI! Come on, Princess, it's time to go," he yells out, as he starts walking to her.

"Daddy, look!" Ori yells back at him as she continues to swing higher and higher once more on the swing. Olpha looks around to check if anyone else is in the park. When he realizes it's totally empty, he starts jogging towards her.

"Now, Ori!" he yells out to her. As soon as he says that, Ori stands up on the swing. Once it reaches the top of its arc, she leaps into the air and perform two front-flips. Olpha jumps towards her and spins her already-twirling body more, making her perform a twisting, aerial flip —one that she's never done before. She lands, once again, perfectly on her feet with her father next to her, and begins to cheer her heart out.

The entire time these two been complimenting each other with synchronized twists and flips, Laharin has been looking at her phone, reading an article in the news that she can hardly believe is true. Olpha and Ori walk back to her, with Ori rambling about how cool she is and Olpha happily indulging her. As they approach, Olpha notices the morbid expression on Laharin's face.

"Baby, you ready? What's wrong? Is it your legs?" he asks her, concerned.

"No, no, I'm okay," she says. She then gets up on her own and they all begin to walk towards the elevator to exit the Greenground.

"Mommy, did you see me? How high I went? That was so cool!" Ori exclaims as she struggles to contain her excitement.

"Yeah, that was amazing, honey. Olpha, look," Laharin responds as she hands her phone to him. They enter the elevator, and the article that she just finished reading pops up again once her phone unlocks after it recognizes him remotely via her SHED band. The elevator door closes and they head down towards the street level.

When the elevator doors reopen at the street level, Olpha's face resembles the same one that Laharin has. That's because he just finished reading an article about the now-retired War General, (not to mention, his ex-comrade) Roger Morris, house exploding from an attack by an unknown group of terrorists just earlier this morning. It goes on to say that fortunately, his family wasn't home at the time and that he is currently recovering at Lorentz Medical hospital.

"My god, Paula and the kids ... who could've done this, Olpha?" Laharin looks and lugubriously asks him.

Before he can answer, a three-inch long, thin, metallic pin flies directly by his ear and pierces the brick wall millimeters from his daughter's neck. He's startled by the sheer speed the projectile was moving and is the only one who notices it. He looks back, and sees a folded note pinned between the metal pin and the wall next to him.

Beep-Beep.

The driver that escorted the Chambers to downtown Monachopsis, has just pulled up to the curb next to them.

"Baby, come on the car is here. Come on, Ori," Laharin says to her fiancé and daughter before heading off to the car.

"Coming," he signals back to her.

Before following them, Olpha walks to the metallic pin that's in the wall and upon closer inspection, notices that behind the penetrated note, a deadly hornet, with its curved stinger still fully erect, has also been pierced directly through its thorax by the precisely-thrown, sharp object. Olpha soon realizes that this hornet was but a half a hair's breadth away from stinging his own daughter in the neck. He removes the pin from the wall, unfolds the note and reads it:

You've been slacking, Nero.

Olpha looks up at the hundreds of rooftops around him, to only notice that nothing about them is out of the ordinary.

"It can't be ..."

Chapter Five

JUMOPIKWARIS

April 14th. 1:53 P.M. (CDT)

THE SUN now hangs directly above the wandering creature at early noon, it who can't stop looking up at it, seemingly unaffected by its overbearing brilliance. Since leaving the home it just learned so much in, the creature has now been walking in the same direction along a road for a little over three hours. After enduring such a trek, in hopes of absorbing some new data about the people of this area but unfortunately not finding it, the creature finally comes across something that may aid in such a task. A blue sign that has REST STOP written in bold, white letters, announces an establishment where people gather, must be nearby. The creature figures it'll slip in and observe everyone while it blends in, hoping to extract more information about this place and its inhabitants.

After walking for a bit longer, the creature finally sees what it thinks is a small house named *EXPRESS DINER*. Interpreting this as a sign of where a community may be present, the creature walks into the establishment, hesitantly at first, only to soon realize that no one is paying any attention to it. So it drops the obvious inconspicuous act and walks to a seat at an empty booth, several rows down from the entrance—just to be safe. Upon sitting, it spends a significant amount of time paralyzed by the different aromas and sounds coming from an assortment of different breakfast foods being cooked at the same time. These 'firsts' that the creature is experiencing does wonders to its senses. Suddenly, the creature's trance-like focus is broken by a large woman who's quickly approaching.

"Coffee?"

The woman's voice is amongst some of the most unpleasant sounds the creature has heard up until now. Still, the creature looks up at her, silent, but mostly confused. The waitress continues to hold the cup of coffee with the small tea dish under it, as she waits for her customer to answer her. Not too much longer after, the waitress just put the coffee and the proper accommodating spoon and fork down in front of the creature, writing the nomadic visitor off as just another weirdo who was up all night experimenting with psychedelics, like many people her age around these parts are known to do. The creature watches the waitress all the way until she walks back behind the counter to resume her restaurant duties.

The creature finally averts its gaze from the boisterous woman, mostly because watching her didn't cause it to have any mental flashes of any sort, and fixates on the hot cup of coffee now in front of it. Before it peers inside of the dark brew, the creature watches the steam from the cup dance and twist up into the air before disappearing. Mystified, it closes its eyes and smiles. Clearly, the creature just experienced another flash.

After the episode, it sits back up straight, not exactly knowing what to do with the beverage that sits on the table in front of it. So, it looks around the establishment hoping to find some sort of clue that'll help it solve this puzzle—and it finds plenty. Everywhere it looks, every so often, every single person around the creature eventually picks up a cup that's similar to the one in front of it, brings it to their face, and pours the substance inside of the cup down into their mouths. The creature watches this for a little while in an effort to see if that is all there is to it. Once it concludes that it has a good idea on how to proceed, it looks back down at its own cup and preps itself to do exactly what it saw everyone else just doing.

Carefully, the creature reaches for the mug and immediately notices something—the closer its hand gets to the cup, the hotter its hand becomes. This delights the creature. With its curiosity now taking over, the creatures starts to wave its hand over the top of the cup and notices the air is much warmer there than anywhere else. Anxious to learn more about this foreign beverage, it takes a finger and puts it entirely inside of the cup. The heat from the coffee burns the creature's finger and it pulls it back even quicker than it put it in. It then stares at its finger to inspect it for any damage. All it notices is that the moment it removed its finger from the liquid inside of the cup, it immediately started cooling back down. The creature then puts its finger in its mouth, and immediately, the explosion of grounded coffee beans, milk, sugar and water excite every single one of its taste buds, causing another shockwave to surge through its head. The creature shuts its eyes tightly as it allows the frenetic activity in its head to run its full course.

When it finally ceases, the creature opens its eyes and the first thing it notices is the fork and spoon resting on top of a napkin next to the coffee. The creature pauses and takes a moment to once again reflect on the tumultuous events that occurred with the armed soldiers last night. A lot had happened in that short amount of time. Of all the unfamiliar things that came its way, the one that currently stands out the most to the creature is when the small metal projectiles that were being shot at it, mysteriously slowed down in their path right before they were about to hit it. Up until that moment, the creature had no idea what was it that was causing the loud rattling that made the dirt and rocks around it shatter and break apart. And though it still has no idea what a bullet is, it does have a slight idea of what its material is made of. Right now, of all the different materials present around the creature, the fork sitting in front of it, comes closest to matching it.

Much like when man first stood erect and began to run the first of their experiments to quench their curiosity about how their environment worked, the creature decides it's going to run one of its own experiments right here in this restaurant. So slowly, it picks up the fork —admittedly, a little surprised it can even do that much to something that resembles something that seemed designed to take its life. To the creature, this must mean it could've picked up the bullets from earlier that were flying towards it, if it so pleased. The creature then checks its surroundings and swallows hard, involuntarily. Once satisfied that no one is paying any attention to it, the creature tosses the fork upward into the air, directly above it. As it comes falling down aiming directly for its head, the fork suddenly and drastically slows down in speed and floats about a foot and a half away from its face—just like the bullets did—while the creature and everything else around it continues to move at a normal pace. The creature makes a yelping noise from what it witnesses, and immediately snatches the fork out of the air. As strange as the creature itself is, an object in motion that slows down in time once it gets close to it while everything else continues to flow at the same rate, is something that even *it* finds strange and unfamiliar. Deciding not to spend too much time mulling over this phenomenon, considering it has already previously witnessed its capabilities when trying to escape from those soldiers from last night, the creature then takes its free hand, lays it on the table, and with its other hand, grips the handle of the utensil tightly, making sure the teeth of the fork is pointing down.

It waits for a brief moment, both to make sure again that no one is looking and also to brace itself, then suddenly takes a violent stab at its own hand with the fork. Immediately, the fork again, like the bullets, reduces it speed dramatically in free space, yet the creature's hand somehow continues onward at its normal speed. This causes the creatures hand to slip off of the fork and slam down on the table, causing a loud noise to resonate throughout the diner. Frightened, the creature freezes and waits for a few seconds, before slowly glancing back over its shoulder to see if it drew any kind of attention that it desperately doesn't need. Everyone looks over at the creature's direction for a second or two before turning back to whatever they were doing—they, too, are probably just dismissing the creature as some young, obstreperous troublemaker.

After concluding it hasn't caused any unwanted attention, the creature turns back to look at what happened to the fork and what it sees next blows its mind. Though its hand didn't slow down in the least, the fork, along with a glob of coffee that spilled out when its hand accidentally banged on the table, continues to descend ever so slowly towards the creatures resting hand, independent of it pushing on it. The creature watches this miracle unfold before it as its human-looking mouth remains slightly hung open. The creature touches the glob of excess coffee currently flowing through the air also, causing it to break up into smaller globs and droplets of dark-brown liquid. Anxious to see the conclusion of the fork's voyage, the creature reaches out and grabs the handle and starts forcefully pushing down on the fork in an effort to speed up its descent, being careful not to let its hand slip this time —which surprisingly, isn't so easy.

The creature's influence on the fork only causes it to speed up its trip towards its hand very, very slightly, but eventually it reaches it. Immediately, the creature lowers its head above its hand to get a better, up-close view of what happens when an object moving this slow comes into contact with its body. As it carefully watches, the teeth of the fork gently touch the top of its hand. In an effort to be safe, it removes its right hand from pushing down on the fork any further; irrespective of this, the fork continues to press down further into its hand. The creature continues to watch in awe, and then it starts to worry. The fork still has not stop descending into its hand, and it has now begun to press into the creature's skin. The creature immediately grabs the fork with its free hand and attempts to pull it up, however the effort is superfluous. With the fork now attempting to puncture the creature's skin and with no other options left, the creature quickly yanks its left hand back away from the fork. Because the momentum and force that was originally given to the fork when the experiment was first conducted is conserved, the fork slams into the table at the speed it would've had the creature's hand not been in its way.

This causes a second loud noise to erupt from the booth, and the waitress, who was secretly watching the creature from behind the counter, is now storming her way to the creature's booth in a huff. Without even looking back, the creature can tell the waitress is hurrying towards it, evident by her loud footsteps, and the creature braces itself for whatever strife this woman is about to bring its way.

"Um miss, just what the hell is going on over—"

Before the waitress can grab the creature's shoulder, she's frightened by the loud sound of several plates crashing onto the floor from near the eating counter she was just at.

"Ay dios MIO!"

A second waitress that was carrying a steaming breakfast platter containing multiple plates of grits, eggs, sausages, bacon and toast, has dropped all of it, at the sight of what is being transmitted from the flat screen television that hangs above the eating counter. The creature and the disgruntled waitress both turn around to see what all the ruckus is.

"What in the hell is *THAT?*" says the creature's waitress, as she looks up at the television.

The footage of dozens of foreign, alien-looking beasts attacking and pummeling on the bodies of soldiers and scientists that occupy a set-up base camp, that was built around one of the meteor crash sites, has caused every single customer in the diner to stare at the television mortified at what is currently being shown on it. The unspeakable acts of horror, arguably too gruesome to be shown on public television, continue for about ten seconds until the newscaster who's showing the footage, pauses on the face of a man they consider to be the sole person responsible for what they can only define as a freak attack on the base; a man leading and commanding a new type of animal species *never before seen*—as the newscaster describes them.

The creature immediately notices that the man who remains in the still-frame boasts the same exact smirk as the man who was on Apophis with it. Only now, he's dressed head-to-toe in a formal two-piece gray suit, with a skinny, black tie to match his shiny, black dress-shoes. He wears the same kind of hairstyle you would find on one of the Beatles at the height of their popularity in the 1960's. All of this does absolutely nothing to sway the creature from speaking the name of the being who has changed his appearance to also look like one of these humans, just as she did.

"Jumopikwaris," the creature says out loud to herself, as she remains in an intermittent state of shock. Her voice is about as normal of a woman's voice as you can get—boasting no particular idiolect or accent.

Soon the creature shakes off the initial shock it got from seeing its familiar partner, and instantly begins to contemplate its next move.

Chapter Six

BREACH OF CONTACT

April 15th. 9:39 A.M. (EDT)

"WE'VE GOT the place surrounded, Vincent! Do us a favor and just come on out ... you won't get hurt if you just come along peacefully!"

Lieutenant Garrett, along with six other Opia police officers surround apartment 6B—the place where Vincent Wolfe has barricaded himself inside of so he can have one last stand off before he or a few of the officers outside his door are blown away.

"Come out? Why don't you just come in and get me, how 'bout that?" he yells out to Garrett and the officers in the hallway. "Even though, I don't think that'll be a very good idea for any of you!"

"Vincent, listen to me, it's not too late for you—you robbed a few pharmacies, so what? You're not looking at any real hard time!" Lieutenant Garrett responds back to him, doing his best to make Vincent reconsider his next action.

"You think I'm worried about jail? You blowhards don't know shit!" Vincent shouts back.

"How about you tell me what it is about then?"

"Of course. Come on in and I'll tell you *exactly* what this is about."

"Sir, we aren't getting through to him, we are going to have to breach," the squad sergeant tells his lieutenant.

"I know, but I really need this guy alive. I was trying to wait for

Nerosion to show up, but it doesn't look like that's going to happen," Garrett admits to his team.

"Hey! It got awfully quiet out thereeee! Hey Garrett, you planning to breach? Well, come right on in—I need all the target practice I can get! Don't worry, it's only a 12-gauge, so my aim might be a little off!" Vincent teases.

"Alright, we breach on my command," Garrett says to his squad sergeant.

"Yes, sir."

The squad leader silently gestures to the other officers to wait for his signal.

"Do it!"

Lieutenant Garrett gives the command, and one of the officers triggers the mini-explosion that blows the locks off the door. However, a microsecond before this happens, Nerosion, aka the Tyrant, bursts into the apartment through the window that Vincent is holed up in, and grabs the elusive perp from behind. Because of all the commotion, the men cannot tell that Nerosion has entered the apartment and immediately opens fire on both Nerosion and Vincent.

The breach by the officers genuinely surprises Nerosion, something that almost never happens and he, almost by instinct alone, ducks down and out of the way of the incoming volley of bullets, avoiding making contact with any of the shells. None of the bullets hit Nerosion, but the rubber shotgun rounds that smack into Vincent's chest carry with them enough force to send him flying backwards. Normally, such shots would've simply knocked him out but still kept him alive nonetheless, however, the momentum sends Vincent stumbling back, and he trips over Nerosion's crouched body, sending him out of the now wide-open window that Nerosion busted in through a moment ago. Vincent plunges six stories down and lands inside of the alley below—the fall killing him instantly.

Nerosion and the police officers both stare at each other confused and upset—each side wanting the next to explain what the hell just happened. Lieutenant Garrett enters into the studio apartment, observes what just transpired, and lets out a quiet but disappointing sigh.

"You gotta be shitting me," he says out loud as he places his pistol back into his holster. "*Now* you come," he says to Nerosion, clearly annoyed, before he walks over to the window and peers into the alley below.

"I got the call late," Nerosion, now filled with regret, admits. "I'm sorry. Was that Wolfe?"

"It *was* him, yeah. And I needed him. Now we got nothing," Garrett tells him.

"What do you mean—you still have Trunt."

"Ah man, Trunt ain't tryna talk to anybody."

"He didn't tell you anything?" asks Nerosion, genuinely surprised.

"Seven hours with him and all we learned is that Wolfe would rather kill himself before telling us a thing." He looks down into the alley. "Guess he wasn't completely lying."

"Give him 'til the end of the day. Something will turn up," Nerosion says reassuringly.

"The only thing that's turning up is the number of meetings I have to now go to explaining what the hell went wrong here. I hope you plan on showing up to some of them yourself—after hearing that Trunt hasn't been cooperating, the chief hasn't exactly been in his rosiest of moods. You skip out on them and it might get ugly. I suggest you show your face—or your mask or whatever," he says to Nerosion, before turning and conferring with the other officers in the room.

On top of being part of the reason Vincent Wolfe is now dead, hearing about Trunt's unwillingness to cooperate, especially after the little talk they had, causes Nerosion to grow more upset than he usually is while he's on duty.

"Oh, I almost forgot to tell you," Garrett says to Nerosion. "Remember Randy Gallen? Well it turns out the Exile he was on wasn't normal. What you saw was a man who was hit with a concentrated dose."

"Concentrated?"

"It turns out that Randy was a guinea pig for an experiment to test for the performance of someone on a concentrated hit. Normally, a mild dose of the drug will allow you to experience all sorts of things that results in making a person feel as if they're invincible. They say it's like being in a dream."

"Doesn't sound like a problem to me. Most criminals already think very highly of themselves," Nerosion remarks.

"Yeah. The only problem is that extreme doses of Exile makes the user feel like their dreams are actually their reality. As a result, people on it can hit harder, and take harder hits—I'm sure you can confirm that after your little scuffle with him."

Nerosion nodded. "They were others like Randy?"

"Yeah. Plenty. We just didn't know it at the time. Every so often, we'll get a report about a bunch of officers struggling to take down one man. Or a perp who is completely unaffected by our tasers."

"That's not all that unusual. It happens all the time," Nerosion appropriately reminds the shrewd lieutenant.

"It happens all the time with *one* taser. Not *fourteen,*" he retorts, causing Nerosion to completely acquiesce his attention. "*Strawmen* is what we call them. We still don't know where they're getting the Exile from."

"Trunt knows. Offer him something."

"We did. We did offer him something—everything. And he turned it down. All of it. I don't know what else to tell you."

Garrett walks away and leaves Nerosion standing by himself, so he can be alone with his thoughts.

4:15 P.M. (EDT)

At Prosopa Penitentiary, many of the inmates are spending the first of their two free hours a day participating in one of the few recreational activities that the penitentiary offers to its inhabitants. Amongst the hundred or so playing basketball, lifting weights or just loitering about in the yard, is Ivan Trunt. The man who has refused to take a plea deal or volunteer any kind of information in relation to the Pharmacy Heists, is now confined to the facilities offered at Prosopa up until his trial date. Though it's only been a couple of days, Ivan has found himself easily adapting back to a place he has frequented more times than he cares to remember. He even meets up with a few of his old cellmates, some of whom have been there since he was last there over four years ago. His time spent so far in the pen hasn't been as unsettling as most would assume. That being the case, the likelihood of him telling anything the police wants to know is now practically nonexistent. He knows this better than anyone, so he smiles as he finishes up his last set on the bench before he takes a quick smoke break.

"Hey Ivan, I gotta admit, I'm little surprised to see you here," one of the other inmates around the workout bench says to him as he finishes.

"And why's that?"

"I'm just surprised someone like you got caught, that's all. I thought I'd never see you back here after your last bid. You must've bumped into the Tyrant again."

"You're funny, Ricky. Actually, he bumped into me," Ivan says to the inmate before placing the heavy barbell back on its prongs and standing up.

"You know, you should write a book—I hear they're letting people out early now for completing one ... part of some new Prisoner's Rights Act or something. You can write a self-help guide on what to do when you run into the Tyrant. Shit, I'll buy it, hehehe," Ricky quips.

"Yeah—and maybe you can write a self-help guide on how to be funny," Vincent shoots right back before taking off back to his cell.

With everyone outside, he figures he can finally get some time alone to enjoy his cigarette and contemplate what he plans on doing once he gets out. He reaches his cell and tell his bunk mate, who's quietly sleeping on the top bunk, to scram so he can have some peace and quiet while he relieves himself.

"Hey Lenny, it's my cell time and I need to take a dump so hit the yard for a few for me, will ya?" Ivan says as he pulls down his prison pants and sits on the toilet. "I'm about to light a cigarette and I know how you feel about that. Come on seriously, it's my time now, get the fuck out," he says to his cellmate, who still hasn't responded back. "Fuck it."

Ivan spends the next few minutes relieving himself while he puffs on a cigarette in total silence. The splashes from his excrement falling into the toilet are especially loud now that most of the noisy inmates are outside. After a few more relatively minor colon expulsions, Ivan gets up, wipes himself and pulls his pants back onto his waist.

"Yo, Lenny!" he says much more loudly.

Now losing his patience, Ivan steps up to bed and uses the lower bunk as a step-ladder to reach up to Lenny so he can shake him out of his sleep if necessary. "Yo, Lenny! Wake up man, this is my time! Take your ass outside, I need the cell."

He starts to shake him and when even that proves to be insufficient in waking him, he yanks on Lenny's arm, pulling him over so he can punch him right in his jaw to wake him.

Fed up, he turns him over with his left hand while cocking back his right fist. When he gets a glimpse of his face, he goes to swing but stops when he realizes someone literally beat him to the punch. Ivan, who quickly realizes Lenny isn't sleep but unconscious, notices Lenny's jaw is swollen and slightly unhinged.

"Lenny ... what the ...?"

Immediately, Ivan slowly begins to panic as he starts to remember the Tyrant's promise from when they last met. He gets down from off of the bed and backs up from it. His six-by-eight foot cell suddenly becomes a lot more cramped as he steps back and bumps into a firm, broad object behind him. He turns around slowly and the last thing he sees is the faceless mask of the monster who put him inside there. Ivan closes his eyes for a second, perhaps hoping he's dreaming.

When he opens up them again and looks up into the sky, he only sees a city floating above him, and he concludes that this must be the case after all. But it takes him a few seconds to realize that no, he isn't dreaming, and that yes, the city of Monachopsis is indeed really floating above him—only it's upside down for some reason. The wind, combined with the blood now pooled inside of his skull, and his internal balance, all remind him that something's off about this picture much sooner than his own logic does. When it finally sets in, he can't help to let out a frightful scream when he realizes he's actually dangling seventy stories above the breathtaking city, upside-down. The Tyrant lets him scream to his heart's content, because at this height and time of day, absolutely no one in this city can hear you over their festivities, and even if they did happen to notice him, they more than likely wouldn't care. After all, this isn't the first time Nerosion put on such a display for the citizens of Monachopsis.

Nerosion, being the versatile craft master he's known to be, has used his wired staff to suspend Ivan in such a way that allows him to dictate whether or not he stays tangled, safely seven hundred feet above the ground, or from being the second scumbag to help paint the sidewalk red in the span of a day. In other words, he can easily escape at any time, the only problem is that freeing himself means falling to his death. To change this circumstance, he has no choice but to oblige the requests of the Tyrant, he who sits on the edge of the rooftop directly next to his defenseless prey.

"Oh my god, please. Get me down! Get me down! HELLL-LLPPPPPP!" Ivan screams out helplessly, which causes the wiring around his body to loosen a bit more. "Oh shit!"

"I wouldn't move. When you fall, I'm not catching you," Nerosion blandly tells the erratic prison escapee.

"What do you mean *w-when?*" Ivan whimpers out.

"Before you do though, there's something I need to know: I gave you two days. Garrett told me you didn't tell him what he needed to know. Why?"

The wire loosens a bit more and Ivan slips a tad bit further down.

"Please, God, help me. Please," Ivan cries out.

Nerosion, unsatisfied, gets up and starts walking away.

"Wait! WAIT!" he yells as he slips even more. "WAIIIITTTTT!"

Nerosion stops, turns around, and walks back towards the edge.

"The bands, the SHED bands! That's why we were breaking into the goddamn pharmacies! We were getting messages of the addresses of the locations we were supposed to hit from some unknown number. We were told to go these places and take as many different types of medicines from them as we can. But we had to put on these modified SHED bands first. They never explained why; we were just told to wear them while we hit the stores. Then they'll put money in some account that was already set up for us," he shares as he slips a little more. "Oh fuck!"

Nerosion listens to him intently, then starts walking away again without saying a word back.

"Hey, Tyrant ... wait, come on man, where are you going? I told you everything I know, man. I fucking swear." Ivan's voice quivers as he does his best not to slip any further. Nerosion stops again.

"I asked you *why* didn't you tell Garrett what he needed to know. Not *what,*" he says to him before walking away once again, this time not turning back.

"What? No, wait. Nerosion, wait! Don't leave me, I'm sorry man, I'm sor—!"

The wire trap that Ivan was ensnared in finally untangles completely and sends him plunging down towards the street. By the time he reaches the twentieth floor below he can barely see anything, thanks to the tears flowing from his eyes as he screams his lungs out from the sheer terror of coming to the conclusion that this is really going to be the way he's going to go.

He's about five stories before he smashes into the pavement before the wire coiled around his ankle becomes taut and breaks his fall. The wire then rebounds and begins retracting itself with Ivan still attached to it, reversing his direction back upward, moving him almost as fast as he was when he was falling. Ivan is dragged back up to his original spot where he hung upside-down from the crane. Except now the momentum from the retract causes him to shoot over the entire roof before dragging him back down on the other side.

He completely arcs over the entire building in reverse, letting out screams in a pitch that even surprises Nerosion. The wire finally detaches from his leg and the momentum sends him flying above the city. Before he smashes into the side of a building six blocks from where he was flung from, Ivan closes his eyes again and when he opens them, he's back inside of his cell.

Chapter Seven

TWO IN THE CHAMBER

April 16th. 5:55 A.M. (EDT)

"MOMMY? MOMMY, WAKE UP. MOMMY? MOMMY!"

At 5:55 in the morning, a time unfamiliar even to the sun, little Ori Lorraine makes her best attempt to wake her mother up per her request, so they can get ready for her first day back to school—a decision she can tell her mother is starting to regret a little.

"Hmmm?"

Laharin lets out a soft coo as her daughter gently shakes her back and forth in her bed. After several attempts, she fully climbs in bed and on top of her to get a better grasp.

"Mommy, it's six a-clock, you told me to wake you up for school today."

"Hmmm? Where's your father? Is he up already?"

"Daddy's not here. He forgot to come home last night," Ori tells her.

"He did, didn't he. I swear imma hurt that man, I told him we both have to go down to your school today to re-enroll you," she says while yawning out the words. "And he's not even here. You still want to go?" she asks her dutiful child.

"I don't know," Ori says to her mother after mulling over the idea. Laharin can tell she does, but she can also tell that Ori only wants what's best for her mom. And right now that's sleep. What an angel.

"Hmmm? You don't have to if you don't want to," Laharin says after considering Ori's feelings.

"Okay!" Ori immediately exclaims.

"No, matter of fact, come on. I be damned if I let some asteroid keep my baby from learning."

"But Mommy, what about your legs?"

"Mommy's legs are fine, baby. Start getting ready."

"Are we waiting for Daddy?

"No, Daddy'll meet us there."

"Okay."

It takes a little over an hour for Laharin to complete her morning routine, always saving the part where she must take her medicine for her legs, last.

"Coming up at seven—Unknown Creatures Destroying Crash Sites," a channel 9 newscaster says between commercials on the television in the living room.

"Ori, you almost ready? Ori?" Laharin calls out to her daughter from her bedroom. In the past, the mundane task of getting dressed was easily accomplished by the war vet. In fact she used to take pride in performing such tasks because she remembered that things like eating and getting dressed quickly were part of her daily regimen while in the Armed Forces.

Laharin was always one who actively made sure to take the things she learned in her life that most people overlooked, and find a way to pragmatically apply them to her everyday lifestyle. She saw the benefit in everything, it was one of the key factors that allowed her to prosper in the Air Force. If she had to get up early, the benefit would be that she gets to have more of her day. If she didn't get up early, the benefit was that her body would get more rest. She applied that philosophy to every single facet of her life and does her best to continue to even as she struggles to put her pants on by herself. Although, since her accident, the benefits haven't really been as easy to extract as they once were. It's pretty difficult to find the joy in things when your legs have a timer attached to it that determines how long you can use them.

Ori, as expected, is fully dressed and ready to go. With the extra time she's accrued, she does what she's known to do best: watch television. Laharin calls out again from the bedroom and realizes the reason she doesn't get a response is because Ori is transfixed on whatever program she's watching. Nine out of ten, it's *Madly Dote!*

Ori can hear her mother's footsteps coming down the hall—she who, once again, emerged victorious in her morning bout with her jeans which incidentally makes Ori happy and sad at the same time, so neither a smile nor a frown appears on her face. If anything, the two emotions cancel each other out.

"Ori, didn't you hear me calling you?" she says as she walks into the living room to find her daughter cleaned, groomed and ready for school, and not to mention—spellbound. She walks into the kitchen and the indentation on her refrigerator automatically produces a glass of water for her to drink. Laharin grabs the glass and opens a nearby cabinet to grab her prescribed morning medication. She looks over to her daughter and notices she still hasn't averted her gaze from the television.

"Ori, turn the Cupid off and let's go. You know how I feel about you watching that show. I didn't even know it came on this early in the morning," she says to Ori as she opens up her bottle of pills.

"I'm not watching Cupid, Mommy, I'm watching the news," Ori corrects her.

"The news? Oh, that's even worse," she says to her before looking at the pills and placing them back into the bottle she got them out of, instead of swallowing them.

"Look Mommy, Daddy's on the news!"

"Really? Who he beat up this time?" she says before gulping down a glass of water, minus the medication. She looks down at her SHED band and notices that their driver has arrived. "Ori, come on, get your book bag. Leander's downstairs."

Laharin places the glass back into the refrigerator compartment and goes to get her jacket and purse.

"Mommy? What kind of animal is that?" Ori says as she points to the television. "I've never seen that one before."

In her haste, Laharin finds a second to quickly glance at the television and the images that's being portrayed makes her do a double-take and stop. The reporter who was up until this minute all but inaudible to Laharin, now comes in as crystal as a bell. She walks over to where Ori continues to sit and looks at the television intently. She presses a button on her band and the volume on the television goes up.

" .... footage from the second meteor crash site to be attacked. Again, many people are calling what they can only describe as some sort of "alien-wolf", as the reason for this second attack. As with the last site, the entire staff and personnel were completely wiped out—no survivors, and the same unknown man showed up again after the attack who, like last time, appears to be looking for something "

A slight uneasiness comes over Laharin as she does her best to understand what those animals are. She looks down at her daughter, maybe to find some clue of an answer, then continues to watch.

"As you can see, Gina, dozens of these animals, if not hundreds, just absolutely lay waste to everything in their sight. Judging by the video, though the creatures are shown to be biting on their victims at times, they don't seem to be focused on consuming any of the bodies that lie around them during or after their onslaught. It's hard to tell what the true intent of these unknown beings are or who is the man that shows up with them each time afterward. Hopefully, this second attack in addition to the first, can help the proper authorities begin to piece together exactly what may be going on."

The second news correspondent jumps in to make sure to warn the viewers of what she feels is some very important information.

"And let us also remember, Gary, that the local authorities haven't said anything official about the attacks being planned or coordinated in any way. In fact, when asked about the attacks, the local police department was quoted as saying that there's a good chance these unidentified animals are just shaking up by the events of the asteroid and because something like this has never happened before, we are bound to see some unprecedented behavior from many different species all around the world. Celebrity Theoretical Physicist Arthur Bouya spoke from a panel yesterday in Washington, where he shared his viewpoints on the recent events:

The news coverage suddenly switches to footage of a conference held by notable members from the scientific community.

"The overall uniqueness of this event has allowed the world to witness some very exotic activity, including the emergence of a new species—the likes of which have never been discovered or observed in nature," famed theoretical physicist Dr. Arthur Bouya says to a crowd from a large panel on a stage. "I've been hearing countless rumors that these animals are from outer space. Rest assured, these creatures are definitely homegrown—they are from planet Earth. To think otherwise is an investment is irrational reasoning," he concludes. The video ends and switches back to the newscasters.

"Also, the second attack which has occurred about eighty miles west of the first is being dubbed as an 'unfortunate tragedy' by the scientific community, and poses no direct threat to anyone here on the East Coast. When we come back, we find out what happened when Secretary Cooke visited Russia during her—"

Familiar Channel 9 news correspondent Gary Singh's voice is cut short thanks to Laharin remotely de-powering the television from her SHED band.

"Come on, let's go," she says to Ori.

"What was that, Mommy?" Ori asks, still looking for clarification of what she just saw on the television.

"I'm not sure. Here, put your book bag on."

"Is Daddy coming with us?"

"Daddy called, he said he'll be there to pick us up when you get out of school later, Okay?"

"Okay."

Ori puts her book bag on with a few books in it designed for third graders along with a couple of pencils. She grabs her lunch, and goes to unlock the front door for her mother. They both exit and the door closes behind them, with the electronic lock automatically engaging after a few seconds.

Chapter Eight

DRIVING MINUTIA

April 16th 5:56 A.M. (CDT)

OF ALL THE things the creature can think about while it continues to walk for hours down one of the many desolate roads etched throughout Iowa, it chooses to only fixate on the image of the man it saw on the television in the diner—its former acquaintance from Apophis—Jumopikwaris. Who he was to the creature prior to them crash landing on Earth no longer matters, because all the creature can think of now is where he plans on striking next. That question bothers the creature the most, even more so than *why* he's attacking these meteor sites in the first place. The creature is no doubt the only person on the planet who knows the answer to that question, and such knowledge doesn't come without cost. The creature feels that it is absolutely imperative that it obtains what its partner seeks from these sites before he does because if it doesn't, those foreign beasts will be the least of this planet's worries.

It's hard to imagine how someone from another planet will have a destination on a foreign world, and let alone know how to get to that destination without some sort of guide. Luckily for the creature, such a setback is all but gone thanks to the exorbitant amount of data it's been absorbing since it's been here. Every few minutes, the horrible seizures the creature experienced when it first started interacting with the environment, are now replaced with a mental wash that hits it like a cool, oceanic breeze. With each soothing episode, the creature becomes more and more familiar with the planet and all of its people. In a sense, it's thinking about all the memories it's created while here except it's never been here; it's almost as if the creature is remembering a life it never had. Because of this phenomenon, one thing continues to come more and more into focus in the creature's mind: the location of a special artifact it protected before the asteroid it rode in on exploded.

The brisk early mornings that Iowa are known for around this time of the year doesn't seem to do much to affect the state of the creature. It's clear that it has a much larger tolerance for temperature than most people. Even after walking for fifty plus miles, the creature doesn't appear to be the least bit winded or irritated. It is, however, well aware that its mode of travel is very inadequate considering the gravity of its new mission. Just as the creature started dwelling on this setback, it notices two tiny, white orbs appear in the distant horizon in front of it like two small dabs of white gouache tapped against the backdrop of a fresh, black canvas.

The creature stops in her tracks and watches the two floating orbs move ever so slightly in the distance, hoping to trigger an episode that will enlighten it on whatever it is that continues to rapidly approach. As the orbs gradually become bigger and bigger, more of what allows the two orbs to remain suspended in the air and move at the same time slowly starts to reveal itself. A distinct rumbling now accompanies the approaching orbs and the speed of the orbs are reduced when they finally arrive next to the creature.

A spanking, brand-new Ford Mustang stops on the other side of the road next to the creature. The driver's window rolls down and a single man, no older than thirty and wearing glasses, pokes his head out and looks at the creature directly in its eyes.

"Hey there, you lost?" says the helpful gent to the creature. A surge of energy races through the creature's skull as images of thousands and thousands of cars of every type and model swims through its mind. The creature closes its eyes for a few seconds to absorb all the new information and realizes that these machines can move many, many times faster than it can.

"Yes. I am," the creature responds back to the driver. The sound of its voice throws the driver off more so than he would've ever anticipated, not because it's drastically different from any he's ever heard, but that it's drastically more pleasant than any he's ever heard. Maybe the creature's coy, yet approachable appearance had a little to do with it.

"Well, I wouldn't mind helping you get to wherever it is you're trying to go," the obviously smitten driver responds. His response triggers another, yet much lighter episode which the creature registers as flirtation, or in other words, the verbal marker that humans use to indicate that they are infatuated with someone, and as a result, are more likely to be swayed to do something for someone else's benefit. "It's pretty late out and the next town isn't for another eighteen miles. At the very least, we can stop there and then figure out where it is you're trying to get to."

The creature doesn't say anything, it just smiles and looks down. It still isn't a hundred percent on how social engagements work, so though the creature wants to use this person's machine to aid it in its journey, it doesn't want to say something that'll inadvertently ruin its plans of obtaining it.

The creature continues to stand there smiling while looking at the pavement. The man, sensing its shyness, finally comes to his senses when he realizes how rude he's been.

"Oh god, I'm so sorry!" he says as he hastily gets out of the car. "I'm Glenn. What is your name?" Glenn says as he holds out his hand to shake the creature's. Puzzled, the creature looks at it for a second or two before experiencing another minor episode. It then sticks its own hand out to meet his, grabs it and shakes it kind of weirdly.

"It's okay. I'm uh, Kayelimneusia," it says to him. Glenn chuckles as he does his best to register what this foreigner just said out loud. But it's to no avail.

"I'm sorry, what?" Glenn says as he leans his head closer to the creature's mouth, signaling that he didn't quite catch whatever it was the creature referred to itself as.

The creature realizes that even though it did its best to translate its official designation to the English language, it still doesn't come across as anything this man has ever heard before.

"You said something kay-el-*Minutia*?" he says to it still trying to interpret that garbled mess it just spit out to him.

"Yes, *Minutia,* you can call me Minutia. My, uh, friends call me that. Yeah, that's what all my friends call me anyway," the creature says as it decides to roll with the part of the name that he seemed to grasp.

"That's ... different. I don't think I've ever met anyone named Minutia before. Doesn't even sound like a real name."

"No, it's extremely real, believe me! An earth name doesn't get any more real than that. It's a very common name for a girl ... here ... on Earth." the creature says as it forces an awkward chortle, which comes out for the first time as a clicking snort.

Glenn's eyes widen at the insect-like sound and he pretends to ignore it as he goes to remove his hand, and stops when he realizes she hasn't loosened her gripped yet which causes him to chuckle, yet again.

"I'm going to need that to drive," he says to her as she continues to hold on to his palm. She smiles and when she realizes what he's referring to, she immediately loosens her grip.

"Oh," she says, unaware that she made some sort of mistake.

"Heck, if it was up to me I would never let go, hahaha!" Glenn says to her as he forces out a laugh in an effort to break the awkwardness, which only does the opposite of everything he thought it would. He silently scolds himself for the corny line.

"Then why did you?" Minutia genuinely asks him in an effort to learn as much as she can about social interactions. However, Glenn interprets her question as one of profound depth which causes him to have a mini-existential crisis about how much of a slave we all are to these social structures that none of us really created.

"I...uh," he begins before going completely speechless. In all his years of living, Glenn has never once pondered such a question. The awkwardness from earlier that he attempted to extinguish has now evolved into a palpable poison mist that he even chokes on a little bit, judging by his inability to currently speak another word.

"Is this your car?" Minutia asks as she walks towards the vehicle.

She speaks not in an effort to break the tension, but because she learned from one of her episodes earlier that humans find it inappropriate for someone else to talk while they do, and it's best to wait until they are done before starting the conversation back up. Again, her question is one full of sincerity.

"Uh, yes.. yes it is," he says, suddenly remembering that he's a man, and that it's the man that is supposed to leave women speechless and not the other way around. He quickly tries to relocate his mojo. "You won't find many of its type here in Ida Grove."

She enters the car through the open, driver side and sits inside. She stares out of the front window with her hands down at her side like she used to do back on Apophis. Glenn laughs and walks up next to her.

"Oh, you drive a stick?" he asks her. He might as well not be speaking at all, because Minutia didn't understand at all what it was he was asking. She attempts to as she thinks of sticks and driving but can't seem to find a link between the two in the least. She looks up at him slightly confused which he takes as her being embarrassed. Minutia's scatterbrain expression makes Glenn bashfully shake his head as he's overwhelmed by just how darn cute she is. Nevertheless, he vows not to let his feelings get the best of him this time. Glenn decides he wants to play along so he walks around the car and enters through the passenger side.

"You wanna drive?" he asks her when she doesn't say anything. She only continues to stare blankly at him and smiles again.

"You're not really that talkative, huh? Well, I'm glad I can make you smile at least. I swear you're like an alien or something. Well go on, *take me to your leader,* hehehe," he chuckles to her jokingly. His last sentence causes her to frown again. He scolds himself twice as hard this time for his inability to stop being lame.

Trying to remember the position Glenn was in when he rolled up on her, Minutia carefully puts her hands on the steering one at a time, looks over at Glenn to make sure she's doing the right thing, then pushes on the steering wheel with her body. Glenn looks at her slightly puzzled and amused. When she continues to jerk forward and backward in her seat, he completely loses it.

"HAHAHAHAHA!"

Glenn's sudden outburst of laughter is as sincere as they come, considering it would be impossible for most people to mimic such a distinct type of laughter, as such a unique laugh can only belong to him. "What was *that?*"

She begins to chuckle with him. "Was that wrong, hehe?"

"You're hilarious. No, not at all. Just relax. Here, give me your hand," Glenn says as he places his hand on top of Minutia's and guides it towards his stick. Confused, Minutia immediately becomes defensive as she remains clueless to his actions. Suddenly she feels a hard object inside of her palm. Immediately, she closes her eyes and an influx of memories rushes into her head. She vigorously opens her eyes again and firmly grabs the stick he put her hand on top off.

"Whoa!" he yells out. She engages the clutch pedal and yanks the stick into first gear. "Yee-ouch!"

Glenn startled, quickly removes his hand off of hers as Minutia takes full control of the car and performs a burnout in an effort to swing the entire car around to perform a U-turn. Glenn almost falls out of his seat as he watches this sweet, awkward weirdo, handle his brand-new Mustang like she drove rally cars for a living.

Soon they peel off and Glenn watches on as Minutia speeds down the road, perfectly upshifting and switching between each gear with staggering precision. Minutia's eyes contain a fire that Glenn didn't, up until this point, think was possible to be ignited from within her. She looks over at him with the expression of someone who has a lot to lose, and then cracks that familiar smile that his life will no doubt now be different without. Glenn forces a smile back, sits up and buckles his seatbelt. He dares not tell her to do the same.

Chapter Nine

SITIO DEL ACCIDENTE DE METEORITO

April 16th. 7:52 A.M. (EDT)

LEANDER ESCORTS Laharin and Ori through the city of Monachopsis as they continue to make their way to her school. Mondays in Monachopsis are usually filled with people doing the same things at this early hour: either heading to some place to learn, or heading to some place to teach—a great deal of the time, neither of those places are educational institutions. As Ori stares out the window as she's driven through the city's streets she's become quite familiar with, she notices that on this particular Monday morning this normally monotonous experience is more or less the same with one exception: she doesn't see nearly as many children walking with their parents to school. Even the older kids known for wearing their fancy, customized SHED frames are nowhere to be found, and there are usually a particular group of them who always meet up at the same train stop every weekday morning.

"Mommy, where are all the kids?" Ori asks as she voices her concern for the absence of other children like herself on this early morning.

"What's that honey?" Laharin is currently preoccupied in her own thoughts.

"I don't see any kids waiting for the train to go to school. Where are they?" she reiterates to her mother. Her biggest worry, more so than any other, is that her best friend Cassandra won't be there.

"Well, maybe their mommies and daddies decided not to take them to school today, Ori."

"Is it because of the Apophis?"

"Yes honey, that's most likely the case. I swear these people in Mona kill me ... your father was right—everybody's quick to shop and support their own greedy habits, but when it comes to education, all of a sudden 'school is too dangerous for my child.' Bunch of rich dummies, I swear. Well rock or not, we're still going to school. And we gon' go every single day as long as it's open," Laharin voices aloud.

"Okay, Mommy," says Ori in response, though Laharin was just bellyaching out loud and not necessarily looking for her daughter to agree with her. Ori continues to stare out of the car window wearing a dour expression and as she does so her ears happens to catch the news on the radio once she hears it mentions her father's superhero alias.

"Mommy! Mommy! They're talking about Daddy on the radio! Tell Leander to turn it up!"

"Uh, Leander?" Laharin calls out to the driver from the back seat of the car.

"Yes, Mrs. Chambers?" he says back to her.

"Can you please turn up the radio for us? I'd appreciate it."

"Of course, ma'am," he says, politely acknowledging her request.

Life in Monachopsis hasn't been the best but it certainly hasn't been the worst, especially considering the place Laharin was six years ago. The only problem Laharin had with living amongst rich people here was getting used to their privileged lifestyles and ways. In fact, she mostly despised it. To her, being on the run from the federal government wasn't all that bad a life considering what she now has to put up with. At the same time, Laharin also realizes that much of her angst comes from how she feels about her stupid legs. Thankfully, having Leander as a driver was one of the few perks that she enjoyed as a citizen of Monachopsis. She thinks all of this to herself, even choosing to refer to herself in the third person within her own thoughts. How crazy she is, she thought to herself, to even refer herself to herself in her own selfish mind.

"Again, rumors continue to swirl throughout Opia after recent footage has emerged of what appears to be a man hanging upside down from a crane that he's somehow got entangled in, seventy stories above the ground. In the video, you can see the man slowly losing his grip to the point to where he falls and is then immediately shot back up into the sky. Many people are saying Nerosion is the one who's responsible for this as a similar occurrence has happened in the past, even though he's nowhere to be found in the video."

"Yeah, it was him," Laharin says out loud to the radio which makes Leander chuckle.

"Again, this is the only video out right now of this incident, so no one knows what really happened. Police haven't yet given a statement regarding..."

"Thank you, Leander," she says to him, prompting him to turn the radio back down.

"Mommy, you think that was Daddy? Or the man that killed the bee?"

"*Killed the bee?* Watchu talkin' about?" Laharin asks, thrown off by Ori's seemingly random statement.

"The man that killed the bee! He has long hair, a ripped jacket, and dirty boots, and he kills bees with his needles!" she exclaims.

"Girl, what are you talking about, what man killed what bee?" she asks her normally sensible daughter. "That's it Ori, you ain't watching that Cupid show any more. That thing is messing up your mind worse than my own," Laharin says to Ori, which causes her to pout at the fact that her mother has no idea what she's talking about. The car pulls up to the front of the school, and Ori notices something is very different about the usually crowded area. Though the front of the parochial private school is normally filled with a crowd of people around this time on weekdays, this isn't nearly the same type of crowd that Laharin and Ori usually pulls up to.

Ori looks out the window and sees a bunch of people who look like they haven't been near a school in a decade and a half, holding up picket signs and posters while chanting a bunch of different, incoherent things. Ori has never seen anything like this. Though much of the wording on the signs are different from one another, all of them seem to have a very similar theme between them: *Keep Your Children Home.*

As the car pulls up to the curb, hundreds of angry faces from the mob peek and snarl at the occupants inside of the car—particularly Laharin and Ori.

"Come on, Ori. Thank you, Leander."

"Do you need me to come inside with you, Mrs. Chambers?"

"No, Leander, we'll be fine. Thank you," she assures him.

Laharin and Ori don't exit the car until the local school safety officers make a path through the crowd for them to be able to safely walk through. It's evident to Laharin, by the faces of the officers, that they didn't expect anyone to bring their child to class today.

Laharin exits the car first. The crowd's sneering grows somewhat louder once she emerges. That could be due to the fact that she simply opened the car door, or due to the fact that it's she who happened to exit out of it. She then walks around to her daughter's side on the curb and opens the door for her. Ori exits the car and the crowd's booing and jeering grows substantially louder as the crowd becomes more erratic.

"Take that child back home! She shouldn't be outside during this global crisis!"

"The end is upon us! Keep your kids safe!"

"Children should have a choice to be schooled! Stop forcing your children to be outside the safety of their homes while we are facing a global crisis! PUT THAT CHILD IN A SHELTER!"

Many of the screams and shouted comments coming from the crowd, derive from the mouths of the many self-righteous, unenlightened hipsters living in Monachopsis—they who, Laharin assume, have nothing else better to do than to protest against a contrived, fabricated non-issue such as "Forced Schooling" during the aftermath of a national crisis.

"Is this for real? Are they serious?" she says as she grabs Ori's hand.

"Mommy, what's going on?"

"Nothing, baby. A bunch of lowlifes with nothing better to do doesn't want you to get an education, that's all. Come on."

Laharin and Ori begin walking towards the entrance of the school using the path that the school safety officers have created for them.

"Maybe it's because they don't have educations, Mommy," Ori shrewdly submits.

"Yup, exactly."

"I think people just like being around other people who are like they are," Ori says as she continues to watch the behavior of the unruly crowd. "Occupy. Educational. Freedom." Ori reads aloud the words of one of the signs she notices amongst the many. "What does that mean, Mommy?"

"It just a fancy way of saying 'Hey, I'm a jackass, so I desperately need everyone else to be, also.'"

Laharin's quip causes Ori to giggle. She loves when her mother swears every now and then, especially when it's directed at someone besides her father.

Laharin and Ori finally make it out of the outside noise and inside of the comforting, quiet lobby of the school. Not that she was exactly expecting it, but Laharin can't help but to be a little surprised that no one is there to greet them. Considering all the commotion outside behind them, you would think there would be a team of people ready to provide them with some necessary information on what's in store for any parent and child who attends their school. But nope, no one appears.

Mostly unbothered, Laharin proceeds with her child to the main office as Ori looks around at the familiar environment she hasn't seen in the last three months. She's surprised to see it's exactly as she remembers it: unimaginatively bland. Most grade schools in Monachopsis are catered to a unilateral, indoctrinated style of learning than they are to promoting and catering to a child's individual learning style. As a result, many of the things that would normally be found in normal grade schools outside the city—like colors for example—are generally absent on the walls inside the halls and classrooms at the Del Cora Private Art School for Girls. For a school that's centered around building the artists of tomorrow, there sure seems to be an extreme disinterest in the field present throughout the building.

When Laharin and Ori entered the main office they were greeted by an office staff member who wasn't at all anticipating any parent showing up with their child. In fact, none of the staff even noticed her when she first entered, which is surprising, considering that some of the workers were candidly sitting on top of the desks they should rightfully be working at. Their idle chatter, which more than likely has nothing to do with the education of First to Eighth graders, was abruptly interrupted by a sharp, intentional throat clearing by Laharin.

"Heh-MM-MM-MM-MMMMMM," hocks Laharin to the hard-working staff. "Good morning guys, I'm baaaaacccck. Miss me? Ha, nah I'm just playing, I know y'all do," she vocalizes almost farcically. "Well, as you all know, school was officially opened again today, so—woo hooo! I wasn't a hundred percent sure myself, but that big crowd outside basically confirmed it for me. So, here we are, hehehe."

For a good, few, long seconds, no one speaks or addresses Laharin as they are now much too upset to find out that they just may have to work today after all. It's the office secretary that is the first to finally speak out.

"Hello, Ms. Tahilri, I'm surprised to see you ... today. I didn't think you were going to bring Ori to school."

"Really? Why not?"

"Well, considering everything that has happened over the past couple of days, I figured your concern for your child's safety would be heightened because of this whole asteroid business," the office secretary tells her.

"Hi, Mrs. Piven," Ori says to the familiar woman.

"Hello, Ori," she blandly but politely replies back.

"Really? I thought you knew me well, Mrs. Piven. I'm here at every Parent-Teachers conference, every after-school function, every school play, why wouldn't I be here? Shoot, y'all here, I wanna be here too. Ain't no rock gon' stop my baby from getting an education, ain't that right, baby?" she says to Ori.

"Mommy said Apophis can't stop us, won't stop us, Mrs. Piven," Ori says to the secretary.

"You tell em, baby," Laharin says, proudly.

"Mrs. Piven, where are all the kids?" asks Ori, noticing she has yet to see another child since she's entered the school.

"Most of them aren't here, Ori. Their parents didn't bring them in today."

"Oh. Why not?"

"Because many of their parents didn't want to put their kids in any danger," she replies, while tossing a soft indirect jab at Ori's mom. One that Laharin picks up on but doesn't in the least let phase her.

"Oh, I see. Did Cassandra come to school today?"

"Yes, she did, Ori."

"Yes!"

"See, Cassandra's mother brought her in, why are y'all so shocked we here too, then?" Laharin poses.

"Well, Cassandra's mother happens to work in the school, Ms. Tahilri. It works out for her to have her child attend every day since she's here also."

"Well, this is Ori's first year, so I'm sure y'all will agree that it's important she's here as often as she can be. Especially considering that she's younger than all of her classmates and this is her first experience in a school setting ever. Being a five-year-old amongst third graders is a tough thing to have to get used to. She gon' need all the experience she can get while she can. And now that that rock is gone, we can finally get back to her getting on top of her studies," Laharin dishes out not only to Mrs. Piven, but to the entire staff behind her.

"Ms. Tahilri, I totally one-hundred percent agree with you, believe me. The only problem is, it's not just the students. Many of the teachers haven't returned either. There are only a handful here."

"So, where's Cassandra?"

"She's in Mrs. Aronson's class."

"Okay, then Ori can go there until her teacher shows up."

"I'm sorry, but Mrs. Aronson teaches the fourth grade, that class is much too advance for Ori."

"Oh really? Would it be too much trouble if we took a look?" she asks, mostly innocently.

"Uh, sure, but I don't see how that's going to—"

"Come on, Ori," she commands, her tone suddenly switching.

Laharin, Ori, and Mrs. Piven proceed to Cassandra's class on the fourth floor. They walk until they reach classroom 4-403.

"Cassandra?" Ori calls out to the girl who she assumes to be her best friend. A pretty, lively, dark-skinned girl turns around to see who it is that called her name.

"ORI!" Cassandra yells out before getting up and running to greet her dearly missed friend. They hug each other like they haven't seen each other for years, and Cassandra pulls her to her table.

"Mom, this is Ori Lorraine, is it okay if she stays here? She's very smart!" Cassandra pleads to her teacher.

"Oh, I can tell she is just by looking at her. Hello, Ori. Sure, you can have a seat at Cassandra's table if you like. The work may be a little advance for you, but don't worry, you can hang out here until your teacher, Mrs. Riley, returns. She should be back sometime this week."

"I can keep up, Mrs. Aronson. I love geometry," the erudite student says back to her. Cassandra leads Ori to her table while Mrs. Aronson joins Mrs. Piven and Laharin for a brief conference by the door.

"Hi, I'm sorry, I'm Mrs. Aronson," she says to Laharin as she offers her hand for a shake. Laharin meets her hand and exchanges only her first name. "Nice to meet you, it's just been so crazy here. Before the school doors even opened those people were already outside crowding the entrance, shouting and yelling. This Apophis thing has really got everybody losing their minds. I must admit, I'm a little surprised to see you bring Ori to school so soon after the event. Most of the kids who are here parent's work in the school," Mrs. Aronson shares with Laharin.

"Asteroid or not, I just want my child to get the education she needs, and this is one great way to show her that she should never let anything or anyone stop her from learning. As long as the school remains open, she will be here," Laharin strongly reaffirms.

"I admire that so much, Ms. Laharin. It'll be my pleasure to help your daughter get the education she deserves while she's here."

"I appreciate that. Ori, come give your mother a kiss before she goes," Laharin says loud enough for the entire class to hear. Because Ori hasn't yet matured to the age where such an action by a student's mom in front of a classroom of students would be considered top three most embarrassing things that can happen to a fourth grader, she obeys her mother's endearing request without ever second-guessing it.

Obliviously, unlike her classmates, some who watch in slight disgust, Ori runs and hugs and kisses her in front of the other students. Laharin realizes she has about a full year left before her genius butterfly realizes that a mother's public affection to her child is considered a cardinal sin in any normal school setting, so she tries to make the most of it while she still can.

"You're going to be staying with Mrs. Aronson until your teacher comes back ok? She'll be back soon."

"Okay, Mommy," Ori happily squeaks.

"I'll be here to pick you up when you get out at 2:15, okay?"

"Okay, I got it Mommy. Bye," Ori says to her mother. She prematurely ends their conversation, both so she can hurry back to Cassandra, and because five-year-olds aren't yet much knowledgeable in the area of proper social etiquette. Besides, Laharin realizes three months is a long time to go without seeing your best friend. After all, it's been almost ten years since she's seen any of her own. Laharin begins to choke up a little before stepping out the class and she waves her final goodbye to her daughter before she sees her again in six hours.

6:58 A.M. (CDT)

Minutia and Glenn continue to speed down the open road. Even after driving for a good fifteen or so miles, she continues to impress Glenn by keeping the speedometer over eighty and almost never dipping below that mark.

"Hey," Glenn says to his adrenaline-junkie driver. "Pull over."

"Huh? Pull what over?" Minutia responds as she has trouble understanding Glenn's figurative choice of language. So, he points at the sign indicating a gas station is coming up soon.

"Oh!"

She still doesn't really understand what he meant, but she goes along with it and acknowledges his request with a simple nod, one she's performed numerous times since they've been driving, almost as if she's practicing how to properly use it. The whole ride up until now has been mostly silent as most of Glenn's attempts to strike up a conversation were either dismissed by Minutia's inability to effectively communicate using modern colloquialism, or from Glenn's inability to talk about anything worth elaborating on—or perhaps from a combination of both. For the first time since she's gotten behind the wheel, Minutia decelerates and rolls the car into the nearby gas station. She pulls in near a pump and keeps both hands on the steering wheel like a Nascar racer who's just pulled into a pit stop and is anxious to get back on the track.

"Hey," Glenn says to her. She looks at him and nods again. At this point it's no longer cute to him—in fact, it's a little annoying now. "We need gas," he says as he points at the gas gauge in the dashboard. "You can relax now."

"Okay, no problem," she says back to him clueless to what it is that made him say she can relax now. "I can relax now."

He looks at her then at her hands which are still clutched tightly on the steering wheel. She notices this and finally removes them.

"You're a mysterious one, aren't you?" he says to her in a lighthearted way, pushing his glasses up back onto his nose in an effort to lighten up his mood now that they've finally took a break from being on the road. She takes her hands away and places them flat on her lap.

"You can turn the car off now, too. Don't worry, it'll start back up when it's time to go. Take a break, love," he says to her. His colloquialism still throws her off but she's getting better at catching his drift. So she turns off the car and suddenly she realizes just how quiet the area is. In fact, they both pick up on that.

"Where'd you learn to drive like that?" he says to her after a few seconds of silence.

"Drive like what?" she says back to him which causes him to smile. He mistakes her obliviousness for sarcastic modesty. Nevertheless, it makes him smile so he indulges her.

"Most ... *women* I know," he says, carefully choosing his words, "don't drive quite like you do. With such ... I don't know, passion," he tells her. Minutia has no idea what he's getting at so she responds in a way that he's come to accept as non-sequitur.

"Sometimes we have to learn to know when to pull over," she says to him. And she's stumped him yet again, only this time he can't tell if this woman is exceptionally wise for her age or out of her damn mind.

He shrugs the thought off and squints his eyes at her before asking another question.

"I know it's a pretty rude thing for a guy to ask a lady, but you never told me your age," he says to her. She waits for a question to come and it never does. So she nods in agreement to his age statement. "How old are you?"

"Oh!" she exclaims although she still doesn't produce an answer. With nothing to say, she reverses the question to get an idea of what age is.

"How old are *you?"*

"Thirty-three," he says after lightly chuckling.

"Thirty-three?" she repeats. Though she knows the number, she doesn't know what it applies to in this case.

"Yeah. Why, I don't look it? Most people think I'm much older."

"No, you look it. Thirty-three. Just like I thought."

"And yourself?"

"Me? Forty-three."

"What?" Glenn shrieks. His reaction causes Minutia to panic a bit. She's not sure if she said something wrong which she thinks she most likely has, but she runs with it anyway.

"Yep. I have a lot more ages than you do. Why, *I don't look it?"*

"Forty-three? You look more like you're twenty-three, love. Barely."

"Oh. Okay, twenty-three. You got me, hehehe."

"Whatever you say. You want to pump the gas or should I?" he asks her.

Before she can answer he takes her silence as a clue that it'll be wiser for him to do so. "Never mind, I'll take care of it."

Glenn grabs the keys and gets out the car. Thinking he's abandoning her, Minutia gets out right with him and follows him closely while doing her best to not make it seem like she doesn't know what's really going on. They reach the pump and he pulls the gas pump from its holster. She stands much closer to him than she has yet as she watches him fill the tank up, which causes her to have another slight mental episode. The whole transaction starts becoming a little more clearer for her as a result.

"Are you hungry?" he says to her as he opens the little door that covers the gas cap on his car. This question she understands completely.

"No, I'm fine. Are you?" she asks back from behind his shoulder. Glenn can't help to mistaken her sudden proximity and tendency to flip his questions back at him, as her genuinely caring about him.

"No, I'm also fine, also," he answers with a chuckle. "Thank you."

"You're welcome, Glenn."

"You still never told me where you need to go. You just got in the car and started driving."

"Oh right. I need to go to the *Sitio Del Accidente De Meteorito,"* she tells him. She's not sure if that's what people are calling the areas where the meteors made impact with the Earth, she just know that's what the guy on the television in the diner called it.

"What, you speak Spanish, too? Wait, what did you say? *Meteorito?* Is that meteor? Did you say meteor?"

"Yes!" she exclaims, overjoyed that he understands what she's talking about. "Meteor!"

"You want to go to the meteor? The site? Is that what you said? You wanna go to the meteor site? Why?" he wonders.

"Well, the explosion blew up my mode of transport, but I think my artifact survived."

"Mode of transport? What do you mean?"

"Yes, I think y'all call it an *'asteroid'* here."

"I have no idea what you are talking about."

"Oh. I was on that asteroid when it was attacked, most likely from something or someone from this planet. I then woke up in a ditch and then a bunch of people tried to shoot me. So, I ran to this diner and saw someone I know on the television. Then I realized he's looking for the artifact, also. I need to go the meteor site and find it before he does."

"...."

Glenn stares at Minutia slack-jawed, as if she really was speaking nothing but Spanish.

"Are we ready?" she asks him.

"Ready? Ready for what?" he responds.

"To go to the meteor site."

"To the meteor site," he repeats. "For what?"

"I told you, to find the artifact before Jumopikwaris does."

"..."

"I mean, before...Juu-mm-oo does. Before Jumo does," she clarifies.

"Jumo. Who's Jumo?"

"The man from the video in the diner. With the...hmmm, what *would* you call them here?" she says after dwelling on it a bit. "*HY-Lokans,*"

"Man, I give up," Glenn says, feeling defeated at trying to understand what it is he's hearing this woman say.

"Didn't you see the video of the HY-Lokans attacking that site?"

"The HY-Lokans? You mean those alien-wolf looking things that killed all those people?"

"Yes! Those!" she exclaims.

"You know what those beasts were?"

"Of course, they belong to Jumo. But they're not really beasts. They're not even really alive. It's kinda hard to explain."

"And Jumo is that man at the end of the video?"

"Yes!"

"And you know him—how?"

"He's from where I'm from. He was also on the asteroid with me when it exploded."

"So, you're not from Earth?" Glenn asks her sort of seriously; which surprises even him.

"No. Not at all," she shares. She then hesitates before attempting to pronounce the name of what her original home would be called in this language, knowing he won't be able to comprehend it. "I'm from a nearby star system."

"Nearby. How nearby?" he asks, trying to hang on to something she says that he can acknowledge as sensible.

"By your terms, 8,458 light-years that way," she accurately answers while pointing towards the horizon behind her and not necessarily the sky above.

"Mm-hmm. And you flew here on an asteroid?" he continues to ask. Adding more layers of sarcasm with each question.

"Yes, and it was blown up by some weapon on this planet a few days ago."

"And this asteroid was called Apophis?"

"Apophis?" she tries to remember where she heard that name before and remembers it being said in the diner on the television. "Yes, exactly!"

"So, you're an alien?" he asks her. She takes a second to process what does the word 'alien' mean to human beings.

"Uh, yes—I guess," she says, not entirely sure.

"Oh okay. And how do I know you're an alien?"

"What do you mean?"

"Like do you have special powers or something?"

"Special powers?" she repeats, perhaps looking for him to be more specific.

"Nothing," he replies.

Glenn finishes pumping gasoline into his car and places the gas pump back into its station holster. He then walks to the driver side of the car, confusing Minutia.

"*I'm* gonna drive this time—if you don't mind, of course," he says to her. She nods and walks to the passenger side. They both get in and the first thing he does is tell her to put on her seatbelt before starting the car.

"Are we going to meteor site?" she asks him while they drive.

"I told you I'll take you wherever you needed to go so yeah, let's go. First, I have to make sure we go to the right one."

"There are more?" she asks, surprised to hear this.

"Yes, hundreds more. When the government shot that missile at Apophis, it blew it up into thousands of little pieces. A lot of people believe a lot of the debris fell back to Earth but they're mostly denying that."

"Yes, of course! Let us go to the closest one then, I need to find the artifact before Jumo does!" she exclaims, excited to finally get back on the road.

"Okay!" he agrees as he goes to shift the car back into first gear. "Oh, can you do me a favor really quick, can you hand me that map from inside of that compartment, it'll show me what road is closest to the next impact site," he says to her as he points to the glove box.

"Sure," Minutia says with a smile as she takes off her seatbelt and leans down and feels for the latch that opens the glove box. As she does this, Glenn takes his right hand and hits Minutia in the back of the head as hard as he can. As a result, her head knocks against the dashboard, knocking her completely unconscious.

Glenn drives about a mile before he pulls over to the side of the road. At seven in the morning on this particular dirt road, there isn't a soul in sight who can witness what he's about to do. So, he gets out the car and walks to his trunk. He retrieves a silver roll of duct tape and now walks to the passenger side where Minutia lays unconscious. He pulls Minutia's limp body out of the car, and begins binding her arms and legs with the tape. Glenn then picks up her body and places it into the trunk of his car. He closes the trunk and goes back inside of the driver's seat. Before driving off, he pulls out a cellphone and dials a number. The phone rings three times before a man picks up on the other end.

"Hey—you still accepting bodies?"

"I am," the voice responds on the other end.

"How much?"

"Depends. What do you have?"

"A young one. Female. Early twenties. Healthy."

"Okay. Forty."

"Fine. I'm on my way."

Chapter Ten

ORI'S REQUEST

April 16th. 2:20 P.M. (EDT)

SIX HOURS and twenty minutes never felt so long for the students who are currently in attendance at the Del Cora Private Art School for Girls. That is because the one and only teacher that's currently present in the school, finds it'll be fruitless to teach a class laced with students from various grade levels. Especially when chances are this class will soon disassemble either because the student's parents will opt to keep them home when they learn that it makes no sense to continue to send them to a school where no real learning is taking place, or because hopefully, the student's original teachers will eventually return to the school.

Even Ori, a child who can somehow intrinsically extract joy from a learning environment that many others find otherwise academically arid, is finding herself desperately waiting for the dismissal bell to ring, or for her mother to show up—whichever comes first. It's not that Ori isn't enjoying spending time with her friend Cassandra, who she's missed dearly, but it's that her and Cassandra has just about caught each other up on everything that a five-year-old and a nine-year-old can basically catch each other up on in the six hours they spent together. It doesn't help the fact that Ori is way more into learning than socializing anyway.

Interestingly enough, most of what makes Ori affable, at least to a class of fourth graders, is that she's somehow found a way to make academics seem cool. Not in the corny way that most teachers forcefully attempt to impose on their students in the beginning of every school year, with the promise that their "style of teaching" is going to be different than any teacher that came before or will come after them. No, to identify what makes Ori an interesting person to be around, would be like understanding how listening to an interview about why a serial killer decided to do the abhorrent things he or she's done in their spree, is interesting, and then actually finding yourself identifying with or maybe even, sympathizing with the serial killers choices at certain points. To the extent that upon listening to the serial killer's reasoning, what's right or wrong becomes irrelevant, if only for a brief moment. Similarly, what's cool or corny, tends to also become irrelevant once people start hanging around young Ori.

But Ori isn't popular in the least, at least in the traditional sense. If fact, if she can be identified as anything from her classmates, it's that she's notably *infamous*. For example, never before have the students who know her and know of her, have they ever seen a child before her who can avoid being bullied by simply negotiating with her oppressors. She's known to also diffuse the tensions that naturally exist between opposing cliques of students before it erupts into fights; advance through her classes and win over the hearts of her teachers without ever coming across as a kiss-ass; and even choosing at times to hangout with the "loser" students perhaps more so than any other group in the whole school. Overall, part of her infamy seems to stem from her detachment from subscribing to any one particular faction in her school environment.

Perhaps, her tight friendship with her fourth-grade best friend is the best testament to how advance this five-year-old must be. It's not that these events don't at all take place at that level, in fact they may be even more prevalent in the fourth grade, but at that level she is more able to be understood as someone who is fulfilling a role, something she's secretly come to grow proud of, whereas in first-grade, she was simply another student whose biggest accomplishment would be whatever curve of rudimentary, elementary academics she just mastered; just known as another "smart" child who had to spend a week learning single-digit addition when she was already capable of multiplying fractions. It is rumored that when asked by Cassandra whether Ori enjoys being viewed in the way she is by other students or not, it is said that Ori just looked up and said, "who cares but who cares?"

BRRRRRNNNNNNNGGGGGGGG!

The last bell of the day finally goes off and the dead silence that filled the room due to most students exhausting their supply of conversation too soon, and the remaining too tired or bored to keep their eyes open, is broken by the sounds of the chairs and desks being moved by the dozen or so students all hastily getting up at the same time. Chances are many of them won't be returning back the next day. This is likely due to the fact that most schools in Monachopsis are generally occupied with students who have been inundated by most adults in their short lives on how unnecessary school is nowadays anyway, though they continue to send them to it, almost as if it were some sort of prank. As a result, most people who attend schools in Monachopsis, no matter the age, attend them with a collective lack of enthusiasm for learning. And it doesn't at all help that the parents themselves don't really see the point of pressuring their children to go to school at such an early age, as they've come to believe in this new "free-learning" model. A model which postulates that basic knowledge is naturally learned in the outside world through socializing, and only those who wish to become a specialist in some sort of field should then attend special institutions designed to teach them that said skill. Undoubtedly, many parents will feel it's senseless to continue to send their children back there once they learn no real learning is taking place.

Since learning doesn't seem to be on the menu at this point, it's pretty likely that the students who've attended class today are planning on spending a good portion of their afternoon bombarding their parents with their individual versions of how fun their day was, thanks to the lack of instruction going on.

Ori just may attempt to partake in this ubiquitous soliloquy performed by children all across the city. However, her chances of staying home are significantly way less than most other students. The main reason being that just as her enthusiasm for learning happens to be greater than most students in Monachopsis and perhaps in all of Opia, it doesn't even dare to come close to her mother's enthusiasm for getting her child to attend school every day.

Cassandra and Ori exit the classroom together with their teacher behind them and begin walking towards the elevator.

"How'd you like your first day back, Ori?" Cassandra asks.

"It was fun, I guess, and your mom is so cool. I wish my mom was a teacher, too," she replies.

"Nah, I don't think you would. It's not that fun," she says back to her.

"Oh, okay," Ori says incredulously.

"How are you getting home? Is your mom coming to pick you up, Ori?" Mrs. Aronson asks after suddenly remember the situation that existed directly outside the school doors just this morning. Ori nods.

"And my Dad. He's coming too," she surely adds.

"Oh okay, I've yet to meet your father, you'll have to introduce me sometime, Ori."

"Okay, I will when he gets here, Mrs. Aronson."

The class makes it to the main office where other kids' parents are already waiting for them. Ori looks around and sees no one that remotely resembles her mother's esoteric, yet grandiloquent taste or demeanor— and especially no one resembling her father. Mrs. Aronson turns back towards Ori after also failing to spot her mother.

"Did they say where they were going to meet you?" the teacher asks her. Ori doesn't really have an answer. She, like any child, would never entertain the idea of their parents not being there waiting for them when they were dismissed. Amongst the commotion happening in the office, a distant phone ringing in the background is picked up by a staff member after about two and a half rings. In the meantime, Ori is trying to imagine why neither her mother *nor* her father is anywhere in sight. The thought of it upsets her more than it worries her.

"Ori? Ori Lorraine?" a voice behind the main office counter calls out.

"Yes?" says Ori in response to the voice, doing her best to be heard over the noise of the office without blatantly shouting '*I'm here!*'

Ori is too short to see exactly who it was that shouted her name from behind the desk, so she can only wait to see if her voice was heard by whoever is back there. Suddenly a large, heavy-set woman looms over the desk and peers down at Ori like some giant sea creature that was much larger than anyone initially speculated it to be before it fully revealed itself.

"Ori, do you know a man named 'Leander?' He's waiting for you in the front."

The large woman's patience has vanished sometime years ago, no doubt during her long career working as an office clerk or whatever it is she does, evident by how she doesn't even wait for Ori to answer her question. Mrs. Aronson, overhearing the entire exchange, looks at Ori to confirm if everything that was said is true.

"Who's Leander, Ori?"

"He's my driver. You don't have to worry, Mrs. Aronson. If he's here it just means my mother's in the car right now," she tells her.

"Okay, love, well let me escort you to the front just to be sure," Mrs. Aronson says. Ori quickly wipes a tear from her eye before anyone can see it and her, Cassandra and Mrs. Aronson all walk towards the school's entrance where they spot an older, tall, and fit but almost lanky fellow, dressed in what appears to be a driving uniform, standing alone. His missing jacket and hat somehow brings more attention to his balding, curly hair which thankfully makes him appear more congenial than his solemn expression paints him to be.

"Hi, Leander!!" she shouts out to her favorite non-relative adult. The expressionless Leander returns her gesture with a wave.

"Hello, Young Miss. Your mother's waiting in the car for you."

"Oh. Why didn't she come out?" Ori wonders aloud.

"Unfortunately, your mother has used up all of the time she's allowed to walk for today."

"Oh. Is Daddy there?"

"I'm sorry, but your father couldn't make it either, Young Miss."

"Okay," she says, seemingly unfazed by that particular news. "Bye, Cassandra, bye Mrs. Aronson."

"Bye! Come to school tomorrow!" says Cassandra, making sure to remind her one last time before she takes off.

"Take care, Ori. Hopefully we'll see you tomorrow," says Mrs. Aronson to Ori before shaking Leander's hand and seeing them off.

Leander and Ori exit the school doors only to learn that the crowd of protestors from this morning have not only not dispersed in the least, but seems to have grown to some degree. The slew of insults thrown from the crowd has intensified since this morning. These protestors are clearly agitated but it seems as if something has occurred in the interim that exacerbated their rage.

"Leander?"

"Yes, Young Miss?"

"Why are these people so mad at this school? she asks him. "Did the students do something? It seems a bit ... unnecessary."

Leander, perhaps more so than even her parents, understands just how intelligent Ori is, probably even more than Ori does herself. He senses the sincerity in her voice, so avoids answering her prematurely and instead dwells on the subject of her question for a bit as they continue to walk through the schism in the crowd.

They cross the street away from the school and reach the other side where the chanting is now only but a distinct, inaudible noise from where they stand.

"Where's Mom?" says Ori as she looks all around for the distinguished Mercedes-Maybach she's grown so accustomed to riding inside of. "She doesn't drive," she tells herself, still confused.

"I had set the car to circle around the block for a while until I returned with you, Young Miss," he tells her, relieving some of her confusion.

"Ohhh okay."

"No, the students haven't done anything. I believe they're mad because their lives are maddening," he randomly says to Ori.

"Huh?"

"You asked me why are the protesters in front of the school mad, didn't you?"

"Oh, yeah I did. But what does that mean? Maddening?"

"When your life is maddening, it means that there is something in your life corrupting you, or it means that there is something that your life is devoid of," he says to Young Miss, purposely using unfamiliar words with the intent to teach her new vocabulary knowing she'll naturally deduce its meaning.

"So, because they are missing something in their life, they are mad at other people's lives?"

"That's right," he confirms.

"What are they missing?"

"I'm not sure, Young Miss. It's impossible to know what each one of them are missing in their individual lives. In fact, it's not really fair to generalize an entire group of people in that way. Chances are they all may be missing something quite different from one another. Whatever it is though, it has brought them all together to this place. That's the only thing we know. The only thing we can know for sure is that their madness has brought them together," he concludes.

Ori remains silent as she ponders over Leander's insightful words.

"People like being around people who are like they are, don't they," she realizes for certain this time.

"Are you missing anything, Young Miss?" he says to her sensing her slight mental bind. She looks up at him then looks up at the tall buildings that surround them, and smiles.

"No. I think I'm lucky to have my mommy *and* my daddy. I miss him. But it doesn't make me mad. It makes me happy. It makes me happy that he always comes back home to me and Mommy," she says as she continues to stare at the rooftops of the various buildings in her vicinity.

"Madness comes when something corrupts us, or when something is missing from our lives. I hope you never go mad, Young Miss," Leander says.

"Oh, there she goes! I see the car, Leander!"

"I'll hold your bag, Young Miss."

"Leander? Can I ask you for a favor? But you have to keep it a secret."

"Of course."

"Instead of Young Miss, can you call me Young Miss *Nerosion?"* she asks of him. Leander cracks a smile, a gesture usually only seen by Ori.

"How about just Miss Nerosion?" he says back to her which causes her pretty brown eyes to light up in a way he's never seen before. She cheeses and nods feverishly in agreement with her new secret designation.

Chapter Eleven

KIDNAP YOUR BABY, SPIT AT YOUR LADY

April 16th. 1:28 P.M. (CDT)

IT'S BEEN a good twenty minutes since the thumping in the trunk started. Minutia, who was passed out in the back of Glenn's pitch-black trunk, finally regained consciousness and has been annoyingly shuffling and kicking in the tiny uncomfortable area, long enough for Glenn to be absolutely elated he's finally arrived at his destination.

Though she's unable to physically see anything going on outside of the trunk, Minutia quickly becomes aware that the car is coming to a stop. The car stops, and Glenn kills the engine. She listens intently for any sounds for a clue as to where she might be—a mostly fruitless endeavor, considering she hasn't been many places.

At first, she hears nothing except the sound of Glenn rifling through the inside of his car for who knows what. The thought of what he may be doing absolutely terrifies her, but her curiosity keeps her composed and focused. After all, during the car ride, she's grown more confident with her abilities and her knowledge of the world. If she can survive getting hit by a nuke, then a kidnapping should be a walk through the park ... she hopes.

Minutia continues to listen, hopefully for any sounds that might trigger an episode for her—however, not only is she not experiencing any seizures, but Glenn's rustling has also come to an end. Then, she hears something unexpected—the voices of multiple men. Older men. She hears Glenn talking with them for a short while before he gets out of the car. They continue to speak, but no matter how hard she tries, she can't make out any details from the conversation. At last, she hears footsteps approaching—the kind that nobody who's tied up in the back of a trunk wants to hear. The footsteps, which she can only guess are coming from at least four men, grow louder and louder before they stop just outside the car. The trunk pops ever so slightly open, and a large hand opens it up the rest of the way. Before she can even adjust her eyes to the blinding light, a black hood is thrown over her head and she's lifted up out of thc trunk.

"What the hell was that? You felt that?" she hears one of the voices randomly blurt out as they pick her up.

Most people would remain silent in such a situation because they are too petrified to speak, however, Minutia's silence comes from her innate interest to process every single thing happening to and around her. Yelling out, screaming, or even speaking at all would only work against her ability to learn more about her environment. Be that as it may, she can't help but to flinch, yelp, and shake from the entire ordeal as she's pulled by two men towards an unknown location. She's quickly learning that curiosity is a two-sided coin: with every flip, she risks either access to great knowledge or access to great danger.

They all walk for a little while before stopping inside of an elevator. Minutia can tell her surroundings have changed because she can smell just how close the men are to her now. She hears the door close, and the sounds around her begin to whirl. The elevator begins to ascend and now Minutia recognizes that she's inside of some sort of contraption that aides in transporting people on this planet up to higher levels within a larger structure. Interestingly, this actually sort of relieves her.

The moving platform, as she's come to know it, comes to a halt after a good twenty seconds, by her count. She hears the doors open again and immediately the heat and shine from the morning sun hits the woolen cloth over her face and she can tell she has again entered a new area of wherever she is.

She's led out of the elevator into the new room and the guards let go of her arms. A second later the hood is snatched from off of her face. It takes almost no time for her eyes to adjust to the brightness of the room, which is, to say the least, unlike any room she's been in since being on this planet—which has only been three. She decides rather quickly that she has no time to inspect the brand-new environment that surrounds her because what she sees in front of her is a hundred times more interesting.

A single child with a very sophisticated looking, but nonetheless plastic mask of some gruesome-looking creature, bounces up and down on a bed that could fit a dozen of his friends easily. Instead of friends however, two women both of whom are so attractive that if they had their own stock ticker symbol, surely people would invest in them—sit on each side of him as they both stare at Minutia as if there wasn't an eleven-year-old boy jumping up and down next to them.

Minutia looks around in the hope that someone can somehow explain to her what is going on. At the same time, she notices she's suddenly having trouble remembering the details of what happened to her before she landed on Apophis.

"What is this?" she all but blurts out.

"Can't hear you!" the boy yells back, bouncing up and down on the super-sized mattress. His voice comes across synthesized thanks to the mask he's currently wearing—something Minutia is unable to discern.

"I said what is this? Who are you?" she asks, this time much more loudly.

"Calvin. Who are you?"

Minutia looks again at the people around her. None of them respond to her.

"Who am *I?* You brought *me* here," she reminds him.

"Uh, no I didn't," says Calvin still jumping. He turns around to face Minutia. "He did." Calvin points to Glenn who stands behind her. "Catch!" Calvin says as he throws a thick envelope, seemingly filled with money, at an unsuspecting Glenn, who catches it at the last minute.

Glenn looks inside of the envelope. "Thanks, Cal,"

Minutia whose wrists are still bound by duct tape, turns around and stares at Glenn with a puzzling scowl. "Glenn, what is going on?"

she asks, but he ignores her—partly because he really doesn't know himself.

"Glenn tells me you're special," Calvin says, now having stopped jumping. "Is it true?"

"What?" she says before turning and facing Glenn again. "Glenn, why did you do this to me?"

"Hey!" he yells out to her. "I asked you a question. And why do you keep calling him Glenn, his name is Chadwick."

Minutia looks at him again as she experiences disloyalty for the first time in her life as an Earthling. "Are you special or not?"

"No, I'm not *special.*"

"What? Aww man, Chad you lied to me. You said she had powers," Calvin says, now sulking.

"She does. She's lying."

"What? Is that true?" Calvin says, suddenly enthusiastic again, clearly displaying a habit of hanging on to every word someone says to him.

"I have no idea what you are talking about. Who are you anyway?" Minutia asks.

"I told you, I'm Calvin. Calvin Sonder. And I have powers, too. If you show me yours, I'll show you mine."

"What?" she says, almost baffled at what she just heard. With everything that has transpired thus far since landing on Earth, hearing this shocks her the most.

"Ah, Chad, you said she was smart! I don't even know if she can even speak English cuz she keeps saying 'what,'" he says as his anxiousness to see her powers starts to get the best of him. "Fine! I'll show you mine first, but you have to promise to show me yours next, okay?"

Calvin gets down from on top of the bed and grabs the pair of scissors out the awaiting hand of one of the women next to him. He walks up to Minutia and cuts the tape from off of her wrists.

"Okay, hold still, lady," he says to her as he puts his hand out near her stomach. He closes his eyes and Minutia's entire past of where she's from and how she got on Apophis all start flying into his head. He quickly snatches his hand away and falls on the floor.

"Whoa, what was *that?*" Calvin screams as his enthusiasm goes from a nine to a fifty. "You really *are* an alien! Oh, my God, this is so amazing! You must show me more, that Slow Down thing ... how did you do that!? That's even more amazing than The Man in The Dirty Robes who rescued the Star Child!"

"The Man in The Dirty Robes?"

Minutia has no idea who he's talking about, and neither does anyone else in the room.

"You don't know about him? Oh man, you got SO MUCH to learn!" Calvin exclaims.

"Wait ... what did you do to me?"

"Nothing, I just looked at your past," he responds dryly.

"My past? How?"

"Yeah. How? Uh dunno, I just hold my hand out ... like this and I can see anyone's past."

"T-That's ... that's incredible," she says, utterly nonplussed that someone else on this planet also has an amazing gift.

"Thanks. Now can you show me what you can do?" he asks her.

Minutia thinks about his request but then looks around at the armed guards, women and servants all throughout the large room.

"Do I really have a choice?"

"Of course you have a choice—what do you think this is? In fact, you can leave right now if you want to."

"I can? Are you serious? Then why did you bring me here?"

"Because Chad told me you had powers, so I paid him to bring you here. You're not very smart are you?"

"So you're not going to shoot me?"

"What? Um, no?" Calvin says to her, a little confused by the question. "Why would I shoot you?"

He eventually notices Minutia's skepticism is derived from the five armed guards currently behind her.

"Oh! They're just here so *you* won't kill *me*. Sometimes when people are brought here, they freak out and try to kill me once I show them what I can do. I'm actually surprised you haven't done that yet."

"People? You do this often?" she asks, each revelation of information he shares with her leaving her more shocked.

"Uh, yeah?"

"Okay. I'll show you. But can we go somewhere else? Honestly, I'm a little uncomfortable."

"No problem! This is my parent's bedroom anyway. They're on vacation right now, so this is like the only time I can do this. Please don't tell them," he pleads to her. Minutia nods in agreement and they begin walking back to the elevator.

On her way to the elevator, she walks past the guards, but has her eyes fixated on only one person: *Chadwick*. As she comes closer and closer, her piercing scowl becomes more and more intense to him. Finally, she crosses right by him, this time unbound by any tape or woolen hood.

"I'm sorr—" he begins to say to her when she's within speaking range.

"You will be. I promise you," Minutia shares back in a cold whisper. He barely recognizes her voice in her new-found anger. The duo enters the elevator and Calvin presses "4" on the button console. The doors close and the elevator begins to ascend.

"Where are we headed?" she asks him.

"To my room. It's not as big as my parent's room, but it's not as crowded either. You'll feel much more comfortable, trust me," Calvin replies.

"Trust you? You kidnapped me."

"I didn't kidnap you, you're an adult—you can't get *kid*-napped. Besides, it was Chad who brought you here, not me."

"And you paid him for it."

"How do you know that? You're an alien, you don't know what money is," he says dismissively.

"I learned what it *is* when you tossed him that envelope," she says with an attitude.

"I told you, you're free to go. Nobody's going to stop you."

"And I'm supposed to just believe you?"

"Are you going to show me your powers or not?" he snaps at her. Clearly, things like kidnapping and human trafficking are nothing compared to whatever it is a child truly wants, like seeing the abilities of a being from another solar system.

The elevator dings and the doors open again. He walks out first and she follows. They enter a dilapidated room with nothing but a box-spring bed, a single window, a television and a closet. Minutia can hardly believe such a place exists in the same place that the room they just came from exists in.

"*This* is your room?" she says in a surprised tone.

"Yes, AND..? Jeez! It's not *your* room so stop worrying about it," Calvin snaps back at her.

"I have no problem with it, it just doesn't look anything like your parent's bedroom."

"I brought you to my parent's room which was much better, but you wanted to be here, so now deal with it."

"No, it's fine. I'm much more comfortable here," she tells him.

They enter the desolate room and Calvin rushes to the bed and tries his best to inconspicuously remove the toys that were on top of it before Minutia notices what he's doing. Being the alien she is, such attempts at hiding certain customs that would normally embarrass a child whose intent is to appear more mature, escape her entirely. However, she does pick up on his vehemence to perform whatever task he doesn't want her to see, so she allows him to do whatever it is he doesn't want her to notice by pretending to be fascinated by the chipped paint on the walls in the mostly empty room. When she senses that he's done, she looks back at him.

"May I sit here, Calvin?" she politely asks, trying to appear as non-threatening to the things he wishes to hide from her as best as she can.

"Yes, yes come sit next to me," he anxiously says as he dusts off the spot where she'll eventually sit down on top of his bed. She then sits down on the bed next to him.

"Okay, go!" he says anxiously.

"Okay. but before I do I want to ask you something."

"Ahhhh! What is it?" he whines, become increasingly annoyed by her constant deflection.

"Why are you doing this?" she asks him.

"I told you, I wanna see your cool powers," he reminds her.

"I'm not talking about my powers, I'm talking about everything. How often do you kidnap people?"

"I told you already, I don't *kidnap* people, people tell me that they found someone with powers and they always say *'I can bring this person to you if you pay me.'* So, they bring the person to my house and I give them money for it."

"You don't see anything wrong with that?" she asks him with all sincerity.

"I always tell them they can leave. Most of the time, the people they bring never have any powers. They just lie to me so they can get paid," he confesses.

"You know that, and you still do it anyway?" she wonders.

"Yeah. I just want to meet someone else like me," he admits.

"And what do you parents say about all this?"

"They don't really know. Please don't tell them."

"Please don't tell your parents that you pay men to kidnap people against their will?"

"Well, I wouldn't do it if they didn't keep me locked up in this damn room all day."

"What? They keep you locked in here? But you seem so free," she says while looking around.

"Yes, well not locked up *exactly*. When they're home, I just stay in here for the most part. They just want me to watch that freaking television all day to find information about the past or whatever," he shares with her.

"That's horrible. I'm sorry, I had no idea."

"It's okay. It doesn't really work anyway. My powers that is—it doesn't work that way. I can only see the past of a person or a thing, like the TV itself—but not the shows *on* the TV. My parents don't know that because they're stupid and are always on vacation."

"I see. Is that why you have so much money?"

"Basically. People pay them to learn about their history. So they bring them to me and I just tell them what I know. Most of the time I just lie. They don't care, as long as they get paid."

"I see. You have an incredible gift, Calvin. I'm sorry it's been used in this way."

"I don't mind, my life is pretty okay most of the time since they're hardly here and all. Now are you going to show me your powers?" he asks her once again.

"Can't you just look into my past and see them yourself?"

"I can but when I did earlier, I didn't really understand what I was looking at. It was very confusing."

"I see. Calvin ... you ever thought about leaving?" she asks.

"What do you mean?"

"I mean, getting away from here and going out into the world."

"Uh, why would I do that?"

"Plenty of reasons."

"You know what, I'm starting to think that you don't have any powers. Besides, I'm just a kid."

"I know you are, but I'll protect you, and who knows we just may be able to meet others like you," she tells him.

"So, there really are *others?* Like The Man in The Dirty Robes?"

"I'm not sure who that is, but if you have seen him, then I'm sure he exists. I just don't think this is the place for you."

"You're asking a kid to run away with you? I thought you was against kidnapping people and that's the exact definition of it," he says to her, deciding to use this opportunity to turn their back and forth prattling into a teachable moment.

"I found you, so I'm sure together we can find others like us. We can start with The Man in The Dirty Robes first if you like. If you come with me, I'll help you find him," she tells him.

"Oh my god! Really? Please don't lie to me, Minutia!" he says, suddenly excited.

"Toss me that toy," Minutia says as she gets up and points to the series of action figures located on the other side of Calvin's bed—the very ones he tried to hide from her. Calvin embarrassed at first, reluctantly reaches behind his bed and picks up one of the larger ones.

"Catch."

Calvin tosses the action figure at her and then watches as it slows down in mid-air and appears to seemingly rest there, but moving ever so slightly towards her.

"No way!" he says, bewildered by what he's looking at. He hasn't been this excited since he first had visions of The Man in The Dirty Robes. Minutia grabs the toy out of the air and sits back on the bed,

this time much closer to Calvin. She grabs his hand and wraps it around the toy that her hand is in.

"Stay close to me, and I will never let you fall, Calvin," she sternly but softly tells him.

"Okay!" he says with a new sense of purpose in his head. "I'm ready, Minutia. Let's go."

They enter the elevator and proceed down to the garage floor where Minutia first entered the building at.

Ding! The doors open, and they take two steps out only to realize that they are surrounded by the very gunmen that were hired to protect Calvin. Chadwick steps out into view, having revealed that he's the reason behind this treason.

"You!" Minutia growls upon seeing her once-trusted friend.

"Chad, move! I'm leaving," Calvin tells his kidnapper-for-hire.

"I'm sorry, Calvin, I can't let you do that," Chadwick responds.

"You're not my DAAAADDDD!" Calvin shouts, his voice cackling thanks to the electronic damper on the mask he still hasn't taken off.

"I'm not, but I informed your dad on what's currently taking place, and he's advised me to see to it that you don't leave the premises until he returns."

"He did? When did you call him?"

"Right after you threw that toy in your hand at your new friend," he says to him.

"You were watching us," Minutia interjects.

"Yes, as per his father's request with all of Calvin's guests. Normally, we let most people go with no problem. One, because ten out of ten times, they never have any powers, and two, because they have no idea where the hell we are. So, not only are you the first person in history that we brought here who actually has some gift, but with Calvin now with you, it won't be long until you learn of our location. So, I'm sorry but I can't let you leave," Chadwick tells them.

The gunmen all raise their guns and cock them.

"What are we going to do, Minutia?" Calvin says hoping Minutia has some sort of plan. After a couple of seconds, she looks down at him.

"Remember what I said Calvin, stay close to me and I'll always protect you," she says back to him.

"No, you said stay close to you and you'll never let me fall," he says, correcting her.

"Come on, really? You know what I meant. Ready?"

Calvin electronically gulps then nods.

Suddenly, with Calvin holding her hand, Minutia starts running directly at the guard in front of her. The gunman aims and fires a single bullet at her. Much to the gunman's surprise, the bullet slows down and she moves out of its path. He lets off two more shots and they both do the same. Not at all anticipating this, the gunman is completely thrown off and Minutia catches him with a sloppy right hook. The punch connects directly with his face, causing him to stumble and his weapon to fall. She winces from the painful but effective punch, then tells Calvin to keep running and that she'll be right behind him.

Every single gunman in the parking lot is now firing upon her as she continues to follow Calvin through the underground parking lot.

"Why didn't you pick up the gun??" Calvin says when she catches up to him.

"I've seen what those things can do and I'm not trying to kill anyone," she replies.

"But *everyone* is trying to kill us!" he exclaims over the loud gunfire.

"They won't," she promises him.

As they run, Calvin is amazed at how beautiful the bullets—that he's never been able to see in flight after being fired from a weapon—are all now flying around him, slowing down long enough for him to see them, and disappearing as they fly off again.

"That is so cool!" he says to himself out loud.

"Where are we going?" Minutia asks him as they continue to speed through the underground parking lot.

"To my mom's car! She lets me drive it sometimes when my dad isn't home!" Calvin yells out over the loud rattling of the automatic machine guns firing at them.

"What kind of car is it?"

"I don't know, I can't pronounce it!"

They turn a corner and waiting outside in a sectioned off area is an elegant Wine Red, 2015 Koenigsegg Agera.

"There it is!" Calvin says to her, pointing to the sophisticated vehicle.

"That's your mom's car??"

"Yeah, she rarely drives it though, she's more of a collector!"

"I see!"

Though Minutia is probably used to handling technology that is literally light-years ahead of anything anyone can produce on this planet, even she can't help but to be amazed at the fine piece of Swedish craftsmanship that sits before her.

"Can you drive?" he asks her, hoping her answer is of course.

"A little!"

"Can you drive manual!"

"That's stick, right?"

"I guess."

As they continue to run towards the vehicle, Calvin pushes a button on his wrist-mounted SHED band which causes the car doors on both sides to lift up and the engine to automatically start. They both hop into the car and he presses the button on his band again, triggering the doors to close.

Minutia takes a moment to gather herself and notices something very familiar is missing.

"Hurry up, they're shooting at us!"

"This isn't a stick shift!" Minutia screams out as she searches for the gearbox that the last car she was in contained but that this one is clearly missing. "Calvin, what is this?"

"You said you can drive manual!" he shouts.

"Well, where's the stick then? There is no stick!" she shouts back.

"Oh, there isn't?" he says to Minutia. "I could've sworn this was a manual."

Minutia can't believe he bungled something that was so important to ensuring their escape. She starts jolting herself back and forth in the car like she did when she first tried to drive Chadwick's Mustang, while pressing all types of buttons in an effort to get the car to move.

"What the hell are you doing?" Calvin says in response to her erratic movements.

Most of the armed men find their way to their position and begin firing at the vehicle and Minutia pushes Calvin's head down onto her lap.

"Hey, what are you doing!?" he screams.

"Saving your life!" she says as she keeps his head pressed down.

"This hurts!"

"Calvin, do something! I can't drive this thing!!"

"Ugh, hold on!"

In that same moment, Calvin closes his eyes and sticks his hand out in front of the steering wheel. Meanwhile, bullets continue to fly towards Minutia, puncturing holes in the car before slowing down when they enter her vicinity. But at this point, even some of the bullets slowing down are beginning to touch her clothing, with some now about to touch her face. Unable to move thanks to the bubble of bullets her entire body is encased in, she helplessly remains frozen as she waits for Calvin to figure something out.

"Calvin, please hurry," she cries out to him.

"I'm trying!!"

"I thought you said your mom lets you drive sometimes!"

"She never taught me how to switch to the first gear!!" Calvin suddenly opens his eyes. "Oh yeah!" He takes Minutia's hand that's currently on the steering wheel, and places it on top of the right paddle directly behind the steering wheel.

"Brake, now!!" he screams out to her. Minutia immediately engages the brake pad and the car switches its gear to Drive. Minutia acknowledges this by the unique sound the car makes when it transitions gears.

"Shoot the tires, you dolts!! SHOOT THE TIRESSSSS!" an encroaching Chadwick screams out.

Minutia then engages the gas and the car peels off out of its parked spot where it reaches upwards of sixty miles in less than three seconds before hitting the main road and leaving the premises.

Chapter Twelve

WELCOME TO VESTO MELVIN

April 16th. 4:14 P.M. (EDT)

"HOW WAS SCHOOL TODAY, HONEY?" Laharin asks Ori once she's in the car and they start driving away.

"Not bad," Ori dryly responds.

"I'm sorry I couldn't come inside to get y—"

"Where's Daddy?" she interrupts. Laharin caught off guard, takes a moment before she answers.

"Daddy couldn't make it," she tells her inquisitive daughter.

"Why?"

"He's working, honey."

"Okay."

"Are you upset?"

"No, as long as Daddy's at work it doesn't bother me."

"Well, that is a really mature thing for you to say, honey," Laharin tells her daughter, impressed.

"Mommy?"

"Yes?"

"Is Daddy missing something in his life?"

"What do you mean?"

"Nothing," she says, dismissing the question. "Mommy, can I watch T.V.?"

"Sure, Ori," Laharin says to her.

Ori presses a button on a console located next to her in the car, and a thin screen pops out of a compartment in front of her. The screen turns on and Ori starts flipping through the channels.

After surfing through a few she stumbles onto her favorite show *Madly Dote!* Immediately, she takes the two plastic, disposable, wireless tabs out of a small compartment by the T.V., and presses them against the back of her ears. She turns the screen towards her before her mother can see what she's watching. Laharin is too busy texting on her cellphone to notice anyway.

"Uh, Leander, dear?" she calls out to her driver.

"Yes, Mrs. Chambers?"

"If you don't mind, I would like to make a quick stop."

"Where to Mrs. Chambers?"

"Vesto Melvin," she answers. Leander pauses for a moment before speaking.

"Are you sure, Mrs. Chambers? If I'm not mistaken, I believe Vesto Melvin is still under martial law. I'm not certain that's a wise choice considering your condition."

"Yes, I'm sure."

"Is there any particular place you wish to visit?"

"Borick Valley," she tells him. Leander looks at Laharin through the rearview mirror when he hears the name of her destination.

"As you wish, Mrs. Chambers," he says as he dutifully adheres to her request.

4:59 P.M. (EDT)

Back at Del Cora Private Art School for Girls, Olpha hastily makes his way to the main office where he's expected to meet his fiancée and daughter.

"I'm sorry Mr. Chambers, but Ori's been picked up already by her mother."

"What? Are you serious?"

"Mr. Chambers, that was over an hour ago."

"I...Okay. Thank you."

"Should I contact them and tell them you stopped by?"

"No, that won't be necessary."

Olpha's SHED band begins to vibrate indicating he's received a message.

**URGENT* Report to the 43rd OPD Precinct ASAP.* The message scrolls across his band continuously until he marks that he's read it. Olpha lets out a sigh and walks out of the school. A great deal of the crowd of protesters has dispersed since Ori was picked up by her mother. Still, Olpha can't help but get irritated that there are people out here who are really trying to prevent his daughter from getting an education. Having to head to a meeting to explain why some lowlife lost his low life, does nothing to assuage his irritability and pushes him to want to confront one of the protesters—which he does. Wearing a grimace, he approaches one of the occupants and faces him.

"What are you doing? This is a private school for children. You need to get out of here, right now," he says to the contentious protester.

"Sir, it is people like you that is what's wrong with this city! Children should NOT be forced to leave their homes to go to school while the country is facing a global disaster. Parents need to stop this overt, brutal campaign on forcing their children to having to be exposed to imminent and avoidable danger, just so they can feel accomplished as a parent. Children are not asked to be born! It's the adults that irresponsibly force them into this world, and then impose on them what they desire them to do for them. It is unfair! A child is an individual with rights just like everyone else! They are not your own personal servants, the likes of whom you can just choose what they can and can't do academically to the point it puts their life in danger! Enough is enough! We are not going to stand by and allow irresponsible parents to continue to put children in harm's way for the sake of their own selfish gratification. It's time children learn that they too have rights and their rights should be represented and upheld!" the forward protestor spouts loudly.

"Listen to me carefully, you insufferable piece of shit," Olpha says as he gets closer to the man's face. "Stopping my child from getting an education is the greatest harm of all. And I'll die first before if I let any one of you deranged derelicts come close to robbing her of that opportunity."

"You can't stop us. You can't stop the sharing of *true* knowledge," his stubborn contender affirms, not at all appearing to back down. "The time where you selfish parents choose which information your child has access to is finally coming to an end. If you had your children's best interest in mind, you will tell them exactly why it is they should have a choice as to whether they come to school or not. However, it is a known fact that parents continue to willingly keep information that can ultimately benefit their children from them, just so they can fulfill their own personal agendas. No more!"

Soon the rest of the crowd joins the single outspoken occupant in his affront.

"My daughter will be here tomorrow. This crowd better not be. I am not playing," Olpha growls to the disgruntled occupant. "You've been warned."

"You do not intimidate me, sir! I am NOT your child!"

The protesters start to interrupt their own trite, repetitious chanting, to instead use colorful language to remind Olpha of all the things he is and represents—none of which are pleasant.

5:02 P.M. (EDT)

What's interesting about the borough of Vesto Melvin, is that during the time of the infamous Melvin Riots, many of the residents (something like ninety percent of the population) of the time, had united on a scale yet unseen before anywhere else in the country. When Kenopsia had decided that it was going to use the income generated by the citizens of the borough to fund developmental projects for Monachopsis, the people of Vesto Melvin knew that the time for peaceful protesting was officially over, and the time for a revolution had to take its place. It was at this time that the Einstein-Rosen Bridge & Tunnel that connected Kenopsia to Vesto Melvin and Monachopsis had to be seized, and if necessary, destroyed. This act would prove to be the defining moment where the state and federal government will finally take action against the residents of Vesto Melvin, and it is also here that the residents of Vesto Melvin knew they were going to have to fight and maybe even die to be taken seriously.

A common misconception is that the conflict that existed in Opia at the time was between Vesto Melvin and Monachopsis. In actuality, the only enmity that existed at that time was between Vesto Melvin and Kenopsia directly. Monachopsis learned very quickly that by not getting involved in such affairs, they would only stand to benefit from such a conflict—even more so if Kenopsia emerged as the victor. Of course, that didn't happen, and as a result, Monachopsis became a target once the people of Vesto Melvin realized that their so-called neutrality was really just a ruse for them to be able to benefit altogether, regardless of who emerged victorious from the conflict.

Years have passed since the Melvin conflict, and as far as the country knows, tensions between the three districts have diminished to the point to where they can now coexist peacefully, hopefully for many years to come and thereafter. What isn't known too well by anyone not living in Opia, is that since the inception of Apophis, these once dormant tensions have begun to resurge throughout the county. The sudden emergence of various "movements" have once again popped up around the districts in Opia at an alarming rate.

The Einstein-Rosen Bridge & Tunnel, a.k.a the ERBT, or Wormhole as dubbed by Opians, as it stands today, no longer just represents a tether that ties the districts together by which people can use to travel between Monachopsis, Vesto Melvin and Kenopsia. It also stands as a symbol that acknowledges the bond that now exists between the three boroughs. It is looked upon as a promise from the people of Opia, to never again use violence to influence politics or economics, send a message or even make a point. This is why now, today, with the help of Nerosion's presence, violence on a macro-scale hasn't been a concern for the most part within the city. That is until Apophis became a national headline.

But where large egregious acts of criminality rarely reared its ugly head, the insurgence of a passive-aggressive animus has taken its place in the form of numerous socio-political campaigns and movements. On the surface, they only appear to serve the mission statement of its cause including but not limited to: a child's right to choose an education; a prisoner's right to choose where they serve their sentences; privacy rights, and many others. The truth is however, is that these movements only seem to exist, so people can use them as a guise under which they can continue to incite hate, fear and violence throughout the region, as they did so well years ago. At least this is what Laharin firmly believes and thinks about as she reads the highway sign that says: '*Welcome to Vesto Melvin - The Marble Botanic*' as she, Ori, and Leander make their way to their destination located in the district. And right now, it's going on an hour since the crew started making their way towards the tempestuous borough.

"How much further, Leander?"

"We'll be in Borick Valley in two minutes, Mrs. Chambers."

"Thank you."

"If I may ask Mrs. Chambers, what is it you're hoping to find out here?"

"I don't know. An answer ... maybe," she says to Leander which makes him slightly turn his head. "Ori," she says, as she taps her daughter, who's currently entranced in her show. "Take those off, I want you to see something."

Ori does as she commands without a fuss and Leander gets off at the exit that'll take them to Borick Valley. At first, Ori isn't too intrigued as to what she sees around her. There isn't anything in Vesto Melvin, let alone in Borick Valley, that a child who was born and raised in Monachopsis can hope to find interesting. However, Ori wasn't your typical child, and Laharin knows this.

"Mommy, where are we?"

"Earlier you asked me is Daddy missing something in his life, right? I can only guess that you probably asked that because he's always away, as if he's always out looking to find whatever he is missing. If he is missing something, then this is where he goes to find it," she says to her daughter while staring out of her own window. Ori turns and looks at her as she talks, then looks at the passing streets out of her own window.

As they cruise through the borough of Vesto Melvin, they both stare out of their respective windows, seemingly searching for a clue to whatever it is that draws the most important man of their life here.

"Daddy comes ... here?" Ori reluctantly asks. She can't seem to make sense out of the words that escape from her mouth as they don't match the reasoning that exists in her head. Why would her perfect hero head to a place as destitute as this?

As they continue to cruise through the vast housing neighborhoods sprawled throughout the borough, Ori's attention to her surroundings has peaked, and she now observes every passing activity with unhindered focus—even though there aren't many. For the most part, the streets are relatively empty, at least compared to the average bustling street in Monachopsis. Maybe it's because the streets are wider. Maybe. She can't tell what the reason is, she just knows it's emptier here. The buildings are much smaller; that she knows for sure. It must not be too exciting for Daddy to swing from them. Even the design of them aren't too interesting to look at for the most part. The entire town, from what she can tell, almost seems to be painted in the same bland color palette: gray. She's sure it's just the area they happen to be driving through at the moment. It is sure to change—her father would never find anything he thinks he may need, here. In fact, it *has* to change.

"Why are we here, Mommy?" she asks as she turns away from her window to face her mother.

"I told you I wanted to show you something," Laharin answers. "Make a right, here, Leander."

As Leander makes the right, Ori scoots up to the middle of the car to get a better view of what they're now approaching; a single burgundy building with the United States and Opia flags sitting on top of it. Laharin looks at Ori to answer the question she never asked.

"My old school."

"You went to school here, Mommy?"

"I did. From the sixth grade to the eighth. I spent most of my days here inside of the halls of Victor Hess Junior High School."

"How was it, Mommy?"

"It was ... enlightening, baby. It's what made Mommy want to become a soldier. Even your father doesn't know that I went here. So you better not tell him."

"Wow," Ori says, amazed her mother possesses such a secret.

"Why is it you've never shared this part of your life with your husband, Mrs. Chambers?" Leander asks, displaying some curiosity of his own.

"Contrary to what he'll have you and everyone else in this city believe, Olpha is very sensitive. If he found out I used to attend a school in a district he only wishes to rebuild, it'll more than likely affect his work here. There's a sort of bliss knowing that my king is helping restore a place I used to consider an empire, back to its former glory—even if he's unaware that he is doing so. It makes me honor him even more. I want him to work at his full capacity, so it's better if he didn't know. When the dust settles, I'll make sure to tell him then. Who knows, maybe after all this is over, we may be able to move back here. Would you like that, sweetie? If we all moved to Vesto Melvin?" she says to her uneasy daughter.

Ori takes a good while before responding and looks outside again with a pensive expression before she answers.

"If this is where Daddy's happy at, then I want to be here with him," Ori responds.

"It'll look a lot better when he's done, trust me. Honey, come help me get out the car, I want to see if the school's still open."

"Mrs. Chambers, should I join you?"

"No, that's okay, Leander, I'll only be a minute. And Leander, you can save the *Mrs. Chambers* handle for when I've officially earned it. Until that day, I'm still a Tahilri."

"As you wish, Ms. Tahilri."

Laharin and Ori head to the front of the school. Ori helps her mother up a few steps to reach the entrance. Laharin gives the front door a nice tug and realizes it doesn't budge and probably hasn't budged since she was last here fourteen years ago.

"I knew it," she says, disappointed. "Oh well, come on, Ori."

"Wait Mommy, say cheese!" Ori says as she catches Laharin off-guard with a candid picture.

"Oh Ori, come on I wasn't ready," Laharin chuckles as she fixes herself this time for a better one. "Okay, take it again, baby."

Ori holds up her mom's phone and snaps another photo. She runs back to her mom and shows her the results, the likes of which came out spectacularly. Ori grabs her mother's hand and helps her back to the car. They get back inside and take in one last view before they begin to head home.

"The entire borough is under a police state," Leander shares. "It's a good chance most, if not all, schools here are closed."

As they pull out from the curb, a speeding car almost sideswipes them and Leander blows the horn excessively as it swerves by. Leander's blatant regard for following the rules of the road must not sit well with the passing motorist, because they immediately slam on the breaks once they realize some other car had the nerve to honk at them for speeding.

Leander, who's still struggling to pull out of the car spot, decides he's not going to focus on inflaming any kind of potential petty transgression that may unfold between the two motorists. He's just going to focus about getting Ms. Tahilri and her lovely daughter back home safely.

Suddenly, the white lights that indicate the reverse gear has been engaged, lights up on the other car, and the car begins moving backwards at a considerable speed towards them. It stops about a yard away and five young, rash, male passengers hop out of all four doors of the vehicle. The music blasting from their vehicle is especially loud, now that all the doors are open. Because the windows on the vehicle Leander is currently driving happen to all be up, it's tough for him to hear the obscenities the five males are currently hurling at him. However, the windshield is more than adequate at allowing him, Laharin, and Ori to see all five men now approaching their vehicle.

"Leander, get us out here," Laharin tells him, with a slight worrying inflection in her voice.

"Right away. I don't know why I squeezed into this tiny, tight spot anyway," he says to her back, trying to offer a bit of levity to their situation. Laharin silently scolds herself for telling him to park there so she can get out of the car closer to the school.

"No, it's my fault," she says as she forces a chuckle. "Let's just go."

"Mommy, what's going on?" Ori asks as she watches the men get closer and closer.

"Nothing, sweetie. Leander is just a little stuck right now," Laharin calmly replies to her child.

"Who are those guys coming?"

Laharin stays silent and she curses her disability more than she ever has in her life; the ex-soldier inside of her however, chooses to instead curse the heavens, asking why couldn't this predicament happen nine and a half years ago when Ori didn't exist and neither did her disability. In fact, nine and a half years ago, she would've gotten out of the car first. Now all she can do is rely on Leander to pull off a miracle.

Tap! Tap! Tap! One of the men finally makes it to their car and begins tapping on the windshield, while the other four ruffians flank the sides.

"Looks like your old ass is having some trouble. Funny, you were just in a rush pulling out but now you can't move. Need some help? Why don't you let down the window, so I can help you," the driver of the other vehicle suggests to Leander from outside the window.

The rest of the men have fully encircled the car and are now staring inside of the back windows, luckily the dark tint on them help prevent the men from getting a good view as to who's inside. However, Ori can tell that her mother is feeling uncomfortable about the situation, considering she pulls her closer to her once the men begin peering inside.

"I said open the fuckin' door!" threatens the man at the driver's side as he pulls out a pistol and points it directly at Leander's head from the other side of his window. Leander notices this and immediately puts his hands up. "Get out of the fuckin' car old man! You bitch-ass Mona motherfuckers think you can just roll through here and do whatever the fuck you want? Get out, nigga! I'm takin' this shit!"

Not wanting to make the situation worst, Leander complies with the gentleman's every request. He figures if he's outside of the vehicle he can greatly reduce any potential harm currently facing his passengers.

"Okay, okay, calm down. I'm getting out. I'm getting out," he says calmly as he exits the car. Laharin and Ori are surprisingly quiet during this ordeal. Laharin's silence stems from a culmination of anger, overall helplessness and a natural fear for her daughter's life, while Ori's seem to derive from her natural sensibility to stay calm in these type of situations, coupled with her penchant for being brave in the face of adversity. Also, she's secretly developed a dash of intrigue for the entire ordeal. Leander fully steps out of the car and over to the side, hoping to get the gunman to point his weapon anywhere except near the vehicle.

"I should kill your bitch ass right now. The fuck your old ass doing in Borick Valley, huh? I can tell by your whip that y'all from Mona. Prolly downtown Mona, too. And who that in the back witchu?" the gunman asks as he make an effort to look over Leander's shoulder and peer inside of the backseat windows. "Look like you escortin' somethin' nice back there, too," he says now waving at Laharin with his free hand. "Oh okay, hey boo ... I see you—in the back all dolled up, being chauffeured around and shit. Your sexy ass—whatchall tourin' through here or sumthin'? You ain't welcomed here, nigga," he says back at Leander. "Yo, I asked you a question."

"We was just visiting an old landmark is all. Nothing fancy," Leander says as he does his best to keep the situation under control.

"What, the school? Your old ass ain't go to this school, this shit wasn't even here when you was a kid, fuck u talkin' bout? Ohhhh, wait a minute, this ain't *your* old school, no, sista girl in the back used to go here. Say word! I went here too—we prolly had the same teacher, shit, lemme go introduce myself," the assailant says to Leander before he begins to walk towards the back of the car.

"Wait, no!" Leander screams out to the gunman as he reaches out and grabs him on the arm. Once grabbed, the gunman reacts immediately and snatches his arm away from Leander's grip and then delivers a swift pistol whip to the back of Leander's ear, effectively knocking him down to the ground.

"LEANDER!" Laharin screams from the back of the car as she watches her beloved friend collapse from the blow. The gunman hears the shriek and reaches for the door and when he realizes it's locked, he signals for her to open it. However, Laharin is much too focused on Leander's well-being to even notice the man's request. Feeling ignored, he grows annoyed at her defiance and strikes the window with his gun, shattering the glass and exposing Laharin and her daughter to everything he is. This action redirects Laharin's attention back to the gunman and she can now clearly hear all of the whooping and hollering that the gunman's delinquent friends are doing after each heinous action he commits. He takes his time unlocking the door from the inside and then opens the car door himself. He squats to get a better look at them.

"At first I just wanted the car but now," he says as he enters into the vehicle, now sitting right next to Ori and Laharin, "I think I wouldn't mind keeping y'all two, also. How bout it? You wanna come live with Rotty for little a while? You look like you can cook your ass off, too. We can be one big happy family, just the three of us," the gunman says as he lackadaisically waves his gun around as if it were just his finger. Laharin holds Ori up against her tighter than she ever has. "Oh and don't worry about Pops out there, Rotty'll make sure to drive you wherever you wa—"

Suddenly without any warning, the gunman is violently snatched out of the vehicle as if a bullet train threw a lasso around him as it passed by at two hundred miles an hour, making the car rock extremely hard as a result. The suddenness of his disappearing act makes Laharin jump harder than she has since the men started harassing them. She takes a few moments to collect herself so she can hopefully understand why is it she no longer hears any whooping or hollering from any one around the car. Ori opens her eyes and is suddenly more excited than her mother expects her to be.

"They're gone Mommy, they're gone!" she exclaims as she begins to crawl out of the car.

"What? ORI COME HERE!" Laharin screams to her daughter as Ori carelessly crawls across the broken glass on the seat. She can't help but to remain fearful and uncertain of whatever is out there.

"It's okay, Mommy—the Bee-Killer took them away," Ori confidently replies.

"The what?" Laharin says as she scoots over to the other side of the car so she can get a better look at what has transpired in only an instant. What she sees is anything from what she expected—not one of the men that were just terrorizing them is anywhere to be found. The only things that contain any evidence that they were even there is the pistol that belonged to the gunman, that of which now lays on the ground not too far from Leander, and the abandoned car the group arrived in that's still in the same place it was when everything went down.

Ori immediately runs to Leander's side to assist him. Laharin, who remains debilitated from her disability, can only watch from the car as her daughter moves with a boldness that reminds her of herself when she was younger.

"Ori, is he okay?" she says, the worry in her voice just now starting to fade away.

"Wake up, Leander," Ori whispers in his ear after squatting down next to him. "We're going to be okay, the Bee-Killer saved us from the bad men."

For some reason Leander begins to come to after she says that to him. Though hurt and a bit disoriented, he finds his ground and allows Ori to help him to his feet. He picks up the pistol on the ground and begins to limp back to the car with his hand over Ori's little shoulder.

"Oh my god, Leander, are you okay? I already called EMS, they'll be here soon," Laharin tells him when he makes it to the car.

"I think I'll survive, hehehe," he quips as blood continues to trickle down the back of his ear. "What happened?"

"The guy who you was with hit you with the gun, then—"

"Then the Bee-Killer came and saved us! It was SO COOL!" Ori excitedly interrupts.

"What?" Leander says as he chuckles along, something he's been doing a lot lately. "Who's the Bee-Killer, Young Miss?"

"Daddy's friend with the long hair," she confidently shares with him. When she says this, the expression on Laharin's face instantly goes from concerned to morbidly shocked. She stares at her daughter without uttering a word, or even blinking, while her mouth remains slightly agape.

"Oh okay," Leander says, going along with whatever the hell this child is talking about, but just happy that he still has full use of both his ears.

In record time, the sirens of a police car can be heard approaching. Leander puts the pistol in his pocket and sits on the hood of the car.

Meanwhile, Ori leans in between her mother's legs and rests her head on her chest.

"I can hear the police, Mommy. You think Daddy's with them?" she says to her comforting mother. However, Laharin remains completely silent as she tries to make sense of her daughter's description of her father's "friend", and gently continues to run her fingers through her daughter's short, curly hair.

Chapter Thirteen

DEVIL MAY CRY

April 16th 7:37 P.M. (CDT)

"We made it, Calvin!" an overly enthusiastic Minutia exclaims to her passenger and current escapee.

"Yeah. Barely," Calvin says back to her, hesitating to share in her overzealous joy. Minutia notices that though they now share an entire stretch of road alone with no other vehicles, Calvin continues to look over his shoulders as if someone can catch up to them at their current speed.

"You can relax now," she assures him. "I think I finally got the hang of this car, which I must admit isn't like anything I've ever seen."

"Really? That's shocking. I'm sure nothing on this planet compares to anything where you're from," he responds. Minutia takes a moment to consider this and actually agrees with him, albeit silently.

"Well, I have yet to see anything like this *on Earth,*" she says, correcting herself.

"Well, you've only been here a few days. How could you?"

"I guess it doesn't really matter how long I've *physically* been here, there are things about this place that I just naturally know about. Yet, for some reason I can't seem to remember them."

"What do you mean?" he asks in response to her cryptic statement.

Evidently, his eleven-year-old mind has trouble understanding what she's trying to say.

"Okay. I'm not sure if it works the same way, but what you people call 'memories'—or the ability to recall events—doesn't really work the same way for me. I shouldn't have any memories of this place because I've never been here, but I have tons of information on various things that continue to sort of awaken in my head every now and then. Does that make sense?"

"Um ... what do you mean by, '*you people?*" Calvin sharply addresses.

"Huh?" she asks back, thrown off by his quirky, off-kilter question.

"Nothing," he continues. "*You people* are weird. But yes, I guess that makes sense. I guess that explains why you are able to drive this car so well."

"Exactly! So why do you keep looking back? There's nobody that can catch us at this speed," she confidently says, which makes Calvin chuckle a little. "What's funny?"

"You. The fact that you didn't know about this old ass car worries me a lot."

"Why?" she says while looking around the inside of the car. Wondering how machinery this exquisite can be considered "old."

"Because this car is a piece of junk. It's absolutely nothing compared to how fast cars can go today," he tells her. Minutia remains silent and she now can't stop herself from looking into the rearview and side mirrors, also.

"Don't worry, we should be fine. Here, put these on," Calvin says as he reaches into the glove box and pulls out a pair of glasses.

"What are these?" she asks, looking at them while she continues to try to focus on the road.

"SHED frames."

"Shed frames?" she repeats, quizzically.

"Yeah. SHED band," he says, lifting up his left wrist. "SHED frames," he says, holding up the glasses in his right hand. "Let me guess, you have no "memory" of these either?"

"What are they?"

"Oh my god, you never heard of SHED frames? That's crazy! Lady, you are missing out! They're basically a pair of glasses that can identify things about your environment. They can like scan whatever area you're in and give you information about it. It can even scan objects or whatever. It's kinda like a super Google for your eyes. Here, let me show you—one second."

Calvin puts the frames down and finally begins taking off the mask that he's worn since they've met, which astonishingly, begins to freak Minutia out so far more so than anything else on this planet has yet.

"HEYYYY! AYYYYY! WHAT ARE YOU, DOING? STOPPPPP, NOOOOO! AHHHHH!" she shrieks out loud in a panic as Calvin yanks the mask from off of his head.

"OUCHHH! My damn ears!! What the hell are you screaming for, lady!?" Calvin shouts back at her, his real voice matching that of a prepubescent preteen, his natural face finally in full view.

"W...w...b-b-but you took your head ... off. How ... did you ...?" she stammers, trying to understand how he now suddenly has a new face.

"That wasn't my head—that was a mask you degenerate! See!" Calvin snaps as he picks up the elaborate, life-like mask to show her how fake it is. Her mini-freak-out caused Calvin to drop the frames somewhere beneath his seat, forcing him to now search for them again. As he puts the mask back down and continues to look for the SHED frames, Minutia can't help but to stare at Calvin's brand-new face. She can't believe how young he looks compared to everyone else she has seen so far. She admires his unkempt, but stylish jet-black hair that's surprisingly in order considering all of the running and racking they just finished doing.

"There they are!" Calvin says when he finally finds the frames, which he immediately places on his face. "See!" he says to her pointing to the frames on his face, and when he does, something about them becomes immediately familiar to Minutia.

"Wait a minute...can those things scan people, too?" she asks, now with a sudden worry in her voice.

"Um, yes? Well ... no. Well, not exactly—what they can do is pick up on people's 'shedding."

Minutia stares at him with the same blank expression one would had a vampiric scarecrow's stillborn just asked her in latin for a large valuer bag of crushed-up paintball pellets for it to inject into its neck.

"Ugh! Shedding is basically when a person lets other people learn things about them through their SHED frames. The more a person 'sheds' about themselves, the more you can learn about that person."

"I knew it!" she suddenly blurts out.

"Huh? What? You knew what?" Calvin responds, slightly frightened by her sudden outburst.

"Those glasses! That Chadwick guy had them on when I first met him! He was shedding me the whole time!"

"No, *you* would be the one shedding *him* if anything." he corrects her. "And yeah, that's how he knows who to kidnap and bring to me.".

"But I'm not from here. There shouldn't be anything about me on there," she figures.

"And that's why he took you. Basically, everybody in the world has a SHED profile. Remember Facebook?"

Minutia's blank stare returns for a second, then disappears when she acknowledges that she in fact does somehow know what he's talking about this time, so she nods. "Oh, you do remember Facebook. I didn't expect that. Well, SHED nowadays is like what Facebook was back then—just about everyone has it. So, when Chadwick notices that you didn't have a SHED profile, he knew you had to be crazy."

"So, he kidnaps me? I'm sure that everyone that doesn't have a SHED profile doesn't get kidnapped," she posits.

"No, but the ones who wander in the middle of Iowa alone, telling strangers they flew to Earth on a giant asteroid, generally are. Besides, people go out of their way to create a SHED profile mainly because it prevents things like this from happening."

"So, by being more public, society has become safer?" she postulates.

"Basically. People gave up their privacy for safety. They say that when no one no longer have any secrets, then there will no longer be nothing to really fear. Everything is recorded nowadays, so murderers and rapists don't really try to do any of that stuff anymore. Everything's out in the open and people like it that way," he explains.

"That sounds ludicrous. No wonder I don't have any memories of this."

"Well, what is it like where you're from?"

"Where I'm from?"

"Yeah, is there like murderers and kidnappers and stuff?" he asks her, suddenly eager to learn more about her home world. He turns his body in his seat and faces her directly, waiting for Minutia to fill his mind with stories of her alien civilization.

"Actually, I don't really remember ..." she says with a hint of remorse, almost shocked at the words she just uttered out of her mouth as she comes to terms with whether this is the truth or not.

"What a wonderful, beautiful convenience," he sarcastically replies.

"Well, you're the one who looked into my past. Why don't you tell me? Speaking of which, you never explained to me h—"

Minutia's attempt to learn more about her passenger's unusual gift is suddenly interrupted when her passenger suddenly reaches out and grabs the steering wheel, turning it sharply to the right as a rocket-propelled grenade shoots by them, just missing the rear of their car by inches. The rocket flies off for several seconds before exploding in the distance.

"WHAT WAS THAT!" she screams out as she watches what's known as an explosion, go off for the first time.

"A ROCKET? ARE YOU KIDDING ME? A ROCKET? WHY WOULD THEY SHOOT A ROCKET AT *ME?"* Calvin frantically yells out.

"From where!? I don't see anyone!" she yells again, this time much more panicky.

"From a helicopter most likely," he tells her.

"What's a helicopter?"

"It's like a big car that can hover! That's why I told you to put the glasses on! Here!" Calvin picks up the SHED frames from off the car floor and hands them to her.

"I'm not wearing those disgusting things," she says as she takes the glasses and throws them down.

"Hey, those are my mom's, be careful!"

"I can't see anybody, where are they?!" she asks again, doing her best to locate the source of wherever that rocket came from.

"There are probably pretty close to us, they're driving using a stealth-infrared mode most likely, so you won't be able to see their lights or hear their engines," he shares with Minutia, as he hands her the glasses again. This time she places the frames on her face. "Keep those on! It'll help you see where they are."

"Fine!" she finally agrees.

"You'll be able to see whatever they shoot at us!"

"These things can do that?"

"Not the regular ones, no, but these were my mom's—and with your powers you should be able to track whatever they shoot at us and get out of the way! In the meantime, ..."

Calvin pushes a button on the console near the steering wheel and a compartment opens, brandishing a loaded submachine gun. "I'm going to try to hold them off!"

Calvin grabs the gun from its compartment and cocks it. He then begins letting down the window. The sight of the gun immediately makes Minutia feel uneasy.

"Where'd you get that?" she nervously asks.

"It was my mom's!" he shares with her. With a third of his body now out of the window, Calvin begins unleashing a barrage of hot steel from his mother's submachine gun, but mostly only at complete darkness. However, his shots must be somewhat accurate, because he can hear the sound of multiple vehicles swerving as if they are trying to get out of the way of his blind firing.

Minutia does her best to quickly get used to the SHED frames and finds the glasses' capabilities completely astonishing. Like Calvin said, she can see information about most of her environment and even pinpoint the position of where the cars that are chasing them are, even at the ninety plus miles they are currently cruising at. All this and more is possible by just looking at the rearview mirror.

"Calvin!" she screams out to the young boy currently spitting hell-fire at anything parallel to his current position. "Calvin!"

"What?" he screams back from out the window.

"How far is eighty meters?"

"What!? I don't know!"

"Because that's how far away the closest car is!" she informs him.

"How fast is it going!?"

"A hundred and fifteen miles per hour!"

"Punch it!" he yells back to her.

"Punch what?"

Minutia, who's slowly getting used to tracking some of the gunfire that is coming from the black void behind them, immediately swerves the car from an incoming bullet that would've surely ended young Calvin's life. The momentum of the swerve forces Calvin back into the car.

"Hey, keep this thing straight. I can't hit anything out there if you keep swerving like that," he tells her, slightly agitated.

"You're going to die out there," she responds.

"I'll be fine. Stay close to you and you'll protect me. That's what you said, right?" he reminds her. Minutia thinks about this for a second.

"Come here," she instructs him.

"Come where?" he asks, suspiciously.

"Here," she says as she motions her head to her lap. "Get on top of me."

"Ewww, no! I'm not getting on top of you, you freak. What do you think this is?" he exclaims in disgust.

"Calvin, I can't protect you from all the way over there! Get on my lap and shoot from here so I can dodge these bullets more easily!" she says to him. Calvin isn't a fan of the plan, but he goes along with it although very hesitantly. The pair now sit facing each other, with Minutia's hands and eyes on the steering wheel and road in front of them, and Calvin hands and eyes on his mother's gun and the road in back of them.

"This is uncomfortable," he complains.

"I'm sorry but it's the best we can do."

"I knew I should've first read the description of this side mission. Even if I did, I still bet it would've not said anything about mounting no alien. Ugh. I swear I better get a lot of XP for this," he murmurs entirely to himself as he tries to get comfortable while on top of her.

"What?"

"Nothing. Hang on," Calvin says as he turns around and hits a switch on the dashboard. When he does so, the entire roof to the car begins to recede backwards. The cool breeze is welcoming for Calvin as he embraces his new-found freedom of movement.

For the first time since she's gotten behind the wheel, Minutia decides to see what this car can really do. The SHED frames do a great job at listing all of the functionalities the vehicle can perform by just engaging the paddles on the side. She puts her foot down and the car begins taking off like a rocket. The digital speedometer's numbers on the dashboard and in the HUD of her frames, tick upward at a speed that no one would rightfully be able to track. When she stops accelerating the display reads 169, which is no speed for any car to be moving at on these roads.

"That's what I'm talking about, Mom...uh, Minutia!" he says, growing more excited as this side mission goes on.

As she speeds off, the gunfire from the vehicles around them become more intensified. Because they're no longer driving with a roof, Minutia can now physically see multiple bullets riding along side of her, above her head, and directly outside of the car door as if they too were trying to escape from the mad men behind them. Regardless of how fast the Agera takes Calvin and Minutia through these deserted back roads, the bullets continue to inch forward unremittingly at a slow, steady pace until they reach a point where they return to their original velocity and disappear from sight altogether. Even the SHED frames glitches out every time it tries to make sense of what Minutia looks at, especially every time she glances at the bullets as they slow down and pass her. To describe what she sees is akin to a cruise ship filled with tourists waving at the people along a nearby harbor as they pass by, before jumping into light-speed. Such a ballet has never before been witnessed by anyone before Minutia came to Earth.

Calvin ducks his head back down and grabs a fresh magazine from the compartment from where his mother's gun was originally stowed. He picks his head back up, only to now be looking directly into the eye of a rocket that floats in mid-air no more than a mere fifteen inches from his nose. His mouth hangs open as total fear envelops every cell in his body. He is so shaken by the sight that he doesn't even entertain trying to get his larynx to produce the sound necessary to properly call out his driver's name, considering the act of breathing itself has become one of the toughest tasks he's ever had to perform in his life currently.

"Mi...nu...tia?" he whimpers. Minutia glances into the rearview mirror and notices what it is that has Calvin paralyzed.

"Oh shit," she utters. Her swearing is probably the only thing more astonishing than the sight of an ever-approaching rocket that is set to put an end to this duo's escape. "Calvin. Calvin! Get back in the car," she calmly tells him once she has his attention. Calvin sits back down in his seat and quietly gesticulates the sign of the Holy Cross across his chest.

She knows that swerving out of the path of the rocket will cause it to speed back up and explode into the ground next to them. Because the resulting splash damage is sure to kill them without a doubt, she crosses that option off her short list of contingency plans. Minutia decides that her only other option is to drive fast enough to hopefully escape out of the vicinity of the rocket and the inevitable, resulting explosion. So she begins accelerating.

170. 175. 190. 210. Minutia realizes that with every mile per hour she adds to the speedometer, she increases the risk of losing control of the vehicle. Be that as it may, the rocket still inches towards them. Not only that, but its trajectory has changed also. By now it should've at least either passed them, hit them or landed behind them—but it just continues to slowly follow them.

Her face displays a worrisome expression of battered confusion—something Calvin notices as well.

"Hey," he says with his head down, but while pointing at the rocket behind them. "It's a heat-seeker."

"A what?" Minutia asks. Unfamiliar with the terminology, she inspects the HUD of the SHED frames for any information shedding light on whatever a "heat-seeker" is. She finds it.

"Oh, no," she utters to herself.

"Oh, no," Calvin also utters to himself, right after her once he sees what's coming up ahead.

The long stretch of road that has aided the duo in their escape so far, comes to end in about seven hundred meters. A tunnel in front of them, which would normally under the given the circumstances be considered a good thing, spells unequivocal disaster because it contains a wide turn that they are traveling much too fast to handle.

225. 235. 240. Minutia, nonetheless, continues to push the car to its limits. 250. 260. As fast as she tries to push the vehicle, the heat-seeking missile still invariably inches closer to them.

"I need more speed!" Minutia cries out.

"Hold both the paddles for three seconds," Calvin says to her as he starts putting on his seatbelt.

"And then what!?"

"Then pray," he tells her before whimpering to himself. "I knew I should've saved my progress, man!"

She follows his advice and after the third second, the car lets out a loud roar and it suddenly receives a large boost, taking the vehicle from a speed of 265 miles per hour to 330. This boost propels them ever so faster to the mouth of the tunnel. Minutia and Calvin are pierced into the back of their seats by the sudden jump in g-force from the boost, which frightens them just as much as an exploding missile does.

Microseconds before they enter the tunnel, Minutia engages the emergency and regular brakes, and turns the car as hard as she can, doing her best to round a seventy-five mile per hour turn at about two hundred miles per hour. The missile has trouble following this sudden change in direction and though it flies into the tunnel with them, it misses striking the car and instead explodes on the side of the tunnel wall. Thanks once again to Minutia's inexplicable gift, almost of all the splash damage from the explosion is completely avoided.

Minutia and Calvin slam into the state-of-the-art, impact-resistant guard rail extremely hard. Because impact-resistant guard rails are designed to handle the forces of cars traveling up to speeds in excess of 150 miles per hour the most, it does help absorb some of the impact of the crashing Agera, but ultimately fails in keeping the car from spinning out of control and flipping over twice. Luckily, the car lands on its wheels and is still somehow still intact.

The violent crash causes Minutia to forget that she isn't alone for a while. Once she collects herself, that fact returns to her and she worriedly turns to check on her young passenger.

"Calvin! Calvin! Are you okay?" she cries out.

"I think so," he says as he rubs his forehead. When he removes his hand Minutia notices blood has trickled down the side of his face. Seeing human blood for the first time causes Minutia to have one of her mini-seizures. When she returns, she realizes the seriousness of such a sight.

"Oh no," she says as she unfastens her seatbelt and reaches out, but he waves her off, letting her know that he's alright and that they currently have more important matters to settle.

"I'm fine. We have to get out of here," he says to her, causing Minutia to look back to see why he's in such a hurry. The SHED frames inform her that two vehicles are rapidly approaching their location. Immediately, she tries to start the car and the engine refuses to turn over.

"It's not going to start," he tells her. "We need to go."

"How do you know? Where can we go? We're trapped in this tunnel."

"I have an idea. Follow me," Calvin says as he begins walking while slightly limping towards the entrance of the tunnel they just came through. "Hurry."

"Calvin!" Minutia calls out as she begins to follow him. She takes a few steps then stops and looks at the submachine gun from earlier lying on the ground before her. She silently curses to herself before picking it up and catching up to Calvin.

"What are you doing?" he asks when he sees what she's picked up.

"Saving us, hopefully," she replies. He looks at the gun in her hand and looks back ahead. "That won't be necessary."

Thankful, but still worried nonetheless, she throws the gun on the ground and continues to walk. They make it near the place where the rocket that was tailing them exploded, and stand in the middle of the road. Because it's so quiet, they can now hear the cars approaching.

"What are we doing, Calvin?" she whispers out loud to him, frankly feeling stupid standing in the middle of a tunnel that cars are about to come speeding inside of.

"I'm not sure," he replies to her.

"You're not *sure?*" she exclaims.

"No, not really."

He moves closer and stands right next to her. They can now hear the car's wheels squeal as they turn the corner at a speed which is probably also too fast for the guard rails to absorb. However, these cars happen to have superb handling and traction control which probably automatically adjust their speeds to provide the maximum speed a car can travel up to without spinning out or crashing. The SHED frames that Minutia still wears clocks the approaching cars at around ninety-five miles per hour. Calvin aptly grabs Minutia hand tightly.

"You might want to duck a little bit," he calmly says to her. Minutia, still clueless as to what this kid's plan is, follow his directions anyway.

The first car comes into view far enough away to where the driver can choose whether to drive around the idiotic pair standing in the middle of the road, or run their asses right over. If Calvin knows these guys—who had up until now been firing rockets at them—he knows they will never waste an opportunity to add to their personal kill count. He knows it is part of an ever-long quest to see which of them can achieve the highest score in some sadistic game they've made up years ago.

The car speeds towards them and the driver suddenly turns on his high beams, using his lights to blind the duo before he sends them to the light at the end of their own respective tunnels. Minutia winces from the sudden brightness, and right before the car smacks into them, its high speed is suddenly reduced by over ninety-nine percent. The amount of force that is created from an object that goes from around ninety-five miles an hour to about one mile per hour in less than a nanosecond, forces every single occupant inside of the car to first be crushed by the seats, planes of glass, and chassis of the car, and then ejected entirely out of the vehicle, which flies directly over Calvin's and Minutia's heads (thanks to him telling her to duck earlier). Whatever happens to be left of their bodies after it exits the car is propelled outward, where the wall turns their corpses of mangled bones and shredded ligaments into a cadaverous pile of human slop.

Minutia's chest becomes extremely heavy and she lets out a blood-curling scream at the sight of the gruesome horror show unfolding before her very eyes in real time. Reactively, Calvin holds Minutia's hand tighter from the overwhelming display of horror unfolding before both of them, and the child, while still holding her hand, leads her a few steps to the right after the bodies fly out, to allow the slow-moving vehicle to pass by them as it normally would've had she not stepped in its way.

As the second car begins to round the corner, Calvin, still holding Minutia's hand, leads her back into the middle of the road. At this point, she's sobbing uncontrollably. For the first time, real tears are now careening down her alien face.

Just like the first vehicle, this one also turns on its headlights in an effort to blind them. Minutia is no longer engaged in the activity as she is too overwhelmed by what she just saw happen in front of her a moments ago. Unlike the first vehicle however, the driver of this car notices the fate of the first car. In a last-minute attempt, the driver tries his best to swerve around Calvin and Minutia and for a moment, and it seems as if he is successfully going to get by them. Noticing this move, Calvin suddenly and violently pushes Minutia without any notice, directly into the path of the swerving vehicle, knocking her on the ground in front of its path. As it should, the vehicle continues to press forward, but before the car can run her over, the bottom of its bumper makes contact with Minutia's special spacetime-warping, invisible bubble, causing the passengers and the front of the car to instantly stop, but the back of the car to shoot upward, as if its just been subjected to some unexpected software glitch in a video game. Because the back of the car is now moving faster than the front of it, the difference between the two forces causes the front of the car to rip apart from the rest of the rear, upward traveling part.

The bumper, dashboard, grill and thousands of pieces of glass and debris all appear to float above Minutia, while she continues to sob uncontrollably on the ground with her face laying on the asphalt. Calvin steps away to the side to watch this entire debacle unfold in front of him. He never fathomed just how amazing the destruction of a car that takes place at two totally, drastic different speeds can look. The bisected vehicle eventually ricochets off of the ceiling, ending the life of everyone in the car and finally lands behind Minutia in a fantastic explosion.

Calvin looks in awe at what's left of the burning car and mound of death placed behind them and amongst all things, smiles. He then looks over at Minutia, only to find her still laid out on the ground, silently, but intensely weeping.

Chapter Fourteen

YOU DOWN WIT OPD?

April 16th. 9:17 P.M. (EDT)

MUCH LIKE PROSOPA PENITENTIARY, the inside of the 43rd Police Precinct, located in west Monachopsis, is one place many have come to understand as both a haven or a hell, depending on what type of citizen the Opia Police Department consider you as. It is here, where two OPD detectives talk about one of their favorite citizens, who they have had the honor of sharing some of their warm hospitality with recently.

"I heard Trunt finally talked," Detective Hamilton enthusiastically shares with his partner while gnawing on a classic, Opia-styled chicken gyro.

"Get out—Ivan Trunt? He talked to the L.T.? When? How?" his partner responds.

"Over the weekend. Saturday, I believe. They said he just woke up early in the morning asking to speak to Garrett. The meeting was long, too."

"I don't believe it, wow. Ah, come on Richie, you're getting white sauce all over my desk here."

"Yup," Richie says as he uses his hand to wipe up the glob of sauce, whose ingredients remain a mystery to all who can't get enough of it, from his partner's desk. "They're saying the reason is because the

Tyrant threw him off of a building over there in Faraday Bay, damn near killing him."

"Yeah, but nobody saw that," his partner quickly replies, clearly demonstrating that he's either a die-hard Nerosion fan or just not a fan of unsubstantiated rumors.

"I know. But a few of us saw him knock Wolfe out that window the other day. Ever since then, they don't trust him. That's why *they're* here now," he says, as he points to the Internal Affair agents in the next room. "They're waiting for him. He was supposed to be here over an hour ago."

Just then, the band of detectives and police officers who all sit in their chairs in some fashion or another, many even sitting informally atop their work desks, all turn their heads. They notice the all too familiar Ventablack outfit complimented with its trademark ultra-white, clothed belt, which ties around his waist multiple times before draping down to just the back of his calves, ensemble. An outfit which characterizes the Tyrant as he walks into the main administrative area of the precinct.

It is indeed a rare sight to see Nerosion, period, let alone in this manner—inside of a building with adequate lighting, simply walking around like a normal human being—and not swinging from a window ledge or cartwheeling off of the side of a speeding, runaway tram. It is almost enough to make the officers there feel uneasy. Judging by the variety of expressions currently plastered on their faces, emotions must range from some geeking out from seeing their favorite super-hero, to some wanting to scold him. Others wanting to shake his hand, some wanting to condemn him, some wanting to lock him up, and some wanting to praise him. Still more wanting to take a picture with him and some, maybe, even wanting to sleep with him. Of course, nobody dares vocalize their inner most sentiments.

There is another certain class of people in the world that are known to elicit similar feelings from people: celebrities. And it is not at all uncommon that many see Nerosion as such, even if he is technically on the same payroll as many of these men and women, though he makes most of their yearly salaries in a month. As true as this may be, disbelief often goes unsuspended when seeing an icon in person, and people seldom allow themselves to reach any point pass their initial, primitive feelings to acclimate to his presence.

The collection of officers continues to watch Nerosion waltz through the room alone, his regal passage rendering the entire hall to a complete silence. The range of emotions that currently permeate the air now contains enough energy to cause a power outage in the room if it so desired. Of all of the disparaging and simultaneously uplifting, contradictory feelings sprinkled about throughout the room, there is one common emotion that is surely shared between all of the men and women currently present in this police station—that of confusion. It's as if they all were watching a celebrity eat a hamburger on film, and their subsequent emotional response to such a sight derive from their inability to understand why a great deal of the world would call *this* art, or how a great deal of the world can't understand why it's considered as such.

As the Tyrant presses on, he walks along the pathway that'll send him directly into Lieutenant Garrett's office to be amongst the three people that await him. Not like anyone can readily tell, considering his mask doesn't contain any holes for his eyes to see out of, but Nerosion keeps his gaze fixed in front of him as he makes his way to the office. Before he enters, one of the fellow officers speak out to him.

"Hey, Tyrant," the officer says out loud, the use of that nickname indicating that Nerosion has in fact spent some leisure time with at least one of them in the past. "You can take the mask off, you're amongst friends here."

Surprisingly, instead of ignoring him, Nerosion looks back at the officer.

"I would if I could, Jim, but thanks," he says back to him, shocking most to some degree from the fact that he spoke at all. He then turns the knob of the office to his destination, and walks inside.

"You certainly took your sweet time getting here," says Lieutenant Garrett as Nerosion closes the door behind him. He takes his time before reacting to the lieutenant's sarcasm.

"Traffic was horrible on the Worm," Nerosion says. "Or so I heard."

Looking to put an end to light-hearted banter and ready to get down to more serious matters, one of the IA detectives steps in to introduce themselves.

"Good Evening, Nerosion. I'm Lieutenant Macy and this is my partner, Detective Rothwell."

The first to speak is none other than the recently promoted lieutenant, Rachel Macy. Since the Melvin Riots, Macy's presence has become somewhat of a common sighting, not just in the 43rd Precinct, but to the entire Opia Police Department. During those times, departmental corruption was at an all-time high, as many officers didn't see the benefit of fighting a losing war. The city, during those times, was on the edge of collapse. Many of Opia's Own, aka the OPD, felt that if they couldn't receive the resources they needed from the government to help combat and bring order to the chaos that ran rampant throughout all three districts, then it would be senseless for them to not at least try to exploit the out of control situation for their own benefit. This was of course done under the guise that the police force intended to do everything in their power to bring peace and justice between the warring boroughs. At the time, many in Opia's police force didn't immediately think that their tactics were all that wrong—if a boat was sinking and you had no tools to fix it, then you'll just have to do what you can to patch up the holes —even if that meant using the passenger's bodies to do so. That stood as a rough paraphrase of the brutal rhetoric many of Opia's Own felt during those harsh years.

During her tenure working the Riots, the then Detective Macy usually found herself four out of five times outclassed, three times outsmarted, and twice almost out of work. Not to mention, almost always staring face down the barrel of unsolicited derision, and even one time staring face down into the barrel of a .45 Colt Python Magnum—and from a fellow officer of the law no less. Notwithstanding the overbearing opposition she faced everyday trying to right the wrongs of those who are tasked with righting most wrongs, her unyielding fervor for exposing truths, combined with her intrinsic affinity for justice that her eighty-year-old parents can attest that she had since she was a child, superseded any alliance she had developed over the years as a fellow soldier-in-arm. Because of this, the life as an officer of the law hadn't been the smoothest for the intrepid lieutenant. If one didn't know any better, it would appear as if today she lives to spitefully overburden those she meets every day, with the same misery she must go to sleep with every night.

As Lieutenant Macy sticks out her hand towards Nerosion to formally greet him, Nerosion begins to realize that he's in a rare situation where he's about to deny or confirm everything he's heard about the congenially, callous woman. For the next hour or so, he will either be making a new friend or a new foe.

Nerosion hesitates for a moment, mulling over the implications of what'll happen if he doesn't shake her hand, then silently chuckles to himself of how funny it'll be if he doesn't. He's already decided he's going to find ways to amuse himself during this "emergency meeting."

"Pleasure to meet you, Lieutenant Macy," he says, firmly grabbing her hand and shaking it. He turns and shakes her partner's hand right afterwards.

"Please have a seat," she says to him after they all finish exchanging pleasantries. If Nerosion has learned anything since being a government agent, it's that when they tell you to have a seat, nine out of ten times it's so they can hit you with something that'll knock you off your feet and effectively reduce your height to that of someone they can tower over--like a parent over a child. Nerosion has been known to employ this tactic himself in the field to many-a-criminals. However, when he does it, it's usually with a hard, stiff, physical punch and not a hard, figurative, sucker punch. Cowards.

"Thanks," he says before sitting in the chair furthest from the door. "You look happy," he sarcastically quips to Lieutenant Garrett once he's comfortable in his chair.

"That's eleven cups of coffee you're looking at, not me," Garrett dryly responds.

"That amount of coffee can kill you ya know."

"Why do you think I drink it?" grumbles Garrett before downing and finishing his twelfth, causing Nerosion to chuckle under his mask.

"So ... why are we here?" Nerosion asks, addressing everyone in the room. "I know it's late, but the sun usually rises in Vesto Melvin around 10 P.M."

"Well, we contacted you earlier when the sun was still out here in

Mona, and unfortunately we can't put this off any longer," Macy says to Nerosion, responding to his charm with a little of her own. "We want to talk about the events that occurred on the morning of April fifteenth."

Nerosion looks over at Lieutenant Garrett after she says this. He then looks back at Macy indicating to her that she can proceed.

"According to the police report, Vincent Wolfe had barricaded himself inside of an apartment in Highwater Gardens. Lieutenant Garrett along with a SWAT team, was dispatched to the location to apprehend the suspect. After a careful assessment of the situation, Lieutenant Garrett then gave the order to breach and neutralize the suspect by force if necessary. Upon breaching, that is when you entered the premises through the window located directly behind the suspect. So far, does this accurately reflect the account of events as you remember them?"

"They do," he confirms.

"Good, then I'll continue. Upon entry, you immediately acted to apprehend the suspect by grabbing him. It was then at the same moment, that Lieutenant Garrett and his team had entered the apartment with their weapons drawn. Unaware that Garrett and his team were planning to breach, the commotion caught you off guard which made you stumble and fall behind the suspect. Unaware of your presence, Garrett's men immediately opened fire on the suspect, successfully hitting him with a well-placed rubber bullet to the chest. The impact from the shot forced the suspect backwards, where he trips," she says as she closes her folder, "and falls out of the window to his death."

"That is arguably the most accurate police report I have ever seen filed. No, I am serious, I am impressed. Who submitted that, was it Romanoski? It had to be," Nerosion says, once she concludes her retelling of his events.

"What were you doing in Highwater Gardens that morning?" she sternly asks him, not finding his words at all amusing.

"Well, as you can see, I was trying to capture a dangerous criminal," he starkly replies.

"Were you in Highwater for any other reason?"

"Any other reason?" he repeats, confused at the intent of the question.

"How did you know the whereabouts of Vincent Wolfe?"

The question makes Nerosion look at Garrett before he answers, this time presumably for a different reason. When he doesn't speak right away, Macy senses his hesitation and so presses on.

"Several police officers have went on record saying that no one notified you on the operation that morning. So, how was it you knew exactly where Vincent Wolfe was holed up?"

"Well, after doing a little investigating of my own—yeah, I tend to do that time to time—I was able to pinpoint the suspect's location. Once I was able to confirm that my information was correct, I moved to apprehend the suspect, unaware that Lieutenant Garrett and his men were already planning to do the same."

"This 'investigating' you did, can you elaborate a little on it?" she says as she takes her pen and crosses out a line on her notepad.

"Sure. A source of mine located in Highwater confirmed that they witnessed a man who matches the description of the suspect going in and out of the apartment—usually very late at night. From there, I went to the place myself to confirm what I was told. It was then that I decided I was going to wait until after nine to apprehend Vincent, in order to decrease the likelihood of him escaping."

"That's 9 A.M. or P.M.?"

"A.M. Criminals in this city tend to like to sleep in on Sundays."

"So, you had no idea Garrett and his team were planning on breaching at the same exact time?"

"No idea at all. Lieutenant Garrett and I had collaborated on multiple infiltration assignments in the past and almost always do they go off without a hitch. If anything, it would've been easier for us to team up to capture the suspect especially considering we had similar information."

"Can you tell us a little about this source?"

"Unfortunately, I can't," Nerosion replies, much to Macy's dismay.

"And why is that?"

"The people who choose to work with me do so with the understanding that their personal information isn't exposed to anyone, especially anyone in law enforcement. Considering the kind of relationship the police have with the citizens of Vesto Melvin, it's somewhat understandable why they wouldn't want y'all knowing who they are."

"And what kind of relationship does the people of Vesto Melvin have with the OPD?"

"Well, there's currently a martial law in place in the borough. I'd venture to guess that the people there aren't too happy with their new neighbors in blue."

"Nerosion, we fully understand that because of your status within the Lamarch administration, you technically aren't under any obligation to work with, or even disclose, any information about your operations to us. However, giving the coincidence of the events that happened on Sunday, it is of the utmost importance that you choose to cooperate with us. As it stands, no foul play seems to have occurred during the operation, but Vincent Wolfe's family has already made a move to file a wrongful death suit against you and the department."

"Oh, really?" he says letting out a soft chuckle. "I'm not worried about that."

"Maybe not. But you should be worried about the other person looking to press charges against you: a mister Ivan Trunt," she shares with him, as she places a folder on the table in front of him.

"It seems Mr. Trunt had been telling everyone that you paid him a little visit in his cell, where you then kidnapped and tortured him until he gave you certain information—perhaps even the location of his partner-in-crime, Vincent Wolfe. You can now understand why it's suddenly in our interest to discover how you knew exactly where Wolfe was located during Sunday's operation," Macy's partner adds to the discussion.

"I know I'm not about to learn that you're taking the words of a glorified stick-up man—seriously? Trunt's been in a cell since he was caught. Are you saying I infiltrated one of the most heavily guarded penitentiary's in the nation, kidnapped a prisoner, and tortured him just to obtain information about his little heist buddy?"

"No, but there *is* surveillance footage of a man hanging upside down from a building suspended from what looks like one of your devices, and Trunt's bruises are also consistent with that of someone who was tied up," she informs him.

"Well, can't his cellmate vouch for his disappearance?" Nerosion replies to her.

"Apparently, his cellmate was asleep the entire time he was gone, resting from an apparent accident he suffered while working out," her partner informs him.

"Cameras, security footage?" Nerosion asks, trying to find some consistency in the testimony of a man who's been known to exaggerate and fabricate stories.

"It is well understood that you possess the capabilities of getting around undetected by such devices," she asserts, after an uncomfortable throat clearing.

"I see. So, *this* is the real reason you're here. Y'all already decided the Wolfe thing was open/shut. You're here to question me about the rambling of some nut, and some grainy rooftop camera feed," Nerosion says as he starts to clap his hands. "Now I'm *really* impressed."

"Contrary to what you may believe about us, we actually want to help. But we can't do that if you don't cooperate with us," Macy reveals to him.

"Help with what? I haven't done anything."

"With protecting you from any potential charges that may come your way."

"Oh, you're going to arrest me?" he chuckles.

"We? No. But once the D.A. gets involved, it's completely out of our hands."

"If it ever comes to that, I'll be sure to cooperate in any and all ways I can."

"You're an ally, one the president highly recommends, and one we've come to greatly appreciate. We want to keep it that way, if it's all the same to you. We'll be looking forward to speaking to you again soon, Nerosion," she closes.

Lieutenant Macy and Detective Rothwell turn and exit the office. Lieutenant Garrett sees them out and closes the door behind them. He lets out a sharp exhale and places his hands on his hips.

"You're playing with fire, kid."

"What are you talking about? And by the way, thanks for telling them you didn't inform me about the Wolfe operation."

"They were investigating us, you know I can't lie to IA."

"I didn't say to lie, but volunteering information doesn't help me either. I was trying to save the man the OPD was trying to kill. Now I'm being questioned as to why I was trying to do that? I've seen the crime scene—that rubber bullet was one amongst sixteen live rounds."

"You're fine. Like you said, the Wolfe thing is open/shut. It's the other thing I'm worried about," Garrett shares.

"What? Trunt? Please, don't tell me he has you entertaining his B.S. also," Nerosion says with a resounding scoff.

"You know I don't give two damns about what you do out there. My concern is you getting caught doing it."

"The man said he was kidnapped from his jail cell. Even to me, that sounds crazy. Why are you even entertaining this mess?"

"Because the D.A. is starting to believe him. And they, more than anyone, knows how to get information out of people to get answers that may help their cases."

"I swear, ever since this asteroid blew up, this whole city has started to turn on itself. Maybe I should call out for a few days and see how much my presence is appreciated when I'm not around," Nerosion smugly shares.

"We're playing for the same team Nerosion. Remember that."

"Yeah, well, I guess I just haven't been feeling the team spirit lately," he says before he walks out and accidentally shut the door a little harder than he intended to.

Chapter Fifteen

THE MAN BEHIND THE MASK

April 16th. 11:40 P.M. (EDT)

"O-Dog, what up, baby? Long time no see!"

"Hey Reg, what's up? Work man, you know how it is—how you been?" Olpha blandly responds while fist-bumping the enthusiastic lobby attendant behind the large desk.

"Ah man, you know me, I can't call it. You seem a little down tonight, brother—everything okay?"

"Yeah, I'm fine, just a little tired. Long day, you know?"

"I hear you, man. Alright, well enjoy the rest of your night, don't be a stranger. Give Laharin and Ori my best."

The brief exchange that happens when Olpha enters the lobby of his high-rise building, occurs between him and Reginald, the long time front-desk attendant of the building where the Chambers family, and many other high-profile families and visitors, stay. Reggie is a favorite to many of the residents that lived there over the years. His charismatic and upbeat attitude gives life as a privileged denizen of Monachopsis a certain quirky edge that many of the residents feel you won't find in the lobby of too many other buildings in this city. The way he blends his charismatic 'coolness' with his proficiency of service has allowed a deep rapport to be developed with not only him and the residents, but the residents with each other. His lively attitude breaks any tensions that every so often begins to build amongst the usually private renters, to the point where once upon a time many of them came together to fight on his behalf to keep him as their warm, convivial, concierge.

Reginald is the heart that all the blood in the building must pass through whether they want to or not, and just like a heart, he keeps the place alive and thumping in a way that only he can. This is why it is perfectly understandable why he's able to notice that one of his favorite residents of the past four years is not as upbeat as he normally is. Olpha glumly heads to the elevator and enters it and from his desk, Reggie inconspicuously watches him by looking off of the reflection of a series of an interlocking mirror system located in the lobby—the same one he has used for years to his advantage to secretly gain insight to the emotional state of most of the residents in this building.

The ride to the 32nd floor allows Olpha to spend a few moments going over the events of the past twenty-four hours. However, instead of using this time to focus on that, he winds up wasting it, thinking about how much this slow elevator ride reminds him of how he should always just enter his house through the window. Interestingly enough, the elevator gets him from the ground floor to the 32nd in a speed that would surprise anyone who's not use to riding in them. This may be due to the fact that in addition to moving up and down, the elevators in Monachopsis are also known to move side to side through buildings. But to a man that can leap thirty-two stories into the air faster than a man can hit the ground falling thirty-two stories from the air, these elevator rides seem to take eons.

The elevator bell dings once it reaches his floor. Normally, this walk to his apartment door, especially around these hours, is mostly quiet except for when he and Ori have an impromptu race to see who can get to their house door first. This isn't the case this time, as once he exits out of the elevator, he can hear faint chatter coming from nearby walkie-talkies located inside of the other elevator adjacent to his, whose doors coincidentally are closing when his just happened to be opening. Though he can't make out exactly what was being said, he can tell by the type of garbled cadence belonged to men from the OPD. He tries to use the training he's learned in Chapter Five to expend some extra bio-kinetic energy to allow himself to hear exactly who is it that is currently in the elevator that closed when he arrived at his floor. Unfortunately, there is too much interference coming from the sounds of the mechanical whirring inside of the elevator shaft as the elevator descends, which precludes him from learning anything useful.

He turns the corner leading to his apartment's hallway and notices that his driver, Leander Davis, is at the other end of it, walking towards him.

"Leander?" Olpha says when he sees his loyal driver.

"Good evening, Mr. Chambers," Leander casually responds.

"Leander, what's going on, what are you doing here so late?" Olpha asks him as he tries to remember if he's ever seen him on this floor at this hour without his knowledge.

"Everything's fine. Ms. Tahilri asked me to wait with her until you've come home. Once she saw you downstairs, she said it was okay if I left. It's been a long day, I'm sure Ms. Tahilri will share everything with you in full detail once you get in. Goodnight, sir."

"Ms. Tahilri?" Olpha mutters to himself, perplexed by Leander's sudden decision to start calling his future wife by her maiden name.

Olpha watches Leander walk off and doesn't move until he's completely out of view. Knowing Leander, if there was anything out of control happening during his absence, he would've no doubt contacted him. It is then Olpha looks down and realizes he's not currently wearing his SHED band, and it doesn't help that he hardly ever brings his phone with him while he's working. After a few seconds of just standing in place, perhaps ruminating over the implications of what Leander's words meant, he proceeds down the hall towards his apartment. He takes another second to rub his face before he grabs the doorknob, which automatically recognizes his hand print and unlocks, allowing him to enter.

"Laharin? Ori?" he calls out loud, before fully entering into the apartment. "Baby?"

"We're in here," Laharin calls out.

"We're in here, Daddy!" Ori says right after her mom.

Ori enters view first as she sits up on the couch rubbing her mother's legs while she lays down watching television. "Hi, Daddy."

"Hey, Pumpkin, what's going on here?" says Olpha, as he points at the little tactile therapy session happening on his living room couch.

"Oh, nothing, just a little massage after a long day," Laharin responds.

"Oh, you too? What happened, your legs gave out again?" he says as he starts hanging up his jacket on the nearby coat rack.

"Yeah, but it's my fault, I kind of over did it. Nothing to worry about. How was work?"

"Pretty smooth. I got caught up in a meeting with Lieutenant Garrett and some of his friends."

"Oh, really? What friends?"

"Couple people from Internal Affairs wanted to talk to me about Vincent Wolfe," he says as he sits down next to his family. Laharin sits up and Ori moves down to give him some space.

"Why?" his fiancée wonders.

"Apparently, his family thinks I pushed him out of a window and now they want to sue me and the department," he says, sort of wryly.

'What? Really?"

"Yeah, can you believe that? I was trying to save the guy and that's the thanks I get. By the way, honey," he says, now looking at Ori. "I am *so* sorry I missed picking you up today."

"It's okay, Daddy. You was busy working but it's okay because your friend saved us, so it all worked out," Ori sweetly replies.

"Huh? My friend saved you, what are you talking about?" Olpha asks with a quizzical smile, switching his gaze from Ori to Laharin—then back to Ori.

Laharin glares at Ori like she's ready to pop her damn lips off. It appears she's about to violate an agreement that her and her mother made earlier where she was directed not to, under any circumstances, discuss today's events with her father. Ori notices her mother's piercing glare and pursed lips, and remains quiet thereafter.

"Ori, what are you talking about? Who saved you?" he says to her, this time with a bit more serious tone. Ori looks at her mother again fearfully, unsure of what to do next.

"Your friend?" she leaks out, her voice now possessing a slight whimper to it.

"Who's my friend, Ori?" Olpha sternly, but gently asks his daughter.

"Uh, Olpha, um, where's your SHED band?" Laharin interjects out of nowhere, trying her best to change and hopefully derail the subject. It's sort of effective as it causes Olpha to instinctively look down at his wrist.

"I don't know, I must've left it at the meeting," he quickly responds, trying to get back to this 'friend' matter Ori blurted out.

"How did you leave it at the meeting?"

"Laharin," he says over her, getting annoyed. "Who saved you, what is she talking about?"

"How could you leave it at the meeting, Olpha? You always do this!" Laharin presses on.

"I don't remember, I must've forgot I.." he stammers.

"Oh, what a surprise!"

"Laharin!" he screams out, silencing everyone in the room. When he achieves the effect he expected, he again addresses his daughter, calmly.

"Baby, who saved you?" his says again, his voice immediately returning back to the soft pitch he uses when speaking to his gentle daughter.

"Um ... your friend," she shares.

"And who's my friend, honey?"

"The Bee-Killer," she says.

When Ori says that name again it causes Laharin to let out a frustrated sigh and Olpha's expression immediately changes. Though he knows the answer to the next question he's about to ask, he asks anyway to try to find out how is it that his daughter knows what she currently does.

"W-Who's the Bee-Killer, honey?" he asks, not looking at all to abandon his quest for further enlightenment.

"Olpha, you know who's she's talking about," Laharin says without warning, looking to put an end to all this torturing compunction Ori is currently dealing with.

"Laharin, please! Baby, who's the Bee-Killer?"

"Um ... he's the man with the long hair and the needles! *Shink!*" she says while crossing her fists and making the same action pose Wolverine does when he makes an 'X' with his claws.

Olpha sits back and turns his head to look at Laharin, who has her body comfortably turned at a three-quarter angle. She rests her cheek on her hand using the top of the sofa to hold her elbow up as she stares straight at a depowered television.

"What happened?" Olpha says now with a much lower, remorseful tone.

"We were attacked," she answers very calmly. Her answer sends Olpha's head to the back of the top of the couch's headrest, as he exhales out a very strong, frustrated breath of air.

"By who?" he asks, looking at no one directly when he does so.

"Some punks trying to carjack us. It was nothing serious," she says, looking to alleviate some of his mental anguish in the same way a loving fiancée ought to.

"Are you hurt?" he asks her.

"No, we're okay," she reassures him. "But Leander got knocked out trying to defend us. But he had no chance—they had a gun."

Each answer Olpha receives from one of his questions makes him proportionately more upset.

"Where did this happen?" he asks, his expression stoic. Laharin doesn't answer this question as she knows the answer may undo whatever little relief her answers just brought him.

"Laharin ..." he calls out again.

"Yes ...?" she responds.

"*Where* were you?" he asks again, ten times more emphatically. This time, Laharin lets out a sigh of her own as she preps herself for what's to come from her answer.

"We were in Borick Valley," she says after letting out a quiet huff.

"Borick Valley? In Vesto Melvin?"

"Yes," she says, looking away from him.

"Laharin, what the h—" he begins before stopping himself and begins to rub the edge of his eyelids with his thumb and middle finger. "Laharin, *why* were you in Vesto Melvin? It's under martial law."

"I was just going for a ride," she tells him.

"Why would Leander even take you to Borick? *That's* why he hurried away from me just now in the hallway—wait until I see him."

"Oh, leave Leander alone. He was just listening to me. I'm the one who told him to take me there, don't take your disappointments out on him," she says condescendingly.

"My disappointments?" Olpha almost screams out.

"Yeah, that's right. You're mad that your so called arch-enemy did something that you should've rightfully been doing yourself. And now you want to place the blame on someone else," she affirms.

"You put my daughter in harm's way and you think this is about my ego? I told you to never ever *ever* go to Vesto Melvin, especially in your condition. Not only do you disobey me, but you put your own child at risk. Ori could've been hurt! All of that for what?"

"For you?" she quietly replies.

"What?" Olpha asks. Though it is unclear if he didn't hear her, or if he's thrown off by her response.

"For you, you dummy! For you. I miss you, Olpha! She misses you!" Laharin says as she dramatically points to Ori. "You're hardly here anymore. You can't even pick your own daughter up from school like you promised. So instead of you coming to us, we went to you. We went to visit you at work, or maybe even to, I don't know, pick you up from work," she dolefully reveals to him. With nothing to say, Olpha lowers his head in response.

"Ever since this asteroid came into our lives, you've been gone from it. This city has had their hero for far too long. Don't you think it's about time we got *our* hero back. Come back to us, Olpha. We need you ... now more than ever," she concludes as Ori crawls closer to her.

Choosing to no longer look at her through the periphery of his vision, Olpha turns his head as he watches Ori crawl under her mother's arm, which causes the tears that almost formed in Laharin's eyes to recede back into their reservoir.

"I'm sorry. I'll be there from now on, for us. I promise," he says before gently placing his hand on top of hers, and Ori placing hers on top of theirs.

Chapter Sixteen

FUTURE REFERENCE

April 16th. 10:52 P.M. (CDT)

"THERE, IT'S FIXED," Calvin says, finally getting the Agera to function again. For the past half hour or so, he has been working to get his mom's car to start to hopefully continue to assist them in their journey. The time it took for him to get the car to start would've probably been cut in half, had Minutia helped him to some degree. Instead, she continues to sit in the driver's seat of the vehicle totally silent, still recuperating from the emotional trauma she experienced from the brutal events that took place a short time ago.

"Hey, thanks for the help. You sitting in the car helped keep it steady, while my eleven-year-old mind and body did what it could to learn on the fly how to properly fix a broken automobile. So, thanks for the assistance," Calvin says from outside the car before walking to the passenger side to enter. Once inside, he continues his sarcastic anecdote. "I mean considering you're an alien and all and you can probably download all the instructions on how to fix a car into your brain, it makes sense that you let me do it instead—alone," he quips, as he starts buckling his seatbelt.

"So, where to?" he asks his expressionless driver. "Helllllloooooo! Earth to Minutia. Hey, lady, we have to get out of here and get back to the main mission. I was able to remove the tracking device from the car, but by now I'm sure Chadwick has went back and told my father that he failed to capture me. If you noticed, he wasn't in any of the cars in that tunnel. I'm almost certain he has already sent some more people to find me," he informs her.

Without saying a word, Minutia starts the car and the engine responds with a deep, rumbling growl. The Agera, though moderately damaged, is finally back in order. Calvin whistles a familiar theme from a famous Role-Playing Game released in 1997, that plays anytime the main character completes a challenge.

"I have to go back to my crash site," Minutia suddenly shares with him.

"Wait a minute, you promised me you were going to go take me to see The Man in The Dirty Robes!" he exclaims to her. Minutia looks at him saying nothing, then looks forward at the stretch of tunnel that lies before her, and takes off in that direction.

The pair exit the tunnel and enter the on-ramp of a nearby highway that Minutia instinctively knows will bring her closer to where she needs to be. In the passenger seat, Calvin remains silent and upset, sporting a pout unlike any Minutia has seen from him before. After driving a few miles without talking, Minutia finally addresses him. She does so not because of his somber attitude, and not because it's best to initiate a conversation when an awkward silence has taken hold, but only because she has some questions of her own that needs to be answered.

"How did you know?" she asks after minutes of silence between them.

"Know what?" he asks back, hardly even looking in her direction.

"In the tunnel, how did you know that those cars wouldn't kill us?"

"Uh, I know how your powers worked, and I kinda just went with my gut based off that," he says, all of a sudden appearing a little uncomfortable as he does so.

"No," she says, immediately dismissing his answer. "You knew exactly where to stand in order for neither of us to get scratched. It's like you knew exactly what would happen. Knowing how my powers work has nothing to do with knowing whether or not we would be ran over by two speeding cars."

"You're really reaching here. In the car, when I got on your lap, the bullets that flew next to me stopped in the air just because I was near you. You even showed me in my house ... it's not that hard to figure out," he replies with nothing but snark.

"Now that I think about it, you even knew that a rocket was about to hit us before you could even see it, and you swerved the car out of the way even though it was pitch-black behind us," Minutia explains before pausing. "You can't see the past ... you can see *the future.*"

"This lady is crazy," Calvin says out loud but to himself.

"But why would your father be trying to kill you if you can see the future?" Minutia says as she poses another theory. "Unless, he knows that you can't be killed," she concludes, answering her own question. "Why would you lie to me about how your powers work, Calvin?"

"I can't be killed? Wow, you have really lost it, lady. I'm going to sleep," he responds.

"Wait a minute, did you know you were going to meet me? Did you kidnap me on purpose!? Why?" Minutia's attention is now at a hundred while Calvin's is at zero. "Calvin?"

Calvin continues to pretend-sleep as Minutia repeatedly calls his name. After the fourth or fifth time, Minutia decides to put her theory to the test. "You know what ...?"

Minutia begins accelerating the car, eventually reaching speeds that's much too dangerous for a car to be at on a freeway. The loud revving of the engine wakes Calvin up out of his false slumber.

"What are you doing?" he asks, clearly worried about her choice to suddenly speed up.

"You don't know the future right?" she yells out over the loud engine. "Okay! Let's see if that's true."

"Minutia, wait ..." Calvin mutters nervously. She has now exceeded the speed limit by at least fifty miles per hour, and her impeccable driving skills will only allow her to continue on but for so long before she inevitably crashes. "Minutia please. T-That's not how my powers work. Please slow down, you're going to kill us," he begins to plead.

"Huh?" she yells out. "I can't hear you!" She starts swerving between cars at breakneck speeds.

"Okay, okay ... you're right, I can see the future but it's not how you think! Please stop!" he says, this time much more loudly.

"Not how I *think?* Not how I *think?* I *think* I don't understand!!" she yells out, pressing the gas pedal even harder now. The car responds with an even higher-pitched whine. "Why would you lie to me about how your powers work, Calvin? Tell me now!"

Amazingly, she blazes through traffic without colliding with any cars, but at this point she's only barely missing each and every car that she passes by inches. Horns blare and lights flash as she continues to barrel down the freeway.

"I can't see the future," Calvin all but screams out. "I can only imagine it!"

"What do you mean? You're not making any sense!" she yells out as she crosses the line that separates the direction of which cars are going and which cars are coming.

"I can only imagine what's going to happen and if I'm right, then I can see it! Please stop!" Calvin begs the psychotic motorist. After determining that his words possessed some value, she decelerates back to the speed limit, sharply turns back onto the proper lane and waits while Calvin catches his breath.

"What the hell is wrong with you?" he cries out.

"I was driving even faster when we were running from those madmen, and you seemed to handle it perfectly fine. If I had to guess, I would go as far as saying you was even enjoying it."

"That's because I had a good idea we was going to be fine," he says to her, still panting and trying to find his breath.

"How?"

"Because I've imagined that future right before we got into the car," he tells her.

"What do you mean you *imagined* it? You knew one day I was going to come and break you out of your house and we were going to be chased and shot at?"

"No, it doesn't work like that. Like I said, I can't see the exact future. I can only imagine a possible future, and if what I imagine winds up happening, then I've already seen it. But even then I can't see who's in it," he tries to explain.

"That's not seeing the future, that's just guessing what will happen. Even I can do that. I know if I drive this car on to the other side of the highway we'll eventually crash and burn."

"Except you're only *guessing* that's what'll happen. What I see isn't a guess, it's the truth. I knew none of those bullets was going to hit us earlier because I saw the future of this car," he clarifies, able to think more clearly now that his life isn't in mortal danger.

"So, you 'imagined' yourself being in a car chase?" she asks, unconvinced.

"Something like that. I just told you, I can't see who's in it and I have to be very specific in my thinking in order to see something. Plus, I can only look into the future of objects or areas. So, yeah, one day when I was home, I kinda just started to imagine what my home would look like if I tried to escape. So, I looked into the thousands of possible ways that may happen by looking into the future of my house. And all I kept seeing was bullet holes all over the parking lot. So that gave me a clue that there will be a shootout sometime soon in the parking lot of my house. I had no idea if I would be involved in it or not or whether I die because of it."

"But how did you know the future that you saw—the one with the bullet holes in the parking lot, was the correct one?"

"I didn't. I have to keep looking into the nearby future to make sure that what I saw a long time ago, continues to be right. That's why I try to never look too far into a future I imagine because it doesn't really help much. When we were surrounded by Chadwick's men, I looked again and saw the same bullet holes from months ago. It wasn't until we got in the car that I could see a little further, or I should say, a little clearer. I can't see your future or my future exactly, but I was able to start imagining what the future of the car we were driving was going to be like," he elaborates while Minutia does what she can to process all of this elusive information. "And even then, I can only see up to a particular point depending on how big the thing or area is. The bigger it is, the less ahead in time I can see of its future. And because the future isn't clear, the things I do happen to see also isn't clear. Or so my mom tells me."

"What do you mean?"

"I don't know, it's hard to explain. It's like, take this car. Like I said, I know for sure what will happen if you were to drive on the other side of the highway."

"Crash and burn, like I said," says a confident Minutia, trying to one up Calvin. Calvin promptly responds to her assumption by holding his hand out and closing his eyes.

"Actually, if you wouldn't have turned just now, we would've made it about 625 feet before we hit a pothole, clipped the divider and spun into a ditch," he says after opening his eyes again. "I know that because I didn't just look at the car, I also had to look at the future of the highway. If I just focused on the car, all I would see is it start to swerve and then dent up ... but I wouldn't know how that happened to it. Also, after about 2,000 feet, I wouldn't be able to see any further. That's the other lame thing, I have to look at as many futures as I can all the time, so I can be ready. It's really annoying. Also, when I imagine a future, there's nothing telling me that it's *my* future. That's why I had no idea you were coming to get me," Calvin expounds before he points to the steering wheel. "I can tell you what's going to happen to the car if you drive down the other side of the highway, but if a sniper happens to shoot us from a building far away, then we're screwed."

"But you said you can see the future of the car."

"Yeah, but I can't see the future of the *people* inside of the car. So, if he's good, then the sniper would shoot us," he says, pointing to his chest and making a finger-bang gesture. "Directly."

"Well, just look at the bullets then, like you did when we were being chased."

"Ugh, you don't get it. Anyway, to not get shot, I would have to first imagine a sniper shooting us, then I would have to look around the buildings for him, well not really *him,* but his sniper rifle or something. It's like trying to watch five blurry movies at the same time that you've never seen before and trying to tune their pictures while you do. And the more of them I watch, the harder it is to pay attention," he shares.

"Is that why you dodged the rocket at the last minute? Or, why you didn't see the 'heat-seeking' missile that could've killed us?" she asks.

"Oh yeah, I wasn't really paying attention, sorry about that. But the first rocket—I never imagined my own mother shooting something like that at me. I guess I don't know her as well as I thought."

"But wait, you said you can't see the future of people—"

"Exactly. Just like how your Slow powers can't slow people down, just objects," he smugly says back to her. Her brief pause indicating to him that she's shocked that he's discovered that about her.

"... so, in the tunnel, how did you know we would survive?"

"I told you I didn't. But *I did* imagine what would happen if a car that's traveling at ninety miles per hour were to suddenly cut down to two in a second. Then I started looking at the tunnel itself ..." he says sinisterly. "And what I saw was magnificent! But what actually happened ... now that was beyond anything I could've *ever* imagined," he says, his eyes wide-eyed and glistening.

"Why'd you say your *mom* shot the rocket? I thought it was your father that was after you?" Minutia asks him seeking an answer. But something about this revelation renders Calvin speechless. Whether she's incapable of sensing the sensitivity of the subject or just very adamant about learning the truth, Minutia presses on anyway with a different question. "Why is she trying to kill you? Aren't mothers on this planet supposed to protect their children?"

"You would think so, right? The truth is, she isn't really trying to kill me, exactly. She's just trying to train me," he tells her.

"Train you? For what?" Minutia asks him, unable to associate what they just went through with something that's designed to strengthen you.

"I'm not really sure, actually. See, my dad keeps me around because of all the money I bring to our family. But my mom, ever since I was little, she always talked about preparing me for something greater than that and all this other nonsense. Like I'm some special warrior or something. My mom and dad fight all the time over me and my "purpose." Plus, it doesn't help that he's an Adaptist and she's an Accurist.

"She's a who and he's a what?"

"An Adapti—ugh, it's a long story, I'm not even going to begin to get into all that. Anyway, I'm pretty sure it was my dad who sent those men after me—but to rescue me. And I'm pretty sure it was my mom who told them to try to 'kill' me."

"That's awful."

"I'm used to it. This isn't the first time this has happened."

"What? She does this all the time?"

"Pretty much. Sometimes she asks me to come with her to pick up laundry or go food shopping, and most of the time that's what we do. But every now and then, the same men that was just chasing us will start shooting at us on our way to the market. And she calls it 'training.'"

"*That's* training? What does your dad call it?"

"Attempted murder."

"Oh," Minutia replies, not expecting such an answer. "What do you call it?"

"It's life I guess. The craziest thing is that it actually does help me —a lot. At first, I used to be scared to death to go anywhere with her. But on our trips, she always speaks to me and give me advice about how to focus and control my visions. Sometimes she would blindfold me and say "*bullets really hurt, so don't get shot. Because we don't have health insurance—just life,*" he says completely in Mandarin, which Minutia somehow completely understands.

"Have you ever got shot?"

"No. Never. We can't afford to be "on the grid" as she would say. A hospital is "on the grid" so if I got shot then I would probably just bleed out."

"But you're rich, you can afford any doctor you want."

"Oh yeah, that's true," he happily agrees before suddenly switching to a somber tone. "Minutia, I lied to you because I'm ashamed of how much I suck at seeing the future. My dad thinks my mom is wasting her time with me."

"Where is she now?"

"Home. Probably," he speculates.

"Home? Where we just came from?"

"Yeah. She was in the kitchen cleaning when you were there. I'm sorry, I should've introduced you. I know my mom, she would love you."

"Guess she's not on vacation after all. Isn't she worried about you?"

"No. I mean she shouldn't be—at least I don't think. I told her I'm going to go see The Man in The Dirty Robes one of these days. She said okay, just make sure I'm not gone too long. So, we have to hurry so I don't get in trouble."

Minutia ponders all of this exposition and wonders if this is really the normal dynamic parents have with their children on this planet. She wouldn't know any better herself, so she has no choice but to go along with it.

"Okay. Calvin ..."

"Yeah?"

"I want you to know that you don't ever have to lie to me. No matter how bad a situation may seem, just promise to always be honest with me," she decides to share with him.

"Okay. I promise."

"Thanks. So, The Man in The Dirty Robes, do you know where he is?" she asks him.

"Nope. No idea," he says, as he puts his hands behind his head and leans back in his seat.

"Then how do you suppose we find him?"

"I don't know. I know he knows about Apophis though."

"What? How?" Minutia exclaims.

"Um, because he was there—I think."

"Are you sure?"

"God, lady, you ask alotta freaking questions!" he suddenly blurts out.

"Tell me!" Minutia blurts right back, anxious to hear more about what Calvin has seen.

"I don't know! Every time I think about him, I see him in space next to a blown-up space station. Jeez."

"You mean the International Space Station?"

"What's that?" he asks her.

"It's a space station," she answers.

"Yeah, that," he confirms.

"Then he definitely was there. That must mean he had something to do with the explosion."

"I guess. Hey!" Calvin cries out when Minutia suddenly pulls a risky lane switch to reach an exit that'll put her on the road to where they need to be.

"We have to go back to the area I landed at," she says in response to her sudden move.

"Why?"

"Calvin, do you think you'll be able to find someone by examining a particular area? I ask, because there was another person with me on Apophis right before it exploded. The night I woke up, I realized that the person who was on the asteroid with me was able to escape before the rock got hit by the nuke. If we can find the vessel he escaped with, then we can find him—and chances are he knows where The Man in The Dirty Robes is. We'll secretly follow him and he'll lead us right to him!"

"Uh, I never tried to find anybody before," his skeptical attitude forces him to admit. "But okay, I guess."

Minutia then looks at him and her smile is complemented with a look in her eyes that one would have when they see great possibility in their future together with a comrade.

"We'll start by going back to the area I first woke up from—there's bound to be some parts of the asteroid I overlooked. I see great possibilities in our future together, comrade," she suddenly tells Calvin.

"Oh okay," Calvin acknowledges before whispering to himself. "Creep."

The duo takes off and heads straight for the area where Minutia first awoke.

Chapter Seventeen

PROTEST CONTEST

April 17th. 9:05 A.M. (EDT)

SINCE THE DAY Apophis was officially considered a global threat, President Lamarch hasn't been getting the minimum amount of sleep one would think is required to manage an entire country. His wife Marjorie, possessing the background of that of a retired nurse, can't help but to feel helpless considering all of her tactics to ease her husband's stress thus far haven't been successful. She's known to overreact over things her husband rightfully considers trivial, however, considering all that has happened in the past year, even the president can understand his wife's concern for his mental acuity.

It is why now, the president has called for another press meeting, not only to hopefully over-exhaust his body to the point where it'll have no choice but to shut down, but also to address the voracious attacks on the meteor base camp sites by these unknown creatures and, with them as always, the accompanying mysterious Man in the Gray Suit.

At least that's what the headlines of all the news outlets who are reporting on this press conference seem to believe. No matter which news channel one would use to tune in to this conference, each of the outlets have headline titles something along the lines of *President Calls*

For Emergency Press Conference to Address Unknown Camp Site Attacks, more or less.

After a brief ten-minute interval since the White House press secretary left the podium to give way for his president to address the nation, or a long ten minute interval depending upon how emotionally involved one may be with these attacks and the leader of their country's subsequent response to them, President Lamarch finally enters the stage to orate to the people he represents on these matters.

"Good Morning, everyone. First, I want to thank those on my staff for being able to quickly pull together this impromptu conference on my behalf—as always, I am sincerely grateful for their expeditious efforts. That being said, I'm sure it has been made abundantly clear to everyone why such a conference was suddenly summoned. Last night, our country had to face yet another attack on one of the many base camps around the country, designated to supervise many of the meteor landing sites to protect the public from any foreign elements that may have come with the residual meteor fallout," he begins.

"Many of the men and women that were delegated to serve at these sites—many of them scientists, soldiers, and public servants of this country—have lost their lives in the wake of these unprecedented attacks. It is very clear that we are facing a threat, the likes of which we have never faced before, that comes at a time where we as not just a nation but as a people, must stand in solidarity through our continued crisis. Though we know very little about the creatures that are causing these attacks, the intelligence gathered so far has determined that whatever it is all center around the single individual that we have come to know as the Man in the Gray Suit. Because of the seemingly unexplainable actions of this unknown assailant, as of today, or until we gather more information as to who this mysterious man may be, he should now henceforth be referred to as an Unidentified Sentient Life Form, or simply *UNSELF,* for short.

"It is important that I remind you that this does not classify nor confirm the unknown person in the video as some outside visitor to our planet, it simply grants those responsible for taking charge in capturing him, a better understanding of how best to proceed as they do so. Once we are able to identify the national origins of where this person comes from, he will, like any other human being, be treated and subjected to his basic human rights.

"Because of the randomness of these attacks, local law enforcement agencies around the country have deemed it imperative that you are to avoid this man at any and all costs, as he is considered extremely dangerous. If you happen to spot this individual, you are to immediately report his location to 911, or your local police department and remove yourself from the premises. After receiving and analyzing all the reports sent in to my team thus far regarding these nationwide atrocities, I have the utmost confidence that the threat of this man along with his legion of godless creatures will be captured and brought to justice. Thank you, God bless the world, and the United States," President Lamarch says, concluding his address to the nation.

"I thought they were saying they were some unknown animal we haven't discovered yet, but now they're saying they're creatures of some unidentified life form? What does that even mean? So, let me guess, he's going to bring these creatures to justice, too?" Laharin says aloud to the television that's showing the press conference inside of their car. "What he gon do, handcuff them and put them on trial? Have them testify in open court and what, rat out their buddies so they can get less prison time? That man sounds stupid."

"Honey, take it easy, that man is the reason you and I aren't rotting in a cell in Prosopa right now—or did you forget?" Olpha responds to his fiancée's rant from the front seat of their car.

Though Laharin has been incessantly prattling on about the conference since it started over a half an hour ago, it is this statement from her fiancé that makes her finally shut up—if only for a few moments.

"I guess. I just wish he would be more upfront and just say they're aliens," she resumes.

"Maybe because they're not aliens. I see no reason why Allen would keep that from us."

"Daddy, are those creatures in our city?" a curious Ori asks her father from the backseat.

"No, baby girl. They know better," he assures her.

"Yup. They're scared of Daddy and his Mowwer Power Trolly Kite. Right, Daddy?"

"That's right, Princess," Olpha says, reaffirming what his daughter avows as uncontentious truth.

"His what?" Laharin interjects, looking for clarity on what her daughter just tried to pronounce.

"Daddy's stick, Mommy."

"Oh. Hahaha, I almost forgot about that little stick," Laharin chuckles.

"It's not a stick. Don't call it a stick Ori, it's not a stick," Olpha says as he goes to quickly defend the honor of his combat staff.

Just as they go to finish watching the president's broadcast, Olpha's SHED band rings out that all-too-familiar beep—the same beep that all SHED bands come with pre-programmed when they receive a notification. Laharin's attention immediately goes from the president's address to her fiancé's reaction to his incoming message.

"You can't be serious," Olpha mutters from the front seat. He turns fully around and looks at his longtime partner.

"What happened?" Laharin asks him. Olpha can't help to laugh at what his office has called him in for this time and chuckles first before answering her.

"Another riot," he says. "Can you believe it?"

"Are you kidding me? Where?"

"Kaluza Plaza."

"What, they can't handle a little riot by themselves?" she asks, clearly annoyed that the OPD is now infringing on some much-needed, quality family time.

"I guess not. They said it started as a small gathering last night and now it's a full-blown thing."

"I swear the OPD has officially been on vacation since we moved to this city."

"Leander, open the roof," Olpha instructs to his driver.

"Honey, you don't even have your outfit. You can't go out like this," she says to Olpha as he looks around to see if it's wise to leap across buildings nine o'clock in the morning. He realizes Laharin is right and decides against it.

"You're right. As a matter of fact, forget the roof and pull into that alley for me," Olpha says pointing towards a narrow passage between two large buildings. Leander does as he's told and pulls into the nearby alley. Olpha exits the car and walks to the side that his daughter is on.

"I'm sorry I have to go Princess, but I'm only going to be gone a little while. I want you to take care of your mother while I'm gone, and I'll promise to be there when you get out of school today, okay?"

"Yes, Daddy," she says as Olpha leans in to kiss her on the cheek.

"Listen, I need you to take it easy today," Olpha pleads to the mother of his child. "I can't have Leander ready to take a bullet for you every time you want take a stroll. You know he has a bad knee."

"I heard that," Leander drolly says from inside the car. "Knee's bad. Ears ain't."

"Okay," Laharin complies.

Olpha leans in to kiss his significant other. He then steps back from the car and looks around.

"How are you getting home? You're definitely going to be seen at this time of day," Laharin says, leaning her head slightly out of the car as she watches Olpha walk away with no apparent destination. She then sees him stop and crouch down. He grabs on a grate that leads to the tunnels below the street. After applying a little strength, the small bolts that pin the grate to the ground bends and snaps, and he lifts the grate from the ground and gently lays it to the side, careful not to drop it lest he brings attention to their whereabouts.

"Subway, of course," he says to her before smiling and disappearing into the earth below.

12:10 P.M. (EDT)

The Return Of The Shee Is Upon Us! Repent Before Our Deliver Arrives To Receive His Blessing! Our Divine Lord Will Unite The World Once Again! Shee and Mankind Alike! All As One, Under Our Savior!

When Nerosion finally arrives at the location where the riot is taking place in Uptown Monachopsis, also known as Vellichor, these are some of the sayings on the dozens of picket signs he sees bobbing up and down from within the large crowds. The wording on these particular signs stand out to him for some reason, and it's not because the indelible messages on them have little to do with the reason these riots have even emerged. According to the information Nerosion received on his way to the area, the main reason for this outbreak is because the self-righteous people of Monachopsis have had enough of the unfair and brutal martial law the OPD has imposed on the citizens of Vesto Melvin. No, the real reason why these specific signs stand out to Nerosion as he descends towards the large pool of citizens only dozens of feet below him, is because he can't recall the last time he has seen a crowd of this magnitude come together and mention anything related to the *Shee,* of all things. Clearly, he thinks to himself, there's more than meets the eye to this crowd than what appears.

"There he is!" screams out a voice from the sea of disgruntled protestors as a hand points in the sky towards the direction where Nerosion is approaching from. "There's the bastard responsible for all of this!"

Nerosion retracts his staff mid-flight and lands behind the phalanx of OPD officers that are currently preventing the mob of protestors from entering into the mayor's home.

"Fancy meeting you here," Lieutenant Garrett greets the resident hero. "I figured you'd have your hands full with those PHADSYN folk right about now."

"I was in the neighborhood," Nerosion responds to Garrett's statement. "Thought I drop in."

"You're just about the last person these people wanna see right now."

"I was told that this was a protest against the state of affairs in Melvin."

"Just about," Garrett confirms.

"So, what's with all the Adaptists?" he asks.

"Oh, you haven't heard?"

"Heard what?"

"They believe the Shee has finally arrived. And they believe Apophis was the spacecraft that they used to fly in on. And when we blew it up, we also blew up their ship. That's why those alien-wolves have been attacking all of those military camps. The Adaptists believe those creatures were on the rock we destroyed, and now they want revenge," Garrett shares to the Tyrant.

"But some of these people aren't even from Vellichor. And from the looks of it, none of them are from Vesto Melvin. These are Choppies —so why are they here?"

"Well, besides the fact that their good ol' mayor happens to live right here in Vellichor, they also know that we found one in Melvin."

"One of the creatures?" Nerosion asks, not expecting that.

"Yep. And he isn't letting anyone get close to it," Garrett confirms as he withdraws a loose cigarette from his shirt pocket and starts fondling it in his own idiosyncratic way.

"And lemme guess, they've already concluded that the reason for the martial law is really to hide the secret of that creature from them."

"Ex-actly," he says, swinging his finger like a game host does when someone answers a question correctly.

"These people don't even *live* in Vesto Melvin and they're still out here protesting for them. Unbelievable."

"Come on, you know the people of Vesto Melvin and Monachopsis are like bridges and toll booths—you can't cross one without paying for it," Garrett zings, forgetting that he currently has an unlit cigarette dangling from his lips.

"Sounds like you believe them. Is it still alive?"

"The creature? Nope. A couple of truancy-dodgers found it on their way home from school. Get this—when they found it, the creature was injured and was trying to crawl away from whatever hurt it. But there wasn't any trail of blood."

"What did the autopsy say?"

"There isn't any. At least if there is, they're keeping a pretty tight lid on it. In fact, chances are that if there is one, it's doubtful you or I will ever get our hands on it," Garrett tells him.

"I see. I'll get a hold of it, Bryanton won't keep that from me," Nerosion says as he begins walking towards the crowd of angry protestors in front of him.

"You've seen those things, I don't know many people besides yourself that can even keep up with them, let alone kill one."

"I guess there's only one way to find out what really happened," Nerosion tells him, looking at the crowd.

"My guess? Strawmen."

"Great minds guess alike."

"I thought talking wasn't your strong suit. Besides, you know how far out there these Choppies can get in their assumptions."

"Ex-actly," Nerosion says, mimicking Garrett's finger swing from earlier as he start making his way towards the protestors. "Great minds also assume alike."

"You just want your drugs, man," Garret says while kissing his teeth.

"You know me so well," Nerosion says back, agreeing with him.

Chapter Eighteen

THE BOUYA EFFECT

April 17th. 1:50 P.M. (CDT)

MINUTIA AND CALVIN continue their quest to find this acclaimed Man in Dirty Robes. Though the sub-par patch-job performed by Calvin to get his mother's Agera to start driving again has gotten them a good three hundred miles towards their destination, Minutia can't help but to start to notice that weird noises are coming from the back of the car—the likes of which she's never heard from a car before. Naturally, to help understand what may be occurring under the back of the car (where the engine is located) more easily, she starts slowing down and begins waking Calvin up, he who's been snoring like a mammoth for the past six hours.

"Calvin. Hey, Calvin," she says while gently shaking him.

"Wha-Wha ... hmmm? What? What's going on?" Calvin responds even though his eyes haven't fully opened yet.

"Wake up. We have a problem?" she reveals to him. She can tell by Calvin's expression to her saying that, that he already knows what it may be.

"Where are we?" he asks her after letting out a big yawn.

"I don't know, some place called Chicago," she says as she pulls the car over.

"What? Chicago!" he yells out.

"Yeah. See, that's what the sign says: 'Chicago six miles. Stay Right,'" she says while pointing to a nearby sign.

"How the hell did we end up here?"

"What do you mean, you told me to keep driving east!" she yells back—a natural defense mechanism people tend to use when they become aware that they've done something wrong and don't want to be scolded because of it.

"Because that's where you said your landing location was!" he yells back.

"It is!"

"Okay, then where is it, Minutia? Huh?? Where?" Calvin says, waiting for Minutia to point at the place where she told him she landed at.

"I don't know, all the signs kept saying head east. So, I thought that if I kept heading east, eventually I'll get there."

"All the signs? What happened to your 'Instinct' map?"

"My what?"

"You said you knew how to get there without a map. Didn't you know in your head when was the right time to get off of the highway?" he says, almost sounding as if he's her parent.

"Well, yeah ... but I thought cars have to stay on the road when driving."

"Yes, that's true, but—"

"So, I thought if I kept driving, eventually I would reach a highway that will lead me directly to it," she shares confidently.

"Oh my god. I'm too young for this," Calvin dramatically acknowledges.

"But you're almost twelve," she says. Calvin doesn't even dignify her comment with a response. He just promptly opens the passenger side door and exits the car, to see what, if anything, he can do to at least make it to the nearest rest stop, so they can maybe call a mechanic.

After a quick inspection of his mother's 2.2-million-dollar car, which is the original retail price of the car without counting the expensive, advanced customizations added to it, he concludes that there's no way it's going to make it to any auto-parts shop anywhere that can help them get this thing fixed.

"We're screwed," he hopelessly concludes.

"Is that good?"

"Just get out," he replies frustratingly. "I can't even call a mechanic because my father cut off my SHED service. Ugh. We have to walk."

"Walk? Why?"

"Because that's what you do when you wanna get somewhere that a car can't reach."

"Oh."

Calvin's sarcasm flies over Minutia's spacey head, so she gets out and joins him on the side of the empty road. The two begin their six-mile hike into the city to find the nearest place they can settle down and hopefully get a bite to eat. After only about a quarter mile into their trek, Calvin turns around and begins sticking his thumb out. This telltale sign that lets passing cars know that he needs a lift, only registers as some strange, foreign gesture that Minutia has never seen before.

"What are you doing?" she asks him, grossly confused at his new gesture.

"I'm not walking six miles. My feet weren't built for that," he replies with an attitude.

"Your feet weren't built at all ..." she first confidently posits, but doubts after he doesn't immediately respond. "... right? And what is sticking your thumb out going to do to help that?"

"That's what we do here on Earth when we need to catch a ride. Why, how do drifters hitchhike on your planet?" he asks her, wanting to know the answer the more he thinks about it.

"Hitchhike? Wait, you mean have someone pick us up in their car? Oh no, no, no, no. I'm not falling for that one again."

"Wait a minute, don't tell me you're still upset about that Chadwick thing."

"Upset? Yes, I'm upset! I ... I trusted him," she cries, her emotions suddenly flaring up for a second.

"Fine. I guess we can just walk then."

After a brief spat between the two, the pair finally find some common ground amongst them and beneath their feet, and they use it to walk in tandem towards the heart of the Windy City. It's not long before the lengthy trek begin taking its toll on Calvin's mental state.

Delirium is an interesting ailment that human beings are time to time subjected to for a plethora of reasons, none of which can really be said to be the direct cause. When afflicted, the mind begins to fluctuate, and as a result a person's mental function can decline severely. In very rare cases however, it's been observed that when delirious, a person can also become much more sensitive to ideas that they previously never entertained and as a result, are able to become overly immersed in these concepts allowing a wealth of insight to emerge from such an experience.

This rare occasion just may be what Calvin is currently experiencing, as he and Minutia continue to walk their six-mile journey to wherever it is he feels he needs to be. During this trek, for some reason, it's starting to become fairly understandable to Calvin why time itself would seem to pass more quickly for a person who tends not to get tired or physically drained from walking long distances, such as Minutia. That's because compared to someone who *does* happen to get tired from walking those same lengthy distances, time slows down to a crawl —especially when all one would desire is a nice, comfortable bench to sit upon so one can rest his weary feet. And ideally, of course, in front of this bench, would be a heavily-desirable restaurant that serves literally anything capable of being eaten right at this very second. Anything. When either thing becomes more and more of a fleeting dream with each aching step taken, it's not hard to imagine why time wouldn't, at this point, just completely stop for the person who experiences a time contraction due to traveling at such a hungry speed. After all, people are known to associate time with distance, so it is again understandable why Calvin hasn't yet given up on thinking that the more distance he travels, the more likely it'll be time for some place he can sit down and eat at, to just pop up. Because he had fully committed to these new laws of special relativity after walking five and a half miles, the next natural, logical thing for him to do, would be to just sit down on the ground beneath him. In his mind however, he knows that though time is now moving slower for him than anything else around him, it is still inexorably moving and therefore an eventual burger joint HAS to pop up for him, so at the very least and as hard as it is getting to be, he doesn't want to even begin to imagine what ceasing to continue to adding distance would equal for him—as both elements are required to create the phenomenon known as 'Juicy Rib-Action At A Distance.'

"I'm so hungryyyy, I don't know how much longer I can go on," he whimpers while panting.

"Can't you just look into the future to see when you're going to eventually eat?" Minutia asks, hoping to give him an idea he hadn't yet thought of.

"How many times do I have to tell you that I can't see anything that involves people?" he responds with an attitude.

"Wait, so does that mean you won't see this!" Minutia says as she flicks the back of Calvin's ear.

"Ouch!" he winces, flinching from the flick. "What the hell is wrong with you, lady!?"

"Or this!" she says as she playfully pinches his nose, this frivolous behavior bringing her untold amounts of joy and laughter.

"Cut it out, you creep! Don't play with me, Minutia, I can kill you with just a thought if I wanted!" he threatens her.

"Oh really, how? You can't see my future," she promptly reminds him.

"That's because you won't have a future if you don't leave me a—"

Calvin stops short of his threat when his eyes discover something he almost can't half-believe he's seeing.

Because Minutia doesn't experience the smallest feeling of fatigue from mundane tasks such as walking, she also doesn't experience the sheer amount of unbridled excitement that Calvin expresses when he finally sets his eyes on a small pizza place sitting on the horizon.

"J-Juicy Rib-Action At A Distance?" he mumbles to himself as a lob of drool finds its way out of his gaping mouth.

Immediately forgetting that he's been traveling with a buddy for the past twenty-four hours and thanks to his pseudo-experience of time dilation, he immediately takes off running towards the tantalizing establishment he may very well only be imagining is there, with no regard for Minutia whatsoever—she who is currently entranced by the numerous skyscrapers that gives the city its signature look. Whatever. If time is stipulated to work the way Einstein's equations postulate they're supposed to, then thanks to him, Minutia can stand there and stare at the skyscrapers forever, and never fear he dying from old age thanks to the blazing speed at which he starts running towards the restaurant.

"Isn't it amazing, Calvin," she says to him, unable to take her eyes off of the gargantuan, towering marvels. "Calvin?"

When Minutia reverts her gaze back to the place where she last saw Calvin dishing out his threats, she notices that he has already sprinted a good eighty yards towards the direction of the pizza shop, with no regard for what terrain he's crossing in the least. He goes as far as even blindly running across an eight-lane highway to get to the side necessary to get a whiff of one of Chicago's most famous cuisines. His sudden spike in energy is way more unbelievable to Minutia, than the fact that not a single car even so much as honked a horn as he dashed across.

Unlike Calvin, Minutia must proceed through something like a highway with way, way, WAY more care and attention. An eight-lane highway is more of a circle of hell for someone like her to just be running across or even standing next to for that matter. One misstep could turn a pretty standard commute into a landscape that appeared as if a foreign enemy had come and attacked it with a fleet of aerial bombers. One thing's for sure, the day will definitely be one that'll be remembered in infamy.

Considering her history with cars on this planet that other people are driving, Minutia makes the conscious choice to take the long way to get across the road in order to get to the other side. Doing this however, requires her to make her way back to the entry of an overpass, that of which will successfully bring her over safely, where she can hopefully catch up to Calvin. When she looks back to see just how far she would have to walk back just to get to the overpass, she realizes that by the time she gets across, Calvin may very well be out of her sight—which he almost is. And if there's anything she's come to learn about eleven-year-olds, it's that when they have their hearts set on something, they lack the awareness to understand that that doesn't mean everything else all of a sudden, no longer matters anymore.

Against all of her better judgement, Minutia decides crossing the highway directly might just be the best way for her to keep up with her traveling partner. As she walks up to the shoulder of the freeway, she realizes that regret is slowly becoming the next thematic emotion she's experiencing for the first time as an Earthling. Though she doesn't necessarily need oxygen to breathe, she lets out a very sharp exhale anyway and rubs her hands together very similar to the way humans do right before they perform some nerve-wrecking task that they usually regret shortly afterwards.

"Calvin, wait!" she screams out to him in a final attempt to stop him before the top of his head disappears over the horizon in front of her, completely disappearing from her view.

Half of her expects that to fail and the other half expects that in the time she spent calling his name, every single car on the freeway would've inexplicably stopped in their tracks to allow her a safe passage across. Stranger things have happened, surely.

Carefully, Minutia lifts her right leg over the short concrete wall that separates the highway from anything that isn't considered a part of it. As if stepping onto a fresh frozen lake, where the superficial ice can crack and split at any moment, Minutia enters onto the highway via the shoulder lane with the highest degree of care. Though it's fairly common for people to feel a little uneasy when standing on the shoulder of a freeway, never before in the history of man has something like a passing car become so foreboding for anyone the way it currently is for her.

Even when she decided to pull that stunt to scare Calvin into revealing the truth of his powers to her, was she not as terrified of speeding vehicles the way she is now. She knows that with every passing second that she spends worrying about not necessarily herself, but the fate of the innocent commuters— they who probably don't even so much as believe in aliens, let alone believe one is trying to run across the highway in front of them, she increases the risk of their lives, those of which can perish in the blink of an eye just by being in her mere presence, being lost. Immediately, the images of what she saw in the aftermath of that tunnel in Iowa, rush into her head and almost begins choking her as a result. Not wanting to let the thoughts of that grim experience paralyze her, she clenches her jaw really tight, forcing the thoughts out of her head and preventing another episode of Tears, an original Lifetime miniseries, from beginning again.

"Okay," she says to herself after locating some composure within.

Though she's no fortune-teller, Minutia has grown quite adept at anticipating danger around her and learning how to evade it. If she can treat the cars passing to and fro like bullets, she trusts that she may be able to slip by without harming anyone. The only difference now is, where before her mind was set on essentially "catching" the bullets so she can purposely slow them down, here she decides she's going to focus on dodging them entirely. How wonderful it would've been, she thinks to herself, if she could just simply catch the cars also.

Minutia starts watching the vehicles on the freeway intently as they blow past her, trying her best to find a pattern she can exploit—if one happens to exist. While looking, she can notice the expressions on some of the drivers face as they look at her when they pass, and she can tell that a great many of them are hoping she isn't planning on doing what they fear she might be; perhaps Calvin isn't the only fortune-teller on this planet. She nods her head instinctively, as if answering the questions none of them can possibly ask her at this particular juncture, before preparing to cross.

"Four. One. Three. Four. Two. Two. One. Three. Four. Three. Four. One. Two. Three."

Minutia counts out loud the number of cars as they pass her, resetting the count every time a small gap appears before the next batch arrive.

"Now!!" She suddenly sprints across the highway, and by some miracle, makes it to the divider without a scratch to her or any of the commuters. Though she's absolutely elated that she's made it this far, she knows she doesn't have the luxury to celebrate or even rest. Not because she still has another four lanes to cross, but because of her precarious position. Unlike the shoulder, the median she now stands at is dangerously thin and leaves her body within the vicinity of any cars that pass her on the lanes closest to her. In other words, the longer she stays here, the shorter it'll be before the coroner have to bring a mop with them.

Cars now honk incessantly as they shriek pass the hapless daredevil. Her first introduction to the Doppler Effect—the difference in pitch she hears before and after the sound of something like a car-horn shrieks past her—simultaneously disorients her and fascinates her and initializes one of her mini-seizures. It paralyzes her to the point to where she almost doesn't notice that a car is approaching her on the innermost lane near where she stands.

At the last second, she shakes herself out of her trance and dives out of the way, causing the passing horn-blaring to triple in intensity, and lands in the middle of the other side of the freeway which thankfully has no cars approaching at the moment. Now panting, she quickly gets up from off of the pavement and makes a dash towards the other side and towards her freedom. With mere feet to go before she reaches the opposite shoulder, Minutia begins to fill up with joy, as evident by the smile she prematurely expresses before she makes it across.

Much to her amazement, she makes it across all four lanes with only a scratch from when she took that dive earlier. The only weird thing now is that, instead of the four-lanes-plus-the-shoulder-lane layout that the side she just came from had, this side appears to have five lanes in total. Normally, this wouldn't be that peculiar to her, except that she only noticed it because she found herself running a bit longer than she did on this side compared to the other. It isn't until she sees the sudden approach of a vehicle appearing on this fifth lane that the party in her head comes to an early end, as if the DJ stopped the record once he was told that the cops just entered through the front door.

It turns out that the fifth lane of this side of the highway is a lane reserved for cars looking to exit the highway—the exit ramp. Because she didn't see this happen at all during her analysis earlier, she didn't anticipate any of this happening. Now, a burgundy Toyota Camry approaches her seconds before she can hurdle over the concrete slab to exit the veritable shooting gallery she's become entrapped in.

She realizes that the car will make it to her before she makes it across, so like a jackrabbit spotting a hungry fox making a beeline towards it, she breaks off to the left and runs as fast she can before the car meets up with her. To the left and only to the left because every other direction besides up, back into outer space, is the only direction that doesn't spell utter disaster.

"Crazy bitch!" the driver of the burgundy Camry yells to his windshield once he looks up from sending a naughty text to someone who didn't ask for one. The driver immediately hits the brakes and the car begins to swerve as a result. Trying to reduce sixty-five miles an hour to zero in only fifteen feet is a tall order for any vehicle to pull off besides a Formula One race car.

Minutia continues to run away from the encroaching vehicle as fast as she can. From the outside, it appears as if she runs to save only herself, but any passerby who assumes such couldn't be more wrong.

Even as she presses on, the mere seventeen miles per hour speed that her legs allow her to achieve, does almost nothing to outrun a car traveling three times as fast—even if that speed is rapidly decreasing. It is this basic principle of *speed* and *distance* over *time* that under normal circumstances would've most likely knocked Minutia out, if not killed her upon contact. Instead, it's the driver who is knocked out by the entire ordeal, a rather fortunate occurrence for him considering what happened to the last person who tried to avoid crashing into her at the last minute.

After tripping and falling some distance sometime during the incident, Minutia lays on the ground covering her face with her arms, in the same familiar way she did not too many days ago inside of the tunnel. Afraid to look back at the certain devastation she caused, she gets up only when she hears the voices of those around her saying that they think the man in the vehicle is okay. She looks back astounded that the car is exactly where it stopped, in relatively good shape and not in the condition of a crushed soda can with its driver's body splattered across the road. It isn't long before another person stops their vehicle to rush to Minutia's side to check if she, too, is okay.

"Miss? Excuse me, Miss?" calls out the man currently hovering above her. Minutia looks up frantically, but not from the terror of almost dying, but from the terror of thinking someone else did. "Are you okay?"

"That man, is he ...??" she asks the stranger, ignoring his effort to check to see how she's doing.

"What?" the man asks, unable to anticipate her line of questioning.

"Dead?" she nervously asks.

"Dead? From what, he didn't hit a thing. It does look like he passed out though."

"Oh, what a relief," she says, letting out the held air she doesn't ever need to hold in.

"I'm surprised you're not more worried about yourself. After all, you're the one who almost died. If he hadn't stopped in time, you would've been roadkill, miss. You should thank your lucky stars he saw you," the man tells her.

"My lucky stars?" she says, still dumbstruck by the figurative language spoken so frequently on this planet.

"Yep. Somebody up there likes you. Here, let me help you up," he says as he reaches out his hand towards her. As he rushes to do so, he can feel the sleeve on his shirt and his watch slightly slide up and tighten around his arm for a brief second. Meanwhile, Minutia looks up to the sky and wonder if he was talking about Jumo when he said that bit about somebody up there liking her.

"There we go," the man says while groaning a bit. Thirty years ago, he could've lifted her up over his head, now he struggles a bit just to get her to her feet. "I'm Arthur by the way, Arthur Bouya—I'm pleased to meet you."

"It's a pleasure to meet you, Arthur," she says as if this greeting exchange had been rehearsed by her some time ago. And just like a practiced rehearsal, she knows how important it is that she conducts the next step flawlessly, which in this case is to shake the man's hand immediately after. What she doesn't readily know or just downright forgot, is that it's pretty common for a person to share their name to someone after they've done so. It's because of this standard social etiquette that Arthur continues to shake her hand while he waits for her to do so. At the same time, Arthur also realizes his hearing isn't what it used to be, so he's now thinking that she already has shared her name with him but he just didn't hear it.

"I'm sorry, what was that? I didn't catch it," he says to her while pointing his ear towards her, slightly creeping her out.

"Catch it?" she asks.

"Huh? Gretchen, you said?" he sort of yells out.

"Gretchen?" she repeats, unable to follow his line of questioning.

"It's a pleasure to meet you, Gretchen. Wow, I haven't heard that name in years. I knew an alligator named Gretchen," he says, chuckling a little.

"What?" she asks, confused.

"I said I knew an alligator named Gretchen. She was very friendly, don't worry."

"My name isn't Gretchen."

"Oh, I'm sorry!" he says as he busts out laughing. "Forgive me, my hearing has never been worse. What is your name?"

Before Minutia answers, she recalls what happened the last time she told a stranger her earthly designation and everything after that came with it. It took that for her to learn that it isn't wise to share personal information with people you don't know on this planet lest you wind up duct taped in the trunk of someone's Mustang.

"It's Joelle ... Joelle Grace."

"Joelle Grace. Did I say that right?" Arthur repeats.

"Yes, Joelle Grace. That's my name," she assures him as her palms grow sweatier by the second. Whether this is due to her lying for the first time in her life or because Arthur and Joelle hands have yet to separate, is anyone's guess.

"Really? I knew a dolphin named Justin," he cracks to her, trying to diffuse the awkwardness. Unfortunately, Joelle doesn't get the joke. "Ahem, anyway, what were you doing running across this freeway, Joelle," he says as he finally is able to set his hand free from her grip. "Are you crazy?"

"No, I was trying to get to the other side," she tells him.

"Hahahaha, that's funny—you're funny," he chortles. Again, Joelle doesn't get the joke. "Why, what's on the other side?"

"My friend, Cal ... uh, Sonder, is," she tells him, almost letting the first name of her partner slip out, not knowing that sharing someone's last name can potentially work against her even more.

"I see. There are much safer ways to get to your friend, dontcha think?" he rhetorically asks her. "Like via that overpass behind you."

It is at this moment that Joelle realizes Calvin is probably several miles from her by now and is only steadily getting further with every second she wastes chatting with this deaf weirdo.

"Oh, no. I gotta go!" she suddenly realizes.

"Not so fast, child. You hit that pavement pretty hard, you should go to the hospital just to make sure you don't have a lucid interval, or anything," Arthur recommends.

"It's my friend.. uh, well he's really my brother, I mean ... he's in trouble."

"Oh, dear. What kind of trouble is he in?" he asks, suddenly concerned but for a different reason now.

"He, uh, he can die at any moment if I don't get to him right now!" she shares with him, lying for the second time as an Earthling—sort of.

"Where is he?" Arthur asks her, growing increasingly worried as she is. To answer him, she just points to the city in the short distance in front of them.

"That's where you were running to earlier?" Arthur asks, baffled, to which Joelle simply nods to.

"Well, dontchu have a car?" he asks her.

"I did, but it broke down," she informs him.

"Clearly. Well that's what trains and buses are for, Joelle," he says to her, not knowing Joelle doesn't know what either of those things are. Her facial expression comes across as if the idea to use such things to get to a person or place in a timely manner, let alone quickly, is ridiculous. Arthur reads this as such, and nods in agreement.

"Hmm, good point. Come on, I'll take you there," he offers.

"What?" she asks, suddenly becoming defensive.

"I'll drive you to where you need to go."

"Oh nononono."

"What's the problem?" he genuinely asks, unable to deduce the many disturbing implications that may come from an old man offering a free ride to a beautiful, young woman such as herself—she who may very well be dozens, if not, hundreds of times his age. It takes a second for him to realize where her hesitation stems from, and once he does, he immediately makes an effort to dispel her alleged worries.

"Oh, my child. Don't be silly, I'm happily divorced. Even if I wanted to try something, I'm not exactly as spry as I used to be, and I would hate to embarrass myself during what I'm sure would be a very pleasurable experience."

If it was any other girl besides Joelle having this conversation right now, their creep meter would've spiked at the end of that last comment, but because it's Joelle, nothing registers in her head as alarming from such a statement. Her reasons for hesitating couldn't be more off-track.

"You said your brother is in danger right? Well, let's go!" he demands, making Joelle realize that a car ride through that thing she pointed to earlier that she doesn't know the name of but can certainly register the magnitude of, would be much more convenient than walking. Arthur begins walking back to his car and Joelle, hesitant at first, eventually starts to follow. The two enter the car and Joelle is surprised to see that the seat belts automatically latched themselves on to you when the engine starts. It kind of reminds her of something she saw while on Apophis.

"Where did you say he was again?" Arthur asks once they're seated in the car.

"Somewhere in there," she says, again pointing to a vague area in the large city.

"In there? You don't know where he is?" Arthur asks, confounded by her response.

"I do, he's in there," she reassures him.

"Where are you from, love?"

"Uh, where are *you* from?" Joelle asks back, reversing the question back at him in an effort not to look more stupid than she can tell she's already beginning to look.

"Me? I'm from New York, I'm just here in Chicago for a conference regarding the escape pod that shot out from the side of Apophis."

Hearing these words in that order causes Joelle to purge almost every negative thought she had against this stranger.

"I'm from New York!" she suddenly yells. Her sudden pitch in volume, Arthur feels, wasn't warranted in the least.

"Uh, okay," he says while mildly chuckling. "What brings you all the way out here to Chicago then?" he asks as he begins driving in the rough direction Joelle is still pointing at. "You can put your hand down now, dear."

"My brother and I were on our way to the conference about Apophis," she says as she blatantly lies to him. A move judging by the way her lips curled up, is something she isn't at all comfortable with doing.

"Say what? You're kidding!" he exclaims.

"Nope, we've been so interested in learning as much as we can about Apophis, so once we heard that there was a conference being held out here, we decided to make our way here."

"You drove all the way from New York to Chicago? Jeez, that must've been rough. No wonder your car broke down."

"Crazy, right?"

"Crazy indeed, well how about this ... how would you and your brother like to be my honored guests at the conference today?" he congenially asks her.

"Honored guests?"

"Yes. My treat. If your enthusiasm about Apophis is anything like mine, then it'll be my privilege to have you two in the front row so you can hear all about everything Apophis related."

"Really? Thank you! Thank you, so much!" she says, no longer feeling so bad about her untruthfulness considering the rewards it's currently producing for her.

"But first, we have to find your brother. What did you say his name was again?"

"It's ..." she begins before stopping herself for some reason. "Sonder."

"Got it! Hold on, Sonder, we're coming."

Chapter Nineteen

THE BEE-KILLER

April 17th. 5:23 P.M. (EDT)

"HEY, Tyrant! Keep it moving, we know exactly what you represent, and it ain't us!"

Addressing the concerns of a raging group of protestors is likely the last thing you would hear someone say when they speak of Nerosion in earnest. However, with all that's been going on in his life recently, and like any great martial artist, Nerosion is never above adapting and learning from his circumstances to try to use a different approach to secure a victory. This is why of all of the obscenities that continue to be hurled at him as he approaches the crowd, he still presses forward. He believes he may be able to learn more about Exile by speaking with these folks; punching people has only gotten him but so far, so a part of him doesn't really have a choice at this point but to proceed diplomatically.

Even the plethora of news cameras, that now part like the Red Sea to allow him passage to confront the legion of concerned citizens before him, is no longer enough to turn him away from this situation. Though they do step aside for him, as much as he wishes that they'll turn their cameras off as he attempts to address the crowd, such a thing is as likely to happen as him finding out where the source of the Exile is coming from just by speaking to one of these infuriated gatherers. It is almost laughable that he even dreams that such a thing would happen in his favor. At the very least, he appreciates the small amount of solace that's granted to him, knowing that due to the unique blackness of his outfit, his appearance on camera isn't always the easiest for producers to transmit appropriately to their salivating viewers at home. Often times he appears as the two-dimensional shadow of an organic mannequin when on camera, and often times people at home have complained about their television playing tricks on them whenever he's on their favorite news program.

Nerosion raises his arms before he addresses the crowd—a move not many, including himself, see him performing often, if at all.

"If you all will hear me for a moment, I would like to talk with you about some of the things that have been troubling you over the past weeks. I know as of late, especially since Apophis introduced itself to us, it seems as if our city has been divided—divided in a way it hasn't been since the Melvin Riots. Because I wasn't around at that time, I only pray that my presence now can be one of the factors that help restores Opia's balance and prevent us from ever going back to those dark days," he projects loudly to the crowd. A most rare occurrence.

"Balance? Aren't you the same guy who sat by and let them impose a martial law on us?" one outraged citizen screams out from the front of the crowd.

"I didn't let anything of the sort happen. Contrary to what you believe, I am merely an officer that operates under the law. I am in no position to enact any district-wide impositions on the citizens of this city or any other," he informs his audience.

"Don't give me that crap! You do whatever you want in this city and don't ever receive any punishment for it!" another outrage citizen spats. This one coming from the left side of the fourth row of people.

"We know exactly which team you're playing for. You pretend to stand for the people of Vesto Melvin but it's a lie! We know you killed Vincent Wolfe! You would never do that to one of Mona's own!" says another.

"Vincent Wolfe was a notorious thief and armed robber whose death came by his own hand," Nerosion replies back. "He made an already disenfranchised borough even more dangerous for its upstanding citizens to live in and—"

"So that gives you the right to kill him? Man, that's some bullshit!" a fourth one calls out, this one eliciting a heap of agreeing cheers with his outcry. Soon the controlled crowd that Nerosion has attained devolves back into a slightly noisy one.

"Jesus, he's terrible at this," Lieutenant Garrett mutters to himself.

"Please everyone, I just wanna help. There are some very dangerous drugs out here in the streets of Opia. Drugs, that if in the wrong hands, can make our lives much more difficult than they already are. I have reason to believe that these drugs are linked to the creature that was found in Twin Parks. Help me find where they're coming from, and I'll do everything in my power to removing the martial law that is currently subduing the people of Vesto Melvin."

As Nerosion submits his concerns to the crowd, he can hear them slowly beginning to calm down again. The self-appointed leaders of the anti-establishment groups displaced throughout the large crowd are starting to heed his words, and are subsequently hushing the people in their respective sections to allow Nerosion a chance to offer something in return for what he asks.

"I know why most of you are here. Over the years, I have come to respect the people of Vesto Melvin more than any other I have ever had the honor of protecting. It is why, as you've come to know, I have been spending most of my time patrolling the areas that have been subjected to facing the worst that this city has thrown their way. I am not here to make the lives of those who do the right thing over there any worse; I am here to protect them while they continue to do the right thing. They who deserve the most protection and acknowledgement for their strength. Because it is they who we have come to know, fight the hardest in the face of the adversity that time after time again, continues to ravage them. It is why I risk my life every night, to ensuring that those who, despite the harsh circumstances they continuously find themselves in, still rise up every single day to go to work. To go to school. To open their shops and stores to serve their people. I am but a servant, nothing more, nothing less. So again, I beg of you ... please. Please help me continue to help you. Help me find the source of these drugs poisoning our streets, and I promise you I would do everything in my power to help liberating the people of Vesto Melvin, even if I have to take off this mask and stand with you hand-in-hand, while we march down these streets together."

Judging by the collective mumbling going on between the massive amounts of people inside the crowd, Nerosion can tell he didn't fail, yet he can't tell if he succeeded, either. One thing he knows for sure though, is that he didn't fail.

"Hey Nerosion," a man suddenly calls out to him from the crowd, causing a great deal of people to look back. "I think I know where the Exile is coming from!" he says when he gets the hero's attention.

Though it's impossible to tell, thanks to his expressionless mask, and judging by Nerosion's reaction, he's probably smiling harder than he has in over a month.

"Stay right there, I'm coming," Nerosion yells back at him before looking back at Lieutenant Garrett and nodding. He then starts to walk towards the man's location.

"Excuse me, don't push me. I said don't push me! What the hell is wrong with you!" a woman from somewhere in the back of the crowd suddenly yells out.

"Hey man, get off of her! What are you doing!" another yells—this time a man who's witnessing the unspecified activity.

"What's going on back there?" Garrett says to one of his men over his radio, looking to get an idea as to why there's suddenly a bunch of shouting coming from within the large crowd.

"I'm not sure. There seems to be some sort of commotion within the crowd by the southeast side. It's hard to tell exactly what." an officer communicates back over the radio. *"I'll check it out."*

"Get the hell off of her, what's wrong with you! Hey!" a voice can be heard saying somewhere in the crowd. As Nerosion continues to jog towards his unexpected confidant, he slows down, and notices the commotion coming from within the crowd.

Two OPD officers close to where all this disruption is occurring have no choice but to jump into the crowd to assist the woman, who as far as they can tell is being attacked by someone. From where Nerosion currently stands, he is unable to tell exactly what is happening.

Seeing that the situation is doing everything but deescalating, Nerosion looks at Garrett for answers that neither of them currently have. Suddenly, a gunshot goes off.

"Shots fired! Shots fired!" an officer near Garrett yells out as just about all 2,000-plus people in the area immediately lower their heads at the same time.

Nerosion immediately leaps up into the air towards the area in the large crowd where all the commotion is occurring. The large crowd begins to disperse as chaos begins to unfold. He lands to find a man shot on the ground and one of the two officers holding the still smoking gun.

"What the hell did you do?" Nerosion harshly asks the frantic officer.

"I ... I don't know. He tried to attack me ... it all happened so fast," the cop cries to Nerosion. It isn't long before more shots are heard from another section of the crowd. At this point, full chaos has ensued, and the entire police presence has run into the crowd to try to get control of the situation. It doesn't take long for the relatively small crowd that lingers around Nerosion that has witnessed what this cop has did— shot and killed one of their own members—to lose their composure. As a result, they collectively attack the nervous cop in a blind rage as they all try to tackle him *and* Nerosion at once. Luckily, Nerosion grabs the officer and leaps out of the way, leaving him in a safer area before heading to the location where the other shots rang out. He lands only to see another victim lying in a pool of their own blood, as he tries his best to scramble and scan the crowd to find this other shooter.

"Who's doing this?" he yells out to one of the panicking protestors currently running away.

Unnrff! Out of nowhere, a man delivers a right hook square into Nerosion's jaw, causing him to stumble back and almost fall from the unsuspecting blow. When he looks up, he sees no one. Wasting no time, Nerosion quickly regains his footing in order to find the culprit who dazed him, but there's no way of telling which one of these people running away struck him.

"He's got a gun!!" someone yells from another part of the crowd.

Nerosion gets there in a single bound and grabs the barrel of the pistol that some man is holding and using to take aim at one of the protestors.

Nerosion attempts to perform a swift arm-takedown move to successfully wrestle the gun away from the shooter while simultaneously pinning him on the ground. When he does so however, the shooter somehow anticipates his movements and reverses the hold. He shakes Nerosion off of his gun long enough for him to get another shot off, which finds its target in the back of another protestor.

Nerosion is more astounded from the fact that a mere man has countered one of his holds, as opposed to seeing another innocent person get shot. Looking to not let it happen a second time, he swiftly delivers a glorious, roundhouse-kick combo which connects with the shooter's gun, chest and head in that order, disarming him while knocking him out cold. Nerosion takes a look at the man to see if he's ever come across someone so skilled before and notices he has the same look as Serota and Randy Gallen did after he fought them. This man is clearly high on Exile.

"Oh no," he mutters to himself. Garrett approaches Nerosion to tell him what Nerosion has no doubt already figured out.

"It's the Strawmen! They're here!" Garrett exclaims to him.

"I know. And I'm getting to them too late," Nerosion regretfully admits.

"Can't you locate them?"

"It's too much commotion. It's hard to focus. How do I find them?"

"There is multiple groups of them shooting people with semi-automatics. We gotta get rid of this crowd quicker. Wait for my signal," Garrett says, making his way to the middle of the crowd.

Nerosion leaps to the nearest rooftop as he waits for whatever it is Garrett has planned. Moments later, hundreds of gun shots ring out from all of the police officers in the area. As expected, the already-dissolving crowd begins dispersing much faster than before. Nerosion isn't sure what he should be looking for, until he notices that there are several people who aren't running away from the sound of the gunshots. Immediately, Nerosion blasts off from off of the top of the roof directly towards the nearest Strawman, like an arrow that's just been fired from a giant bow.

He delivers a high-flying kick to the first Strawman with super precision, which knocks the man back several meters. Surprisingly the Strawman isn't completely knocked-out, so Nerosion extends his Mauerbauertraurigkeit and promptly slams the better part of the staff into the skull of the struggling perp.

With most of the crowd gone, the Strawmen now have a good look at Nerosion's position and a few dozen of them begin rushing towards him.

"Thank godddddd," Nerosion whispers to himself, overjoyed at the fact that they're dumb enough to bring the fight to him and he no longer has to chase them.

The Strawmen finally reach Nerosion's position and they begin throwing a fury of blows at him in a way that he's never seen a human attack another before. Each of the punches that he swiftly dodges and counters are delivered with a force that would make their arms explode if any of these punches connected. He even finds himself dodging just as many head-butts, many of which connect directly with the pavement, thanks to his nimble movement. Judging by their suicidal fighting style, Nerosion quickly learns that this isn't a fight in which these men are trying to walk away from—the objective, as it appears, is for them to completely destroy themselves as they destroy whatever their target is.

Most of the bones broken on the men from this unorthodox scuffle isn't because of Nerosion at all. The style of fighting performed by these Strawmen would be worth applauding if it wasn't so dangerous. Though none of them has been able to successfully touch Nerosion so far, he finds himself backing up more so than he cares to admit. Because of this, he decides he must quit trying to not hurt these guys and get a bit more serious. He draws his staff and now wields it, assuming a signature stance, one that presumably dictates that he's now serious about taking care of these guys. As he does so, a few of the men who previously were thought to be incapacitated, stand up—which is particularly strange considering a few of them have at least one broken leg, a few broken collarbones and ribs.

Not like they can tell, and if they could tell it isn't likely they'll care, but Nerosion is currently smiling under his mask—a peculiar, but not all that difficult for someone to grasp, action for a man who chooses to fight essentially blindfolded to do. After all, choosing to brutally beat up groups of criminals on a daily basis while blindfolded, has to be enjoyable on some level for the man who chooses to approach such a task in such a way.

The Strawmen all finally find their grounding again as they all begin to circle around Nerosion even without communicating their actions to one another. Like many formidable families of predatory creatures dwelling in the ocean, these men all seem to instinctively know what kind of formation they should go with for their next attack. All of this done without a single one of them uttering a single sound. Even as the large portion of them hobble and limp into their respective spots to unleash their next attack, Nerosion can almost smell the inhumane relentlessness of these Strawmen's stench.

They attack all at once, yet Nerosion doesn't budge an inch. The first attack is countered in a way that is debatably impossible for a martial artist to do, let alone a human. Looking to seize this moment, Nerosion leaps over the rest of them, causing a few of them to collide into one another. He sees his opportunity to end this fray altogether and while in the air, transforms his staff into a whip-like state, where all the sides are fully extended with exception to the hilt. The men look around and can't seem to find where their prey has disappeared to —the exact response Nerosion expected to occur from his swift act. He lifts the hand that wields the whip-like staff into the air and spins in a way that allows the whip to build up a substantial, yet non-lethal amount of force, designed to bring a quick end to this band of nuisances. The twirling end of the whip is met by the twirling heel of Nerosion's right foot, and the tail end goes flying down towards the confused bundle of Strawmen.

PUH-KLANK! The fast-moving tail-end of the whip never finds its way to the bodies of the Strawmen. That's because the moment before the final blow touches the body of any of the men, the whip is deflected by some unseen object that sends it back towards Nerosion in the air.

"What the —" Nerosion says out loud as he is now both confused and slightly pissed that he missed his target.

As he now begins to fall from the apex of his leap into the air, he turns to see what in the hell is fast and accurate enough to deflect one of his signature attacks. A bullet is just about the closest thing, but considering that he's been trained to easily anticipate the path of a bullet fired from virtually anywhere like it was a giant steam engine coming from a mile away, there's no way that he would've not noticed it. At this point, all he can do is scan the area of whatever that object was, came from. When he does, the silhouette of a man with long hair swaying in the breeze is staring directly at him, standing along the edge of a nearby rooftop. There is no other beast on the planet who can simultaneously cause what just happened *and* fit that description.

"SURII!" Nerosion screams out upon landing. The millisecond his foot makes contact with the pavement, he springboards himself right back into the air, only this time in the direction of his elusive nemesis.

"Nerosion! Where are you going?" Lieutenant Garrett shouts, watching the only man who can contain such a crisis expeditiously, abandon the area to, as far as he knows, chase a pigeon.

Because the Strawmen still have to be dealt with, Lieutenant Garrett doesn't currently possess the luxury of focusing on Nerosion's abandonment, especially considering most of the Strawmen have now shifted their focus onto him.

"Goddamn it," Garrett murmurs to himself before grabbing his radio to update his officers on the new situation. "All units, we have multiple 10-78's at my location. All available units converge on my position on the southeast side of Manor and Patelly!"

Only a second has passed by the time Nerosion makes it to the rooftop, and it only took a second for the silhouette to make it four blocks away from him. Because he knows there's only one other person in the world that can travel as fast if not faster than him, he's sure now more than ever that the man he's about to pursue is none other than Surii, the Elusive Cheshire, himself.

The chase begins across the relatively low rooftops that blanket Vellichor. And what such luck, as Surii won't have much of a chance hiding between buildings and houses of such low heights. Even if he does manage to make it to one of the many larger ones that stand out around Vellichor, they are so spaced apart from each other, it'll actually put him more at a disadvantage, if he attempts to run towards one. He knows this, and he knows that Surii knows this also, so he allows this truth to calm him down and pace himself if he is to catch up to this man.

"Relax, Nero," he says to himself as he takes in and lets out a breath of equal strength. Amazingly, a single breath is all the time it takes for him to clear about five rooftops in a single bound. Though his nerves are now relaxed, and his heart rate has almost returned to normal, Nerosion is finding it hard for him to get his adrenaline back under control. Performing such a feat at will is generally deemed impossible by normal standards—after all, epinephrine is guided by an autonomic function of the nervous system, which indicates that only some stress-inducing event can trigger the release of adrenaline into the body. However, those well-trained in the arts of Mahze Du tend to have the ability to allow or prevent the release of adrenaline in their bodies at any time they wish. Be that as it may, those trained in the arts are fully away of how dangerous it is to abuse such a skill, which is why the members of the Hannibal Article almost never willfully access it. Considering that Nerosion is still trying to get his adrenaline under control, a function that his body will naturally do on its own if he would just let it, it's clear that the sight of his old friend has him a bit off of his game.

"Surii! Surii! I know you hear me!" Nerosion yells out to the nimble buttinsky. Though Nerosion pushes onward with great effort to catch up to his old friend, the distance between them hasn't shrunk in the least. "Why are you here? I know you can hear me—why were you near my family, Surii? Answer me, goddamn it!" he screams.

At first, the only feedback that Nerosion has been receiving since his pursuit and subsequent line of questioning began, is the soft ticks that Surii's boots make when he lands from one of his lengthy leaps. It's almost mind-blowing that he can almost completely mask the sound of his 185-pound body smacking the edge of a rooftop, after falling from heights upward of forty feet. It's a weird thing for Nerosion to see someone just as skilled as himself performing stunts that he is usually doing. Throughout this chase, Nerosion finds himself being reminded just how remarkable it is to see someone do the things he's come to overhear from the everyday folks living in Monachopsis.

One time I saw Nerosion jump off the top of a truck just to catch some little girl's balloon from flying away.

Crazy! I remember it was snowing one time, and Nerosion was running on top of people's heads just so he wouldn't get snow on his boots.

Man, that's nothin' lemme put you on ... I swear one time I saw this mofo Nerosion backflip out of the bathroom window of my man's kitchen, just to catch the train before it went underground. Shit had me buggin'.

Though at this current moment Surii isn't exactly replicating any of those feats, Nerosion can see just by the way he's moving, why people have given such testimonies about his own capabilities. However, all this drifty thinking Nerosion has found himself preoccupied with, must soon find a new home inside of the gray matter that occupies the space within his skull. That's because the second type of response Nerosion receives from his old sparring partner is in the form of an unsuspecting, hazardous attack on the citizens the dwell below them.

"Surii, what the hell are y—"

Before the question can be delivered out loud in its entirety, Surii has cut through the metal prongs that hold up a restaurant's lighted signage that is already in the midst of collapsing on top of some unexpected dinner guests. In the length of a single heartbeat, Nerosion has already extended his staff and whipped it around the legs of the chairs where two love birds who share a single dish of Creme brûlée, with one spoon no less, comfortably sit. He then yanks on the hilt and literally sweeps the couple off of their feet, allowing the swinging sign to safely pass over them and crash into a nearby parking lot.

"Are you crazy?" he shouts at Surii, following that lightning-quick ordeal.

After receiving no response, Surii raises his arm to prepare for another attack on the helpless Vellichorians below.

"Surii, stop!"

Before Nerosion's voice can even reach his eardrums, Surii has already thrown his U.R.O. off the side of a street light with enough strength to cause the pole to bend in half. It ricochets off, striking a manhole cover and popping it open before the device returns back to his palm.

The sewer lid now sits inside of its own hole, except now its edge is sticking upward; the approaching taxicab driver is completely oblivious to the new condition of the familiar street he surely has traveled down well over a hundred times.

Seeing the impending doom this is surely to cause, Nerosion leaps towards the street, temporarily abandoning his chase, and jumps towards the cab. Before landing on the trunk of it, he chucks his staff at the vehicle with considerable force, successfully piercing the back of the trunk. He then tethers the cab via one of the thousand tensile, nigh-indestructible, disposable cables housed inside of his signature weapon, to a nearby pillar. After successfully executing the nifty procedure, he leaps off the trunk the moment he lands on it and rejoins the pursuit, not losing so much as an inch of distance in the entire act.

He moves in such a haste and with such precision that he doesn't even get the chance to see how it looks, when the wire he placed goes taut and nearly rips the entire trunk from the back of the cab. Judging by the sound however, he can tell that a moment's hesitation on his part would've caused at least one certain death. The thought of continuing to play it this close disturbs him rather deeply. This torturous game of having to save lives while trying to capture one, finally forces him to yell out in frustration.

"Ahhhh! I just wanna talk, Surii! Enough, please!" Nerosion pleads. He knows the longer he continues this pursuit, the greater the chances of someone getting hurt.

"Heyyy, Nero! Didn't see ya back there," Surii turns around and yells back as he removes his pink headphones from his ears. "Anyway, whatchu wanna talk about? As you can see, I'm a little busy here," he responds as he continues to dash across the rooftops—a response of this sort being the last thing Nerosion expected, until he realizes again who it is he's talking to. Even under the given circumstances, Nerosion can't help but to be a little thrown off after seeing his old friend for the first time in over five years, especially considering a part of him believed he was dead.

"Well," he begins, not really knowing what to say now that he has his attention, or at least a portion of it. "First off, can you please ... please, just stop what you are doing."

"Argh. Fine," Surii says as he tucks his U.R.O. away.

Nerosion lets out a soft sigh of relief. "Why are you here in Opia?"

"I can't come to Opia?" Surii asks him instead.

"Obviously, you can. I'm trying to figure out why? I don't think you've been here since the city opened."

"Oh, I don't know. I heard you were struggling over here, so I figured I come and lend you a helping hand. Yeah, that's it," he says to him as they continue to dash across rooftops at the same speeds that Nascars circle a track.

"That's bullshit!" Nerosion spats.

"Oh, okay," Surii says as he turns back around and raises his U.R.O. again, delivering a visual promise to his pursuer that if he doesn't control that temper of his, it'll be his fans that'll have to pay for it.

"Okay, okay!" Nerosion says compliantly.

"Hey look," Surii says as he lowers his arm. "Don't ask questions you don't want the answer to."

"Is that what Boluscant told you? After you saved him? That I needed *help?*"

"Saved him? Who Ol' Bo? *Pfffffffft!* Now does that sound like something I will do?"

"That's funny, I said the same thing," Nerosion says, almost chuckling while he does.

"Is *that* what the good general told you? That I *saved* him? You know you can't believe anything that man says—we all know he hasn't been right in the head since he went all commando on us."

"Boluscant may hate us, but I don't see him lying to me—especially to protect you."

"Protect me from what? From you? Ha!" Surii dramatically scoffs.

"So why don't you clear it up for me, then. You came all this way, I'm sure there's something you want to get off your chest."

"Okay, we may have bumped into each other, but I didn't *save* him. And I told you already ... I'm here to lend you a hand," Surii responds.

"Oh, 'because I've been slacking', right? Is that why you saved Laharin?" Nerosion asks, causing Surii to sigh before answering.

"I could've sworn I told them not to say anything," he quietly mutters to himself. "You know Nero, she was *Laharin* when you stopped me from killing her in New Mexico. It's okay to address her as your wife now. Don't worry, no one can hear us from up here—you can drop the act. Are you sure you should even be up here right now? Away from her? This is how I caught her alone the first time. Careful—once you take the 'us' out of 'housewife,' what remains is likely what she'll become."

Nerosion's silence to Surii's affront says much more to him than his words ever could at this moment.

"Unless ... ohhhhhhh. I see. You still haven't put a toe-ring on it, huh. What's wrong? I've never taken you for the superficial type, so I know it's not because of her military-trained legs."

"Surii, please don't talk about my family," Nerosion pleads, growing sensitive about whatever direction Surii is about to and is known to go at times.

"Oh, here we go with the family shit."

"Surii ..."

"What's crazy is, even though y'all aren't married, y'all still made a baby together. Man, you and Ol' Bo don't be giving NO FUCKS about the Article, I swear. ZERO! But y'know ... I secretly respect that. I mean the masks. The children. The desertion—you are one *brave* soul, boy. Gotta respect it."

"Surii, what are you doing in Opia?" Nerosion, unamused, asks again.

"Jeez. Seren was right—you do ask a lot of questions. Oh, I forgot, you're a detective now. I guess it makes sense, then. And before you ask, no I wasn't with her. I just happen to see y'all on y'all little play-date the other night. Man, can that woman handle a rifle. Oh, and don't you dare try any of that ole 'pinning me into a corner' stuff you attempted against her—because the results may vary," he informs his ex-accomplice.

"What were you doing around my family?"

"Family? What family? Ya'll don't even have the same last name. Lahrain's not a *Chambers* yet, is she? Wait, would it even bc Chambers? What *would* would her last name be if y'all got married? I know Chambers is the name your government *gave* you, but it isn't your government *name*. You didn't even have a government name before they gave you one—it was just *Nero,* right? Or was it? How does that even work? Is that why you haven't proposed yet? Because you don't have a last name to give her. Oh damn, now *I'm* being the detective. Man, that's no fair that you don't have a last name; I always thought that was so damn cool," he rambles before suddenly making a discovery. "Ohhhhh —Nerroooooosion ... I finally get it now."

"I see ..." Nerosion blandly remarks.

"See what? What that mask on, I doubt you can see anything. Nice nod to the Article though, at least you kept up with some of our customs."

"... you're serving Odem again, aren't you?" Nerosion submits.

"Say what?" Surii asks.

"You kill me, Surii. You always pretended as if nothing affects you. Like you're above it all. All the things you knock us for, you in fact desire the most—it's written all over you. I get it now—you miss it."

"What the hell are you rambling about?" Surii spats at Nerosion's apparent non-related statements.

"Chapter Five. The Hannibal Article. Gloria. You miss it. All of it. You miss your family."

"Oh! Eh, perhaps you're right. But over time, I've come to appreciate the benefits of not having a family," Surii says as he carefully observes the denizens he soars over. "You see unlike you, I don't live in a constant state of delusion in order to make my life easier to cope with. When things change, I simply roll with it. I adapt—like my DNA instructs me to do. I don't do the impossible and desperately try to resurrect something that has died a long time ago—that's just downright pitiful. Let me ask you something, you honestly think that that spoiled, decadent apartment that you call a home—that you hastily pasted together to fill that shallow void inside of you—is any more important than the thousands of spoiled, rotten homes below us?"

"What?"

"Just look at them. Look at how many of them are down there. Afraid of change. Afraid to adapt. Just shamelessly relying on one another to get ahead of one another. And proud of it too. They don't even *pretend* as if they were born alone. They don't even pretend as if they can't attempt to fix things with their own two hands," he says while chuckling. "Which in itself, is really nothing to be ashamed of. In fact, I like to think it's our greatest resource—selfishness. And plenty of them are selfish—but they hide it. I don't get that. The problem is that many of them also pretend as if there is more to them, as if they aren't selfish at all. You see that's the part that kills me, Nero—the pretending. As if they wouldn't just move on to another support system the second theirs fell apart. Look!" he says as he points his finger at all of the blurry ants they continue to fly above. "Haha, there's no shame at all. Any and everywhere you look—no shame. I swear you gotta love it."

"And what's wrong with relying on others? Unlike you, Surii, I know I can't do it all alone. And unlike you, I don't pretend as if I can. I'm not afraid to appreciate just how important having a family is in this world."

"Oh, I do appreciate how important it is. But I don't believe for a second that *you* do. In fact, it is so very clear to me just how much you don't understand the true importance of it. Maybe *that's* why I'm here. To remind you."

"I never forgot, Surii. Why do you think I built my own?"

"Because you are a coward. You call that a family? You know what you are—you're a scared little boy who hides behind the very people he's sworn to protect. As you know, during the Edits, we wore blindfolds to increase our ability to see the world around us for what it really is, by using all of our senses and all of our devices to see the truth—and not just rely on what only our eyes can perceive. However, I can tell that you wear that mask just so you can blind yourself from the truth," Surii relays to his former comrade.

"What truth?"

"That you need these people way more than they will ever need you."

"Oh, is that so? You really need to grow up already," Nerosion tells him while shaking his head.

"Oh, it's so, bro. And I'm going to prove it to you."

"Surii, I'm tired of this nonsense. Tell me what are you doing here in Opia? I know Odem is seeking to bring Gloria back to life. And I know he is responsible for the sudden influx of Exile here, also."

"You know a lot I see," Surii tells him.

"You can tell our former *master* that I'm not interested in re-joining his gang. You can quote me on that."

"Heh. Boluscant said the same thing. You see that's your problem—you think everything's about you. Chapter Five is and always was larger than you and your tiny world. It's sad I have to even remind you of such a thing. Odem isn't worried about you. I told you, I'm here to lend you a helping hand. Basically, doing what you couldn't—protecting your family. And how pitiful you must feel—you put on that disgraceful suit and pretend you live to protect the people of this city when it's really you who needs the most protection. You really have been slacking off. What happened to you, brother? Even with all your skill, you couldn't even protect those who you say mean the most to you. All that power you possess, and you couldn't even protect your own precious, little Ori."

"I SAID, THAT'S ENOUGH!"

Nerosion screams at him louder than he has probably ever screamed at someone since he first donned his mask. With a great deal of his might, he extends the edge of his staff straight towards Surii's exposed back. What seems to be a surely-connected attack, is effortlessly deflected by Surii via his U.R.O. at the last second.

"Seriously? Do I look like one of these fiend-out, Exile junkies to you? You better come with something a little better than some baton, brother."

"You're mine!" Nerosion says, no longer looking to control his rage. He starts dashing across the rooftops even faster now.

"SAID THE JUNKIE TO THE HELPLESS CHILD AND MOTHER!" Surii randomly yells out.

"What?" Nerosion says as he snaps back to his senses.

"In your ever-long quest to seek validation, you continue to run from the places where it resides. You're a fraud, Olpha Chambers. You can scare these people into believing you're some guardian angel, but you're not. You're no better than those junkies you beat down—doing anything just for another fix. Even now, you disappoint your girlfriend and child for the second time in record time, just so you can get another dose of that false euphoria."

Nerosion now begins to pay attention to Surii's rambling more closely.

"You know what's the greatest thing about being an addict, Nero? They always come back for another hit."

It takes all but a second and a half for Nerosion to process this statement before he instantly stops in his tracks and leaps off in the direction of downtown Monachopsis, where the Del Cora Private School for Girls has just dismissed their students.

Chapter Twenty

PIZZA PARTY

April 17th. 5:02 P.M. (CDT)

"Is *this* the place?" Arthur exhaustively asks Joelle as they pull up to the sixth pizza shop in the past forty minutes.

"Hold on, let me go and check it out," Joelle says as she exits the car and heads inside of another pizza joint for the sixth time. Inside the premises, she looks around to see if she sees anyone resembling a spent, belly-ached, eleven-year-old boy with tomato sauce on his face. When she doesn't notice anyone fitting the description for the sixth time, she realizes that with every random pizza shop they stop in, Calvin is most likely getting farther and farther away from them. So this time, she decides she's going to ask someone who works there if they have any information about him.

"Excuse me," she calls out.

"*Slice?*" is the response the busy cook behind the counter says to her addressing him without ever looking up. As usual, her lack of understanding of modern English colloquialism leaves her stupefied by his reply.

"Uh, no ... Calvin?" she says back with hesitation.

"Calvin?" the busy cook replies. "Are you looking for him?"

"Yes! Yes, I am," she says, excited that he recognizes who she's talking about.

"Hold on. Hey, Calvin! There's someone here looking for you!" the cook yells out to the back, which elicits a rush of exuberance from inside of Joelle's body.

"Who is it?" shouts back a rugged voice from the backroom.

"Oh, what you said your name was?" the cook asks, finally looking up at the person he been engaged in conversation with.

"Oh, it's—"

Joelle realizes she has been going by a new name since Calvin ran away from her, but she's also afraid of giving this stranger her new, unofficial name. "Wait, is that really Calvin back there? It doesn't really sound like him."

"Woman, you're killing me. I got work to do," the disgruntled cook spats, who is unable to afford to be the messenger between her and their seemingly mutual friend. "Calvin, come out here and get your broad, man!"

"Broad?" Joelle thinks to herself. Understanding the term only as an adjective and wondering why he's using it as a noun.

"Come on, July, you can't even get a name for me?" the man from the back says to the cook as he emerges from wherever he was.

"You see me working here, go on with that stuff, man!" July clearly irritated, spats back. Joelle can't help to wonder why the voice from the back refers to this particular man as one of the twelve months of an Earth-year, and not a person.

"Hey, what can I do for you?" the man from the back asks Joelle as he makes his way to the counter. Now standing in front of her is a husky fella wearing a smock that appears as if he's been eating the tomato sauce instead of adding it to a flattened layer of dough.

"Y-you're not Calvin," Joelle states, rather assuredly.

"Uh, yeah I am," he corrects her. "Who the hell are you?"

"I'm Joelle," she tells him.

"Joelle who?"

"Joelle Grace. I'm looking for Calvin."

"I am Calvin, lady. What do you want?" the man who's obviously losing his patience firmly asks her. At this point, because this man is using terms that the Calvin she knows have used in the past, coupled with the fact that he claims his name is also Calvin, Joelle is inclined to believe that something has happened to the Calvin that she knows that made him grow into the mongrel currently standing in front of her. After all, stranger things have happened since she's been on Earth and it doesn't help that she doesn't know that more than one person on this planet can indeed possess the same name.

"Calvin? How did this happen to you?" she says, now convinced that this man is her friend, as she softly places her hand on his new, large, burly face.

"I don't know," he responds with the charm of a six-year-old. "But I've been so alone, for so long."

Big Calvin puts on a sheepish act and decides to roll with whatever weird thing this chick walked into his pizza shop with, hoping it'll bring a little entertainment to his otherwise dismal, daily, structured life.

"It's okay, Calvin. I'm here now. I'm going to help you get better," she promises, with a deep concern for his health now present in her voice.

"Okay, that's enough," a seasoned, almost-feminine, ragged voice blurts out from the same room that Big Calvin just exited from. Now in view, is a dingy-clothed, slim woman who's probably been listening to the entire conversation before she felt she had no other choice but to intervene.

"How can we help you, child?"

Though higher in pitch, the woman's voice is exponentially more unpleasant than that of Big Calvin's. Each word that rattles out her throat is like something heard when unexpectedly ripping the eyelashes off of a possum that was currently giving birth. Only this possum cries out from the pain in English.

"I'm looking for my friend Calvin," Joelle says after slightly wincing from the unpleasant voice. "He's a young kid who loves pizza."

"You mean that boy with the fancy watch? Yeah, I remember him, he ordered a whole pie for himself and ran out before paying. Well, guess what? He's not getting these back until I get the money for those slices," she says as she holds up Calvin's SHED frames. "I actually been dying to get a pair of these for my grand-baby for a while. Now I can't wait to make him a little SHED page and everything. Woot!" she says, sharing the details of her nefarious plans to Joelle.

"You can't do that," Joelle affirms, not at all appreciating what the woman has just shared with her. "Those are Calvin's glasses! Give those to me!" she passionately demands as she throws her hand out in an uncharacteristic display of bravado.

"Sorry, can't help you there, honey. Unless you cough up the money for those slices, I'm holding on to these things. You should be happy I didn't call the cops on your little friend," the woman indirectly threatens.

"Money? I don't have any money. But I need those glasses so I can find my friend."

"You must be dumber than my son is if you think I'm about to give you that boy's frames back after he done stole from me," she says while cackling.

"Your son?" Joelle thinks to herself, wondering how is it possible someone of her size can possibly pop out anything bigger than a cherry, let alone this oaf in front of her.

"I'm sorry, but I'm going to have to take those from you," Joelle respectfully warns her.

"Oh, you're funny little lady. Calvin, get rid of her."

"Okay, Ma," Big Calvin pouts as he reluctantly agrees with his mother's command. "Come on, honey. Show's over," he says as he makes his way from around the counter to escort Joelle out of the store. Big Calvin lifts up the section of the counter that separates the cooking area from the seating area and allows a person to enter and exit, and goes to grab Joelle by the arm. She immediately ducks under his grab attack and crawls behind him, making her way behind the counter to the cooking area. She now stands between the frail woman and the room where the woman was trying to escape to. Immediately, the woman picks up a wooden rolling pin and threatens Joelle with it. Big Calvin, desperately longing for some much-needed entertainment in his life, does nothing to further circumvent the growing discordance between his Ma and his lover.

"Bitch, you better move out my way if you knew what's good for ya —because if you touch me, I'll beat your ass worse than July beats that dough over there," she promises Joelle. Joelle glances at July to get an idea of what exactly does that mean, only to see July punching and smacking the pizza dough to create its elongated shape as he continues to mind his business, showing absolutely no interest of getting involved in the fray next to him.

"I'm sorry, but I'm taking them," Joelle says to the woman as she takes another step towards her.

The moment she does, the irate woman swings the rolling pin at her with all her might. It is only a second after this moment, that the woman screams out in shock as the rolling pin suddenly stops in mid-strike, and her hand bends and slips off of it, while the pin itself remains suspended in the air.

"What in the devil ..." the woman whimpers to herself as she sees the rolling pin still hovering in front of her—perhaps more surprised by the fact that Joelle isn't nearly as shocked as she is than the fact that the rolling pin she's used for years to threaten customers, is now floating in front of her. "Ju..Ju...li..o?" she quietly calls out.

"Oh, *now* you know my name!? No, no, don't call me now, I'm busy —I'm busy with my customers and you busy with your *Diabla,*" July says as he keeps his back turned to the whole ordeal as if stuff like this goes down in here all the time. Joelle looks around to see what customers July is referring to only to realize that there aren't any.

Just then another person enters the store. Joelle quickly snatches the rolling pin out of the air when she notices it is Arthur who steps inside.

"Hey. Everything alright in here, Joelle?" he says as he walks in.

"Yes, Arthur. I was just asking this woman if she's seen my brother," Joelle says as she quickly turns around and addresses him.

"Then why are you behind the counter, child? I didn't know you were hungry, you should've told me. Come on over from back there and let's get something to eat."

"Wait a minute, I know you. You're that man that be on T.V.—on all of those science programs, aren't you?" the rawboned woman says after staring at Arthur for a bit.

"Dr. Arthur Bouya. It's a pleasure to meet you," he politely tells the upset woman.

"Doctor?" Joelle whispers to herself. Immediately, another mini-seizure is triggered.

"I'm sorry for barging in, but me and my friend here are looking for a friend of ours. We were hoping you can help us," Arthur shares with the woman.

"That's right, Dr. *Boo-yah!"* she exclaims. "So, you're with this devil, huh? Yeah, no wonder she's looking for that little thief—they belong together. Yeah, I've seen that little demon, but he ran out of here without paying for his food," the disgruntled mother practically regurgitates out.

"Oh, heavens. Is that true? I am so sorry for the inconvenience. Here, let me pay you for what he took," the generous doctor says as he reaches into his wallet and begins sifting through several bills before removing one. "Will fifty dollars cover it?" he says as he brandishes the crisp note to her.

"Why, yes doctor, it will. Thank you, very much."

Joelle notices the sudden change in the woman's demeanor upon looking at the particular piece of green paper. A similar sentiment Chadwick displayed upon receiving the same thing.

"No, thank *you*. Come on, Joelle, we have to keep searching for Sonder," Arthur insists.

"No! That woman over there has something that belongs to him! She has his SHED frames!" Joelle suddenly yells out as Arthur begins motioning her to the exit.

"Oh," he says, stopping in his tracks. "I'm sorry ma'am, is that true?"

"I don't know what that crazy bitch is talking about," the recalcitrant woman shares with him.

"You have my brother's frames, return them, now!" yells Joelle, growing more furious by the minute thanks to the woman's obsessive lying.

"I really hate to further trouble you ma'am, but it is of the utmost important that we bring my friend all of the belongings he had with him when he entered your place of business."

"Ma, just give them the damn glasses!" Big Calvin suddenly shouts to his mother, apparently growing tired of this entire back and forth spatting, especially when he didn't benefit from it in the least.

"Fine!" she yells back to her son before sloppily shoving the glasses into Arthur's awaiting hand.

"I really appreciate your kindness, ma'am. Oh and if it isn't any further trouble to you, would you mind pointing us in the direction he went when he left?"

The woman looks at Arthur with a side-eyed at first, then decides her beef isn't with him necessarily, so why not help.

"Well," she begins after rolling her eyes at Joelle and letting out an exasperated sigh. "From what my son tells me, the little thief ran off down that street. Ain't nothing over there but a few stores and the aquarium. Chances are he went there. It's a popular place to visit around this time of year."

"Thank you so very much again, and for your warm hospitality. And again, we apologize for the trouble. Take care. Come on, Joelle," Arthur says before nodding at her and grabbing Joelle's hand so they can leave together.

"Yeah, it's okay doctor—you're fine, you ain't gotta thank me, you can get whatever you want from me anytime. But as for that DEVIL BITCH OVER THERE!" she says, referring to Joelle, her voice suddenly switching back to its previous, ugly tone. "You make sure you lock her ass up in a dungeon somewhere, doctor! She is performing all types of voodoo and magic and I don't know what-the-fuck! She sprayed all that demonic shit all over my food now I gotta throw out ALL MY GODDAMN TOMATO SAUCE I JUST BOUGHT, YOU DEMON BITCH! She lucky you walked in here when you did, doctor! Wanna be stoppin' rolling pins in the middle of the air and shit wit'chur voodoo magic bitch, I got some magic for your ass too! Come back around here again! Stoppin' a rolling pin ain't nothin', remember that! I wanna see if you can stop a bullet from flying in your ass next time!" she spews.

The pair exit the parlor and enter back into the car.

"Jeez, what was all that about?" Arthur says as he starts his car and chuckles.

"All what?" Joelle asks him, downplaying everything that has just transpired.

"Oh, you're going to pretend like that woman didn't wanna tear your head off just now?"

"She did?" Joelle says, continuing her charade which may very well not be one at all.

"I know you're from New York, so you're probably used to those kind of brouhahas as am I, but in my sixty-nine years of living, never have I ever heard someone go off on someone they don't know with such vitriol before over pizza. And all that voodoo-magic talk—what did I miss?"

"Nothing. She was just upset that Sonder was dishonest to her—as anyone would be. Anyway, I got the frames, now I just need to use them to find Sonder's location."

"How are you going to do that?" Arthur wonders as he hands Joelle back the item she almost went through hell to get.

"She said he had a fancy watch on. I'm assuming she was talking about the SHED band on his wrist. Sonder told me that these frames are always linked to his band. I just gotta pull up the Locator like this, and it should leads us directly to him," she says as she attempts to do what she just explained. "Got it! It says he's at the Shedd Aquarium ... uh, what's an aquarium?"

"You've never been to an aquarium?" Arthur asks her, half-thinking she's joking. "Oh darling, you are in store for a heck of a day. An aquarium is a huge vivarium where many creatures of the ocean are kept and taken care of in. And people from all over can come and look at the splendid marine animals in their natural habitat. If we hurry now, we can get there before they close."

"Do you need a pair of SHED frames to look at them?" she sincerely asks.

"Look at what, the animals? My, no ... at least, not that I'm aware of," he says assuredly at first but then second-guessing himself when he considers that it's been a few decades since he's been to an aquarium, so he may not really know for sure.

"Then why is it called the *Shedd* Aquarium?"

"You know, I'm not even sure. But I'm certain it doesn't have anything to do with those silly glasses."

"Then we should get out of here. Here, put these on, it'll show you how to get to Sonder," she instructs him.

"Alrighty," he says as he takes a good look at the glasses she hands to him. "Whoa, these are amazing. How do I look?" Arthur says as he puts the SHED frames over his own glasses. Joelle can't really generate a genuine response considering she's genuinely confused about how he really looks. After all, she's never seen someone wear glasses on top of glasses before.

"Normal," is the first and admittedly only response she feels is adequate in both masking her inability to give an accurate opinion, and masking her lack of taste in fashion.

"Great! Let's go," he says before pulling off.

Chapter Twenty-One

AD HOMINEM ATTACK

April 17th. 6:13 P.M. (CDT)

"SHEDD. AQUARIUM."

Joelle reads the sign out loud as they pull up to the location that Calvin has absconded to. Unable to get over the coincidence that the name of the aquarium also happens to share the name of Calvin's glasses, it prompts her to put them on to see if reading this sign with them will reveal anything special about this place. And of course, it doesn't.

"Fifty-one dollars for parking!? I swear you better be able to claim one of these dolphins on your taxes or something for that price," Arthur suddenly exclaims after reading a nearby parking sign. "Unbelievable."

"Is that a lot of money?" Joelle asks him, choosing to keep the frames on as she slowly comes to appreciate how they look on her.

"To park? In this day and age?" Arthur responds before taking a moment to think about if the price of parking is truly that expensive in this day and age. He let's out a small sigh. "Nah, not really. The fact that you had to even ask that tells me you're definitely from New York. Have you seen how much the train fare is there now? There isn't enough science in the world to make sense of that travesty."

"I know, right?" Joelle says as she pretends to know what he's referring to. At the very least, she does now know what a train is. "That's why I usually walk to wherever I need to go."

"That's good. I mean it's good we've cut gas prices in half, but now the prices of the charging stations are rising. And that's not even because the cost of the electricity is higher or anything."

"Rising? How come?"

"I don't know, some hoopla about maintenance and service costs. Ever since we've perfected the crafting of solar meta-materials and started utilizing its benefits on a wide, domestic scale, most of the things we used to use gas for have started to become obsolete. Especially cars. Solar-powered cars are on the rise and for good reason—you don't even have to go to a station to refuel them—they're just always powered up and ready to go. They're unfairly expensive, but I'll be lying if I said the price wasn't worth it."

"So, what does that have to do with charging stations?"

"Nothing much, at least for now. But we all know that good ole SHED tech never fails and just like what the SHED band did to the cellphone, or heck, what the cellphone did to the house phone ... or what T.V. did to the radio, or what the MP3 did to the CD player, or what the CD player did to the cassette player—solar-powered cars are about to be the next best thing in a year or two, which means everyone who's not already in that market has already started scrambling for a way to survive. And like usual, we're the ones who are left footing the bill."

"What is SHED tech anyway?" Joelle asks him, yearning to learn more about the term she's grown quite accustomed to hearing.

"Smart, helio-electronic device. It's just a type of technology that has, for all intents and purposes, pioneered and accelerated the utilization of solar power for everyday living convenience."

"Oh. So somebody owns it?"

"In a sense, yeah, hehehe—a giant corporation named Newform Industries."

"And who are they?"

"A very influential global conglomerate in the military industrial complex. SHED is just their tech branch. Chances are if you hear or see something related to advanced technology, like the ability to record your dreams for example, or speakers that can cancel out any noise in the area, it was more than likely conceptualized by Newform."

"I see."

"Okay, here we go," Arthur says as he drives into the parking area next to the aquarium. In the meantime, Joelle keeps the SHED frames on, but this time it's because she's afraid that she'll lose sight of Calvin if she doesn't.

"It says he's above us, two floors I believe," she says, updating her driver on her friend's location.

"Okay. Then we should hurry," he suggests.

Arthur and Joelle exit the car and make their way to the elevator that'll presumably take them to Calvin. As he presses the button and waits for the elevator to arrive, Joelle can't help but to reflect on the moments that occurred shortly after the last time she found herself inside of one of these metal boxes. An eerie feeling washes over her that she dismisses as nothing more than the jitters. Arthur notices her sudden clamminess and tries to raise her spirits a little with more questions about her experiences.

"I still can't believe you've never been to an aquarium. I'm curious—what places have you visited before?"

"Um, not many I can say," Joelle says as she does her best not to reveal too much about herself. She carefully thinks about all the experiences she had since she's crashed on this planet, and not one of them are appropriate to discuss with this stranger.

"Okay. Well lemme ask you something else then, what is it that has you so interested in this asteroid?" the inquisitive doctor asks next. This question, Joelle didn't anticipate at all. However, she finds herself wanting to tell him the complete truth considering just how important it is to her but alas, she knows she cannot.

"I believe ..." she begins. "I believe that there is more to Apophis than we've been led to believe."

"Is that so? What leads you to say that?" he asks, looking to hear more from the curious, young girl.

"It's just that ... ever since that asteroid exploded, it's like my life blew up with it as well."

"And here I thought it was just me," Arthur remarks almost inaudibly. "And Sonder feels the same way?"

"Yes! Yes, he does. He desperately wants to know more about it also. He thinks there is some relation to it and his future or something," she tells him.

"I see what you mean. Yes, lots of interesting things have been happening since that rock entered our atmosphere."

"Have you seen the videos of those creatures attacking?" she asks him.

"I have."

"What do you think about them?"

"Well," he starts to say but then stops after thinking about the question a little. "Because of my obligations to the scientific community, I'm not at liberty to really say—yet."

"Oh, I see."

"In fact, my conference here in Chicago is going to also touch on that very thing. If we find your friend quick enough, we should still be able to make it. But I wouldn't worry too much about those creatures though. Evidence suggests that they're just part of an underground species that we have yet to discover. They whom were forced to the surface due to the meteors landing and disrupting their natural habitat," he assures her.

"So, you believe they're from Earth?"

"Of course, don't you?"

"I don't know."

"Don't tell me you're one of those Adaptist folk that believe the Shee invasion has finally begun."

"The who?"

"Good answer. Trust me, aliens coming to Earth is just about the least possible thing that can happen; at least in our lifetime," he confidently tells Joelle.

"You don't believe in other life in the universe?" she asks him with a hint of sincerity in her voice, as if his next answer will determine for her overall how people on this planet feel about such matters.

"Oh, that's not what I'm saying at all. In fact, as a theoretical physicist, I probably wouldn't have a job if I didn't believe in life from another world in some form or another," he shares with her. "However, if there is intelligent life out there and they decided they wanted to visit us, the last thing they'll do is send one of their own to do so."

"What do you mean?" she asks, considering she's here and she's from another world.

"Any species smart enough to perform interstellar travel, undoubtedly has the technology and hopefully, the wisdom, to first send machines or whatever is their version of such a thing, to survey a planet and conduct whatever activity it is they wish to accomplish from such a visit, before they send themselves."

"What if they already have?" Joelle asks after a long pause. The elevator finally arrives and Arthur looks at her with slight intrigue, almost taken back by her sudden perspicacious views in regards to this matter. The elevator opens and the two enter. The doctor presses the second floor button and the doors promptly begin to close right after.

"Well, then we better pray that they're friendly."

7:30 P.M. (EDT)

BRRRRRRRNNNNNGGGGGGG! The final bell of the day signaling dismissal time for the students who attends the Del Cora Private Art School for Girls distinguished after-school program, finally goes off; a program that's surprisingly still running considering the collective disquiet of the country at the moment. In fact, the only thing not surprising about any of this, is that Laharin made sure Ori was the first one there in attendance—as if Apophis wasn't an actual thing that blighted the lives of millions around the country, and was just some hypothetical event that could've only become a reality in some fiction novel.

Unlike before, this time Laharin made sure that she's there in the office to pick up Ori when she's dismissed. Much like her fiancé, Laharin quickly learns how to adapt from an event that previously caused a setback—like the one where her, her driver, and her daughter almost lost their lives. As a result, she's been making sure she arrives early enough to pick up Ori directly from her school, making sure she has more than enough stamina in her legs to wait there and even stand around if she has to, for as long as she has to. Her tendency to adapt to unfortunate situations at times causes her to overcompensate, in this case, arriving at her daughter's school close to an hour earlier than her daughter gets dismissed. Fortunately, she doesn't have to stand around while she waits, as there are plenty of chairs lined up outside of the main office to comfortably sit in.

It is during this time, while she sits in one of the surprisingly comfortable chairs, that she gets her first glimpse at how ugly her daughter's school really is—just as Ori always tries to tell her. As it happens, it isn't even the boring and bland lack of color on the walls in the hallway that makes her feel this way at all. If anything, she happens to be a fan of simplicity. No, it is the voices of those working in the office behind her that allows her to see just how disgusting her daughter's school has come to be. Maybe it is because Laharin told the staff in the office that she's going to go on and head directly to Ori's class to pick her up, that the next set of events happen in the way they do. It isn't until she decided that she needs to stop babying her little girl so much that she decides to take a seat and *wished* she had strapped herself in for something she had no idea was coming.

Whether they realize she can hear them or not, is at this point of no concern to her, as over the course of just a short half-hour, she has already heard just about every nasty thing one can hear a group of people say about the very people they smile in the face of when they pass them in the hallway. Maybe because she's a woman who has spent a great deal of her life on another continent, but these remarks coming from the office next to her that has her shocked beyond belief, only have her as such because she hasn't had the distinguished luxury of growing up around people with such nasty thoughts and feelings towards others they work with. However, no matter if she was born and raised right inside of this school, she can't ever see herself being comfortable with such a clandestine powwow filled with heinous thoughts and ill will towards their fellow coworkers—especially in an environment consisting of children.

But, it really isn't until she hears her own name spoken out loud from the batch of birds behind her, that her feelings of contempt and pity are immediately replaced by blind fury and frothing vexation. And just like anybody who hears their name being dragged through the mud, Laharin's heart rate begins to increase, and whether she realizes it or not, the temperature in her body as well. She doesn't even realize that she's gripping the arm of her chair harder than she's ever gripped her own sidearm pistol while in the Air Force—and yes, if she was still an officer of the military, her training would've surely shook her out of her steadily growing rage. But it's been a good nine years since she's last had to calm herself down from hurting a stranger, so it is of no surprise why, right now, she's already lifted herself a few inches out of her seat and now plans on running straight into that office to put her fist through someone's skull first and ask questions later.

If only she did remember her training during this moment in time, because the proverbial snap occurs the moment she hears one of those prattling crows in the office a foot away from her say her daughter's name. Joking that Olpha hasn't made her his wife yet, or that she sashays around here like she's better than everybody, or even hearing them laugh at the fact that she only walks like that because her legs probably got ran over by a bus, does nothing to her compared to what she's about to do to them, upon hearing Ori's name followed by the disrespectful and vile words that followed it.

Two sequential sentences with her daughter's name in it is all it takes for Laharin to fully leap up out of her seat and barge into the office. She rushes in, seeing only red, and prepares her first and probably last statement before she's carried away to jail for aggravated assault.

"WH—!"

BBBBBRRRRRNNNNNNGGGGGGG!

The bell interrupting the start of her murder spree, is the last thing Laharin remembers as she reflects on the episode that almost happened just five minutes ago. Even as Mrs. Aronson continues to talk to Laharin's blank gaze, Laharin only returns back to the present when she hears the end of Mrs. Aronson's voice pitch go up, indicating that she just asked her a question.

"Huh? I'm sorry, what was that again?"

"I said would you and Ori like to come to the school later to participate in the Back-To-School dinner tonight? I'll be there, as will

Cassandra, and the girls can have some fun together while the parents and teachers enjoy some of the fun and games that's been put together by the students."

"Sure. Sure thing," Laharin expresses once she fully returns from her visceral flashback.

"Yayyyy!" Ori exclaims after overhearing her mother's uncharacteristically low response.

"Great! We'll see you two tonight then."

Without saying anything, Laharin turns and walks away, keeping Ori's fingers firmly interlocked between her own. On her way to the exit, she has no choice but to walk past the doorway of the office that almost changed her life. When she reaches it, she stops, turns and stares inside at the staff who almost became her victims. She stares at them for over ten seconds—an uncomfortably long time to be staring at anyone, let alone someone who you may have suspected now knows you were talking about them.

Ten seconds turn into twenty, and even Ori who was also looking inside the office, though not staring nearly as hard at the staff but still noticing them to a degree, now stares at her mother, both comically and confused.

As twenty seconds turn into forty-five, Ori can't help but to bust out into full laughter at whatever the hell her mother is doing—which makes every attendant in that office even more uncomfortable. To them it must be like witnessing something out of the Blair Witch Project. Maybe it's because Laharin was indeed ready to kill each and every one of them like the Blair Witch is known to—on camera, a device which surely this office contains.

It isn't until Ori's sense of humor is replaced by her easily-accessed sense of boredom that they finally are able to leave. That's because Ori, against her better wishes, begins to pull her mother out of the entrance of the doorway.

"Come on, Mommy."

Ori pulls her mother away from the office, and as expected, her mother follows along without a fight. The only problem is that it seems as if her legs are moving automatically, independent of her will. At least that's what Ori thinks to be the case, considering that her mother's head has yet to turn in the direction they proceed to walk in and instead seems to be magnetized to the faculty in the office.

Considering that the head can only turn but so far before the muscles inside the neck reach their limit, it isn't until this limit is almost alarmingly surpassed, indicated by the accompanying sharp pain that shoots up through the back of Laharin's neck, that of which doesn't faze her in the least, that Laharin swivels her head away from the office southeast of her and towards the exit which lies directly in front.

Even though Laharin has come to confide in her daughter no matter how ungraspable the situation may be for her five-year-old to understand, the reason why Laharin is having such a hard time expressing herself verbally this time is because she happens to be having a hard time unclenching her tightly-locked jaw. It is at the point where tears begin to well up in her eyes which triggers a symptomatic sniffle from her nose, that Ori realizes a lot more has happened to her dear mother than her little mind can readily perceive at the moment. And without ever missing a beat, Ori knows, like any Queen-in-training, that when you see a queen about to lose her footing a bit, you're the one who has to be there to make sure the ground never gives out. That's why when she reaches into her mother's purse to retrieve a fresh Kleenex to deliver to her, she does so near the exit, so that she may never reveal to these peasants that they almost made her Queen's crown tilt for a moment.

Laharin and Ori exit the building together, and this time, Leander is the one who circles the block while Laharin waltzes through the festering crowd of paranoid hipsters. It takes the shouting coming from these blowhards, that she almost forgot about, to wake her back up to the present and all of the joy that comes with living in it.

"It wasn't so many people this morning," Ori says out loud, mostly to herself but loud enough for her mother to hear. For Laharin, leaving from what she just went through only to enter what she has no choice but to walk through, is enough to push someone over the edge. However, somewhere between these two events, she's remembered that any selfish vindication she would receive by impulsively acting on how she currently feels right now, like punching one of these loud-mouths in the nose, would pale by a large margin to the overall peace of mind and comfortability of having her daughter beside her. By comparison, it becomes almost silly to her to even think that anything anyone can do to her can cause a reaction out of her that would result in a frown on her daughter's face. It is then why Laharin begins to smile as she takes her time walking through the parted masses with her perfect, pretty princess in tow. If anything, the jeers from the protesters come across now as cheers, as the crowd clamors in celebration of these two pulchritudinous belles as they warmly grace them with their royal presence. After all, they are the soon-to-be consort and princess of these people's King. It's only right they start perfecting their sovereign appeal.

"That's her right there! That's the wife of the man that got in my face last time! Olpha Chambers! That's Olpha Chambers' wife!" shouts one of the protestors, who was fortunate enough to survive one of Nerosion's assaults—even if it was only administered verbally.

"Olpha was here?" Laharin thinks to herself.

"Mommy, Daddy knows that man?" Ori too, asks, puzzled at hearing her father's name screamed out by anyone but her mother.

"I'm not sure, but I think your father might've introduced himself to him," she drolly quips to Ori.

"Daddy spoke to *him?* Why is he angry then?"

"Angry? I'm trying to figure out why he's still conscious. Your father must've been in a good mood when they met, otherwise that jerk would be recovering in an emergency room somewhere. Either that, or he didn't have his mask on when he met him. No wonder he knows who we are. Lucky motherfucker," she explains to her daughter, taking special care to mutter that last part under her breath.

Protect Children's Rights! Protect Children's Rights! Protect Children's Rights! Protect Children's Rights!

The repetitious, rhythmic chanting coming from a large crowd of protestors are always annoying to those who disagree with its message. The mere sight of seeing someone who disagrees with their message is irksome to anyone who stands with the crowd. Somewhere in the middle of those two points lies a spark that can be accessed by either side daring enough to acquire its power and use it for their cause;

whether the use of it advances their cause or ultimately weakens it won't be realized until the spark is ignited. But most of the time in these kind of situations—where hate and angst have been smoldering for weeks on end, and where this opportunistic spark's destructive potential has increased logarithmically—or basically multiplied several times over since its inception, if such a thing can even be measured at all—the spark seldom acts to ignite the torch to guide either side from their own darkness and back into the light. In fact, the fire generated by the spark is almost always used to burn the opposition, where the charred carcass is used as a symbol of their truth and forthrightness. It's not hard to see what can come from such a case if one of the opposing parties decides to use this spark to ignite their highly volatile gas cloud of rage.

"Where the hell is Leander?" Laharin annoyed, spats out loud to herself, as her tolerance for blocking out the loud rhetoric of the massive crowd behind her slowly begins to crumble.

"Hey! Heyy! Don't push me, what the hell is wrong with you!?"

These are the words that make Laharin look back at the crowd since she's exited the school. It is a single voice coming from the middle of the crowd that projects higher than the rest somehow. A woman's voice.

"GET THE HELL OFF OF ME, YOU CREEP!" the voice yells again, this time twice as loud.

Laharin turns back around and enjoys a little chuckle knowing that these people don't have as much control over their cause as it would appear.

"Hey, you bitch!" a woman near the front much closer to Laharin, yells out to her. "You think it's okay to just subject your children to forced institutionalized learning? You think what they're doing in there ... you think that's learning? That's imprisonment. You should be put away for a long time!"

Laharin is kind enough to spare but a slight glance at the woman before turning her head back towards the street that Leander should be driving down at any time now. She checks the time on her fashionably customized SHED band, and makes a mental promise to let Leander have it when she sees him.

"Hey, you stuck-up bitch, I'm talking to you!" the infuriated woman says to Laharin before raising her arm to throw what appears to be a bottle of some unknown liquid at her.

Before the suspicious bottle can even leave her hand, the entire gate that prevents the crowd from covering the walkway collapses in front of the woman, where she and close to thirty other protestors all go tumbling to the ground as they let out frantic screams and shouts of horror during their spill onto the concrete.

Laharin instinctively tightens her grip around her daughter's hand and takes several steps back as the heap of protesters continue to spill out from their confined positions.

"Mommy!" Ori can't help to shriek. Normally, such an occurrence wouldn't phase her, but considering the couple of events that transpired the other night, those of which will have most likely traumatized her on some level, she can't help but to be on a slight edge, especially at the sight of thirty plus bodies rolling on the floor beneath her.

"It's okay baby, move back," Laharin instructs to her daughter, doing her best to remain collected.

The appointed school safety officers, who couldn't be more unprepared to handle such a situation, are easily overran by the larger crowd, they who have now began screaming and running in multiple directions for some reason unknown to Laharin and Ori.

"Hey! I'm not done with you yet, bitch!" snarls the bottle-chucker from earlier, as she finally attempts to crawl out from the pile of bodies, many of whom carry with them an unpleasant stench due to them festering in their collapsible tents that they've posted around the school and slept in for days on end.

It isn't until the troublesome social justice warrior is on her knees and ready to fully stand up, that her nose gets broken. Out of nowhere, a female Strawman, already in a full sprint towards Laharin, uses the back of the protester's neck as a stepping stool to launch herself at Laharin to attack her.

Besides having her own extensive military background, where Larahin surely completed trial after trial of combat training in her own right, being the fiancée to the most prolific martial arts master known today, allows a gal access to some pretty informal but absolutely effective self-defense classes.

Ask anybody who has been forced to readjust to life after losing the function of their legs, and most likely they'll agree that their arms basically enjoy a status boost thanks to all of the extra work they now have been tasked with completing. This is why the counter-punch delivered by the Tyrant's fiancée to the unprepared Strawman's jaw is executed with such proficiency; it's a wonder why there isn't a *Ms.* Nerosion flying around these rooftops at night.

Unexpectedly however, it doesn't take long for the collapsed Strawman to shake off one of Laharin's punches, even if it did put her flat on her back. If it was anyone else, they'll be out cold right now. That's why a genuine concern now leaps into Laharin's throat, she who was pretty sure that this mongrel wasn't waking up until at least Leander arrived.

"Laaahhaaarinn ..." grumbles the Strawman as she rises back to her feet.

Like someone who's currently in the climax of their high, the woman shuffles for a bit after she gets up—walking around but in no particular direction. She smiles with her head pointed to the sky almost as if there's nothing in the world that can make her feel as good as she does right now. Suddenly, she looks at Laharin again, and her smile disappears once her dilated pupils meet hers.

She instantly goes back into a sprint towards the mother and daughter, only to run directly into the heel of one of Nerosion's beautiful diving kicks, who plants his foot into her chest with the same force of a wooden bat cracking the stitching off a ninety-mile-per-hour fastball. Originally, Nerosion was going to allow his powerful kick to come into contact with this woman's face, it was only at the last second he remembered that killing someone would violate the Nerosion Pact—the contract he has with the government to combat crime in the Opia region of New York state—and decided that he rather let this woman be the first woman in the history of the world to get that close to touching his wife and kid and live to remember it, even if she has to live inside of an iron lung for the rest of her life while she does.

"Daddy!" Ori exclaims once Nerosion lands on his two feet next to them. “Oops!” she yelps as she quickly covers her mouth when she realizes her mistake.

“Hi, Princess,” Nerosion whispers back to his daughter, making sure no one besides Laharin and herself can hear him address her.

“You’re late,” mutters Laharin to her masked savior.

“I miss you too, baby,” he replies with a hint of jocose, which evokes a glare that any woman whose man kept her waiting can and will produce under the given circumstances. Nerosion’s reaction to her piercing, yet adoring eyes is apt given the situation. “Sorry, I was a little caught up,” he says, quickly correcting his light-hearted attitude.

“It’d better be for a good reason,” she tells him while the pandemonium continues around them.

“I bumped into our Bee-Killer—” he shares.

“And?” she says after waiting for him to elaborate more.

“And, he was trying to kill a lot more than bees this time ... more like ants.”

“Did you stop him?”

“Well, I saved the ants, if that’s what you’re asking,” he shares while he continues to put down the Strawmen who keep trying to attack him while he chats with his family.

“So, he got away,” she determines.

“Well, you know ... family first. No worries. I’ll get him next time,” he promises her. “Anyway, what did I miss?”

“Well, a woman tried to throw some milk on me after she found out I was dating you. Besides that, nothing much. Oh, something happened in the crowd though,” she shares.

“What?” he says as he easily disables another Strawman.

“I’m not sure. Another woman started shouting and that’s when everything started going down.”

“Was she yelling something about being touched?”

“Yes, how’d you know?”

“Where do you think I just came from?” he slyly asks before leaping away in order to take care of the rest of the Strawmen that’s harassing this crowd.

“Where’s Leander?” he asks her over his SHED band now that he’s forced to hop around the crowd to put down the Strawmen one-by-one as they all now try to run away from him like he's the kitchen light that made these roaches start scattering back to their crevices—something he notices is starkly different from the last batch of scum he had the unfortunate task of dispatching.

"He was supposed to be picking us up," Laharin communicates back.

"I'll be right back."

"Where are you going?" she asks, confused as to where he can be going at a time like this.

"In the meantime, go back into the school and call a cab. I'll meet you at home."

"Baby, wait!"

The soft thud the band makes to indicate that a call has ended lets Laharin know that whatever it is that Nerosion had to prematurely cut their line of communication off for was probably worth it—like finding out what happened to Leander. With most of the crowd now containing more officers of the law than protesters, Laharin can now make her way toward them to ask if one of them can hopefully give her a ride back to her home. That is, once they're finished cuffing and subduing the unconscious creeps that attacked her and everyone else here, as she absolutely refuses to go back into that school—not now and not ever. In fact, it is at this moment that Laharin decides that neither her nor her daughter would be visiting the Del Cora Private Art School for Girls ever again.

Chapter Twenty-Two

SEARCH AND REFUGE

April 17th. 8:23 P.M. (CDT)

ANYONE WHO IS LOOKING to purchase tickets to enter the famed Shedd Aquarium through any method besides that of a reservation made in advance, is going to have a very difficult time getting in, unless of course you're a well-known theoretical physicist who just happens to be doing some last minute research for his public presentation happening in less than an hour. In fact, if your name just happens to be Dr. Arthur Bouya, then you won't even need a ticket at all—and neither will your accompanied guest.

It is no wonder why Joelle ponders in depth how Calvin was able to slip into this place without trouble. Even as a psychic, he can't see his own future, so just how, she wonders, was he able to slip by the people whose futures he also cannot see? Her focus on this enigma is only broken by the sight of witnessing what can be considered her first aquatic animal: the Bluespine Unicorn Fish, or as Arthur calls it—Naso unicornis.

"Have you ever owned a fish, Joelle?" Arthur asks his guest, as she slowly walks up to the tank that houses the dozen or so species.

"No. I haven't," she replies.

"They make fantastic first pets. Easy to maintain and take care of, and a joy to feed. They can really help restore a sense of calm to your life—really good for someone who appreciates a tranquil environment. Of all the animals I've come across, I find fish are the most enjoyable to watch in their natural habitat. Even though they're always moving, they don't really reveal much, but in that you can learn a lot; they keep life simple and display an ability to appreciate and accept what is. Despite always in motion, they're rarely fussing. Rarely complaining," he poetically shares with her.

"I see. Life on this planet certainly is amazing," she all but mutters to herself, slowly and surely coming to appreciate the abundant variety of life forms here.

"Huh? You said something? Speak up now," Arthur says very loudly out of nowhere, unable to hear her mumbling.

"Oh, nothing. I, uh, said I always wanted a fish."

"Oh. Well anyway, we should continue our search for Sonder. It's best we get a move on."

Even though they now make haste towards the area where Sonder's blip shows up on the SHED frames, Joelle can't help but to be engrossed by the hundreds of different type of fish she passes by in this area alone. That is because nothing like this exists on her home world. The fact that she is witnessing autonomic organisms that move independent of anyone's instruction in their own habitat, is more surprising to her than the fact that witnessing these creatures first hand didn't trigger a minor epileptic episode.

"It says he's at the Aquatic Presentation," Arthur says when he zooms in on Calvin's blip.

"What's that?" Joelle asks, never remotely hearing of such a thing.

"I'm not exactly sure, but it's more than likely the area where you can see different types of animals perform. Namely, dolphins, whales and seals."

"Perform? Like in a show?"

"Exactly like a show. The animals are trained by specialists to perform all kinds of cool tricks and moves that you will never see them do in the wild. People from all over the country come just to see these amazing performances."

"The animals ... do they want to perform these tricks?" she asks, a question that throws Arthur off for a second.

"I'm sorry?"

"The animals that perform, do they like it?" she repeats more clearly.

"The animals? Well, it is generally believed that the animals are taken very good care of and trained to where performing becomes something they enjoy very much," he shares.

"Believed? So, it's not really known for sure."

"Well, we can't exactly ask them how they feel about it."

"No kidding," Joelle says, trying to hide the fact that she didn't really know that. "Why don't the trainers just ask the people how they feel about it then. Since they're the ones who the animals are performing for?"

"Heh. You know, I would love to live in a society where people would be completely honest about such a thing. Unfortunately, we live in a time where as long as something is entertaining us, we'll continue to support it, even if the methods to get that entertainment aren't the most ethical. Many people feel that as long as they aren't the ones who instigated the creation of the entertainment, then it's okay if they enjoy it from the sidelines, y'know?"

Arthur waits for Joelle to say something else, hopefully to reaffirm that this issue isn't as deep as it probably needs to be. When none arrives, he's thankful that the SHED frames he again wears over his glasses update him with a notification on Calvin's whereabouts.

"These glasses are saying that our friend is on the move. Let's hurry," Arthur tells Joelle.

"Take me to this area. I want to see it for myself," she suddenly demands.

"But Sonder is on the move. It says he's now headed for the 5-Sense Coastal Experience."

"I don't care. I want to see the animals in the Aquatic Experience first," she firmly states.

"Are you sure?" he asks before reading the next part of the update out loud. "Listen to this! *Prepare yourself for a high-octane, aquatic explo-*

sion on your five senses unlike any you've ever had, as you traverse through Earth's oceanic history over its 4.5-billion-year lifespan. Even I got to admit that sounds amazing."

"If he's in there then he's not going anywhere anytime soon. We don't have anything to worry about," she assures Arthur.

"I suppose you are right. Okay, if you insist," he relents.

Against his better wishes, Arthur escorts Joelle to the area where some of the most spectacular animal activity in the world is taking place.

They reach the line, luckily right before the last few seats fill up. Arthur is able to purchase a ticket for him and Joelle at the counter, and they make their way to their seats, which aren't the best in the stadium.

Joelle and Arthur make their way to their assigned seats only to enter into a show that's already in progress. The ooh's and ahh's they heard from the crowd, before they had even entered the stadium, helped Arthur feel a bit better about his choice about choosing to attend this show over going after Sonder.

"My, I can't remember the last time I've been to a sea show!" Arthur gleefully reveals. "Look, there's the dolphins, oh, and I think I see a few seals over there. This oughta be exciting, I'm really glad you talked me into this!" he shares, now giddier in his demeanor.

Joelle finally sits in her assigned seat, half expecting a seat belt to wrap around her once she does. After all, attending a show with the reputation that Arthur speaks of, who knows what kind of crazy things one may experience during the performance. This may be the reason why Joelle chooses to focus more on the sea of people in the audience, than the sea animals in the large pool at this time. Or, maybe it's because she's never seen such a large amount of people in one area before. Her observation of them reminds her of the very hair they all contain on top of their heads—at first glance it's just a pleasant looking, personalized lop of styled material, but also, she can count every single individual strand of that lop if she so wished, as could anybody. Unlike hair however, at least as far as she can tell, each person in the audience fidgeted and moved slightly different from the next person. Again, this is something she only noticed when she chose to inspect each person individually and not everybody together as a whole as if they were a wig.

After her captivation with this otherwise uninteresting crowd ceases, Joelle begins focusing on the rich, blue-colored water that fills the pool in front of them. Thanks to a few of her prior mental episodes, Joelle has come to understand what water and all of its properties are to a great degree. Be that as it may, she can't seem to quite grasp why such an environment that houses such large animals is this small and contained. The size of the pool seems unfitting to support the alleged sea creatures that are expected to dwell beneath its surface —at least if the scaled models of these creatures she saw in the previous halls are anything to go by. Nevertheless, Joelle looks on with the same anticipation as anyone would to see the animals at the pinnacle of all of their enchanted glory. Whether they're flying high over a few beams, or leaping successfully though a series of fire rings, even if they're just on the side eating a trout, she's desperate to see at least one, there's no doubt.

And that's when it happens. Suddenly, without notice, at least as far as Joelle is concerned, considering that she nor Arthur was around when the aquatic hosts told the crowd to get ready for the animals' next trick, two bottlenose dolphins leap fifteen feet into the air while performing two spectacular frontal flips in perfect sync. Though they've probably already seen it a few times by now, the crowd continues to be taken back in awe by the relatively simple trick, and their bedazzlement causes them to erupt in a euphonious ballad of whistles, cheers and applause.

Besides the few uninterested children displaced throughout the crowd, whose attention span has long since disallowed them from finding these now mundane marine performances enthralling any longer, Joelle, who's interest in the act is so overwhelming, finds herself currently unable to even voice her thoughts on what just unfolded in front of her. It is this intriguing silence that diverts Arthur's attention away from the show in front of him, as he is overcome with glee, thinking that Joelle is so stunned by everything she just saw that she can't even speak.

"Did you see that? What did I tell you?" he enthusiastically, yet rhetorically, asks her. However, she only responds with a sorrowful glance, her expression resembling not someone who's bewildered, but someone immensely turned off. "Oh, oh here we go. Here. We. Go. Feast your eyes on this next jump, Joelle! Ho, ho!"

Arthur's words prompt Joelle to look back at the large pool as she awaits to see what has him excited in a way she didn't even think he was capable of exhibiting.

Of the four trainers that were in the pool, only three are now visible, and they now all begin to separate from each other and make their way to the far ends of the pool. Joelle watches their actions intently, considering she's probably the only one in the crowd who has absolutely no idea of what's going to happen next.

Maybe it's because she's most likely more focused on what's happening in this show than anyone else, or maybe it's because she's from another planet, but the site of seeing the trainer who was missing now beginning to rise from beneath the surface, doesn't really shock her all that much. It isn't until she sees the large killer whale emerge from beneath the trainer's feet a split-second later, pushing the woman and itself twenty-plus feet into the air, that Joelle is astounded. The huge whale collapses back into the pool and creates a giant splash that washes over most of the crowd. After witnessing such a performance, Joelle receives her first set of goosebumps. Luckily for her, who's space-warping ability would've definitely been exposed by the gigantic splash slowing down in front of her, and unluckily for everyone else, especially someone as enthusiastic about this whole experience as Arthur, almost no one gets wet. She figures this is thanks to the state-of-the-art, protective screens that activate and completely cover the crowd from getting hit with water anytime a large splash occurs.

Joelle turns her head away as quickly as she can once the sea creature disappears again beneath the surface, and once completely gone, she gets up in and immediately heads for the exit. Puzzled, Arthur calls out to her and looks at the people nearby who also saw her leave in jiff, trying to see if they know something he doesn't. Realizing something went wrong during all this wonderful activity, Arthur gets up as fast as he can and heads for the exit to attend to his friend.

After pacing for several minutes through the several corridors that lead into several different areas of the aquarium, Arthur is hoping that because his sight hasn't yielded any sign of his friend yet, then hopefully his failing ears would—after all, with the museum as exceptionally quiet as it is, such a thing might not be all that unachievable. He would much rather hear the sounds of Joelle sobbing, so he can find her and then coax her back to her normal mood, then for her to be perfectly alright but yet still hidden away from him.

Thankfully, with age comes maturity of the mind, but regrettably, with age also comes degradation of the body. At this point, Arthur is starting to wish he can trade all of his wisdom if it meant that his legs wouldn't hurt as much as they are at the moment, considering he's been effectively jogging through these halls searching for Joelle for a good ten minutes now. There isn't any amount of science that's going to serve him better in his search for her, so Arthur decides that at this point all that is left for him to do is go get Sonder. This way, at least he'll be able to half his lost accomplices from two back down to one again.

Unable to enjoy the luxury of a smooth elevator ride thanks to the gravity of his situation, Arthur has to take a moment to catch his breath once he finishes climbing the last step of the two-flight staircase he had no choice other than to ascend. *No worries,* he thinks to himself as he rests on a nearby bench directly outside of the 5-Sense Coastal Experience that the frames tell him Sonder is still inside of.

"Sonder is safely occupied with his Coastal Experience, and as for Joelle, well if that traffic accident earlier is anything to go by, she's great at taking care of herself. Yeah, she's a big girl. Hell, if anything, I'm slowing her down. She ran across a highway and survived—no wonder she ran from me," he says to himself out loud as he continues to pant and catch his breath, the two people walking by most likely writing him off as some looney crackpot. Arthur finds solace in knowing that for the moment, these two temporary disconnected yet somehow apparently, always-intricately connected individuals—Joelle and Sonder, are safe.

"This Coastal Experience is so goddamn awesome! Minutia is missing everythingggggg!" Calvin exclaims as he continues to enjoy having his senses bombarded by taking a virtual trip through the Earth's oceans while it dynamically changes throughout the planet's lifespan.

Of all the virtual creatures Calvin so far has swam with, the one he currently sees lurking in the backdrop behind the large school of fish being devoured by an entourage of swordfish, is unlike any he's seen since the Experience has started. Be that as it may, he chooses to ignore it and dismisses it as some boring sea creature that he's probably already seen, so he can continue to watch the hundreds of bluefish get devoured by their speedy predators. But every time his peripheral vision catches a glimpse of the obscure creature, he notices something new about it. The first thing was that it didn't look like any animal he's seen before, but now he notices that the creature almost appears as if it's walking through the water as opposed to swimming through it like all of the others are. Calvin decides to turn this into a little game and see just how many off-things can he notice about the creature—this creature that also happens to be moving closer and closer to him.

The next he notices is the almost anthropomorphic appearance of the unidentified ocean-dweller—two arms, two legs, he counts. Though it walks as if it were a dog, he can at least tell by the way its body is shaped that it could get up and start walking on two legs if it so wished. In fact, he believes that maybe this is the creature's natural form of traveling because of how remarkable it resembles the anatomy of a person. The third thing he notices about the creature is its stealth capabilities. From this distance he can clearly tell the creature is a predator, yet as it continues to close in on the unsuspecting fish, not a single one of them seem to have acknowledged his presence.

Calvin continues to tally up the different tidbits he's picked up on the unfamiliar beast, adding a new one with each step closer it gets. His playful interest has now turned into a genuine adoration; this creature, whatever it is, is now his favorite of all the others he's seen as of yet.

"Errrgghhhh-aaahhhh!" Arthur moans loudly as he executes a much-needed stretch predicated by his body's tendency to now want to get moving again. He rises and starts to make his way towards the 5-Sense Coastal Experience hall. Though most of the inside of the aquarium sits under a low-lighting setting akin to most museums, it is here that Arthur realizes this place is much darker than any other area he has visited up until now. He must be careful walking up these last set of stairs that'll bring him inside the large room where all the action is taking place, he thinks to himself. Because of this, he proceeds carefully, however, thinking about the fact that he's about to finally meet Sonder brings with it a wind of new energy that powers Arthur's legs in a way he hasn't felt in quite a while. So, he abandons his careful gait and instead opts for a rapid ascension up the stairs. His unabated stride is only halted when his knee bumps into the knee of someone who decided that a pitch-dark staircase that people often use to travel about, was the perfect place to sit down at.

"Ahh!" Arthur yelps out as he stumbles on top of the unknown body. Because his core strength is only a fraction of what it used to be, he fails at trying to prevent himself from flopping directly on top of this invisible person. Luckily, before the fall completely cripples him and renders the rest of his day over, the quick arms of the darkened individual cushion him, they who catch what they can of him, successfully breaking most of his fall and preventing Arthur from breaking or even spraining one of his bones.

"I got you!" the voice of the dark body says to him, one that he immediately recognizes.

"Joelle?" Arthur exclaims once he's seated on the step next to her, using the little bit of light leaking into this area to make out the unique hairstyle and clothing that he's come to recognize her by. "Where did you go? I was looking all over for you!"

"I wanted to get out of here, so I came to get Calvin. But the show is still going on so I figured I'll just wait here until it's over."

"Calvin? Who's Calvin?"

"Oh, right," she says, forgetting she started a lie she no longer has an interest in continuing. "Calvin is Sonder. Sonder is his last name, his first name is Calvin. And my name isn't Joelle, it's Minutia."

"What? Minutia?" Arthur does his best to try to quickly process all this new information as fast as he can.

"But I like Joelle, so please keep calling me that!" she begs of him.

"I ... Okay. W-Why did you leave the show, Joelle?" He obliges her as he decides to focus on matters more important than names right now.

"Those animals in that tank," she begins. Arthur can immediately recognize the hurt in her voice and realize she's in fact been crying the whole time. "They were hurting—bad."

"What do you mean *hurting?*" Arthur asks as he notices something he's never seen on her face before: two, thin purple lines that stretch from just under her right eye before disappearing beneath her jawline, start to faintly glow.

"They didn't want to be there, at all. Not a single one of them, especially the large one. She was in the most pain. But they had no choice, none of them didn't have any choice. It was horrible."

"Joelle ... your face ..." Arthur asks, baffled by what he's seeing.

"I know—I hate crying in front of people," she admits as she wipes her tears, oblivious to the fact that she has two purple lines currently glowing on her face. Arthur decides now is not the best time to press on about the comparatively minor, yet intriguing sighting.

"How could you possibly know that?"

"I felt it. The large one, the orca. She ... she's dying. She's dying, Arthur. How can people possibly applaud such horrible mistreatment? Some of those animals were violently snatched away from their families and forced to live in those tiny environments."

"I don't understand. Did you hear them crying or something?"

"No. I felt their pain. It leaks out of them like blood does from an open wound. I couldn't take it anymore. I can't believe you people are like this ... we have to rescue them, Arthur. We have to set them free. Please," she says as she begins to choke up again.

"Joelle, I—"

CRASSSSSHHHHHHHHH!! A loud scream is followed by a man crashing through the front of the doors that house the 5-Sense Coastal Experience.

"What the heck was that?" Arthur shrieks as he jumps from the loud noise.

Suddenly, all of the lights in the area immediately turn on, and Arthur and Joelle turn around to see the man who flew through the doors land on the same staircase they're on and roll all the way down pass them to the level below, just missing them on his way down.

The man's tumble is followed by the eruption of a crowd of people escaping through a doorway much too narrow to allow the two-hundred or so of them to exit at the same time. Because of this, amongst the fourteen or so that are able to squeeze through at a time, half of them collapse due to the rest of the crowd pushing them from behind. At least that's what Arthur hopes is what's pushing them, and not whatever it was that sent that poor man flying down the stairs.

Unfortunately, Arthur is only half-correct. The combined force of the frantic crowd trying to exit out of the area as quickly as possible, coupled with the mysterious force that propelled that man through the air, has now caused more people to fall and tumble on top of another more than they would have, had their exit strategy not been harrowed by that unknown power.

A pile of screaming bodies now lay wedged in the doorway, preventing even less people from getting out and causing even more of them to become frantic.

"Calvin's in there! Arthur, we have to get through them!" Joelle says to Arthur after shaking off her dreary mood.

"How?" he all but shouts at her, overwhelmed by the mayhem that's currently unfolding before him.

Joelle ponders this question intently as she does her best to come up with some sort of plan.

"Give me the frames!" she demands. Arthur hands them to her without hesitation, now intrigued by whatever plan this woman is coming up with. "Arthur, head back to the pool under the Aquatic Experience. Earlier, I saw an emergency exit that can get us out of here quickly. I'll be there in a few minutes. Go!"

Arthur nods understandingly and Joelle puts the SHED frames on before she proceeds. She waits until the glasses pinpoint Calvin's location before climbing over the pile of squirming bodies and entering the hall.

Unlike in the hallway, the lights inside the Coastal Experience are still dimly lit, making it hard for her to spot Calvin amongst the chaotic screaming and fleeing bodies running around. Thankfully, all she has to do is navigate herself in the dark towards his position by focusing on his blip on the radar. *This must be what playing those video games Calvin was talking about must be like,* she thinks to herself.

As she understands it, her powers seem to work where for some reason, if something non-biological approaches her, it'll always dramatically slow down before reaching her. However, conversely, if she approaches something non-biological, she won't slow down as a result. That's as far as she's gotten to understanding how this 'Slow' ability of hers works, more or less. With this is mind, Joelle understands that anytime someone is moving around her, whether they are running or being erratic, as long as they are moving above a certain speed, which she considers a 'threat' speed, then her Slow ability will automatically activate—which inherently places that person at immediate risk. Because of this, it is more important that at this moment it is *she* who must be careful not to rush, even if her situation requires her to do so. As long as she can stay out of the way of these frenzied individuals, then everyone would be okay. The last thing she wants to see is someone's neck snap by their own turtleneck just from brushing past her.

With this is mind, Joelle proceeds towards Calvin's position very cautiously, making certain to do her best to avoid any and all people still trying to run away from whatever it is that made them freak out like this in the first place. The low lighting in the room not only makes it hard for her to see anyone, but also hard for anyone to see her. This is why after progressing a few meters, she hears a man start to frantically shout like he's being strangled, right after the fabric of what she can only imagine is his sleeve, tears off just from running too close to her. His panicked screams of *GET OFF ME, GET OFF ME* from thinking he's been grabbed by whatever he was running from, is enough to make Joelle's nerves and stress levels immediately spike.

"Goddamn it!" she cries out as she struggles to move away so the man can be freed. Her second swear is screamed under a clenched jaw as she tries her best to hold it together while she continues to tiptoe her way to Calvin.

"Calvin! Calvin!" she screams out, no longer caring if whatever it is she's trying not to alert notices her or not. "Calvin, it's Jo—Minutia, it's Minutia! Can you hear me!?"

"Minutia?" she hears the voice say, returning her call. And it's none other than the pain-in-the-ass she's missed all too much. "Minutia, is that you?"

"Yes, Calvin it's me!" she responds to the darkness. "Where are you?"

"Minutia, help me!" the voice calls back.

"Calvin? I'm coming!!"

Suddenly, Joelle throws caution to the wind and makes a dash for Calvin's position. Amazingly, not one person is subjugated by the space she naturally distorts around her when she pulls off this daring move. According to the blip on her frames, Calvin is located just around the bend of a narrow hallway—literally seconds from her grasp. Joelle turns the corner, and what she sees is unlike anything she's expected—that's because what she sees, is nothing.

"Calvin?" she calls out once more.

"Down here!" a voice whispers from beneath the floor she stands on. It isn't until Joelle takes off the frames that she can make out the familiar hair pattern she's grown to acknowledge Calvin by through the tiny holes on the grate beneath her feet.

"Calvin, why are you under the floor?" she says to him as she continues to communicate with him through the grate.

"I thought this was the bathroom. Nah, I'm just playing—it's actually because of that thing behind you," he says, pointing towards the area Joelle just came from. She turns and looks back to hopefully see what it is that has everyone in a panic.

"I don't see anything," she admits.

"Well, you better get down here before anything sees you. Hurry!" Calvin says as he unlocks the hatch on the grate and slides the floor opening, revealing a small set of stairs that Joelle bypasses by blatantly leaping past them. Though she doesn't land directly on top of Calvin, it's close enough to stagger him.

"Ouch!" he cries out.

"Oh, quiet, I didn't even touch you," she spats upon landing. Once her feet are firmly planted and her mind oriented, she suddenly becomes overwrought with concern realizing she's been away from her only friend for hours now. "Calvin, are you alright? I've been so worried. Have you been damaged?" she asks as she begins to perform what can only be explained as some sort of weird body diagnostics that she performs with her hands, making Calvin extremely uncomfortable after the first two touches.

"Damaged? I'm not a rob—Hey, what are you doing? Get the hell off of me, you creep!" he cries out.

GLLLLRRRUUGGGG-HHHMMMMM. Joelle finally hears the sound of the strange entity lurking in the darkness and tries to process what the hell can make that kind of noise.

"What the hell was *that?*" she asks, growing more and more comfortable with the American English lexicon.

"That my dear, was the boss of this stage. We have to defeat it to complete the level," he tells her.

"This isn't a video game, Calvin."

"You're going to wish it was if that thing finds us—because we have no more continues and my last save point was in that pizza shop. Damn it, it knows where we are—see where all your screaming got us? This was supposed to be a stealth mission. Alright, we have to move. Follow me."

"Move, how? We can't see a damn thing," she says realizing the area under the floor is even darker than the floor she just descended from.

"Frames, please," he says to her.

Joelle hands Calvin the SHED frames and once he has them in his hand, he whistles out the tune that always plays in the video game *Super Metroid* whenever the main character retrieves an item.

"Why do you always do that? You did it in the car when we were being chased also."

"Well, my SHED band would do it on its own, but I have it on vibrate right now," he replies.

"Whatever, let's just go."

At that moment, Calvin, who has already placed the frames back on his face, activates the *Light* function on the glasses, a feature Joelle would've used if she knew it existed.

"This light will aid us in our journey through these narrow corridors," he tells her.

"Wouldn't that thing out there see the light leaking out the floor?"

"No, the light remains invisible until it hits the wall. You didn't know that? Jeez, technology on your planet must suck."

"Calvin," Joelle's voice suddenly becomes increasingly subdued. "Why did you run away from me like that on the freeway?"

"I went to get something to eat. Then I came back to bring you some, and you were gone," he dismissively explains. Joelle, not satisfied with his answer, decides she isn't ready to just let this one slide.

"You don't have to lie to me. I told you that."

"What do I need to lie for!?" he says frustratingly.

"Because you're getting very upset over a simple question."

"What are you, a psychologist now? Besides, that wasn't a question, it was an assertion—you called me a liar. Of course I'm going to get mad when someone calls me something I'm not. Wouldn't you? I came back and there was some sort of car accident. I figured you were okay, and that you would eventually catch up to me."

"How was I going to find you?"

"How did you find me now? With the SHED frames, duhh."

"But I didn't get those until I found them inside of some random pizza shop while looking for you."

"Man, whatever. I see you haven't forgot how to stop being annoying. Yeah, just like a psychologist—annoying, it makes sense now. Freaking aliens, man. Think they know everything." The last part he mutters to himself, and although he does, Joelle happens to still pick up on it.

"To answer your question, no, I'm not a psychologist. But, I am beginning to understand more about you and your people. Why you lie and such. Now, I think I know why."

"Really. Okay, sooo why do we lie, Minutia?" he asks sardonically.

"You lie to protect me. Because you telling me the truth, that you really didn't bring me any food because you know I don't need to eat, would've made you feel a lot worse, and because you were too hungry and tired to come back anyway, you figured I'll be fine. But your conscience got the best of you. I mean, even though you haven't really seen me take a bite of *anything* since we met, you weren't a hundred percent sure that I didn't need to eat, and that I wouldn't just randomly collapse somewhere by myself, all alone. So, you peeked into the future and saw that if you left your frames inside of that pizza shop, an altercation would've ensued over them and they would eventually find their way back to you."

Calvin's silence is all the evidence Joelle needs to confirm her presumptions.

"I don't get it—for some reason, the people on this planet would rather lie to make someone feel good, than be honest with them to make them feel better," she acknowledges.

"Well," Calvin says after a long pause. "If we pass this level, maybe we can finally visit The Man in The Dirty Robes in the next one. I think he might be able to help you figure out why you keep having those seizures," Calvin shares after being stumped by her sudden genius.

"Really? What makes you say that?"

"Well, maybe you're that baby in space that I kept seeing."

"What? There was a baby in space? Where, in your visions?" she suddenly says loudly.

"SHHHHHHHH!"

"Oh!" she exclaims, now in a whisper.

"Yeah, the Star-Child," he says in a rather mild tone.

"How come you never told me?"

"Oh, I didn't? I thought I did. My bad. Yeah, there was some baby floating out there in space right next to the blown-up space station and The Man in The Dirty Robes just comes and takes it. Crazy thing is—I think it was alive."

"What the hell is it with you people and just taking other people that don't belong to you?" she rhetorically asks Calvin, to which Calvin only responds with a smile. "Alright, come on, we have to hurry—there's someone outside waiting for us."

"There is? Who?" Calvin asks about the unexpected information he just heard.

"Someone I want you to meet. He's a doctor," she tells him.

"Great. Another psychologist. That explains it."

"No, not a psychologist—a theoretical physicist. Maybe you can explain to me what that means."

"Okay. Follow me."

Chapter Twenty-Three

JOELLE VS THE BOSS

April 17th. 10:01 P.M. (EDT)

THE POLICE CRUISER that was kind enough to escort Laharin and Ori back to their home finally pulls up to the curb of their building, after a relatively comfortable cruise through downtown Monachopsis.

"You sure you don't want me to come upstairs? Make sure there isn't some strange woman hiding in your closet or anything?" Officer Mavis asks as he puts the car in park, a move that's usually performed by a driver who plans on sitting and chatting for a while before his passenger takes off.

"No, thank you, Officer Mavis. Our doorman will be more than happy to check up on us if I have any concerns."

"No problem, then."

"My daddy says the OPD lunch breaks are longer than their shifts. Is this a lunch break for you?" Ori pleasantly asks the accommodating police officer.

"You're very charming, aren't you? You can tell your dad, thanks to us, he can walk freely down these streets without worrying about getting robbed."

"My daddy says thanks to Nerosion, cops can walk freely down the street without worrying about doing their job."

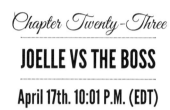

"She's a shrewd little one, isn't she?" he says surprisingly not to Laharin, but directly to Ori herself.

"That'll be all, Ori. Thank you again for the lift, Officer Mavis."

Officer Mavis tips his hat, and the genuine smile that he was robbed of thanks to a little of Ori's harsh criticisms, has been substituted by a permanent scowl he's sure to have developed for her, her father, and especially Nerosion. Any setbacks her father faces from the OPD from henceforth can now be attributed to this moment.

"Your father better be upstairs when we get there. Come on."

Laharin and Ori head into their building and Laharin is surprised to see that her favorite doorman isn't presently behind the counter—instead a new guy has taken his shift.

"Good evening, ma'am."

"Well, good evening, sir. Where's Reginald? Is he off today?"

"I'm not sure who Reginald is. I'm guessing that must be the guy I'm filling in for."

"Yes, he's usually here at this time. Okay, well it was nice meeting you."

"It was nice meeting you, too. Enjoy the rest of your night ma'am."

While Laharin exchanges pleasantries with the new lobby attendant, Ori has already sprinted to the elevator to signal it. Because it happened to already be at the ground level when she arrived, she is now able to hold the door open while her mom takes her time.

After a short ride and quick walk through the hallway, Laharin enters her apartment, where the programmed television automatically turns on upon entry. It's a default setting and one she keeps forgetting to change, especially now considering the programming that's currently being shown on it.

"Madly Dote! is on! Mommy, can I watch it?"

"It looks like we beat your father home. Ori, didn't I tell I wanted you to stop watching that silly mess? That show ain't for no five-year-old."

"But I'll be six in seven months!"

"That show is for big kids, Ori—teenagers. And you'll barely be a pre-teenager in *seven years.*"

"Cartoons are for children Mommy, you know that."

"Well, you ain't gotta worry about no homework, considering I'm pulling you out of that crappy school. So yeah, go ahead. You can watch it until your father gets here. After that, we're all having a family meeting," Laharin reveals.

"Ugh, but we just had a family meeting," Ori laments aloud.

"Well, we having another."

"I hate family meetings."

"You can hate watching that blank screen too if you like."

"Okay, I'll be quiet."

"I know."

9:59 P.M. (CDT)

At this point, it is now Joelle who's becoming quite exasperated with how long her and Calvin have been walking under these floorboards since they've entered them. Unable to see much further than only but the few feet Calvin shines his light on, Joelle is forced to violate her commitment to trust that Calvin is leading them to safety, by asking him just how much longer do they have before they can reemerge safely.

"The blip says just a few more feet," he tells her, sensing how fed up she's starting to become over this whole ordeal.

"Right," she replies dryly.

"Well, it was you who said you wanted to meet up with some doctor, right? That's another side mission that has nothing to do with the main quest."

"His name is Arthur, and it has everything to do with it. He's the one who can probably tell us what's going on right now."

"We're still going to meet The Man in The Dirty Robes, right?"

"Yes, for the hundredth time," she tells him.

"Okay, just making sure. I suppose it won't kill me to rack up some experience points in the meantime then."

"Look, there's an exit, let's get out here!"

"Let's see. Nope, can't."

"What, why not?"

"Well, it appears that if we take *that* particular exit, my frames get crushed and your fancy little sweater is ripped to shreds. More than likely, the boss of this stage finds us. Just a little farther and we'll be good."

A little turns into a lot, at least in Joelle's eyes, and it isn't until she fully believes that Calvin has no idea where he's going, that he finally sees the unique, yet same exact type of sewer-style steps that they've passed over twenty times already, that he finally considers exiting.

"Voila! Here it is, our ticket to freedom," he announces.

"It's about time!"

"Says the girl who can stop time."

"I wish I could stop your mouth. Move."

Joelle brushes by Calvin to be the first to climb out of the grate and re-enter the realm of the living. When she emerges, she looks around and notices something very familiar about the area.

"Calvin, this is the same place we were when I first got here. We been walking around in circles this whole time!"

"Except now the lights are on, and everyone is gone ..." Calvin says as he climbs out of the grate and looks around the room to only realize there's still a few scattered bodies lying about. "... mostly."

"What *did* all this?"

"The Boss. I haven't really given him a name yet. But I'm telling you, that thing can move. I hope your doctor friend found a good hiding spot."

"Calvin ... is this Boss by any chance, one of those creatures that's been attacking the base camps?" she asks him, now suddenly concerned.

"Attacking the who now?

"Those alien-wolves that's been all over the news."

"I don't watch T.V .... well, not for entertainment purposes anyway. That's what my mom calls the news—entertainment. She says it's her favorite reality show because every day there's always a new episode on."

"Great. If that's indeed what has this place turned upside-down, then we need to hurry back to Arthur. He's in extreme danger."

"Right. Where's the RV?"

"The what?"

"The rendezvous point."

"I told him to wait by the area under the Aquatic Experience."

"Okay. Well, you gotta lead the way. I haven't obtained the map for that level yet."

The two comrades begin running towards the place where Joelle told Arthur to meet her in. Thankfully, the pile of bodies that obstructed the entrance earlier have now diminished to just a few unconscious individuals lopped on top of one another. Joelle is slightly appalled at the fact that she's even thankful for such a thing, but considering the situation and what could've been, she has to thank her lucky stars.

The entire museum is now fully illuminated, with little to no thanks to the flashing red lights that has signaled that an emergency alarm has gone off some time ago. It is at this moment that Calvin activates the music on his band to play some background music that he feels is appropriate for their current crisis.

"Would you turn that off? That thing is going to find us thanks to your silliness."

"No, I already looked—both my glasses and your clothes are fine. But we might have a different problem."

"What is it?"

"It's hard to tell—but I can see the building rumbling."

"Rumbling? What causes it?"

"I can't really tell, it's too blurry."

"Is it an explosion?"

"No ... I don't think it's quite that."

"Well, do we get out of here alive at least?"

"You know I can't see that."

"Well do your glasses make it out alive?"

"Yessnooo. Yes. No. No, yes. Yes ... I don't know," Calvin scats.

"Ugh, just stay alert," she finally tells him, after being annoyed by his flip-flopping.

"I knew I should've stacked up on potions," he mutters to himself.

Joelle and Calvin rush down the final flight of stairs that leads them to the hallway under the Aquatic Experience show. This same hallway where one can watch the animals dwell and frolic in their normal environments when not doing stunts for a paying audience.

"Joelle!!" Arthur shouts when he sees his missed friend come dashing into the underground area where he's been standing in for a while.

"Joelle?" Calvin says, confused as to who Arthur is addressing.

"Arthur! You're okay!" she expresses as she rushes to him and hugs him tightly, delivering her first heartfelt hug as an Earthling to another Earthling. Even Arthur can somehow pick up on the sui generis nature of the embrace, but that can be just be due to the fact that no one has really hugged him this tightly in a very long time.

"Is everything okay?" he asks her after they dislodge from one another.

"No, it's not actually. I think one of those creatures from the meteor sites are on the loose. We have to get out of here," she tells him, suddenly rushing her words.

All the while Arthur and Joelle has been embracing each other, Calvin has been staring at the large glass that separates them from the numerous sea animals that from time to time pass by—and it isn't their friendly gestures that has him so fixated on the glass.

"Uh guys, we have a problem ..." he murmurs almost inaudibly.

"What is it?" Joelle immediately turns and ask.

"I'm not sure—but I think this glass is going to break in little while," he says as he walks up to the glass and places his hand on it. "We need to get out of here, ASAP."

"You must be Calvin. I'm Arthur Bouya. Your sister here and I have been searching all over for you for quite some time," Arthur says as he walks over to Calvin with his hand out.

"My *what!?* Calvin practically yells.

"Calvin, what's wrong? The glass looks perfectly fine," Joelle asks in response to the statement he shared with them before almost losing his mind over what Arthur just shared with him.

"Remember that rumble I was talking about? I think it's caused by the Boss."

"What is he talking about?" Arthur asks, unable to follow their non-elucidating dialogue.

"I thought the creature was gone," Joelle shares.

"I never said it was g—oh shit."

Before Calvin can finish sassing Joelle as usual, he sees the creature he's dubbed as this level's boss emerging from the other end of the hallway. His ghostly gaze causes Arthur and Joelle to turn around.

"Oh my. It's one of the UNSELF's creatures. I've never seen one up close," Arthur says, beguiled by the unfamiliar specimen. "They're...."

"Ugly af," Calvin interjects in an attempt to fill in the doctor's blanks.

"Af?" Joelle questions, never before hearing such a term.

"...beautiful," Arthur concludes.

The clear sight of this out-of-world looking specimen is even more disturbing to Calvin, more intriguing to Arthur and far more familiar to Joelle, in person. Even as it slowly creeps towards them, the closer it gets, the more about it Joelle seems to recognize.

"Minutia, we have to get out of here," Calvin seriously warns her.

"I thought we had to defeat this boss to complete the level," she reminds him.

"Defeat it with what? Your powers won't work on it."

"Powers? What is he talking about, Joelle?" Arthur says, his curiosity again suddenly piqued.

"Why does he keep calling you Joelle?"

"Because that's my name," she tells Calvin.

"No, your name is Killuminatti or something like that," he retorts.

"Your name is what?" Arthur blurts out, trying his best to makes sense of what Calvin just called Joelle.

"Calvin, how sure are you about the tank?" she asks, redirecting the subject to the more important matter at hand.

"Uh, pretty freaking sure. That thing is going to go, and if we're not out of here when it does, we're finished."

"Finished? How?" Arthur asks, looking for clarity.

"I'm not going to let that happen," Joelle confidently tells him.

"The hell you talking about, lady? Let it happen? I've already seen it."

"What is he talking about, Joelle?" Arthur asks, the scientist in him needing answers to all the questions he now has.

"I may not be able to see the future, but I don't have to let it control me," she affirms.

"Now this," Calvin quips while rolling his eyes. "The future doesn't care about your feelings, lady. Women—am I right, doc?" Calvin scoffs before nudging Arthur playfully.

Joelle lifts her hand and attempts to sense anything she can about the creature, the same way she did with the animals during the show. Strangely enough, nothing seems to be registering.

"Uh, what are you doing?" Calvin confused, asks her.

"Be quiet, I need to focus."

"Did you learn something new while I was gone? Cuz unless you're going to shoot fire out of your hand or something right now, you look kinda dumb doing that ... and I think you're making that thing even madder," he explains to her. "I mean even *more upset.* Not madder. Sorry."

After appearing not to reach her, he turns to Arthur. "Dr. Bouya, we really have to get out of here."

"What is she doing?" Arthur asks while carefully watching Joelle.

"I was going to ask you the same thing. But we should go."

"And leave her—after all she went through to find you? Are you crazy?"

"Do I look like the crazy one here? Minutia is going to be fine, trust me, it's you who won't be if you don't start moving."

"I'm not leaving her," he asserts to the young child.

"Fine, doc. Well, I hope you can swim."

"What's that supposed to mean?"

"It means you should get down."

Meanwhile, Joelle continues to hold her hand out towards the approaching beast as she inches closer and closer to it. Strangely enough, the creature hasn't attacked her yet. At the same time, Joelle hasn't quite achieved whatever it is she's attempting. As a result, she stops moving towards the creature and instead, begins slowly backing away.

"Dammit. Why can't I feel you?" she says to the beast.

At this point, Joelle can hear the low-pitch growling of the specimen and starts to realize that unlike the animals from earlier, she can't at all feel anything emanating from this one's presence; it's almost as if it isn't even alive.

"Minutiaaaa, that's not workinggg," Calvin worriedly sing-songs to her.

"I knowww," she says back in the same intonation. "How much longer?"

"Eleven seconds," he replies.

"And then what?" she asks, confused.

"Get close to *me* this time."

"Eleven seconds? Eleven seconds, what does that mean, eleven seconds?" Arthur asks fervently, no longer wanting to be left in the dark to the very things that's unfolding before him that he apparently, lacks the vision to perceive.

"It means we either are going to drown, get crushed, both, or neither. It's up to her, really," Calvin remarks, neither quite eliminating nor quite exacerbating the doctor's worries.

"Four ... Three ... Two ..." Calvin yells out as he counts down the final seconds to the end of this level. It is at this point that Joelle can see a massive blurry figure that is approaching her position at an alarming speed, clear up into the form of a speeding whale swimming directly towards her.

"One, NOW!" Calvin screams.

At that moment, Joelle turns and leaps as far as she can towards Calvin and Arthur, who remain crouched near a nearby trash can. At the same time, the UNSELF creature leaps directly at her, executing its signature ram attack that may very well be what catapulted that man through those doors and down those flights of stairs earlier. Unfortunately for the creature, the only thing its formidable head-butt connects with, is the broad side of the large orca that bursts through the glass of its aquatic chamber and pins the oblivious creature under its body.

The sound of the large mammal crashing through its transparent cell, is louder than anything Arthur has heard since he watched a plane slam into the World Trade Center from his apartment rooftop twenty-eight years ago. Luckily, Joelle barely avoids being crushed herself by her gargantuan marine rescuer, and somehow successfully makes it to area where her friends are. However, though she avoids being flattened, the impact from the whale exploding through the glass knocks her back into the wall, where she hits her head hard—the impact temporarily knocking her out. Her body slides down from the wall, and she lands, not-so-gently, on her bottom next to her friends. Not even a second later, does all the water that was contained inside of the tank comes flowing out in all directions, and now a great part of it is cascading its way towards them.

"Oh no!" Arthur screams out right before the huge wave crashes into them. When he realizes that he doesn't even feel a single drop of water touch him, he opens his eyes only to look up and see himself encased in an invisible bubble that's surrounded by water passing all around him.

"H-how?" he whimpers as he looks at the vortex of water surrounding him.

"Even when she's out cold? Man, that is so COOL!" Calvin exclaims when he realizes Joelle's powers work even while she's unconscious. His admiration is quickly cut short when he realizes that some of the water has already begin inexorably falling towards them, though at a substantially slow rate. "Doctor, we have to get out of here."

"How is this possible?" Arthur asks, as he stares at the small droplets of water slowly making their way towards his face, reminding him of the raindrops that are pushed along the windshield of a car speeding down the highway on a rainy day.

"Doctor," Calvin says in an effort to snap Arthur's attention back. "We have to carry her out of here."

"Oh, of course!"

Calvin and Arthur stand up, and even then, he can't get over what he's currently witnessing. By all rights, all three of them should be neck deep in water, instead they are able to move about freely, completely unrestricted. Thanks to the emergency systems of the area, the entire hallway has been shut down, so the water level continues to rise in the hallway as it leaks out of the pool, however the plan is for them to use the emergency exit nearby to safely escape the calamity.

"Lift on three, ready?" Arthur says as he grabs Joelle's legs while Calvin grabs her from under her arms. "One, two, three," they count in sync before lifting her up and making their way towards the emergency exit with her dangling body in tow. Arthur can't help to notice that as long as they keep moving, the water will never reach them—thanks to the fact that their constant movement is causing new water to enter into their vicinity, forcing the original droplets to be swapped up by the ever-approaching wave and causing new droplets to emerge as a result. During all of this extraneous besetment that he's currently confined by, it takes everything for Arthur to refocus long enough to safely exit the premises with Joelle in his arms, as the physicist in him has become overwhelmed by all the new cool science he's just witnessed firsthand.

Chapter Twenty-Four

OPERATIONAL ABANDONMENT

April 18th. 12:34 A.M. (EDT)

KL-TCK!!

Ori is the first to hear the sound of Nerosion's staff clanking outside the window of her house.

"Daddy's home!" she screams out, prompting Laharin to quickly pretend as if she was doing something important, like not sitting on the couch watching the clock to see how many more possible minutes are going to pass until her man finally gets in. Nerosion enters through his bedroom window. Instead of getting up to meet him, Laharin decides she's going to wait until he comes out.

After a long seven minutes with no sign of Olpha, Laharin tells Ori to go check up on him and ask him if he can come into the living room for a second.

"Okay, Mommy. DADDDDDDDDDDDYYYYY!" she shouts, her voice trailing off as she gets up from the floor and heads into her parent's bedroom. After a couple of knocks on the door, Ori enters only to find her father undressed and fast asleep—or more than likely pretending to be.

"Daddy. Daddy wake up, Mommy wants you," Ori says as she continues to shake and wake him.

"Hmm? Baby, can you tell your mother I'm sleep? I'm really tired, today has been a little much for your father," Olpha says to his jewel.

"Tell her you had a long day and all you need is a full night's rest?" Ori asks, making sure that she has the details of her father's message down pat.

"Yes, baby, thank you," he says, turning back over.

Ori promptly exits the room and heads back to her mother, she who continues to pretend to be busy to of course create the illusion that Olpha isn't the only thing in the world she's focused on right now.

"Mommy, Daddy said leave him alone, he's sleeping."

"He said what?" Laharin responds, hoping her tone would elicit Ori to rephrase her message.

"He said," Ori begins again, this time making sure she's clearer. "Tell. Laharin. To. Leave. Me. Alone. Because. I. am. Sleep. Ing."

"Oh, hell no. OLPHA!"

The speed at which Laharin got up off of that couch frightened Ori more than it amused her—which was the point of her instigating this whole transaction as she's known to do from time to time. Still, she giggled to herself anyway, thinking about the hilarity that's about to ensue thanks to her juvenile parent trap.

Perhaps because he can sense what Ori's plan was because he knows his own daughter, or perhaps it's because he can hear everything going on in the living room of not only his apartment but of his neighbor's also, Olpha has already gotten out of bed and started heading to the living room on his own volition. In fact, if he weren't truly as tired as he told her he was, he would've been able to pick up on what his daughter was planning all along before she left the room—which was trying to get him murdered.

Laharin never makes it to the bedroom because she bumps into Olpha in the hallway that leads to it.

"I'm sorry, what was that?" she opens up as soon as she sees his broad frame coming out of the doorway. *"Tell Laharin to leave me alone because I'm sleeping?"*

"I did *not* say that," he says while half-chuckling at how silly and crafty his daughter can be at times. "Ori, imma get you for that," he projects to her in the living room, unable to see her from where he and Laharin currently stands.

"Olpha, we need to talk."

"Laharin, not now. Come on, it's late, baby. I didn't eat, I'm tired. Let's just go to bed. Come on—me, you and Ori together," he begs her.

"Why do you always try to dismiss me when I have legitimate concerns?"

"I'm not dismissing you, or your concerns Laharin, I'm tired. Do you have any idea of what I had to go through today?"

"Uh, yeah, I was there. At least for some of it, remember?"

"Exactly, so you can understand. You seen those men I had to face, I've never fought anyone that difficult before. That takes its toll, babe."

"Olpha, you fought people who were trained by some of the most prestigious military branches in the world, these guys are nothing compared to them—it won't kill you to have a conversation with your family. Besides, you need a shower and I want to know exactly who were those men that you had so much difficulty with."

"It's crazy how you know exactly what I go through out there and yet you still can't fathom how all I need is your care, comfort and understanding when I'm not out there," he reproaches.

"I do, that's why I want to talk to you—so I can get a better understanding of what you are going through; so I can know how to better comfort you."

"Laharin, I told you how you can—and this isn't the way."

The two have already started walking back towards the couch in the living room. Laharin, of course, leading her man by his hand, which isn't all that difficult considering she purposely allows him to get a full sight of her ass while she does so, alluring him into her trap like a siren using her song to lure a lost wanderer to his eventual demise.

They finally make it to the living room and she sits down on the couch completely expecting Olpha to sit next to her, except much to Laharin's dismay, he has opted to sit in the single, winged chair on the other side of the room. It is at this point that Laharin is starting to sense that her sonnet isn't as effective as it once was.

Olpha decides he's going to focus on whatever it is on the television that has Ori so entranced, while Laharin figures out when she's going to stop staring at him and say something.

"You're funny," she opens up with, perhaps looking to get a rise out of him.

"No, I'm tired," he glumly replies.

"Aww poor baby, come here, come lay your head on Mommy's shoulder so you can get you a little nap in," she facetiously offers to Olpha. Unfortunately, her sarcastic attempts to add some levity to the situation falls on deaf ears, and Olpha doesn't budge and neither does his grimace.

"Nah, I need a shower, remember?" he responds, which makes her force a chuckle.

"So, what happened earlier?"

"With what?"

"With you. You said you fought some difficult men. Who were they?"

"I don't know yet. I'm still trying to figure that out, imma have to sleep on it."

"You know they attacked me, right? I had to knock one of them out."

"Are you okay?" he asks her, appearing disinterested.

"Yeah, I managed. A girl gots to take care of herself out here sometimes. Can't always rely on some superhero to come and save her."

"I'm glad you're okay."

"Thanks, babe," she says with a forced uppity tone. "What kept you so long, anyway?"

"I told you, I was chasing Surii."

"No, I know that. I mean, you was with him for a while. All that time and you still ain't get him? You sure y'all wasn't doing anything other than just chasing each other?"

"This is why you have me up right now, so you can be funny? This is amusing to you?" Olpha says as he begins to get up to head back to bed.

"I'm not trying to be funny," she says, prompting him to return to his seat. "I told you one of those junkies attacked me earlier and you wasn't around. I just want to know exactly what kept you so long, considering you was supposed to be there to meet us anyway."

Olpha lets out a large exhale before he indulges her.

"They're known as Strawmen. And Ori's school wasn't the only place they were at. There were twice as many of them in Vellichor before Surii even showed up—I had my hands full."

"So why chase him? He doesn't have anything to do with them."

"I told you, he was trying to kill innocent people. Also, he might. These men came out of nowhere. And now all of a sudden Surii's here also."

"You're saying there's a connection?"

"I don't know. But it's odd."

"What would he have to do with a bunch of dope fiends?"

"That's the thing—"

"What?"

"I shouldn't even be telling you this because it's classified. But those 'dope fiends' aren't on dope, they're on something else."

"Something else like what?"

"Something else called Exile. It's a new drug that apparently makes people stronger somehow."

"No wonder," she says to herself.

"No wonder, what?"

"That Strawman or whatever, when I hit her—it was like she didn't even feel it."

"It was a woman?"

"Yep. A Strawbitch. And I knocked her ass right out."

"Laharin ..." Olpha says to her as he makes a gesture towards Ori, indicating to Laharin that their daughter is still in the room.

"Oh, please," she blurts out dismissively, before going back to her story. "Yeah, it was a woman, you didn't notice when you kicked her? Anyway, I hit her, and I caught her good, too. I mean—I know I haven't served anyone in a while, but my right hook is still lethal. And she just got right back up off the ground, like she just tripped or something."

"This drug somehow grants them incredible stamina, which should be impossible for people of their physical status to achieve."

"And you think Surii is somehow connected to this?"

"Of course. He pops up and all of a sudden there's a new drug on the streets that makes people stronger? That sounds exactly like the kind of planning Odem would have Surii conducting. I think Odem may be trying to bring back Gloria."

"I thought you said Odem was done with trying to bring her back?"

"I wanted to believe that. But I might've been wrong. Ever since this asteroid blew up, so many strange things have been happening around here. And I get the feeling that Odem is at the center of it all."

"So, you're saying the reason you had such a difficult time with those Strawmen is because Odem created a drug to make people stronger, and Surii is recruiting people to test it on?"

"It's not that simple, but yeah, right now that more or less seems to be the case—and why do you keep saying it was difficult?" he suddenly asks her, clearly rankled by Laharin's sly affront. "It wasn't THAT difficult—it was just a lot of them. They weren't *difficult* though."

"You're the one who said they were difficult, I'm just trying to be understanding."

"No, you're being patronizing. It's offensive, this is why I don't like telling you things at times."

"You know, I don't know what it is about Surii, but every time he comes back into your life, you get like this. It's like you become obsessed with him."

"Obsessed? What the hell are you talking about, I'm doing my job! You sound stupid."

"No, you're doing the FBI's job. The man is a domestic terrorist wanted in all fifty states across this country. Your job is to focus on protecting the city, not chasing some man across rooftops," she tells him, which he registers as slightly emasculating.

"And that's what I'm doing—protecting this city! He was in my city, so I was protecting it. Are you kidding me right now? I'm deciding to open up more and share things with you that I rightfully shouldn't be, and this is what you choose to respond with?" he barks to her.

"I was almost attacked today when you was supposed to be there picking us up like you agreed. Instead, you're off somewhere chasing some old comrade from the past just because you feel some type of way about him saving me instead of you. Well, you wouldn't have to worry about that, if you just stuck to your commitment!"

"You don't even know what the hell you're talking about. This is exactly why I don't share things with you. Now all of a sudden you need protection, right? You kill me, Laharin. I did everything in my power to make sure you've been getting the treatment you need so you can get back on your feet. Even when you denied the augmented stabilizers, and opted for this stupid, experimental, muscle-transplant bullshit, I still stood by you. And have you been going to your appointments? No! Have you been taking your medicine? No! So, go somewhere with all that 'I need protection, now' shit. It's not going to work on me. I did everything I had to do to make sure you've been getting the right support you needed. Be responsible for yourself."

"Responsible? Oh, I'm not responsible? Is that why you're afraid to marry a cripple?"

"*We interrupt this program to bring you breaking news ...*"

Suddenly, Ori's favorite program is interrupted by a news story developing within Monachopsis, specifically in Vellichor. It is only until the anchor reveals the details of the breaking news, that Olpha and Laharin stop staring at one another, each of them displaying a very different expression from one another. Apparently, Laharin's last statement created a cloud of tension that neither of them could ignore.

"Breaking news out of Vellichor right now—a police officer and three people have been shot and killed. A peaceful protest occurring in front of Mayor Bryanton's home just earlier today lost control when several people were said to be attacked by a group of men. Nerosion, who was on the scene at the time, was seen fleeing the area after the victims were shot, leaving many to speculate that he may be the sole reason as to why this situation took the grim turn it did."

"I'm the reason they got shot? Are they serious!?" Olpha shouts out angrily.

"Police officials were able to capture six of the men who attacked the protestors—at this time it can't be determine whether or not if there were any other attackers, but an investigation is currently ongoing. Right now, there's no official word on whether or not Nerosion is to be charged for Operational Abandonment, which states that an officer of the law cannot abandon the scene of a crime-in-progress. Under the Nerosion Pact, it is understood that any law

enforcement activity that the hero is involved in must always be carried out to his fullest extent, but many already have decided that he has violated this clause by leaving the scene of a crime. After the OPD was able to get the area under control, Senior Police Lieutenant, Walter Garrett, had this to say about the events that took place during the crisis and has commented on the events that happened just a couple of hours ago—"

"We were able to successfully apprehend several men who attacked the peaceful protest that was occurring here in Vellichor at the time. Thanks to the valor and swift heroics of the OPD, the number of casualties that could've occurred was dramatically lessened, and as a result, many people were able to escape the area safely and avoid any harm," Garrett says to the group of reporters anxious for his thoughts on the matter.

"Was Nerosion present during the protest, and if so, can you comment on his actions once it was learned that the protest was under attack?" one curious reporter asks once Garrett takes a pause.

"Yes, Nerosion was present but had arrived on the scene much after the protest has already started. However, his purpose there wasn't the same as the OPD's, which as a result didn't readily qualify him to have the same responsibilities as them. He wasn't briefed or deployed for any engagements in reference to the protest, and was only there, technically, as a spectator."

"It's understood that he did engage with the attackers once the attack began, and fled while in the middle of fighting them. Does such an action make him liable for investigation?"

"Again, Nerosion doesn't operate under the jurisdiction of the OPD, he operates alongside the OPD. It'll be equivalent to asking why didn't the Fire Department help us foil a bank robbery just because they happened to be in the area, for example. The details of Nerosion's duties are widely unknown, if not altogether classified, and therefore remains unknown even to us. Because of this, I am unable to determine if his actions violated those that other OPD officers would be subjected to."

"Is it possible that Nerosion can be prosecuted for these actions?"

"That's for a judge to decide—thank you."

Nerosion turns off the television, refusing to listen to anymore of the nonsense that's being spewed from it.

"Prosecuted. Are they serious?" Laharin asks once the T.V. once is off.

"Didn't they sound serious?" Olpha responds with an attitude.

"Well, at least it looked like Garrett had your back out there."

"Yeah, it *looked* like it, didn't it? I swear there's always something," Olpha grumbles.

"This is nothing we haven't been through before. We'll find a way out of it."

"Yeah, let me know when we do," he says as he starts walking to the door, and grabbing his jacket off of the coat rack.

"Where are you going?" she asks as she watches him head for the door.

"For a walk."

"To where?"

"The store."

Olpha leaves the house, leaving Laharin and Ori only left with their imaginations as to what store he's referring to, considering the nearest one requires a train ride.

Chapter Twenty-Five

THE HARNESS

April 18th. 1:39 A.M. (CDT)

"CHILL BABE, I told you—she's just my side mission. You're my main mission, c'mon, you know that."

"Calvin?"

Joelle's first word when she awakens is the first name of her first friend.

"Oh, I gotta go," Calvin says quickly, before hanging up the phone on some unknown person, and quickly handing it back to Arthur. "Minutia!" Calvin exclaims, when he somehow hears the voice of his fallen sister over Arthur's ceaseless questions about their origin, and turns to check on her in the back seat. "Minutia, are you okay?"

"Where am I?" she asks, doing her best to readjust to her reality. "Are you okay?"

"Me? I should be asking you that. You bumped your head when that whale tried to eat you," he replies.

"Eat me? Where's Arthur?"

"I'm here, Joelle," Arthur says from the driver's seat. "Are you okay??"

"Yes," Joelle says as she begins to rise up from her lied-out position. "Where are we?" she asks, looking out of the window, as if she would recognize the area even if they told her.

"*We* are on our way to the hospital. This is the second time you've hit your head, I'm not taking any chances this time," Arthur sternly tells his injured friend.

"No, no, Arthur! Arthur, you can't do that," she immediately says back to him.

"Why not? For the past two hours, your brother here hasn't explained one thing about what has happened inside of that aquarium. If you don't want to tell me why water is afraid to touch you, fine, I'm sure stranger things have happened somewhere in the universe, but I refuse to have you walking around here hitting your head on everything in sight without getting a check-up. Hundreds of people die every year after having lucid intervals, and I refuse to have you succumb to one on my watch."

"Arthur, stop the car!" Joelle insists. Her firm demand renders the vehicle silent. After a few seconds of quiet consideration, Arthur pulls over and parks on a nearby street.

"You want to tell me *why* it is you can't go to the hospital? If you're worried about hospital bills, I can take care of that."

"No, it's not that," she says without looking at him even though he's glaring at her through the rearview mirror.

"Then what's the problem?"

Joelle lets out a soft sigh before choosing to share whatever it is she's going to share with Arthur.

"You promise you won't freak out?"

"Freak out? I just saw a freak drown and the only reason we didn't is because water is afraid to touch you for some reason. I'm pretty freaked out already, but the scientist in me will allow me to keep a cool head long enough to brace myself for whatever it is you're about to tell me."

"Okay. You said stranger things in the universe might have happened. What if I'm one of those stranger things?"

"Stranger in what sense?"

"Stranger as in literally *a stranger*—as in I'm not from here, as in the reason why the watch on your wrist tightened when you first met me is because it also was afraid to touch me," she tells him.

"What? How is that possible?" Arthur says while unconsciously rubbing his wrist.

"Because that freak that drowned didn't come from under the ground. It came from above the ground ... way above—as did I."

"So, you're an alien?" he surmises after staring at her for a few moments silently.

"By your society's definition of the term, yes."

"Really? How did you get here?"

"Apophis," she says pointing a single finger to the sky.

"*You* were on Apophis?

"Yes, and so was the UNSELF. Those are his creatures."

"You mean the Man in the Gray Suit—you know him?"

"Yes, I'm his ... associate."

"Associate to what?"

"I'm having trouble remembering all the details, but from what I can recall, I assist him—rather, I used to assist him, on a process that absorbs energy from dying stars. In your language, the process will be known as a Harness."

"A harness? Like a gathering of resources?"

"Exactly."

"Of what kind?"

"The kind that can either save a planet or destroy one. That's why I have to find it."

"Find what?"

"A special artifact of mine that has landed somewhere on this planet," she says.

"What is it called?"

"Well, it doesn't really have a name."

"Well, what's so special about it?"

"Well, for one, if it wasn't important, the UNSELF wouldn't also be looking for it."

"That man, is that why he's been destroying the camps?"

"Exactly. His name is Jumo, and if he finds the artifact before we do, this planet is in a lot of trouble."

"What kind of trouble?"

"That artifact is designed to absorb and preserve the excess energy giving off from exploding stars."

"Gamma ray bursts," Arthur says to himself.

"I'm not exactly sure what his plan is, but he might be trying to reverse the process. You can imagine what will happen if he releases all of that stored energy."

"Is there a reason why he would do such a thing?"

"There is. But I'm not entirely sure what it is."

"How do you know all this?"

"It's what I know. The bad part is that I don't remember much else besides that—like where I'm really from or what I am, even. With as much as I've learned over the past few days, I feel like I'm supposed to know so much more."

"I see. Well, if this is all true, then it's important that we find it before he does," Arthur determines.

"Right. That's the real reason me and Calvin are out here. We're looking for the craft the UNSELF used to escape from Apophis. If we find that, Calvin here might be able to help us find a man who can help us locate the artifact."

"And how will he be able to do that?" Arthur wonders.

"Calvin here has a unique ability, also. Also, he's not really my brother—I had a bad experience once with this guy and Calvin kinda helped me out—that's how we know each other. But he's very special too—aren't you, Calvin?" she says, to which Calvin responds by flashing her the meanest mug.

"Special, huh? And what kind of unique ability might this be?" Arthur asks, now looking only at Calvin. With all the babying Calvin's had to do for this annoying doctor over the past couple of hours Joelle was out cold, he figures why not use him to evoke some much needed 'lols' that he's seriously been deprived of.

"Come on, try to hit mc," Calvin says before exiting the car.

"I-I beg your pardon?" Arthur asks, instantly confused at the odd request even though he exits right after him, with Joelle following.

"Try to hit me!" Calvin repeats, this time more emphatically.

"Uh, are you sure?"

"Calvin, you idiot, your powers don't work like that," Joelle interrupts.

"You don't know me! Go on, take your best shot, Doc."

"Is this really necessary?" Arthur asks as he slowly starts to regret his request.

"You asked for a demonstration, right?"

"Okay, if you insist."

Arthur raises his right hand to swing at Calvin, but then fakes and slaps him across the head with his left.

"Ouch! Hey, that hurt man!" Calvin cries out.

"Whoa, that was some power," Arthur says sarcastically.

"What's wrong with you, you're not supposed to hit kids, you freakin' maniac," Calvin spews.

"No, Arthur, Calvin is just an idiot. Ugh. He can sort of see the future, but not really. It depends on what he's looking at--it's complicated. Anyway, so the plan is to go to the UNSELF's crash site to see if Calvin can look into the future, and perhaps see where the artifact may be."

"That sounds like a horrible idea, if I can be frank," Arthur unexpectedly shares.

"Really, why is that?" she asks, not expecting such a response.

"If this artifact is as special as you say it is, then that means the UNSELF is going to keep attacking different camp sites until he finds it. Your best bet is to head to one of these sites before he does."

"But we don't know if the artifact is there or not," Joelle tells him.

"You don't have to—you can see the future right?"

"No, I'm not falling for that one again," Calvin says as he takes a step back.

"Then why don't you just head to one of the camp sites and look into *its* future. If it isn't there, then you can just move on to the next one and try again there."

"What a minute, that's brilliant!" Joelle exclaims. "Why focus on one area when we can go to different ones and see what turns up?"

"This way, even if you don't find it, at least you will be able to stay one step ahead of that creep."

"That's an amazing idea! If we hurry we might even be able to beat him to it."

"Um, eh-hm, Minu, uh—Joelle? Can I talk to you for a second, right quick?" Calvin suddenly signals to Joelle in an effort to get her to come over to where he now stands.

"One second, Arthur."

"This isn't fair, Minutia, you never told me about any artifact—what about The Man in The Dirty Robes? You promised!"

"We're going to go to him, don't worry. This is just a small detour to see what this guy knows. It's like one of your video game side-quests. Come on, we're killing two birds with one stone this way. And stop calling me Minutia, it's Joelle."

"Joelle? That's not even a girl's name. Why do you keep lying to this man?"

"Lying? I told him everything I know! Besides, you seen what happened the last time I was totally honest with a stranger. I got kidnapped! For you, no less! Just play along for now, until I get some more answers out of this guy," she says before turning back to Arthur. "It's settled, we'll do it your way, doctor. Now we just need the location of the sites."

"Well, our best bet is to try to get to one that isn't near all of the other ones that's been attacked so far. By the looks of it, it seems the UNSELF is randomly attacking sites that are nearby one another. There's supposed to have been a series of meteors that fell along the eastern seaboard," he confirms. "We should start there."

The trio get into the car, this time Calvin sits in the back.

"I must say, all things considered, you're taking everything you've heard up until now very well," Joelle suddenly shares with the doctor.

"I guess that's one of the perks of being a scientist—you're paid to believe the unbelievable. Also, as a scientist, I'm extremely skeptical of everything I have witnessed thus far, so you'll have to excuse me if I take a day or thirty to process what I've seen."

"How can I convince you that I'm being honest with you, Arthur?"

"Well, aside from carving out a piece of your flesh and analyzing it directly, normally, running a few routine tests of these so-called abilities should more than satisfy my dubious concerns. And I'm not even going to begin to talk about your friend there," he tells her.

"Okay, let's do it!" she gleefully agrees to.

"Really?"

"Yes, really."

"But you didn't even want to go to a hospital," the skeptical scientist reminds her.

"The truth is, all these things I'm able to do are new to me also. I want to learn everything I can about these abilities while I have the opportunity. And I want you to be the one to help me understand them, Arthur," she says to him while being uncharacteristically warm.

"Then it's settled," he says as he starts walking back to the car. "I have a lab here in Chicago not too far from where we are, we can go there before we set out for the next site. The better we know what you can do, the better prepared we'll be."

"Wait! Your press conference, we forgot all about it!"

"That thing ended three hours ago. Who knows, maybe with your help, I'll have something a little more interesting than 'space-wolves' to talk about in my next one."

Joelle smiles at Arthur, knowing she can trust that he would never reveal a thing about her to the public.

Chapter Twenty-Six

ZENO'S PARADOX

April 18th. 2:09 A.M. (EDT)

NEROSION SPENDS some time prowling the streets, or rather, the rooftops of Vesto Melvin—not really with any ordained purpose but just to clear his head, mostly; a part of him perhaps hoping he'll bump into Surii while a part of him is hoping he doesn't. While all he really wants to do is find him, he continues to use the excuse of looking for the Exile distribution source as to why he needs to continue to spend more time with criminals in the streets outdoors, than with Laharin in the sheets indoors.

"Available?" the incoming message on his SHED band displays after vibrating.

"Where?" he says, holding the device close to his mouth in order for it to register his words and transcribe them into a text.

"Yunzabit Heights in ten," the next message on his band reads. Considering only about three people in the all of the world has the number to his band, he can only assume it can only be Lieutenant Garrett who's requesting to meet him in the projects at three in the morning, as it's highly unlikely that his fiancé nor the president of the United States would ask for such an obscure request at such a time.

"Anything new on Exile?"

"Jesus, you scared the shit out of me," Garrett says after jumping, once Nerosion shares his voice with the lieutenant before he shares his presence.

"You gotta get a signal for me or something, if I got a text like that while I was home, I'm not sure I would've made it here alive."

"So, you're married?" Garrett asks before chuckling. "I don't know why that's funny to me."

"Yeah, neither do I," Nerosion says in agreement.

"I don't know—you just don't look like the marrying type I guess," Garrett admits, unapologetically. In his voice, Nerosion senses a hint of envy. And in Nerosion's lack of a response, Garrett senses a hint of restraint.

"So, anything?" Nerosion asks again after a half-second of silence.

"In fact, there is. It turns out the source of the drug isn't coming from one location, but several."

"Several?"

"Yes. I wasn't able to trace any of them back to any of the original sources, but we at least now know that there is more than one."

"More than one can mean two. How did you get to several?"

"I like to keep an open mind. Besides, our resident math wizard down at the Four-Three helped corroborate my suspicions with a little statistical data. Twelve attacks in ten days. Each of them coming from a different part of Opia and each one much more destructive than the last."

"Sounds to me as if they're getting desperate," Nerosion states.

"I agree."

"Listen, I want to thank you for not making me look bad out there the other night," Nerosion shares with the lieutenant, suddenly switching the subject.

"Oh, don't mention it. Besides, if it wasn't for you, we wouldn't have Trunt's information, and without that we would still be at square one."

"Is that why you wanted to see me, Lieutenant? To thank me?"

"Actually, no. The real reason I called you out here is because though it hasn't been confirmed yet, it seems Bryanton no longer wants you in his city. I thought it'd be something you might like to know."

"His city," Nerosion says with a scoff. "Have I done something wrong?" he asks, a little surprised by this unanticipated news.

"Are you asking me or him?" Garrett asks him.

"Well aren't you representing him right now?"

"Look, the truth is you left in the middle of a crisis. At this point, I can only assume that his feelings are what's driving this and not because you broke any laws. His house was attacked and a police officer is dead—he's a bit on edge right now and he wants some answers. Chances are, this is not even his idea. If you ask me, it sounds like some of his buddies in D.C. are leaning on him to push you out," Garrett shares.

"Well, I have friends there, too."

"Best friends, I know. Wasn't it Lamarch himself who created the Nerosion Pact?"

"If they have a problem with me, they can take it up with him," Nerosion says, talking as if to himself.

"It's true that the president is perhaps your number one supporter, but he also has the people's concerns he has to address. Fan or not, he still has a country to run."

"And I've made it easier for him to do so. Opia has went through four mayors in ten years, with Bryanton serving the longest so far. Ever wonder how that came to be?"

"I don't doubt your significance, Nerosion, I just know that in politics, it is often emotion and not reason that dictates reform."

"I represent more than just this one city—I also serve as the face of a nation that represents real change. Opia is just one of dozens of places I've cleaned up," Nerosion asserts.

"It's your face, or lack thereof, that may very well be the problem. If you haven't already, you should watch his most recent press conference. He speaks as if he knows something about the great Lamarch that you don't."

"Unnecessary. This is my home now. I wanna see him try to get rid of me," Nerosion says, with the same cadence a threat would pose.

"I don't, and don't wish that upon me, either. We got enough monsters roaming these streets that we need to get rid of—I don't need the biggest one turning against us. Besides, I still need your help pinning them down for me while I continue to convince judges why I need warrants to capture these rats without killing them."

"And what happens when you no longer need my help?" Nerosion asks.

"Well, I would hate to imagine what Opia would be like without you," Garrett replies after a moment.

"Yeah ... so would I," are the last words that permeates through Nerosion's mask before he disappears even faster than he appeared in the abandoned lot that no window faces.

When Nerosion returns to his apartment an hour later, he comes into a house that has the two people he can't live without sleeping soundly in their respective rooms. Be that as it may, even though the walls continue to inhale the soft cooing that his fiancé and daughter make as they sleep, and exhales the ingredient that he breathes in daily for strength, his home strangely feels emptier than it ever has since he first carried a pregnant Laharin inside of it. Unable to determine if he's simply imagining this or if it's empirically true, he decides to spend some time in the living room before heading to bed, in order to do something he hasn't done since his daughter was born—meditate.

When he reaches for the remote to turn off the T.V. that Ori was surely up watching before Laharin told her to go to bed, he realizes that perhaps he should apply a different method of re-aligning and re-syncing himself to his existential coordinates in this giving space and time—that of osmosis. And he decides there is no better conduit to allow this transaction to occur than the very one his daughter uses to locate her own equilibrium—via watching her favorite show, *Madly Dote!*

2:34 A.M. (CDT)

Currently inside of Dr. Bouya's lab, Arthur continues to perform a series of rudimentary, clinical trials on Joelle to further test the limits of her physiology.

"This is absolutely incredible. You've been running for two hours straight and haven't shown one sign of fatigue. No increased heart rate, no sign of perspiration—it's unlike anything I've ever seen before," he says astonishingly, as Joelle continues to run on a treadmill with the same vigor she had when she first started.

"Is that a good thing?"

"Well at the very least, it means I'm no longer doubtful about your origins. You are DEFINITELY not from here. What I can't seem to wrap my head around, however, is although you clearly have a heart, a stomach, lungs, and just about every other organ that humans possess, it doesn't appear as if you need any of them. It's like you were made as the perfect model for us. You even experience pain and fear. Is there anything you remember about how you were born?"

"No ... as I told you, all I remember is waking up on that asteroid, and the few things that was happening when it was collapsing. Besides that, the only things I know about is only what I've come to interact with since I've been here," she shares very clearly, considering she doesn't have to catch her breath to talk.

"That's another thing. It's like someone wanted you to forget where you came from; which is surprising, because you remember everything about the Harness," he continues.

"Yes, but I can't seem to remember anything about what happened during the last event. But I have a feeling those answers will come soon enough."

"Why do you say that?"

"As I told you, the more things I interact with the more of my memory is restored. When I find the artifact, I have a feeling that that's when everything I know will return back to me," she professes.

"I see."

"But what about my abilities, doctor? That's the thing that no matter what I interact with, I can't seem to understand, nor have any memory of whatsoever," she says as she stops jogging for the first time since she's started.

"I still need to run some more tests for that. I must say, all things considered, the only thing more interesting than your abilities, is the fact that they aren't familiar to you in the least. Okay, hold still. If you don't mind, I am going to throw some things at you," Arthur says as he gets up from his chair.

"No problem," Joelle remarks as she steps down off of the treadmill. On the table near where Arthur is seated is a bowling ball, a penny, a feather, a glass, a bat, a tennis ball, and a lawn dart, all spread across from one another.

"Are you sure about this, Joelle? I'm going to be throwing these things at you as hard as I can," he warns.

"I should be asking *you* that, doctor," she replies.

"Alright."

First, Arthur grabs the penny and chucks it at Joelle. As expected, the penny slows down once it reaches within Joelle's vicinity. Next, he throws the lawn dart—it does the same thing. He follows up with the tennis ball, and finally the bowling ball. Arthur throws each of these items at different heights relative to Joelle's body.

"Amazing," he says to himself.

"What is it?"

"I didn't realize this before, but it seems no matter what the material is composed of or how much force they're thrown at you with, they all seem to travel at the same speed. Unless..."

"Unless?"

"Joelle, you can move out of the way of those items now."

She does as the doctor orders and once she steps to the side, the items thrown at her all go crashing into the padded wall and floor behind her.

"Okay, now sit in this chair. I want to try something else. I'm going to swing this bat as hard as I can and try to knock one of the legs out."

"That's not a good idea. Remember what I told you about the lady in the pizza shop."

"Oh, right. Um, ah! I'm going to throw it then. First, get up. We're going to weaken it a little."

With Joelle now off the chair, Arthur starts taking several whacks at its leg. Accidentally, he knocks the entire leg off.

"Oh, dammit. That was not my intention. Alright, anyway this should still work, you're just going to have to sit on it with the leg wedged under it," he tells her. So she picks up the broken leg and helps him place it underneath the chair. Now sitting, they prepare for the next experiment.

"Okay, here we go. Ready?"

"I am."

Arthur launches the bat at the broken leg that is wedged between the chair and floor and misses it completely. Not expecting that, he goes and picks up the bat and attempts this act several more times with no success. Unable to bear this embarrassing display any longer, Calvin finally gets up to perform the task for him.

"Ahhh! If you miss one more time, I'm going to hit myself with that bat. Let me do it," Calvin exclaims, unable to watch this travesty unfold any longer.

"Well I suppose your youth lends you the dexterity I once proudly possessed."

Calvin equips the bat like his favorite baseball player and points the tip of it towards the leg of the chair like he's about to hit a Grand Slam at the bottom of the ninth. He throws the bat at the leg, and the bat slows down as does everything thrown at Joelle. It spins in slow motion, inching ever so forward towards the leg of Joelle's chair.

"It's looking like a hit!" Calvin calls out, already prematurely celebrating.

"Shhhhhh!" Joelle hisses out. They all watch as the middle of the bat is the first to connect with the chair. It successfully makes contact with the leg, forcing it to move from its wedged position. Once hit, the leg begins moving in slow motion as does the bat. However, something unexpected happens: Joelle and the rest of the chair goes crashing to the floor at the normal speed that a chair whose leg is suddenly broke, would.

"Oww!" she winces out when she hits the floor. Her spill caused her arm to knick the handle of the bat, causing its spin to slowly start shifting vertically.

"Well, I'll be a clam's aunt! It was just as I suspected," Arthur exclaims.

"Suspected? So, you knew I was going to fall then?"

"Well, I was more or less hoping you would," he admits.

"I'm glad you got what you wished for, doc. So, what *were* you suspecting?" she asks him.

Instead of answering, he now grabs the feather and ties it to the back of a lawn dart with a rubber band and tells her to stand. He then throws it directly at her. When the dart-feather slows down as it reaches her, the doctor grabs a pair of scissors and walks up to the suspended it and snips the rubber band that kept them together. He then grabs the feather, holds it above her head, and lets it go. Everyone together, watches as the feather floats down slowly from the air, as if her Slow effect had absolutely no influence on it.

"Amazing. Just like with the chair, objects only seem to slow down when they're moving towards you once they achieve a certain speed."

"What does that mean?" Calvin asks, interrupting him.

"Let him finish, Calvin."

"Originally, I thought that when anything came near you, it was affected by a different gravitational field that is only unique to you and different from what everything else is subjected to. But it seems—I don't know for sure as I would have to run more tests—but it seems as if the objects aren't experiencing a different effect of gravity—they just *appear* to be slowing down. Better yet, it's not that they are moving slower, but that the space between you and the objects is stretched enormously almost instantaneously!"

"How is that possible?" Calvin asks.

"Well, while there really isn't any real-world situations I can use as an example, theoretically speaking, it isn't all that bizarre."

"It still doesn't explain why this Slowing effect only happens to her and no one else," Calvin surely reminds him.

"That's true. Hmm, have you ever heard of Zeno's Paradox?"

"Who's Zeno?" Calvin asks. "He sounds O.P."

"What's *O.P.?"* Joelle asks, unfamiliar with another colloquial term.

"I'll take that as a no. Okay, so suppose I wanted to walk across this room to reach the other side. How long do you think it'll take me to get there?"

"Oo! I know! Four seconds!" Calvin shouts, always eager to use any opportunity to showcase his vast knowledge.

"Jeez, I'm not that old. But okay, let's say four seconds. So, logically speaking, how long would it take me to cross half the distance left?"

"Two seconds!" he shouts again.

"And half of that?"

"One second!"

"And half of that?"

"Half a second."

"And half of that?"

"Get to the point, doc."

"But I already did! That is the point. The point is, I will never *reach* the point. There will always be an infinite amount of points I will have to cross to get to the other side of the room, therefore rendering me unable to ever make it to the other side."

"But you *can* make it to the other side of the room," Joelle says, finally joining in on the thought experiment and giving her two cents.

"Exactly! And this dart will eventually make it to your body, if you don't move of course. You know why? Because space isn't infinite! No matter what, we can always add up the sums of the infinite distances and it'll always equal to the total distance it takes to get to the other side."

Calvin and Joelle aren't sure what to say or do next.

"What I'm saying is, thanks to your inexplicable ability to slow things down, the space between you and the dart is exponentially greater than the space between *me* and the dart—but it's not infinitely greater."

"How much greater is it then?" Joelle asks.

"Uh, one second," he pauses to quickly jot down some numbers on the back of an envelope. After mumbling some calculations, he raises his head back up. "Um, about 9,600 meters."

He looks up to see the expression on Calvin's and Joelle's face isn't the gleeful one he expected.

"Meters? Speak English, doc," Calvin advises.

"Well, it was the French who came up with the meter, but I'll convert. Let's see—about six miles."

"Oh, see okay, I knew I knew that," Calvin shares aloud to the group.

"Wait, so you're saying anything that's sent my way has to travel six miles before it can reach me?" Joelle inquires.

"Well, not anything. I'm sure you noticed by now that people can get close enough to you to hurt you—unlike lawn darts."

"Yeah, by the way doc, tossing lawn darts at a person, let alone a girl—yeah, that's not unethical at all," Calvin again says aloud.

"You sure you're only eleven?" Arthur asks the youngling.

"I *have* noticed. What does it mean?" Joelle asks the prudent scientist.

"Well, I can only speculate at this point, but it might have something to do with the atomic nature of living things. All living things are composed mostly of carbon atoms. There must be something about the carbon within them that doesn't get affected by your ... gift."

"Yeah, but then that would mean the UNSELF creature would have been affected by me also and it wasn't," she rebuts.

"As I said, all living things are composed of carbon atoms."

"No, you said *mostly.* The UNSELF's creatures are made up of what you call silicon."

"My word. A silicon-based organism? That's unheard of. I see—so it must have something to do with the molecular structure of living things, then. Unlike normal matter, living matter for all intents and purposes, are entirely much more active than non-living matter. Your 'Gravity' bubble—well, now I think 'Spacetime' bubble is more appropriate —"

"Just call it her Warp Zone," Calvin tells him.

"Where did you get that from?" he asks.

"Uh, um—I made it up, hehe," Calvin says. Neither Arthur nor Joelle are able to determine if he's being truthful or not.

"Sure," Joelle says to Calvin. "I'm sorry Arthur, continue."

"I was saying that perhaps your 'Warp Zone' isn't designed to handle all of the dynamic activity that occurs on a molecular level inside of living things."

"Hey, I have a question—" Calvin suddenly says. "If an object has to travel around six miles before it reaches her, how come the dart doesn't just fall before it does? Technically speaking, nobody should be able to throw a dart or *anything* for that matter, that far."

"That's a good question," Joelle says in agreement.

"That *is* a good question. Yeah, you are definitely not eleven-years-old. Hmm, if I had to guess, I'll say it's because the stretched space that that material is forced to travel through to get to you is a vacuum. Newton taught us that any object in motion will stay in motion as long as nothing is in its way," Arthur shares while still mulling over Calvin's question.

"What can possibly cause all this?" Joelle asks.

"Well, the only other thing I can think of is Dark Energy, but as far as we know, that only affects space on a very large scale."

"Dark Energy? What is that?"

"Hey, aren't you the alien with the super-advanced technology capable of interstellar travel? I should be asking *you* what Dark Energy is because we still don't know. It's a natural property of the universe that causes space itself to expand faster than it should. In other words, there's a force or energy we can't see or identify that is intrinsic to the universe's natural expansion," he tells her.

"Well, you said the space near me is stretched enormously when something comes near me, right? Perhaps that's the reason—maybe this *dark energy* is created anytime an object tries to hit me."

"Hmm. Well, I'll be lying if I said that wasn't an attractive idea. It would explain why the space around you is suddenly shifted."

"Are there any more tests you want to run on me?"

"There are. I still don't know how you survived getting hit by a nuclear missile and survived a 300-mile plunge to Earth."

"Maybe I'm just lucky."

"Or maybe your abilities are more sophisticated than we can imagine. I don't think I've ever met someone who can feel an orca's pain. But unfortunately, we've run out of time. At this point, I think we really should get going. Every minute that passes is one he gains ahead of us."

"Well, how far is the drive?" Calvin asks.

"It's about eleven hours."

"Eleven hours?" he shouts.

"We'll we better hurry to thc airport if we're to get a head start."

"Wait, airport?" Calvin repeats.

"Yeah, airport?" Joelle also repeats, surprised at the fact she doesn't know what this is by now.

"Yeah. I only went back to my lab because my pilot said it was going to be awhile before he lands and refuels the jet. He should be just about done now. Or would y'all rather drive?"

"Nope, I accept this new side-quest. Come on, Joelle," Calvin says as he pushes Joelle out the door.

"What's an airplane?" she whispers to him as he pushes her.

"It's like a big car that can hover," he whispers back.

"Oh, okay. Where are we headed?"

"Opia," Arthur says as he grabs his keys and turns off the lights in his lab before closing the door as he leaves.

Chapter Twenty-Seven

MR. 350

April 18th. 6:37 A.M. (CDT)

"So, *THIS* IS AN AIRPORT?" Joelle says, as they pull up to O'Hare International Airport.

"Yes, you sound like you've never been to one," Arthur surmises, so he naturally feels it's his established duty to enlighten her on what occurs at such a place. "This is where the large, fixed-wing vehicles, known as airplanes —"

During this time, Joelle has closed her eyes to absorb all the information there is to be known about large airports.

"— are housed inside of a large aerodome with facilities for flights to take off and land," she says, completing Arthur's wordy description before he can finish it. "Got it."

"How did you ...?" Arthur stammers, shocked to learn that Joelle has even more abilities he doesn't know about.

"You Googled that. You're not slick," Calvin shares, refusing to believe that Joelle has such an ability. "I'm looking at it now, and you said that word for word."

"I told you, every so often I have these episodes where memories come whizzing into my head, and I learn about something I thought I didn't know anything about just by looking at it," she tells them as they start exiting the car.

"So, that's why you closed your eyes. It almost appeared as if you were having a seizure," Arthur shares.

"Yes, only for some reason after I learn the information, it's almost as if I should've always known about it. It's a feeling like I know something—but I just can't remember what it is."

"Jamais vu," Arthur says.

"Huh?"

"They also got a word for copying information that isn't yours. It's called Play-ver-inem ... playgranist ... wait hold on," Calvin interrupts again then pauses to search for whatever it is he plans on using to show that he's the smartest one amongst them.

"What you're experiencing—it's known as Jamais vu," Arthur elaborates.

"What is that?" she asks, surprised that she never heard of the term.

"Plagiarism!" Calvin shouts after scanning through the information he searched for in his frames.

"It's the opposite of Déjà vu," Arthur continues. "Basically, you've seen something familiar, but you don't recognize it. Then you have a seizure and it all becomes familiar again."

"I guess it's kind of like that," she says, unsure.

"Nope! That's Presque vu," Calvin interrupts as he continues to look up random information on his SHED frames in an effort to one-up the two adults he's with.

"What's that?" she asks Calvin.

"Uh, let's see—" Calvin begins, doing his best to get to the part of whatever search he just ran in his frames that answers her question best.

"It's a situation where you can't recall the name of something, but with enough effort—"

"—IT COMES TO YOU EVENTUALLY!" Calvin suddenly shouts, completing the doctor's words.

"I suppose it's like that also," she admits to Arthur.

"Jamais vu. They call it Brain Fatigue. The theory that surrounds it proposes that the reason we experience it is because our minds constantly need new stimuli to remain active, and on its own it does a

very good job at that. But sometimes, if the receptor is overstimulated by continuously repeating an action, like reading the same word over and over and over again, our minds will deem that action as unimportant, and perhaps even forget it altogether."

"I see."

"Yep, true, true," Calvin adds.

"Joelle, let me ask you something: before you fell onto this planet, did something traumatic happen on your ship before you arrived?" he asks her.

"Well, her ride got blown up by a nuclear missile. I think that's pretty traumatic," Calvin shares.

"Before that."

"I know I was out for a while. But when I came to, the area that I was in was collapsing. Like something hit it or something."

"And your associate, the UNSELF ... you said he escaped long before you did?"

"As I remember it, yes."

"Did anything else happen before the missile hit?"

"The last thing I remember is grabbing the artifact and protecting it from the explosion. Why?" she asks, as she's being scanned by a TSA agent. Though it's her first time, watching Arthur and Calvin go through the procedure without appearing uneasy makes her feel that much more relaxed about going through it herself.

"I'm beginning to believe this man may be the one responsible for your lapse in memory."

The trio make their way directly to the tarmac. Thanks to Arthur's lavish background, they don't have to suffer through the long lines and wait times at security checkpoints most are susceptible to when flying out of an airport.

"WOOOOOO! This is fantastic! This is how you know we really are the main characters in this game—only NPC's fly commercial. By the way, I have a private jet, too, you know ... only, my dad is currently using it," Calvin decides to share as if he had some reason to explain something no one asked about.

"Then how about we board mine until you get yours back, huh, sport?" Arthur responds.

12:39 P.M. (EDT)

"This is your Captain speaking, we should be landing at DeGrasse International Airport in approximately fifteen minutes. At this time, I want to remind you to return to your seats and please fasten your seat belts as we prepare to land."

"Uh oh, Joelle—here comes the scary part I was telling you about—you better get ready!" Calvin says from the other side of the cabin to Joelle.

"I thought you said the scary part was taking off? And that wasn't scary at all."

"Oh nah, that was just the warm-up. This right here, Joelle? This right here? This landing right here, Joelle? This landing right here? Is the REAL DEAL."

"I'm sure it is," Joelle says before turning her head towards Arthur, who is steadily fast asleep, thanks to the super comfortable chairs that comes equipped in most private jets. There's a good chance that if it wasn't for his obnoxious snoring, Joelle would've thought he was dead.

"Arthur ... Arthur ..." Joelle whispers, gently trying to awaken him from his slumber. "Dr. Bouya ... Dr. Bouya, wake up we're about to la—."

Suddenly a large magazine, presumably thrown from across the aisle, lands on Arthur's face, knocking his glasses off but more surprisingly, causing him to jump out of his sleep in total fear.

"Urhh! DON'T PLAY WITH ME! TODAY! HEY, GLASSES! I MISS LAKES!" Arthur yells as he jumps up out of his sleep, scattered, screaming out random words as a Time magazine smacks him across the face. Meanwhile, Calvin hides in the bathroom and tries his best to not let the tears that are currently streaming down his face from sheer laughter get the best of him, as he uses all of his willpower to hold himself back from screaming out louder than he ever has in his entire life.

"Oh, Joelle, it's you. I was startled. This magazine must've fell from the overhead bin," Arthur says as he grabs the magazine and looks up at the imaginary bin that doesn't exist on this plane.

"Yeah, it's me. Who is Glasses by the way?" she wonders.

"Nah, I got them, they are right here. Anyway, where are we?" he says as he sits up to look out the window.

"The pilot said we should be landing in fifteen minutes."

"Oh, wonderful."

"You were really knocked out there, doc."

"Yes, I was. I hope I wasn't snoring too loud."

"It's fine. Don't worry about it."

"I actually had a dream about you."

"A dream?"

"Yes, well, not of you exactly, but of your ... embodiments."

"What do you mean?"

"I may be jumping the gun here, but I can't help but feel that you're here for a reason," he says, getting more comfortable in his chair. He cracks open a bottle of water to fill a glass of ice next to him.

"I thought scientists weren't allowed to believe in fate?"

"Actually, that's a common misconception. Especially considering that the arrow of time—which is romantically linked to fate—may not even flow in a single direction but in fact may exist all the time everywhere and always has. Meaning that all things, living and non-living, are bound to some inextricable fate that can't be escaped. All events can all be accessed somewhere, somehow, in some dimension," he inundates to her. "But no, by reason, I mean—I believe you have a purpose."

"Really?" Joelle says with a light chuckle. "And what purpose is that?"

"While I was asleep, I got a glimpse of what you were capable of and I now believe that what you can do now is only just a small pinch of what's possible. And what I saw was *magnificent*."

Hearing Arthur use the same word Calvin used when they were in that tunnel, makes Joelle feel slightly unsettled. Not unsettled in the way she feels when she sees something she doesn't recognize but surely has seen before, but more in a sense of where she recognizes something she's never seen before, or heard in this case—almost as if she's already experienced what Arthur is only imagining.

"Whoa. Déjà vu," she quietly murmurs to herself.

"The problem is, in science, that word—*magnificent*—it doesn't always mean something positive," Arthur says before shrugging uncharacteristically and sipping his glass of water. Joelle looks at the doctor for a short while after he says this, then looks back and sees Calvin standing outside of the bathroom, where she assumes he's been standing the entire time. A flight attendant soon redirects him to his seat.

The private jet finally lands on the tarmac. Before it touches down, Calvin stares at Joelle with the same goofy look he did when the plane was first taking off, seeing if what surely scared him the first time he ever flew, would do the same for her. Much to his dismay, the action of being on a plane while it's taking off and now apparently when it's landing continues to only bedevil him and him alone.

The trio enter the terminal and head for the nearest place where they can rent a car. Wasting no time, they finalize the transaction and head for the exit.

"This is Opia?" Calvin says upon stepping out of the terminal. As he looks around, he sees nothing resembling the bustling *'Helical Capital'* that many have come to call it. Instead, just about any building that is visible exists much further in the distance, and because DeGrasse International is located east of Monachopsis, Calvin's view of those buildings is obscured, thanks in part to the fact that this part of Opia and the part he has come to glorify, sits on opposite ends of multiple mountain ranges. "What's with all the mountains?"

"Those are the Suburi Mountains. Let me guess, you thought Opia was all skyscrapers and tall structures, right? You've good reason to perceive this great city with such a limited scope, considering that that tends to be the perception this city wishes to be associated by. No, my good friend, Opia is more of a microcosm of the great American experience; it's here where one gets direct access to everything that is to be understood about life in this country. In everything, from its most coveted lifestyles to its unbidden cultural customs, there is nothing in this country that cannot be experienced while living in this city. These mountains here are a reminder of how great is it that the people don't even have to travel to the Midwest just to get a sample of some of the great vistas this country is renowned for. All things considered, though, it's the city behind these rocks that truly punctuates everything one needs to know about living the American Dream—that behind all the beauty that comes with the attractive thought of success and prosperity, lies some sophisticated nightmare that allows it to continue to only be but a dream."

"Sounds like my type of place," Calvin says out loud as Joelle continues to stare at the panorama in silence.

"Then let us go to it," Arthur affirms.

"Arthur, how do we find the site?" Joelle says after minutes of silence.

"I have the locations of all the sites on my phone."

"Working directly with the president clearly has its benefits," she figures.

"It also has its risks. These sites are Top Secret and only known to a select few. If we're caught here, those creatures are going to be the least of our worries," he assures the group.

"I don't care. We have to find the artifact before Jumo does."

"Then we best get moving."

"Hey, Arthur, can I drive? It'll help me focus," Joelle asks once the valet attendant brings the car to them.

"Certainly."

"No, no! Don't do it! She drives like a maniac!" Calvin suddenly exclaims.

"Shut up! No, I don't drive like a maniac, you little twerp!"

"Should I be concerned?" Arthur says, worryingly.

"I drive fine, Arthur. Don't listen to this nincompoop."

"Oh-hohoho-haha. Nincompoop. She got you good, Calvin. Okay, *now* you can drive—courtesy of that zinger," he says while chortling.

"*That* was funny? You guys are pathetic," Calvin spews in repulse.

After obtaining the rented car, Joelle, Calvin and Arthur head for the first site that may or may not contain the thing she needs in order to keep this planet from being destroyed.

"You know Joelle, I've been thinking—what are you going to do once you find this thing? I mean, do you plan on going back to where ever you came from, or are you just like an illegal alien now?" Calvin randomly asks her. "Because I think there are forms and stuff you gotta fill out in order to stay here."

"Up until now, I've obtained a wealth of knowledge about this planet and everything on it. I was already on a course to this place, for some reason, before the artifact was even lost. I have a feeling once I get it back, all of the answers will come to me and I'll know next what to do," she replies. "Why?"

"Oh, okay. No, I only ask because, I mean, like I would invite you to my house to sleepover, but you already know how my parents feel about company."

"That's sweet, but no thanks. Despite what you said, I have a feeling your mom wouldn't like me very much. Especially considering everything that went down the last time I was there."

"What I miss?" Arthur asks, his interest on their discussion suddenly piqued thanks to Joelle's last statement.

"Oh, his mom tried to kill us when I kidnapped him," she tells him.

"She tried to do what when you did *what?*"

"She tried to kill me," Calvin repeats.

"You mean that figuratively, right?" Arthur asks.

"What does that mean?" Calvin responds.

"I guess there's no better time to tell you but, no doc, we are actually on the run. At any given time, a group of hired mercenaries can show up and start shooting at us," Joelle informs the bewildered physicist.

Arthur's reaction when hearing this news would be enough to cause him to have a stroke if it wasn't for the advances in medical science that helps keeps his blood pressure regulated through the form of an encapsulated tablet that he takes twice a day.

"Trained mercenaries? Is that what you said? So, I *should* be concerned. How in the heck are you alive right now? Joelle I get, but you?"

"I told you already—I can see the future. Kinda," Calvin tells him.

"Kinda?"

"Well, I'm getting better at it. These missions are really helping."

"Missions? Son, just exactly what do you think this is?"

"His mom is training him for some sort of ultimate mission. And he thinks everything we do is progress in some video game."

"But IT IS! Just check out our stats on the SHED frames, it's been recording our progress since we escaped. And so far:

- We've traveled 1,312 miles

- Rode in three different vehicles

- Spent 127 dollars. Wait, who spent 127 dollars?"

"We had to pay for your stolen pizza," Arthur replies.

"Oh."

"And pay for parking," Joelle interjects.

"Oh."

"And buy tickets for the aquarium," Arthur adds.

"Oh. Consumed eight pounds of food. That pizza was slamming by the way," Calvin continues.

"Had 1,272 bullets shot at us. Shot 138 bullets back at them bitches."

"Language," Arthur says.

"Sorry. Dodged one rocket,

- Reached a top speed of 331 miles per hour in a land vehicle

- 654 miles per hour in an aircraft

- Slept for a total of nine hours

- Yawned twenty-seven times

- Exchanged 14,511 words. 14,519, 14,52-, 14,530 uh, Jesus, this thing doesn't stop going up."

"That is quite some feature," Arthur says to Calvin, as he is suddenly tantalized by his frames. "May I see your glasses for a moment?" he asks, as Calvin hands them to him. "Oh my, how exquisite!" Arthur says as he scrolls through dozens of categories that the frames has all compiled into legible statistics. "This thing tracks every single stat—from how many breaths we've taken, to how many times I've blinked. It even records how many times I've used a particular word and how many atoms are in the air inside of this car. What an amazing feature, surely this will do wonders in the laboratory," he gleams.

"These ain't no lab goggles, doc. These are state-of-the-art, military-grade—"

"They're his mom's reading glasses," Joelle interjects.

"Shut up!"

"They can even track one's skill level in certain areas by simply scanning them. Let's see here," Arthur says as he looks at Joelle with them on. "This is fantastic. Joelle, I can see almost everything about you—how much you can lift, how fast you can run, even your special abilities, it's all here. I should've used these when we were in my office!" Arthur says to the driver.

"Oh yeahhhh, that's right, I forgot about that," Calvin says.

"No offense, Arthur, but I'm not a big fan of those pervasive glasses. If you don't mind, I rather not be scanned," Joelle says while driving.

"Oooo, scan me, doc, scan me!" Calvin declares, anxious to get a reading on where he stands amongst the three.

"Okay, let's see here," Arthur says as he aims the frames at Calvin and initiates the scanning feature.

"Hmmm. Let's see—it says here for *Strength*, you rate a *0.8*

"*Speed* a *1.1*"

"*Combat Skill* a *1.3*"

"*Defense* a *1.2*"

"*DFM*, hmm I'm not entirely sure what that is ... oh I see, it says *Default Melee Weapon*. Okay? For that, you rate as a *1.7*. I guess that's a factor for how well you can swing a stick at someone or something. Not bad."

"Or stab them!" Calvin adds.

"Or that, okay, relax now. For *Firearms* you rate a *2*.

"*PW*, or *Preferred Weapon* you rate a *3*. Hey, now look at that—a *3*. And just what happens to be your preferred weapon of choice?"

"The .45 ACP caliber, Uzi carbine Model B submachine gun, equipped with a full-automatic, open-bolt option."

"Oh, okay. Well, that explains a lot. Moving on. For *Agility* you're a *1.1*. Now it says something about *Bio-Kinesis*? Any idea what that is?"

"Not really, I've never seen that. You're the scientist, I should be asking you. What does it say?"

"Let's see here. Ah, here it is. *Bio-Kinesis: This attribute determines how much control an individual has over their bodily functions. There are thou-*

sands of functions the human body is capable of performing on its own such as fighting infections, maintaining a structural cardiac cycle, releasing hormones or even multiplying cells. The higher an individual's Bio-Kinesis level is, the more overall control they have of their bodies internal functions."

"Okay. What does mine say?"

"*Bio-Kinesis. 0.7.*"

"Oh. It's probably a glitch."

"I'm sure," Arthur sarcastically quips. "*Wave Sensitivity*? I wonder what that is."

"Who cares, keep going."

"And last but not least—*Special Ability*."

"Let me guess—*1*," Calvin takes the liberty to assume.

"No. It's *350*," Arthur responds, utterly baffled. Hearing this number stuns Arthur and causes Joelle to slightly look back over her shoulder. "That's over three times as high as Joelle's. Think that's a glitch, too?"

"What does it mean?" Calvin asks.

"It doesn't say, but it does explain what a *1* means. *A scale of this factor corresponds to an average human adult standard capability. An example of a person with a 1 in strength is one who is capable of lifting approximately a maximum of ninety-five pounds.* If a *1* in strength means you can lift ninety-five pounds, then I can only guess at what a *350* in *Special Ability* must mean."

Chapter Twenty-Eight

INFILTRATION

April 18th. 8:29 P.M. (EDT)

THE DRIVE to the meteor site takes a little over an hour to get to. It was Joelle's decision to first allow the night to fall over them before they head out, as over the days she's been present on this planet she's come to learn that the dark can greatly aid one who seeks to move about without being seen—something she feels she's going to inevitably have to do no matter how strategic of a plan they come up with upon reaching the base camp.

While not exactly inside of Opia, Opia is about the closest known location to the place where this meteor landed. Arthur instructs Joelle to park the car about half a mile away from where the site is, not because he's suddenly in the mood to take a stroll, but because he knows that General Clemens has recently given orders for the soldiers stationed around these sites to immediately detain or even shoot anyone who comes within 1,000 feet of them.

During the hike there, Arthur has suddenly become overwhelmed with regret when he realizes he should've been developing a plan on how to get inside the base camp instead of playing with some kid's mother's reading glasses.

"So what's the plan, how do we get inside?" Joelle asks apropos, breaking Arthur's daydreaming.

"You must be a mind-reader. I was actually just trying to think of one," he replies.

"And?"

"Well, judging by the readings on Calvin's frames, it doesn't seem likely any of us can overthrow a single one of these armed guards stationed around the camp, let alone an entire platoon of them," he says remorsefully.

"We've faced men with guns before," she asserts in response to his cynicism.

"No, as I've come to understand it, you *ran* from men with guns before. This is different."

"Well, there's the camp right there, so what do you suggest?"

"Wow, this one is much larger than the others. Camp? This is more like an entire facility. They must be expecting resistance. It appears we're going to have to sneak inside," he submits against his better wishes.

"YESSS! Another side mission!" Calvin exclaims.

"Sneak in? How?"

"Well actually, I was hoping Mr. *350* could tell us that," Arthur says, now looking at the Calvin.

"Tell us what? You're going to leave your plan into the hands of a child?"

"If I had a plan, maybe I wouldn't. But this *child* can see things we can't. Isn't that right?" Arthur admits.

"Affirmative," Calvin agrees in a robotic tone.

"Tell me, what can you see, Calvin?" Arthur asks.

"It's strange. The code is somehow encrypted."

"What? The code?"

"Nothing. Um, lemme see. Uh, what do you want me to focus on?"

"What do you mean?"

"I have to focus on a particular thing in order to see its future."

"I'm not sure I understand, but okay. Well, uh, how about that guard? Can you see his future?"

"No. No people. Just give me a situation and I'll tell you if it's a good idea or not."

"So, that's how it works—I give you a scenario and you basically run it in your head from beginning to end."

"Yes, as long as there's no people involved," Calvin reminds him.

"Well, that doesn't help much."

"Fine. We can do it the old-fashioned way then," Calvin says, slightly annoyed.

"Okay, okay, slow down. How about the base, can you see that?

"Yes."

"Okay. What can you see?"

"Uh ..." Calvin says as he peers into the distance where the large base is located. "They have scanners. Lots of them. Focused on all sides of the building."

"Uh, it looks like you're using the frames for that," Arthur wryly says to Calvin, exposing him.

"Alright, fine!" he says, snatching his glasses off of his face.

"Scanners? That means sneaking in isn't an option," Joelle says to Arthur.

"Well, if we can get in, I can disable them but—" Calvin says before stopping and visualizing what were to occur if he did. "Yup, then an alarm will go off."

"Is there a scenario where you see the alarms *not* going off?" Arthur asks.

"Yeah, but it looks like it involves someone likely dying," Calvin shares. Arthur is a bit thrown off by the lack of empathy he displayed when he shared that tidbit of information.

"Okay, never mind. I guess *we are* doing this the old-fashioned way," Arthur decides.

"Which is?" Joelle asks.

"Knocking on the door."

"Then?"

"Then telling them to let us in. I have security clearance—it's getting you two in that's the problem."

"Wait, I have an idea," she suddenly conceives.

After a few minutes of deliberating in a huddle, Arthur, Calvin and Joelle have all agreed on her idea and are ready to set it in motion.

"Okay. Everybody's clear on what to do?" Arthur says, raising his head from the huddle.

"My body is ready!" Calvin strongly asserts.

Now back in the car, Arthur drives up to the gated entrance at the front of the base to a checkpoint booth that all visitors and personnel must stop at before entering. A rather average looking guard comes out of the booth with his flashlight equipped, even though there's more than enough light being provided by the overhead light posts.

Arthur can't help but squint and feel a little nervous as the guard approaches the car. Growing up first as a native of Mali, then eventually becoming a U.S. citizen some fifty years ago, has exposed Arthur to some of the ugly injustices that someone of his ethnic background is often subjected to living in this country. In the past, even a man of his credentials has all too often found himself in a situation where he had a flashlight shining in on the inside of his car from a guy with a gun on the outside.

"Can I help you?" is the first words out of the guard's mouth.

"Perhaps. I think I'm in the right place, but I can't tell with that light currently blinding me, hehe," Arthur retorts.

"I.D.?" the guard sternly replies to Arthur's gaiety. Arthur hands the guard his I.D. that possesses the presidential seal on it, purposely.

"Dr. Bouya? I'm so sorry sir, I hardly recognized you," the guard suddenly blurts out after recognizing the famous icon.

"*Lemme speak to your supervisor!* Nah, I'm just kiddin', it's quite okay, I know all black people don't look alike—just some of us. It's a good thing I'm on T.V., eh?" Arthur responds, making the choice to continue his conviviality regardless of the guard's seemingly intolerant demeanor.

"Pfft, T.V.," Calvin mumbles loud enough for both of them to hear.

"Hehe, I guess so. Just doing my job, sir," the guard chuckles. "I see you're not traveling alone."

"Oh yes, this is my nephew—Calvin."

"Your nephew, huh? The resemblance is uncanny," the guard replies, now choosing to sprinkle a little of his own ironic mirth on the conversation.

"Well, he's my ex-wife's sister's eldest son. He's staying with me for the month while his mother is in Israel. Ain't that right, Rusty?" Arthur says as he rubs his nephew's head.

"Have you lost your mind, old man?" Calvin grimly asks his driver who he now glares at with a death-stare unlike any Arthur has ever seen from a child. Arthur chuckles at how ridiculous he looks now that he's messed up his usually silky-straightened hair.

"Israel? Jesus, I see why he stayed behind. You're going to hate me for this, but, unfortunately, I can't let him in."

"What? Oh, don't tell me that, I woke up in the middle of the night to a random phone call from the White House telling me I need to come all the way out here. I just got off a flight from Chicago," Arthur shares disconcertingly.

"I wish I could help you, but this is coming all the way from General Clemens himself. After the recent string of attacks, he's not playing any games any longer," the guard responds, his slight sympathetic cadence coming across as a bit uncharacteristic.

"Ah, Jesus, what exactly is in there that he's so worried about people seeing? This is the biggest base I've been to yet."

"I wish I knew myself. At the very least, he can stay with me for a bit while you go on in," he offers.

"I see. Hey, Calvin," Arthur says as he turns back to his passenger. "They're telling me that—"

"Put the AC on, turn on the radio and lock the doors," Calvin instantly tells him. Arthur sticks his head back out the window.

"Well, you heard the kid!"

Arthur pulls the car into the small parking area just outside of the base, and leaves everything on as Calvin instructed.

"Well, this is going smoothly," Arthur says when they park.

"Could be worse," Calvin replies.

"Let's hope not."

"Dr. Bouya ..."

"Yes, Calvin?"

"It's dangerous to go alone. Take this," Calvin says as he hands Arthur his SHED frames.

"Uh, okay," he says as he accepts the glasses, obviously thinking Calvin called his name for a reason more significant than that.

Arthur gets out the car and proceeds back towards the booth area. The guard promptly searches him, and once satisfied, allows him passage.

"Don't worry, doc, I'll keep an eye on him," the guard says, assuring the good doctor that Calvin's in good hands.

On the eastern side of the facility, Joelle was able to successfully sneak around to the fence that encircles the perimeter of the base, thanks to Arthur and Calvin keeping the guard at the front gate distracted. Calvin assured her that she wouldn't need the SHED frames to see where the guards were posted who patrol this particular side of the base, as there would be plenty of light that will help illuminate their movements. However, Joelle currently finds herself wanting to use every new curse word she has learned in her short week on Earth, considering there isn't a single light in sight, effectively disabling her ability to see shit.

Possessing no plausible way to tell if whether Arthur and Calvin successfully made it inside, or if she's currently being looked at through the lens of some high-powered scope mounted on the rifle of some sharpshooter on the other side of the roof of the base, Joelle only has her wits, instincts, and luck to rely on to help her continue to proceed with this half-witted, tenuous plan that sounded borderline feasible when it was being discussed, but in action, has and continues to quickly devolve into a system of lamentable regrets.

After a ten-and-a-half-minute interval, a time frame Joelle feels should've been more than sufficient for them to make it inside safely, she begins scaling the barbed-wire fence directly in front of her. Before doing so, she recalls Arthur's instructions to use her sweatshirt as a cushion to protect her from the razor-sharp edges at the top. She removes her top, exposing her black leotard undergarment that even she forgot she wore beneath, and begins to scale the fence, making sure to keep her sweatshirt firmly clamped between her teeth.

While scaling the gate, Joelle finds herself a bit shocked that she's undertaking this task with such verve, even as the risk of her being caught and experimented on remains firmly planted in her head, thanks to Calvin's dumb imagination, where he did everything in his power to try to spook her as to what will happen if she was to in fact get caught.

She reaches the top of the gate, remaining as quiet as a seasoned cat-burglar, this impressing her somewhat, and places the sweater over the barbed-wired as instructed. The trick works like a charm, and she safely climbs over the fence and scales back down on the other side without a scratch. Joelle sees the door Calvin was talking about earlier during their huddle, and makes her way towards a nearby shrub, where she plans to wait until one of the guards exits.

Finally, something goes right in her favor, as she didn't have to wait long until a guard exited the facility. The guard, fully clad in military gear with an accompanying assault rifle strapped around his chest and dangling from his hip, reaches into his pocket and removes two foreign devices she's never seen before: a cigarette and a lighter. Naturally, Joelle experiences another episode or "upgrade" as Calvin has come to call it, which only intensifies when she looks at the fire that appears almost magically in the air from the tiny gadget.

As she sits in the shrub and waits for this man to finish evaporating his cigarette, whether she realizes it or not, it appears that Joelle is, perhaps for the first time, experiencing what it means to be in a rush and now can't help but to gradually grow more and more anxious the longer and longer she waits for him to open the door and walk back in, so she can sneak in behind him. This is apparent now, as her breathing has become more swift and rapid. She can even feel her heartbeat thump harder within the crevices of her upper neck. Clearly, her newly discovered anxiety isn't all in her head. This all could be due to her being in a situation for the first time, where she's forced to wait on someone else to make something happen in her favor—her favor being to remain alive. Never before, from what she's come to know about human beings, has she felt more like one of them.

It isn't too much longer after this episode that the guard, who she watches with the same unshakeable gaze a puppy has when his owner is eating a delicious snack out of a greasy bag, grabs the mostly-charred stick from his lips and makes a motion indicating that he's about finished with his costly stress-reliever. Joelle, thanks to her recent episode, realizes that he's done and is about to go back inside the base.

All that is left, she thinks to herself, is for him to drop the tattered stick to the ground and follow up with the trademark, complimentary boot-crush to fully extinguish the flame on the cigarette in an effort to keep the air a little less toxic. But it never comes. Unpredictably, the man tosses the cigarette, coincidentally, directly in Joelle's direction, which slightly startles her, distracting her, and as a result, causing her to lose focus on his re-entry into the base. By the time she looks back up, the guard has already opened the door back into the base and is currently making his way back inside. Joelle's previous anxiety level is nothing compared to what it currently is, with each second passing only doubling it in intensity. A modicum of level-headedness grants her only a literal second to debate if it's too late to catch this door that is currently closing, or to just let it shut and wait for another guard to step out again for some rapid, fresh breaths of carcinogenic air. She feels the chances are very likely that another guard will come out eventually, so she decides it'll be wise not to run for the door and risk being spotted, and to instead be patient and just wait.

But her mind no longer has the power to control what her body does, so even though her mind was telling her no, her body ... her body was telling her yes. She knows it was, because about half a second ago, while she was preoccupied on how to proceed, her body has already jumped out of her shrubbery hideout and is currently about halfway from stopping this door to her freedom from closing.

If it wasn't for the super-luminous search light that suddenly lit up on her position, exposing her like a flare lit inside of a giant, dark cave exposes the ghastly, yet farouche shadow of a curious explorer, Joelle would've surely kept going and had made it inside the base, probably without even having to touch the door at all. But, this is perhaps what Calvin meant when he said there would be plenty of light over there to help her see. What he forgot to mention was that the light was supposed to be used to help *her* spot the guards, not the other way around.

As she looks up at the bright bulbs, Joelle quickly realizes that this is the second time men with guns have done this to her, and now understands that these bastards do this not to help you see, which light is rightfully supposed to be used for, but ironically, to help blind you. And it does, at least temporarily. The difference between this time and the last, is that Joelle doesn't hear anyone screaming or shouting, nor does she hear the now familiar sounds of clips of ammunition flying out the barrels of automatic rifles. Joelle assumes this absence of gunfire has to be some sort of misunderstanding, because as she's come to learn, men with guns plus a girl without guns always equals *rat-tat-tat-tat-tat*, and that's the way it is. Perhaps, she entertains, it may have something to do with the fact her hands are in the air right now, something she's learned is a pretty standard gesture that people on this planet tend to perform when they have armed weapons pointed at them. Sadly, at this juncture, she can only assume that she has a few dozen pointed at her, as the oh-so-kind operator of the giant spotlight above her continues to make sure she has just enough light to not ever see anything again in her life.

Using this opportunity of what a part of her is assuming must be a glitch in human-to-alien interaction, Joelle begins to slowly back up into the shrubs that her body escaped from without her permission not too long ago. After all, if this is some sort of man-armed/woman-unarmed system malfunction, she might as well capitalize on it.

Two steps back so far, and not a single loud bang yet. Oddly enough, the spotlight follows her the same way her eyes followed every movement of that guard at the door from earlier. Joelle decides instead of making a break for it, she's going to slowly crouch and ease back into the bushes behind her as if no one ever saw her left them, which she realizes in retrospect, tip-toeing could've been the better way to exit out of them when heading for the door, considering that that door took like an hour to close anyway.

"Take the shot."

Joelle was right, at least partially. There was a rifle pinned on her the entire time, but only a single one, and the wielder of such a rifle just received his order to shoot the hostile, that being Joelle, after patiently waiting for the command to do so.

An advance infrared scope tracks Joelle, who now sits as comfortably as she can inside of the bushes she once called a base of operations, and that she probably now calls a magical cloak capable of rendering her completely invisible. Or, if not that, then maybe a reinforced, bulletproof shield that can protect her from any physical threat. Anything except a finicky shrub.

Perhaps it's because of how quiet this area is, and that the guards there wish for it to remain that way lest they ruin their tranquil operations, but the loud bang that Joelle has come to associate with a gun every time one is pointed at her is strangely absent, and has instead been replaced with a soft, yet audible thump—like that of a door closing, when the guard finally pulls the trigger. However, she would be foolish to think that this peculiar, suppressed sound from his rifle is any less lethal than the ones she's used to hearing from others, because judging by how quickly her body dropped to the ground like a restaurant sign cut off its hinges by some unidentified resting object once he shoots her, she is no longer conscious to even realize that the result from the bullet when he pulled the trigger is not only super-effective at completely taking her down, but it also does something that no bullet ever shot at her has—touched her.

About a minute later after the impossible has just occurred, the guard who stepped outside for a cigarette break earlier, has again emerged from the base. Apparently, he's been alerted to the situation and has returned with another guard to apprehend the body that was just shot down.

"She's in the bush over there. Pull her out," the marksman from the roof who took the shot relays to the men below.

"Got it," the cigarette-plucking soldier responds.

"Hey, Sanders? You know that would've been your ass if she got in right? You owe me big time," the marksman says from atop the three-story facility.

"Yeah, thanks man. Whatever you need," he replies.

"I know. Actually, imma need you to file the report. Oh, and make sure you don't leave out the part where you didn't see a woman who was sitting ten feet in front of you, almost sneak up on you," he says as he continues to unhandily scold him for his incompetence. He only stops when he looks up at the night sky after hearing the first humble rumblings of a storm that's brewing.

"Yeah. I got it," Sanders responds unenthusiastically.

"How did you not see her, man?" this time Sanders' partner asks, adding to Sanders' already existential grief.

"Are you serious, Jerry? I can barely see in front of my own two hands out here."

The guards make it to the bushes and carefully move the greenery out the way that continues to hide her face from them.

"Man, she's young. Broad must be from another planet to try to sneak into here with everything going on," Sanders' partner shares. "That, or she's on that Exile."

"Hey, come on, man," Sanders responds to his partner's remarks, indicating that Exile is still a subject that shouldn't be discussed so liberally in the open.

"What? She's knocked out, relax. What the hell were you doing over here, chica? Have you not been watching the news?" Jerry asks the unconscious daredevil.

"Wow, look at the size of these darts, I've been waiting to see what these new Sleep rounds can do. Look at this," Jerry says as he pulls out the tranquilizer dart from her arm. "She's out like an ostrich."

"Out like an ostrich?"

"Yeah 'out like an ostrich.' What, you never heard that—it's an expression here in Opia."

"No, it is not," Sanders asserts.

"Aren't you from Mammoth Cave, Kentucky? You don't know."

"Shut up and just help me with this," Sanders say as he reaches to pull the body out of the shrubs. "And you're filling out half the paperwork because it was your post I was out here covering."

"I told you I'll be back in two minutes!"

The two men together grab Joelle's unconscious body and begin carrying her towards the side door. As they enter the base, the reason why their conversation can only continue to be heard from the marksman on the roof above them outside, is because the door that Joelle had so desperately wanted to enter through earlier, still hasn't closed long after they have already gone through it.

———

"Alright, you're clear," the guard near the front gate tells Arthur after he finally finishes patting him down more thoroughly than your typical, disgruntled TSA agent.

"Well, that took a while," Arthur admits.

"Well, we can't afford to take any chances with everything that has been going on recently."

"No, the attacks, I understand. It actually surprises me that it's only you out here in case such an event were to occur."

"Well, it wasn't always this way, but this site is a little different from all the other ones. Believe me, I'm the only one out here for a reason. We're looking forward to that cock-sucker passing through this entrance. We have just the thing to set him and his friends straight," the guard unscrupulously shares.

"I'm not surprised. If I know Clemens, it's that it was only a matter of time before he found the right weapon for the job."

"And the right one he has. You go on ahead doc, and don't worry about your nephew, I'll keep my eye on him."

"I don't doubt you for a second. Thank you, sir."

Arthur finally picks up his belongings and makes his way inside of the base, alone. Once inside, he's introduced to a large main room that's encumbered with makeshift cubicles, ramps, and hallways, made seemingly of an assortment of sheet metal and plastic—almost entirely opposite of what he thought the inside of this facility would look like. The hallways, specifically, are more like tunnels of bubbled plastic that branch off into other small tunnels that leads to other rooms. Each room it appears, is designed to host some sort of specific job conducive to the overall functionality of the base. It's more so now that he's inside, that Arthur realizes this camp is much more of a hive than anything else—especially considering how many soldiers are present at any given time. Even as a man who is constantly in the presence of the leader of the U.S. Armed Forces, the mere sight of all these soldiers are enough to make Arthur feel like abandoning this mission altogether. Maybe a lot of it has something to do with what'll happen to them if they get caught—after all, he knows first hand how the government treats those who trespass on military installations.

"Dr. Bouya! Dr. Bouya! Arthur, over here!" a voice suddenly calls out. Before Arthur can locate the person of whoever is shouting his name, he hears the rapid click-clacking of high-heels growing higher and higher in volume. Like a child who's attention on anything is suddenly averted by the sound of an approaching ice cream truck, Arthur's gaze goes from searching for a face, to fixating on the matte, black pumps that make their way to his location. It is when the shoes finally come to a stop that he looks up to see that the driver of those pumps is someone he hasn't looked into the eyes of in far too long.

"Beatrice? Oh my god, it's been a lifetime!" Arthur joyously responds with.

"It's been two—of all the familiar places! I'm surprised the president let you out of his little War Room to mingle with us little people," she quips as she hugs him tightly.

"I should be saying that to you. Look at all this—talk about Top Secret. What are you doing here?" he asks her, amazed at how excited he is to see her.

"You sound surprised. Isn't this your field of expertise?"

"My field of expertise is theoretical physics; I study String Theory, not Conspiracy Theory," he jokes.

"You speak as if I know something you don't, which is odd to say the least, considering it's coming from the person who discovered the 'X-Mass' on Apophis. Talk about conspiracies, half of the people here —scientists especially—don't even believe in your so-called discovery.

"I know good and well how my 'peers' perceive any discovery I make, let alone one of a foreign origin. The question is, do you?" he inquires, seeking to see where she stands on the controversial subject.

"Even if I didn't, your enthusiasm, when I finally received a transcript of your findings, practically leapt off of the page as I was reading it. Arthur, your gift was never in making scientific breakthroughs or discovering things, it was in convincing others to be excited about the things that were being discovered," she proudly reminds him. "I was a believer the moment I was told it was you who made the discovery—and I just want to say congratulations."

"I think you might be the only one who believes a congratulations was in order, hehe. But thank you, Beatrice."

"You've always had a way with words, Arthur, but you never needed me to tell you that."

"It's refreshing to know that there's at least two people in here who don't live in an enclosed, military-guarded box. Well, since I have your attention already, how about you tell me what *that's* about?" Arthur says as he points to the large embankment located at the rear of the base, closed off and sealed inside of a large bubble-like structure.

"Oh, that? Heck, I would be more than happy to show you but even we're not allowed back there," she reveals.

"How come?"

"This must be your first camp visit. Even though the last thing you can call this place is a camp. If anything, it's more like a—"

"—a hive. I know."

"Great tin-foil-hat minds think alike, I see. Just look around you, everything and everyone operates like they're protecting a queen or something."

"Yeah, I see what you mean. Lately, I've been extremely caught up in trying to figure out what's the best way to explain to the public what the UNSELF's creatures are—I don't think they're too convinced on the whole 'they came from underground' spiel anymore."

"Oh, me and half my staff almost fell out of our chairs when you said that. The reason I can tell that this is your first time at one of these base camps, is because this is the only camp where even the people who were told to come here can't do any kind of research on the asteroid debris that landed here," she says.

"How come?"

"No one knows for sure. This is one time where the soldiers here have seen more than the scientists. If I had to guess, I'd say it has everything to do with them finally finding something that they've been dying to find."

"What do you mean?" he asks her.

"I used to think these camps were here for us to get a better idea to study what fell from that rock. But it turns out I couldn't have been more wrong. These camps weren't put up to study anything, they're here because these guys are looking for something specific—something that they don't want anyone to see."

"What is it they're looking for?"

"I should be asking *you* that, Mr. X-Mass. After all, didn't you see how stringent the president suddenly became over "protecting" the public from the harmful debris from the asteroid, all of a sudden? Originally ... in fact, for the entire two years leading up to Apophis, not once was he concerned with people having access to the debris. If anything, he encouraged people to put on their hard hats and dig up as much information on the rocks as they can once it crashed. It wasn't until the day after they blew Apophis up, that any and all meteor fragments that fell from the sky were deemed government property and that you could even be detained for obtaining any."

Arthur chuckles. "And *I'm* the one who believe in conspiracy theories?" he cynically responds to the unlikely scheme.

"Well, you explain it to me then. Because if I'm not mistaken, it wasn't until your X-Mass hypothesis was taken seriously, that everyone suddenly started acting funny."

"Maybe he's just worried about the dangerous radiation levels that people can be exposed to from the fragments."

"I see I'm not the only one who watches his press conferences," Beatrice responds.

"All I'm saying is, there could be more than one reason why the president wouldn't want people near any of these rocks. Saying it's strictly because I happened to notice a change in Apophis' trajectory is an unsubstantiated leap."

"Okay fine, but why wouldn't he want any *scientists* that he personally hand-picked to study them, near any of these rocks either?"

"That, I don't know," he admits.

"Well, whatever the reason is lies in that embankment. And so does the answer to whatever your X-Mass is." Beatrice pauses for a moment. "How about you and I go see if there's treasure where the *'X'* is?" she shamelessly suggests.

"Are you crazy, Beatrice? They'll toss us in a military prison til the end of time if we're caught. Where is all this coming from, you weren't like this before. It hasn't been *that* long since I've last seen you."

"Apparently, it has been Arthur, because clearly you forgot who I am. Maybe it hasn't been for you because you've been busy becoming famous, but twenty-six years is a long time. You left, found someone, got married, and then divorced all before I even knew you had a girlfriend. The Academy was over two decades ago, Arthur, so it *has* been that long since we've seen each other."

"The Academy, wow. Now look at us: two ancient relics of the past conspiring to trespass on government property."

"Maybe we don't have to trespass."

"How do you mean?"

"Well, technically aren't *you* government property? If anyone should have clearance, it's you. Maybe that award-winning slick tongue of yours can lead us to the gold," she quips to her former colleague.

"Maybe. But if anyone has a slick tongue, it's you, considering I'm still standing here entertaining this madness."

"Come on, Arthur. It can't hurt to ask. I was always your partner-in-crime, let's do it if not only just for old-times sake," Beatrice practically begs him, to which Arthur lets out a heavy sigh. "What's today, Thursday? Yeah, we'll make it a Throwback Thursday, hehe. Remember that?"

"Unfortunately, yes. I swear if it wasn't for your inexplicable ability to convince me to do things I hated, I would've not gotten into half the trouble we did while in grad school. Alright, come on, but we do this my way okay?"

"You've always been the sun I can't help but to orbit around. Lead the way, Superstar."

Arthur and Beatrice begin casually walking around the facility. With Arthur leading, Beatrice can't help but to feel lost after a while, considering Arthur has already lapped the base twice, seemingly moving with no sense of direction or purpose.

"Arthur, my love? Um, what are we doing?" she asks, now a little confused by her partner's unusual trekking.

"Scanning."

"Scanning? For?"

"Signs of non-intelligent life. Or at least someone who you can sweet talk into letting us take a peep inside the embankment."

"Me, sweet talk? What makes you think I'll have any success with these bozos?"

"Well, because you've already convinced *this* bozo to go on this stupid mission with you. Look right there, he looks just like your type. Let's go, I'll back you up," he says as he rubs her shoulders in an effort to rise her morale.

"Alright, I got this," she says in response to his uplifting words.

Arthur begins making his way towards the guard. Reluctantly, Beatrice follows.

"Excuse me, officer?" she says, her tone suddenly extremely polite and amiable.

"How can I help you?" the officer responds.

"Hi, I'm Dr. Beatrice Medina, and this is my colleague Dr. Arthur—"

"Boo-yah! Wow, I had no idea you would be coming here, sir. It's such an honor to meet you!" the officer shares, his mood suddenly doing a complete 180 once he recognizes Arthur. "I'm Steve Buchanan —uh, First Lieutenant, Steve Buchanan. I'm the lead shooting guard around here—my kid is such a fan of your show *Grazing Incidents.*" Beatrice finally retracts her still extended palm once she realizes it will remain unengaged.

"Why, it's a pleasure to meet you, Lieutenant. I appreciate that very much," Arthur says as he engages in the overly-enthusiastic handshake Steve is currently blessing him with.

"Sure, sure. What can I do for you, doctor?"

"Actually, I do require some assistance. I'm here directly under the president's orders to inspect the—well, you know ... the piece of hardware lying out back there."

"Oh, you mean the—"

"Yeah, you know what I'm talking about," Arthur says, as he puts on a more confident persona.

"I could've sworn he had already sent a team there to inspect, hold on let me relay this really quick to be sure."

"No, no wait, I wouldn't do that," Arthur suddenly says to him. "To be honest, I'm not really supposed to even be telling *you* this but—me being the one who discovered the X-Mass and all, the president wanted me to come down here myself and take a look at the impact site directly. You know our president—even his advisor needs an advisor, and he's not trying to have any more hiccups occur concerning this whole X-Mass thing. He told me to come down here directly, meet up with Dr. Medina, and see what I can find out personally about the crash site."

"I swear that sounds just like him. Alright, I'm not trying to be the fool who denies Dr. *Boo-yah!* access to his own discovery. You two, come with me."

Arthur and Beatrice exchange two silent but ebullient, wide-eyed expressions of elation when they realize their risky, on-the-fly plan worked as they begin following Steve, the shooting guard, into the east wing of the base. After walking down a series of corridors, some with short ramps and steps, they make it to one of the bubble like tunnels Arthur noticed earlier.

"This is some place you guys put up."

"Yeah, this is nothing, wait until you see this weird artifact we found. Unlike anything we've ever seen. Well, technically you're the one who discovered it, so if anyone has seen it, it's you. But I'm sure seeing it on some monitor in space is nothing compared to seeing it up close. Right this way."

The guard leads the two past another two sets of interconnecting hallways which finally leads to the entrance of where the embankment is. The guard hands Arthur a keycard and steps away.

"I'll be out here when you return," he assures them before turning away and heading back down the hall.

Arthur accepts his generous gift, and looks at Beatrice with a look that encompasses a multitude of sentiments.

"Here we go," she says to his ambiguous expression, and without any further hesitation, Arthur proceeds to enter the card into the keycard slot that'll open the door.

WWUUUUUURRNNNNNNNNNN! WWUUUUUURRNNNNNNNNNN! WWUUUUUURRNNNNNNNNNN! WWUUUUUURRNNNNNNNNNN! WWUUUUUURRNNNNNNNNNN!

"AHHH, OH MY GOD, WHAT THE HELL IS THAT NOISE?" Beatrice immediately yells after an alarm goes off inside of the corridor that they're standing in.

"I DON'T KNOW!" Arthur shrieks back while covering his ears.

"DON'T MOVE! WAIT A MINUTE, HOLD STILL, IS IT—I THINK IT'S COMING FROM YOUR GLASSES!" she yells out over the loud blaring.

"MY GLASSES?? WHAT THE—!"

Steve, the shooting guard, immediately turns back and takes Arthur's glasses from him in an effort to stop the alarm ringing from continuing.

On the other side of the base, the two guards who continue to take their time discussing whose job it is to fill out the paperwork before they take Joelle to the appropriate room to process her, are suddenly jolted out of their seats when they hear the same alarm blaring from Arthur's glasses. Immediately, one of them gets up and leaves the room that there are in, before finalizing what should be done about Joelle's paperwork. After waiting no more than a nail-biting fifteen seconds, the second guard also leaves and hurries out the room to inspect the reason for that alarm going off. Assured that Joelle won't be waking up for at least another two hours, he decides that leaving her for no more than two minutes would be of no further consequence to him, and runs out the room also.

"Finally," Joelle whispers to herself after she opens one eye slightly to inspect the room that the guards left her in, making certain no one is around to see her awaken from a drug that should've had her on at least her sixth dream by now.

Joelle sits up and is beyond thankful that the conversation she overheard the two guards having while she was "unconscious" over whether they should or shouldn't handcuff her, ended with the latter. While trying to figure out her next move, considering that everything that just happened wasn't at all according to the plan, she can't help but to spend a second or two geeking over how smart she was for pretending to be hit by those darts that were shot at her, and how swift she must've been to make it look like she was shot by them. All she really did was snatch them out of the air during the same motion as when she pretended she got hit, where she then, while pretending to be knocked out, drained the anesthetic fluid into the ground—careful to do it on the side of her that couldn't be seen by any scope or scanner

—and surreptitiously pierced the empty darts into her arm to make it appear as if they successfully hit her.

The fact that she pulled this off is all it takes for a new sense of valor to fill up inside of her, much like when she was on Apophis and had to save the very artifact she is now currently searching for. With fear now being substituted for confidence, and determination now replacing doubt, Joelle collects herself and finally stands—ready to do whatever it may take to ensure that she leaves this base with what rightfully belongs to her, no matter what.

Chapter Twenty-Nine

REUNITED

April 18th. 9:40 P.M. (EDT)

"I've never seen a pair of glasses with an alarm on them."

"Yeah, I sincerely apologize. I almost forgot they were on there," Arthur says to the guard closest to him inside of the small room.

"As you can tell, his hearing isn't the best anymore," Beatrice interjects, doing what she can to dissipate some of the heat being thrown at her friend.

"Nope, it isn't. So, I had to have them install this darned thing into my glasses so I can even get up in the morning. Believe it or not, it's actually a very common thing many old folks do nowadays. One time I was in the Situation Room and it went off—let me tell you something, I never laughed so hard in my life when I saw General Clemens jump up like that. That man almost had a heart attack and so did I."

"Well unfortunately, we're going to have to hold on to these until you leave, if that's okay with you," another guard inside of the room tells him.

"No, I completely understand," Arthur responds.

About nine or so armed guards currently occupy the room, standing around Arthur and Beatrice while they sit at a table and try to explain the reasoning for the alarm going off.

"Okay, Dr. Bouya, if you and your assistant would come with us, there's just a few more things we wish to check with you before we're done."

"Wait, *assistant?* Hold up—" Beatrice suddenly says, clearly irritated by the inaccurate term.

"Sure thing," Arthur responds to the officers.

"Did he just call me an *assistant?*"she asks Arthur in an angry whisper.

"Not now, Beatrice. They're about to find out about us, we have to do something."

"You know what ..." she says after thinking for a bit. The two get up and proceed to walk with the guards to a room near where the access to the embankment was.

"I knew I couldn't trust you," she randomly blurts out as they all begin making their way down the hall.

"What? Trust who? Who are you talking about?"

"Assistant? Really? That's what you told them? That I'm your "*assistant?*"

"Beatrice, you okay? Come on, let's go, this isn't funny—you're going to get us caught," he whispers nervously.

"I'm not laughing," she confirms before Arthur tries to gently grab her arm. "Don't you touch me, goddamn it!"

At this point, even the guards are confused as they look at each other for answers.

"What the hell is wrong with you, woman?" Arthur suddenly blurts out to her.

"Woman? I know your Hyena-howling-in-the-tall-grass-African ass isn't trying to play me? Oh, so you think because I'm a *woman*, it's okay to tell the president that I'm your assistant, huh? And I bet he went right along with it too, huh? Is that what you told your wife all them nights you had to work late? That you were with your *assistant* working on some lab project, hmm? That you were out late stirring your little spoon inside some beaker, huh? Mixing up some chemicals, tryna get a little chain reaction going, hmmm? Let's get one thing cleared up right now—I'm nobody's *assistant* boo-boo, okay?" she lays on him.

"Beatrice, what has gotten into you?" Arthur asks her, completely thrown-off and confused.

"You haven't! Tuh! Hell, I can tell you what DIDN'T get into me—you! Excuse me officers, this man has been lying to you, he's not here to meet no assistant, he just been trying to get to me all this time—even after I blocked his ass on every SHED and social media app there is, he still always tries to find a way to get to me. He's really here to—"

"Beatrice, please!" Arthur shouts.

"Whatchu calling my name for?" she says before turning back towards the guards. "Like I was saying—he's supposed to be here to inspect the embankment by himself. He only made up that story about him needing to inspect it with me so he can be with me in there alone. He wanted me to go in there with him so he can finally get a chance to get a taste of this concoction. Well, Mr. Celebrity, you will *never* sample *this* mixture. I'm glad you guys are here—if it's okay with y'all, I rather y'all just take him there by himself and leave me out of it, please," she says as her voice starts to break a little.

Surprisingly, the officers fall for this and one of them take Beatrice back to the main area, while the other decides if the fuss of confirming whether or not that this prominent science icon is really here to inspect something he downright discovered is true or not, is more hassle than it's worth. So he hands him back the key card and tells him to proceed. Arthur thanks him with a complimentary smile and silently thanks Beatrice for her sacrifice before he continues along.

Finally back at the keypad, he takes the card and this time is able to use it. The panel beeps as it acknowledges the card, and the doors slide apart allowing Arthur entrance. After proceeding down a small tubular hallway, he finally enters into the large room that contains the embankment and the foreign artifact that many have come to understand as something that can't be explained.

Upon witnessing it in person, Arthur is left entranced by the sight of what he now sees in the trench before him.

"My God," he utters.

Unable to completely take in what he's currently beholding, he takes a seat along the edge of the embankment and sits there as if he's finally reached the edge of the meaning of his existence.

Outside of the base, Calvin continues to play with the radio stations while he wallows in his boredom. It's gotten to the point where he has tried to create new music by playing multiple stations at the same time, similar to a DJ who mixes and overlap different records to try to get a certain vibe flowing. The result, as Calvin acknowledges, is a resounding 'meh.' The single guard outside, he who has eerily continued to alternately look down at his newspaper and look up at Calvin every 3.7 seconds, now appears to be doing something different from before—he has his hand pressed into his ear and seems to be affected by whatever he's hearing over his headset. His face, which up until now has always displayed an immutable scowl, now somehow appears to be even more distraught—as if in addition to finding out he's adopted, he just now learned his wife is really his sister from his original family.

After a couple of head nods, he steps out of his booth and immediately makes his way towards Calvin. Not necessarily worried, but not necessarily completely unbothered either, Calvin remains in his placid position even as the guard approaches him.

Tap. Tap. Tap. The guard arrives at the car and raps on the driver's side window. Calvin lets down the car window on the passenger side only, however.

"We have a situation, you need to come with me."

"Where are we going? Because that booth looks very uncomfortable for two people to be sitting inside of."

"Inside. There's a drill going on," the sullen guard tells him.

"Wouldn't I just be safer in here?" Calvin asks. "I unlocked the door, so you could get in."

"Let's go kid, this isn't a joke."

"Well, I'm hungry, I hope y'all have snacks or something inside. And what's that noise?"

"The alarm for a drill. It's nothing to worry about."

Unaware as to what has occurred, Calvin gets out the car and heads inside of the facility with the guard.

Now inside the base, the guard blindsides Calvin with some new, undesirable information.

"Unfortunately, I'm going to have to keep you in this room until the situation is cleared."

"What? But you said it was only a drill."

"Sometimes a drill can develop into something bigger. This happens to be one of those times. Don't worry, I'll bring you some food. You like balogna? Yeah, you like balogna. I'll be back."

The moment the guard turns his head, Calvin delivers about seven milliamps of electricity into the guard's neck from his SHED band. Though the band definitely has enough power to kill if necessary, Calvin made sure to set it to where this guard won't be getting up for at least another fifteen minutes.

"Sorry about that, but I have a side mission to complete," Calvin shares with the collapsed guard before running out of the room. Once in the hallway, he immediately makes his way to the main hall in an effort to find Joelle before anyone else does.

Back inside the room where Joelle was last seen, the two incompetent guards that were responsible for her continue to argue as to how either of them could've let her escape.

"How could you leave her, you idiot?"

"She was out cold, and an alarm went off! I was only gone for two minutes, how the hell did she wake up so fast?"

"You better goddamn pray she just went to the bathroom or something. Find her, now!"

KSSSHHHHH. The doors that allowed Arthur to witness the very thing his mind is now having trouble believing, has once again opened. This time, three guards enter and address the now depressed doctor.

"Dr. Bouya, we have an emergency. Could you please come with us?"

Joelle, I hope you're okay.

Besides saying these words under his breath and only to himself, Arthur gets up from the edge of the embankment without a peep and dusts off the dirt from the back side of his slacks. Even the noisy alarm that continues to blare doesn't faze him in the least, as whatever he saw in the embankment has effectively robbed him of any and all excitement. He turns and glumly heads towards the guards who wait for him at the doorway. He walks past them, and the doors shut again once they're all gone.

Joelle waits a few seconds before emerging from the place she's been hiding for the past few minutes—which was behind a stack of crates inside the same room Arthur just left. Up until the moment the guards came to escort Arthur out, she was happy to see that he also made it to this place, but more importantly that he was okay, too—at least physically. And once she arrived here and saw Arthur sitting there alone, her plan was to go to him and let him know that their plan—well their consistently, ever-changing plan—was successful, and that she'd also made it in, clearly okay as well.

All of this, she was hoping to do while finding out what's happened to Calvin, and at the very least, praying that he could say the same for himself. However, such things will have to be postponed, as once again, the trio's plan of action has shifted thanks to this alarm, it which as she's probably right to assume, is informing all the personnel in the building that there's an intruder amongst them—and it's most likely not Calvin or Arthur ... but most likely her.

If there wasn't any indication before that the time before Joelle would have to spend the rest of her years subjugated to government testing, or at the very least inside a prison cell, was quickly coming to end, then the now flashing red light and automatic closing of the fortified, reinforced steel gate that is now coming down over the only door that one can use to access this room, would probably serve as the most effective one.

Yet, even as grim as her situation appears, there's something about

Joelle's distinct proclivity for accepting her seemingly dire situations that she's all-too-often tossed in, that grants her an unexpected sense of appreciation. It's this appreciation that may very well be proportionately linked to the importance of her accomplishing whatever task that the powers that be are preventing her from completing at any given time, that causes her to press on without any compunction. In fact, she finds solace in knowing that it is likely only minutes before she's at the mercy of this vile species' whim—they who continue to do whatever they can to prevent her from learning all she can about herself—that allows her to no longer be phased by the many distractions that befall her. The blaring alarm and flashing red light ultimately allows her to approach the embankment in front of her, not with a sense of fear or worry, but a reminder that she's exactly where she needs to be, exactly at the time she needs to be. For as she's come to learn since her short stay on this planet so far, if she's not being chased or shot at, then she's not on the right path.

Joelle begins walking to the trench and is surprised when she realizes it is much deeper than she had thought. From where she's standing, she thought she would have at least seen a part of whatever it is that crashed here. What she has gathered, however, is that whatever fell here was bigger and larger than anything else that came from Apophis—and only the artifact that she's once attempted to sacrifice her life for is dense enough to create such a deep hole. It is here she realizes, that her, Calvin, and Arthur had indeed infiltrated the right camp and even more luckily, they've reached it before Jumo has.

Now only four feet from the edge, Joelle can now begin to see the curvature of the other side, indicating that the hole is at least sixty feet deep. If the artifact she seeks is here, then it's indistinguishable, everlasting shine will surely be noticeable even at that depth.

Joelle finally reaches the edge, then stops. She peers down into the abyss and what she sees drastically changes her expression. Her expression doesn't resemble that of someone who's finally found what they've almost killed or died to find. If anything, it resembles the expression Arthur had when he just finished looking down into the same hole—and now Joelle understands why. Inside of the hole, at the very bottom, is no artifact, no meteor, and not even parts of some alien spacecraft—

all that's there at the bottom, is just a bare, blank platform. And on that platform, is a single UNSELF creature, standing alone.

"I finally found you, Kayelimneusia," a voice says from the loudspeaker inside of the room. This voice belonging to only one individual —Jumopikwaris.

Chapter Thirty

THE MOBILE STATUE

April 18th. 10:10 P.M. (EDT)

THE GATE COVERING the door that leads to the inside of the room housing the mostly empty embankment, lifts up, and the door opens up right after. Rushing into the room is just about every guard in the facility, they all who flank Joelle on every side, making sure to occupy every degree along the circumference of the circle they create around her with a man and a gun. The only people who don't come rushing in but instead walks in together is Calvin, Arthur and of course, Jumo himself.

"In all my nights as an Earthling, I thought I'd never see the day. Kayelimneusia ... is that ... is that really you??" Jumo dramatically asks his elusive friend upon entering the room, to which Joelle gives no response to but instead just wears a face that displays a look of anger and disappointment—and not yet, she's hoping, betrayal.

"Or wait, it's *Joelle* you're going by now, right? Even though that's not your name. You know you could've just went by Kay-elle for all that. *Joelle ... Kay-elle*—almost the same thing. Plus, it kinda sounds like *Kal-el*, you know... like Superman? He was also an alien who landed on Earth! Superman! Clark Kent? You know who I'm talking about? Ah, you don't know."

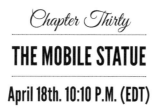

As Jumo prattles on, Joelle continues to try her best to make sense of everything that's happening before her. Maybe it's because they come from the same planet and this just may be an ability of their people, or because Jumo is just good at reading people, but he senses Joelle's desperate yearn for answers and decides to ease her mind a little by filling in some of the blanks.

"Oh, before I forget—here's your cut," Jumo says while handing Arthur an envelope presumably filled with cash. "Annndddd here's yours, Cal. I can't thank y'all two enough for helping me find my friend. I could cry right now—if I knew how to."

This transaction is sufficient in creating the scowl of betrayal that Joelle hoped to death would have never come. Tears substitute words, as Joelle is now hurt worse than she's ever been—on this planet or her own.

"Hey, you got a little something on your cheek." Jumo says when he notices a faint purple glow now emanating from Joelle's face. "So, Joelle —Arthur here tells me that you don't remember much outside of what happened on Apophis. Well, you're in luck, as I am in a very good mood and am willing to divulge some of the things that may have been confounding you since your arrival. But first, however, I'm going to need a favor from you," he tells her.

"What?" she says, after surprising even herself that she still has a voice and one of reason to boot.

"Oh, so you *can* talk. I know that's something we don't do much on Vartiga, but these *saps* around us—well that's just about the only thing they've perfected on this rock and so it's just about the only thing they do around here apparently. So, it might benefit you to acclimate to their way of doing things for the time being. At least until we leave."

"Vartiga? That's the planet we're from?" she asks, her curiosity suddenly piqued by the subject in Jumo's last statement.

"You don't even remember your home star? No, Vartiga is the "star system"—as they call it here—that we occupy. Holy hell, that explosion really did a number on you. Tell me, what *do* you remember?"

"I remember the Harness, barely," she hesitates to share. Though she's too upset to want to do anything to this man besides tear him in half, her curiosity happens to supersede her anger at this given time.

"Okayyyyyy? And what about the Harness ... what's its function?"

"Isn't it a process designed to absorb the energy emitted from dying stars?" she responds.

"Anddddd?"

"And, our people use that energy as a resource for the benefit of our civilization."

"Anddddd?"

"There's more?"

"Are you kidding? If I was grading you on this, you would've definitely gotten a C+. And you're supposed to be my protegèe? Ha!" he says, slightly berating her.

"Why don't you tell me the rest, then?"

"I told you, I'm going to need a favor from you first."

"What?"

"The Man in The Dirty Robes. Big Cal over here told me you know where to find him. Where is he?"

"Calvin, how could you?" she says almost despondently to an uncharacteristically taciturn Calvin.

"Because you lied to me. You told me you were going to take me to see him. All we've done since then was look for your dumb artifact," he reveals, his tone unfamiliar to Joelle but that she detects is nonetheless sincere.

"I was. We were going to go together, as promised. That never changed."

"No! All you did was lie to me so I can help you!" he rebuts, now yelling. "You screwed me after I trusted you. I guess Chadwick rubbed off on you after all."

"Hey, hey, y'all can argue when y'all are dead," Jumo interjects. "So ... where is he, *Joelle?*"

"I have no idea. And I wouldn't tell you even if I knew," she defiantly responds.

"Oh no, you're going to tell me," he assures her.

"Oh yeah, why's that?"

"Haven't you noticed that something that should've been in that hole is strangely absent?"

"I have," she says after glancing into the hole. "As I'm sure you have, also."

"Yuh-huh. And guess who has it? This *Man in Dirty Robes* a.k.a. Aleph Null."

"You seem to know a lot about him," she asserts.

"Well, I know that he's a very dangerous man. And I know I'm going to need your special gifts in taking him down."

"What gifts?"

BLAMM! Jumo immediately fires a single gunshot at Joelle's face from only a few yards away, the sudden loud bang making her jump, and marvels at how it stops just a foot and a half away from her nose.

"I heard the rumors—but it looks so much better in person," he says to her before she side steps the bullet, sending it to the back wall and just missing the face of a guard far behind her.

"Apparently, I'm not the only one who's learn some tricks while on this planet," she tells him after composing herself.

"Oh, you talking about my babies? I could always do that, you even told Arthur that they're made up of silicon. Wow, your memory really is messed up, get it together, hun. But I will admit, there is something about this planet that allows me better control over them. Yeah, Earth is the shit so far. Anyway, I need to find this man, and I need your help in doing so."

"Why do you need me? Calvin is the one who got me even this far. He can locate anyone much better than I can."

"Oh, he's coming too—it was his idea to bring you along, actually. But it's mainly because of that oh-so fancy ability of yours."

"I can reduce bullets to a fraction of their speed—so what?"

"I'm not talking about that, *baka*. Calvin told me you have the ability to learn about things just by looking at them. This Aleph Null fella is not only dangerous, but like you, also very elusive. So much so, that most of the world believes he is dead. If it wasn't for Calvin's visions, I would consider this to be the case also. You know better than I the limitations of Calvin's ability—but you're only beginning to tap into the limitless capabilities of your own. I need your assistance to help me pinpoint Aleph Null's location," he submits.

"Yeah, good luck with that. I may not remember much, but I have a good idea of what you are planning. You want to release the energy from the artifact to destroy the planet. You really think these people are going to let you just do that?"

"Let me? How do you think I found you, my sweet?" he says, smiling. His last statement renders Joelle silent for a few moments.

"Are you aware that this man is trying to destroy your world!?" she turns and screams to the expressionless crowd of armed guards around them. "Are you going to just sit here and let him? Huh!?"

"He's not here to destroy us, Joelle. In fact, he's already saved us," Arthur says as he steps forward from behind Jumo.

"What are you talking about, Arthur? He's killed hundreds already!" she emphatically retorts. A great deal of her intensity more than likely emanating from her feelings of being betrayed.

"You really don't remember what happened during the last Harness, do you?" Jumo asks. "Joelle, you said the Harness is designed to absorb the energy giving off by dying stars. Well, how exactly do you think we do that?"

"I—"

"EEEEHHHNNNNNNN! Wrong. The artifact you so desperately seek, is just the part of the Harness that stores and keeps the energy contained. *I'll take Astronomy for $500.* Answer—'*This titanic, massive object is the only thing in the universe that can absorb the enormous power emitted from a supernova.*"

"A black hole," Joelle says after thinking about Jumo's quirky statement.

"Daily Double!" Jumo screams out after making the sound effects that are made from the television show when someone accesses this node. "There's a reason why we can only absorb the *excess* energy given off by a dying star. The Harness is an entire event, who's planning stages take place over the course of several centuries, but lasts only a moment."

"But we never used a black hole for that. We used the Mavad."

"We attempted to, for the first time ever. And it was a success. After that, the Mavad was no longer needed."

"Why was that necessary? The original method seemed to work fine."

"It was necessary—to protect them," Jumo says as he points to the men and women around them.

"The Gamma Ray Burst from the star that exploded was pointed directly at Earth. If your people never placed a black hole in the pathway of the blast, we wouldn't be standing here right now," Arthur shares to his former confidant. "I know this because the GRB that was absorbed was the one I was studying most of my adult life. When you and Jumo landed, he approached me and verified everything my research has gathered over the years. Since then, we've worked together, and he has taught us many things about the capabilities of the artifact. And together, we have decided were going to use its tremendous reservoir of energy to power the globe. Just a small portion of the energy contained in that artifact is sufficient to provide the energy necessary to sustain mankind for hundreds of thousands of years."

"No. I can't believe that. I remember the explosion on Apophis. You tried to kill me!" she says, choosing to remain a staunch skeptic to Jumo's unexpected true intention.

"Joelle, the condition of the vessel we landed on Apophis with, was caused by our fleet being destroyed during the Harness. We underestimated the effect of these powerful forces at work. I set a course for Earth and landed us on an asteroid that was also on course to pass close to it. Apophis was meant to bypass this planet, when we landed on it however, we caused its path to be shifted back towards it. The explosion that knocked you out was caused by us crashing through their International Space Station," Jumo reveals to her.

"This can't be," she says to herself, unable to relinquish her disbelief.

"I promise you it's the truth. And it's far from the only one. Join me, Joelle—only together can we help their civilizations thrive just as ours have for billions of years."

Jumo holds his hand out and Joelle stares at it. After all, this *is* the man who she's worked with for the part of her life that she does remember. And it's through him that she now knows everything she does, and it's only through him that she can ever hope to learn more.

"Why?" she suddenly asks, with her head facing the floor.

"Why what?"

"Why this planet? Why save this one? The Harness was performed across the galaxy for eons and never once was it to protect a planet from being destroyed. It seems we had the capability to use black holes to protect planets for a long time, so who was it that decided to protect this one? And why did they?"

"I only know part of that answer. They're known as the Vartigan, and they are the overseers of our star system. We—you and I—we are known as *Kun-Veil.* There are many types of Kun-Veil divided into different categories, much like the different species on this planet are divided based on certain characteristics. You and I come from the type of Kun-Veil who happens to resemble humans here on this planet. I've come to believe we look like them for a reason—I just want to be sure that my reason is the correct one. There are many things I can tell you about where we're from, but it'll take time to reveal all. If you like, I'll explain it all to you over the time we spend together from now on. As far as why the Vartigan sent us—*that* I'm hoping you will tell *me* once we get our artifact back. Until then, I won't entertain any other conclusion other than that it was for no other reason besides one that included helping them, like we did when we protected them during the Harness," he tells her.

"You seem to know much about everything except the most important thing. How convenient."

"You're not the only one who suffered memory loss. The difference is, I can't absorb information from the things around me. That's why I need you. So we can truly find out why are we here."

"But I seem to be the only one who hasn't *killed* anyone to find what I'm looking for," she says to him. "You say you're here to save them, and yet all I've seen you do since you've been here is the opposite."

"I know. There is so much about the Kun-Veil I have to tell you. We only *look* human Joelle, but we are the furthest thing from them. There are things about them that they themselves don't even know. But once I show you, everything that has come to past will become clear and more importantly, why it had to. Allow me to share with you the knowledge of our people, and you too would see that my actions up until now has been and will continue to be entirely conducive to the benefit of their kind."

Joelle takes another look at Jumo's extended hand. This time, she considers everything he's said up until now. If this is the way to the answers she seeks, then she must follow her path.

The moment she goes to grab his hand, the ceiling above her and the wall behind her suddenly explodes, suddenly sending seven severely severed soldiers screaming.

"Is my boy in here?" a woman screams out as a small army of men led by an older Asian woman with a bandana tied around her forehead comes rushing into the hole. "Calvin, where are you? I need my glasses!" she screams out with a thick Chinese accent.

"Mom?" Calvin yells out, confused and astonished.

"What the hell is happening?" Jumo yells out. "Kill them!"

"I can't see!" Calvin's mom yells out through the smoke created by the explosion.

"Mom, get down!"

Suddenly the entire room erupts in gunfire as the armed guards of the base and these new radicals that resemble the men that was chasing Joelle and Calvin just a few days ago, begin exchanging bullets with one another as they descend from the ceiling, almost indistinguishable from the heavy rain that now pours inside of the facility. Calvin runs to his mother to go to protect her, while Arthur runs out of the room.

Jumo uses this opportunity to push Joelle, who's currently distracted, into the gaping hole that almost everyone in the room has forgotten about. He rams her so hard he himself almost slips in with her. Before she even hits the bottom, he has already gotten up and made his way to the pallet of crates that she hid behind not too long ago. Appearing heavier than he assumed, he's forced to push the large crate from the back, sliding it across the floor, looking to end her entire existence if he can.

From inside the hole, Joelle seems to be having trouble shaking off that plunge as she squirms from the pain. Before he can push the large crate on top of her, one of Calvin's mother's men takes a couple shots at him, which an Unself* manages to dive in front of, before the bullets find their way to the back of Jumo's skull. The quick-thinking yet sloppily executed dive by the creature, knocks Jumo onto his back. This hit causes the crate to fall into the hole, where it slows down for a while, before eventually landing on Joelle's leg—breaking it first, and then pinning it. The resulting trauma causes Joelle to scream out in anguish before she completely passes out from the pain. Jumo soon gets up, looks into the hole, and decides the hell with it before walking out of the room, with several Unselfs behind him still taking bullets for him.

"FINISH HER!" he yells to the guards before the door shuts close behind him. With Calvin's mom's men occupied with multiple Unselfs, the armed guards who are clearly on Jumo's payroll, all run towards the edge of the hole and take aim at the incapacitated ingénue lying helplessly at the bottom of the hole.

With not a smidgen of hesitation in their bones, each guard unleashes every bullet in their magazines at Joelle. As they watch the bullets stop in mid-air, they know it's only a matter of time before they pierce her skin and end her life. The perverse guards watching soon realize that their fight isn't over as a couple of them are hit by gunfire coming from more of Calvin's mom's men. The large battle spills outside, and the room where the embankment is, finally grows silent.

Not too much later, Joelle awakens to a sight all-too-familiar to her —a symphony of small metal objects, numbering in the hundreds, inches ever so closely towards her—only this time she is unable to move out of their path. After a few unsuccessful attempts of trying to free herself from the heavy crate that sits on top of her shattered leg, Joelle comes to terms with the fact that this is how it ends for her. It is now quiet enough that she can begin to hear the first of the bullets piercing the wood of the large crate. It's unlike anything she's ever heard before. Seeing something like this unfold in slow motion is truly a spectacle to her, and she can't help but to think that every time she looks at the bullets piercing the wood in slow motion, it almost for a moment seems as if the wood is going to stop the bullet in its track the moment it makes contact—only it never does. The shells continue to crack and push their way through the wood, like a drill penetrating through a two-by-four in super-slow motion—only not as loud. If that fork in the diner she felt when she pressed it into her hand is anything to go by, she knows her death won't be painless in the least, so she does what she can to mentally prepare herself for the last thing she is ever going to feel again, and closes her eyes.

With her sight now shut off, her ears pick up something she isn't sure it would've if she never closed her eyes. But what she hears isn't the sound of what she expected—her flesh being penetrated by hot metal—rather it's the shuffling of feet making their way to her position. Yes, it is much worse—Jumo has come to finish the job.

"Joelle, let me help you," Arthur says as he scrambles to make his way to her position.

"Arthur?"

"Oh my god," he says as he watches the flock of shells and now the rain coming from the hole in the ceiling too, slowly descend towards her body. He immediately makes an effort to try to lift the crate off of her legs. After several earnest attempts, it isn't long before he realizes it's been a long time since he had even half the strength to lift this thing.

"Arthur, what are you doing here?" she frantically asks him.

"What does it look like? I'm trying to rescue you, girl. Ahhh! Goddamn, this thing is heavy."

"I don't understand, I thought you were working with Jumo."

"I was working to keep you alive. Jumo knew you were going to be here a long time ago, thanks to Calvin. It is also thanks to Calvin that you're even still breathing," he shares with her before realizing the redundancy of that last statement. "Well, you know what I mean."

"What?" she says, absolutely shocked at what she just heard.

"This whole thing was his plan. You getting caught, the alarms, his mom showing up—everything. He did betray you—but only to save you. When we got separated, he somehow still made it into the base. He found me and told me everything—that *you* must live, so that *we* can survive," he explains as he continues to struggle to lift the heavy object. "As far as me meeting up with Jumo—the only thing true about all that is that the same black hole your Harness created was the same one I've been investigating, but I only met the man today, courtesy of your little brother. I'm sorry Joelle, but there's no way I can get this off of you."

"I had no idea," she says, completely baffled at what he's just told her. "It's fine, just go. Save yourself, Arthur."

"Oh, he also told me one other thing," he says as he stops trying to lift the crate that she's still pinned under. "That one of us will have to die in order to ensure none of us will."

Right after he shares that with her, Arthur gets on his hands and knees, and crawls on top of her.

"Arthur, ***what are you doing?"*** Joelle says as she slowly starts to freak out.

"Please don't think I'm a creep, I loved my wife very much. I couldn't be there to protect her that night like I should've been, but perhaps I can help save one gal before I go."

"ARTHUR! ARTHUR, YOU HAVE TO MOVE!" Joelle screams, as she starts to panic in a way she's never have before. "LISTEN TO ME! ARTHUR, PLEASE MOVE! DON'T DO THIS! PLEASE GOD, NO, DON'T DO THIS! PLEASE!" she hysterically begs of him while starting to sob.

"Your fate doesn't end here," Arthur reminds her calmly as he now gently hugs her, and notices the purple lines on her face reemerging once again. A smile is generated as he can now tell what causes the exotic sight. "Listen to me, don't be upset at Calvin, he's just a kid following what his parents told him. Calvin's mom—she's the real mastermind behind it all. She knew who you were before any of us did. She has been planning for this day since Calvin could talk. As an Accurist, she felt it was her duty to help protect you."

"Protect me?"

"Just listen. Because of his gifts, she initially thought that Calvin was the Warrior of Prophecy—a fighter of legend who is said to prevent an invasion that's to take place any day now on this planet. But some time ago, she realized that her son's purpose wasn't to become that warrior, but instead, to find him—or rather, *her* in this case. *You* are that warrior, Joelle. *That's* why you are here. You came to us to save us."

"What invasion? I have no idea what you are talking about!"

The sounds of multiple shells piercing through Arthur's back can now be heard by Joelle. Her tears at this point are uncontrollable.

"ARTHUR! NOOO ... please, no. I need you, Arthur. Please," she screams out then cries under her breath to the man resting on top of her.

Out of nowhere, the streams of tears flowing down her face begin to transform from a tenuous, hollow, clear liquid, to a thick, viscous silver—like mercury leaking out of a broken thermostat and suddenly freezing in place, becoming solid. The tears, as well as her face, become as hard and solid as the densest tungsten. Unbeknownst to her, her entire body, clothes included, now appear as a statue of reinforced steel. As the tears continue to well up and drip from her eyes, they also continue to solidify as soon as they leave her tear ducts.

"Oh my, there it is—the form Calvin said that you'd take to protect us—it's so ... no—*you're* so beautiful," he weakly murmurs to her. "So, he chuckles, *that's* how you survived a 300-mile fall."

"Arthur, I don't know what to do now," she says as she continues to weep.

"You must go to Opia. In Opia, you will find a man known as Nerosion. He will help you learn to control your abilities. Once perfected, find Aleph Null, it is he who possesses your artifact," he tells her in a dying voice, the blood in his body now dripping from his mouth. As the rain continues to fall in from the hole in the ceiling that Calvin's mom created, Arthur notices something he cannot believe he is seeing —this sight dwarfing even that of her exotic transformation.

"... I don't believe it," he whispers as his voice gets lower and his breathing becomes more labored.

"Joelle ..." he says as his eyes appear to be staring at some imperceptible image that only he can see. "The rain ... the water ... it's no longer afraid to touch you ..."

The last of the bullets that were meant for Joelle, sink their way deep into Arthur's body, destroying every single organ that has granted him a long, worthy life. He exhales his last breath, and his head falls onto Joelle's solid chest. Complete silence once again fills the entire base.

Joelle doesn't move right away, and it's not because the crate disallows her to. After a few moments, she uses her new-found strength to effortlessly moves the large crate that kept her legs pinned, to the side with just her legs alone, being extremely careful not to disturb Arthur in the process. She then stands up and reveals a brand-new body, one that looks like a human made from a molten, then instantly-cooled, carefully sculpted, titanium statue. Her height and weight seem to have doubled and tripled respectively, and it appears as if her clothes have merged with her new form. She stands fully erect, with Arthur cradled within her powerful arms, and looks over to find Beatrice silently weeping—who was there the whole time listening to Arthur as he spoke his last words.

Now holding Arthur in her arms, she looks towards the giant hole in the wall created by Calvin's mom, and makes her way towards it. Once outside the base, she looks up to see that the commotion has died out, and notices Calvin sitting inside of an armored helicopter that's just taking off. Calvin stares at her the entire time from the passenger seat—stoic, silent, almost as in cogitation—while his mom pilots the craft. As the helicopter takes off, the two look at one another as if it's the last time they'll ever see each other.

Joelle looks up as the aircraft disappears behind the gray clouds, and embraces the cool, physical wash that the rain now provides her, for the first time ever.

Chapter Thirty-One

THE ORB CITY

April 25th. 11:06 A.M. (EDT)

"*We have further developments on the new, foreign creature that has attacked the military base just outside of Monachopsis. It's now been a week since the world has learned that we have officially been visited by alien life. Government officials have confirmed that the creature seen here destroying the base camp isn't the same person who's come to be known as the UNSELF. This particular, unknown individual has been referred to as the One-Up, which is as we understand it, is a quip presumably created by the millions of people online who has since watched this video, aimed at the government and how someone finally got a one-up on them, considering how easily the creature laid waste to an entire military establishment in a flash. However, in a recent press release held by President Lamarch in response to the attack, the president is heard referring to the hostile creature simply as the 'Mobile Statue,'"* channel 7 news correspondent Gary Singh, reports to the millions at home tuned in, including the Chambers family. The broadcast quickly cuts to a recent conference President Lamarch held addressing the Mobile Statue.

"As it's come to be understood, this creature, when compared to the UNSELF, is just as, if not, even more dangerous. Unlike the UNSELF and its hordes of creatures, however, the Mobile Statue seems to operate alone and appears to be much more methodic in its actions and movements. Reports have said that the creature was seen violently executing every single surviving guard within the camp, many of whom were already severely injured from a previous firefight that was caused by the creature's emergence," President Lamarch shares.

"It is believed that the destruction that leveled the entire facility was done solely by the Mobile Statue. In some of the footage we've obtained from the site, you can see the creature lifting up a military transport vehicle, the likes of which weighing well over twenty tons, and tossing it several dozen feet into the base."

"That's more than even Roger can lift," Laharin says as she looks at Olpha when the newscaster says that last part, with no clue as to what his reaction would be.

"That's a *lot* more than Roger can lift," Olpha responds back to her without taking his eyes off of the television.

"As of right now, there seems to be no direct relation between this Mobile Statue and the UNSELF. Reports have confirmed that the Mobile Statue was last seen heading in the direction of Monachopsis, but no word yet on its sighting," the news anchor concludes.

Olpha, Laharin and Ori sit around the television screen doing what they can to take in everything they are seeing on it.

"First, we get one alien who destroys camps with space-wolves, and now we got one who can destroy them just by punching them. Baby, what is it about this city that just draws all these weirdos here?" Laharin asks her just-as-stumped fiancé.

"This city was built by weirdos. These aliens are right at home if you ask me," he sharply responds.

"Well, between fighting junkies who know karate, and a walking statue that can throw a truck across the Krauss River, being engaged to a man who can jump a hundred feet high doesn't seem all that weird to me anymore."

"I always told you that being a fugitive from the law was just the beginning of our problems. Now I got three weeks to turn myself in to the OPD or they're going to come after me," Olpha responds to her.

"You're not going to do it, are you, Daddy?" Ori turns from the T.V. to ask her father as she sits on the living room carpet.

"Yeah, this week you've been home has been the best we've had since we've moved here. Hell, it's been the best we had since Final

Chapter if you ask me," Laharin shares with him as she rubs his arm while they continue to enjoy another morning as a normal family.

"It has been nice not having to pick up the OPD's slack for once. But my hands are still tied if that statue decides to show up in Opia," he admits.

"Then let that be the day you put your mask back on. In the meantime, let's make the most of this down time. No worrying about Surii. No chasing exes across the city—"

"Exes??"

"Ex-comrades," she clarifies. "No beating up no Strawmen. None of that. Consider this a vacation until you make your decision. I already started going to my appointments again, Ori can start going back to school again—it'll be nice and simple like how we always envisioned our little family to be."

"That does sound nice," he says while smiling at his beloved, as he remembers why is it he even chose to make her his bride.

"Whatever you decide to do, I know it'll be the best decision for all of us. I'm sorry for saying you was jealous of Surii. The truth is, I was just upset that you were forgetting the very reason why we moved to Monachopsis in the first place—to do this job until you no longer had to, so we can build a life as a family without the hassles you had in Chapter Five. I know the circumstances aren't ideal but, in a sense, this is the moment we've been waiting for, honey. No matter how brief it may appear to exist for, we should make the most of this moment in time and live as if it can all be lost tomorrow."

"You're right. I can't stand seeing Ori missing out on class like this, but I can't send her to school with those monsters still walking around."

"Then go with her. Bond with your daughter—just like you used to when she was just a baby. You don't need a mask for that. I miss y'all two together. She misses y'all two together. Nerosion was always just a way to get in—we're in now; look around you—we're in. You don't have to struggle anymore. Think it over, babe. No matter what your decision is, I'll still support you."

11:29 A.M. (EDT)

"Welcome to Monachopsis: The Orb**ital** **Eccentri**City **of** **Apophis' Doom.**"

Joelle has spent a week walking around Monachopsis, constantly mumbling the quote on the sign that welcomes outsiders to Monachopsis to herself. For first time, for visitors such as herself, the sign unfortunately no longer reads its original text: *Welcome to Monachopsis: The Orb City* thanks, ostensibly, to the tenacious workings of teenagers, whom despite having it continuously erased every two or so days by the city after they put it up, always are sure to return to change the sign to make it say what she keeps repeating out loud.

"Welcome to Monachopsis: The Orb**ital** **Eccentri**City **of** **Apophis' Doom.**"

Having said this phrase well over fifty thousand times, it comes as a surprise to her that someone finally overhears her muttering to herself in a corner booth inside of some diner, subsequently waking her from what at this point could have been considered a transcendental experience. A noteworthy feat, considering she didn't even glance at the woman who brought her a complimentary cup of coffee.

"Pretty clever, huh?" a voice asks her from not too far away.

"What is?" she responds to the unrequested voice that appears to speak to her without ever looking in its direction—which wouldn't at all be of any use in helping her identify the owner of the voice anyway, unless she removed the hood from the fatigued army poncho she now wears, which conceals just about every part of her except her hands.

"That phrase you've been uttering for the past five minutes over and over to yourself," the unknown voice, now accompanied by an unknown man, answers.

"Is it? I don't know. What does it mean?" she says back as she continues to sip her straight-black, piping hot coffee, as if she's been an avid drinker of the common beverage for years.

"I'm not really sure, actually. Some mumbo-jumbo a couple kids tryna make a statement keep changing it to. My guess is that they're saying this city is where that rock came to die."

"That's not clever. It's offensive."

"Offensive? You gotta be the first person in this entire city who actually thinks such a thing. Funny thing is, they only started writing that on there since after that base nearby went all to shit. They think the Mobile Statue came from that rock and is now here to get revenge on us for blowing it up."

"But if we didn't blow it up, we would all be dead," she tells him.

"Yeah, I guess that's true. Most people here however, especially the youth, don't mind the thought of death too much. Not if it meant that it was rightfully someone else's turn to live. The *Iconoclass* is how they're referred to now. People have been going to other people's places and calling it their home since man could steal. I guess when Apophis showed up, the people here felt it was time for someone to finally kick them out of the house that they kicked the Indians out of. These Opia folk are something else, I tell you. The name's Reginald by the way," he says as he sticks his hand out and decides to sit in the empty seat just opposite of Joelle.

"No offense, Reginald, but I'm not really looking to make any friends while I'm here."

"Oh, you're not from here? That's okay, it's not the strangest thing to get blown off by a stranger in this city. Most people just scan you with their SHED frames nowadays anyway, but I'm not the biggest fan of learning about someone without their permission. I guess you can say I'm old-school. So, what brings you to Monachopsis?"

After a brief internal discussion with herself about whether or not she should continue to entertain this man, she decides that with her new-found powers that she's spent a week trying to perfect down at some abandoned subway tunnel but with little success, she has very, very little to be afraid of from anyone anymore. Besides, she could use a little information about who she's looking for.

"I'm looking for someone."

"Oh. I'm assuming it's not going too well."

"What makes you say that?"

"Well, you've been saying that same phrase over and over since you walked in. And that sign is only about a mile away and Monachopsis is about twenty-five miles wide, so I just kinda figured—but maybe I should stop assuming. How *has* that been going for you?"

"Yeah, maybe you should. Actually, it hasn't been going too well," she reveals, corroborating his feelings.

"Well, considering you're not from here, and I know this city pretty well, maybe I can help point you in the right direction to him —or her."

"He doesn't even know I'm looking for him. But I'm told finding him shouldn't be too difficult. So I'm not worried."

"Wait, are you on a DBSD? Oh my bad, I'm sorry for interrupting. No wonder you don't have any frames on."

"A what?"

"Okay, so that's a no. Whew! For a second I was worried about you."

"You don't *ever* have to worry about me," she asserts very firmly.

"No, you have the wrong idea. A DBSD or a Double Blind Shed Date, is basically the "cool" way people date now. In case you are unaware, which is a reasonable possibility considering you're not from here, people nowadays, at least in this city, use SHED frames to scan each other before they talk now. No one introduces themselves to anyone anymore for obvious reasons, as I adequately demonstrated not too long ago. That's bad in itself, but it's not nearly as bad as DBSDs. You still don't know where I'm going with this?"

Joelle's blank stare conveys a resounding no.

"Okay. A DBSD is simply when two people decide to randomly meet up somewhere without either of them wearing their frames."

"Okay, what's the problem with that?" she asks with a wry expression.

"*The problem is,* once you choose to participate in a DBSD, you can't renege on the date," he explains.

"Keep going," she says, afraid to admit that her interest in the subject is slowly building.

"I was hoping I didn't have to. Okay. Once they meet up, a person can choose to "tag" someone who they assume may be the other "study", or person on the date. A "tag" can either be successful or unsuccessful. If it's unsuccessful, then the "tagged" can just go on about his or her day. But if the person who gets "tagged" is confirmed to be the person that's on the DBSD, then they have no choice but to hook-up with the "tagger."

"Okay? I still don't see the issue, you can just say no if you're not interested."

"Well, of course you can, that means you 'shedded' somebody—not to be confused with shedding yourself, which is when a person allows others to scan them openly. The problem is, if you shed someone while on a DBSD after you're tagged, your SHED account is permanently banned and deleted."

"Can't you just make a new one?"

"Sure, if you can figure out how to be born again. One SHED account per individual. No fakes. No duplicates. No matter what."

"That sounds idiotic, why would anyone participate in such nonsense?" she says, finally dismissing the whole concept.

"Because the fun comes when you tag or are tagged by someone you like, or even better—you tag someone who's rich. If that rich person doesn't want to have anything to do with you after you successfully tag them, then it's pretty much over for them. Absolutely nobody wants to be shedless," he shares.

"Who's going to tell?"

"Well, the person who got shedded is, duh. All you have to do is report it."

"What if a person gets whatever he wants anyway and lies that he was shedded?"

"That's what these are for," Reginald says as he holds up his arm.

"A SHED band. You have one," she says when she recognizes the device.

"Oh, so you know about these."

"I've experienced them, yes."

"Not the DBSD kind of experience, I hope."

"No, and I should be saying that to you."

"No. I mean yes, I have a SHED band, but I don't participate in DBSD. The band is there to assure that both studies agree to what has occurred. Both parties have to conduct a series of unique steps on the band that can't be mimicked or copied. It's like entering a unique password to have access to each other. If either one disagrees, then it's a no-go."

"This whole thing sounds like it could be dangerous."

"Actually, without considering the SHED experience as a whole, believe it or not, DBSD has made everything about dating and sex much, much safer. The attention span of people nowadays is so abysmal, that people aren't even getting to know each other's names before they hook up now. DBSD basically says 'hey, if we can agree to get a round or two in and not have to ever get to know one another, then let's make sure it's safe and monitored.' Every DBSD transaction is uploaded to a private server that only you and that person has access to. If you ever hear someone ask 'how many *numbers* do you have, or do you wanna take a number?' that means they want you to tell them how many times you were successful on DBSD, and if not, would you be interested in participating in it. But that's nothing, some people have started calling it Consensual Rape or 'Safe Rape' even. You can even find advertisements for it on T.V., it's crazy."

"Does it always have to end with ... intercourse?" she asks, clearly more curious about it then she was just a minute ago.

"More or less. The original point of DSBD was to find your soulmate, heh—but now if you discover that they don't want you, which happens A LOT, then you can at least sleep with the person of your dreams as a consolation prize. The crazy thing is, nowadays, people sign up for DSBD *only* to get laid, and the consolation prize now is if the person even decides they even want to get to know you after the fact."

"Is it possible to meet someone on there, and not do any of that stuff?"

"It's possible, sure. Though, I wouldn't recommend it if your goals aren't the same as most of the others. People have made careers out of destroying those who 'Filter' or basically, agree to DBSD but not follow through. Wait, you're not thinking of looking for your friend on there are you?"

"Your assumption this time, is correct."

"Are you serious?" he seriously asks her.

"It's my only option. This city is huge—what am I going to do, walk around asking people if their name is Nerosion?" she asks him, rhetorically.

"Wait ..." Reginald says before he takes a breath, evokes a chuckle, furrows his eyebrows, coughs, chuckles again, stops himself short of saying something, and then clears his throat—all in that order. "Your friend's name is ... Nerosion?"

"Yes. Well, he's not really my friend, but I desperately need to find him."

"Then you might need to take a number?"

"What?"

"No, no, not like that! Do you even know who Nerosion is?"

"I know he's some man from this city."

"Some man from this city? Are we talking about the same Nerosion? Nerosion, the Tyrant. *THE* Nerosion?"

"I'm told he's a skilled fighter. Do you know him also?"

"A skilled fighter? Floyd Mayweather was a *skilled fighter,* Nerosion is the demi-god that rules over Opia," he says, half-baffled.

"So, you *do* know him. Where is he?"

"Well actually ... believe it or not, he hasn't been seen in action since that riot went south in Vellichor," he tells her. Joelle stares at him blankly as she waits for something more forthcoming that can help her. "Oh right, that was about two weeks ago. Nobody really knows where he is, which is odd."

"I need to find him. Can we check to see if he's on DBSD?"

"Sister, I don't know where you're from, but there ain't no way in *hell* Nerosion is on there. The man probably doesn't even own a SHED band, let alone a DBSD profile."

"Can we just please check, I need to find him. Please. I have his name, can't we at least just search to see if it pops up?" she says, now sounding much more ingenuous.

Reginald takes in a sharp inhale before he agrees. "Alright, what the hell, it can't hurt," he says as he takes out his SHED frames and puts them on. "But because neither of us have a profile, we're only going to be able to see people who chooses to have their profiles publicly available—which won't be many."

"Thank you," she says to the good-willed gent. "Stranger things have happened, right?"

"Stranger than Nerosion, the Tyrant, being registered on DBSD? Nah, they haven't," he replies.

Reginald scrolls the bios of hundreds of people with the aid of his wrist band, narrowing down and refining the search little by little.

"Let's see ... Nunu, Nuni, Nora, Noel, Nikolai ... Nerosion. I-I don't ... believe it," he says, now in total disbelief.

"See! I knew it! You see, I told you he'll be there," she exclaims.

"I—I do not trust this man, anymore," Reginald says before shaking his head. "This is a damn shame."

"Now, how do we find him?"

"How do we find him? You mean now? I still cannot believe Nerosion ... my man Nerosion, is involved with DBSD. This city boy, I swear."

"Yes, now!"

"Well, we have to see what spots he frequents. His profile should tell us."

"Okay, check it!"

"Okay, it says ... he can usually be found at any time during the day in Copenhagen, Everett Park, or Borh Central. Which one you want to go to first?"

"Uh, which one's the closest??"

"Bohr Central."

"Then take me!"

"I guess stranger things *have* happened."

"Joelle."

"Huh?"

"I guess stranger things have happened, *Joelle."*

Reginald chuckles after another head shake. "This is crazy, let's go."

Chapter Thirty-Two

COPENHAGEN INTERPRETATION

April 25th. 12:51 P.M. (EDT)

AFTER A TWENTY-FIVE-MINUTE CAR ride to Bohr Central, courtesy of Reginald's Uber account, then a thirty-five minute car ride to Everett Park—both locations producing nothing resembling Nerosion has even heard of them let alone ever visited them, Reginald is just about ready to call it quits.

"This is getting us nowhere," he says after letting out a long sigh.

"We have one more location to go, stop giving up so easily."

"I'm not giving up, I'm being realistic—I told you already, no one has seen Nerosion in days.

"So? He probably just called in sick or something and is on bed rest for a little bit and may just now be getting back to his normal self. Better for us."

"Called in sick? No, you see, you really don't know this guy. A man like him doesn't just *call in sick*—it's one thing to not spot him for an afternoon or even a night, but for no one to see him in weeks isn't normal. Something's up with him," he informs her as they continue riding in the back of the cab, coursing through the city.

"Well, maybe he has a family he has to tend to. He's human after all."

"Human? You sure about that? If Nerosion has any family, it'll be to those two aliens they found on Apophis. I wouldn't be surprised if they discover that he's the third one. Also, even if he is still out there, we're not going to find him in Copenhagen."

"Why not?" she asks. Before Reginald can answer, Joelle tells the driver to stop immediately upon seeing a sign that lets her know they've arrived at their location. "There. *Copenhagen*. Let's go."

"Wait, we gotta—"

"There's no time, he could already be on the move," she says as she hastily exits the car. Reginald thanks the driver and tips him before exiting the car. Joelle continues to walk a mile a minute towards the area that the sign told her Copenhagen lies.

"Joelle, slow down—"

"We're almost there. If we don't hurry we might miss—" Joelle's own words are cut off just as the motion in her feet are. "What is this?"

"That's what I was trying to tell you—Copenhagen is a club." he says as they now stand outside of an establishment that has the name of the place Nerosion had listed as a place of interest, written on a large marquee.

"A what? Whatever, let's go in. There's no time to waste."

"You wanna go to Copenhagen at one in the afternoon on a Thursday? You really need to start doing your Googles before you start looking for people, for real."

Joelle enters the club and Reginald follows her reluctantly. Immediately upon entering the large dance room, Joelle is bombarded with the intense music being commanded by the guest-celebrity DJ performing on this particular day. Unfamiliar with the dynamic yet coordinated, rhythmic sounds coming from the large speakers, Joelle can't help but to wince as she does her best to adjust to the abrasive symphony.

"You okay?" Reginald yells out to her.

"What is this noise?"

"Noise?" Reginald chuckles. "That *noise* is called Hip-Hop."

"Hip-Hop? I like it," she surprisingly shares with him. "So, what does he look like?"

"Who? Nerosion? He wears an all-black outfit and a black mask. Think of a shadow."

"A shadow? Really? In this dark place everyone looks like a shadow. Is that a coincidence?"

"If such a thing exists—probably not."

"How do we find him?" she asks over the loud beats.

"You can start by asking someone."

Joelle takes Reginald's advice and taps the shoulder of the first person she sees, which happens to be one of the few people in here who's visible, which Reginald didn't at all anticipate she would've done so suddenly. Before she can deliver the third tap to the shoulder of the man who's dancing by himself, he has already turned around and looked at Joelle with that same typical, smug smirk that most half-drunk oaf's who's been dancing by themselves since the doors probably first opened, hoping some cute chick taps them on the shoulder, is wearing.

"Excuse me, do you know where I can find—"

Understanding that her voice is no match for the volume coming out of the speakers, naturally Joelle leans in on the lucky gent's shoulder to get close to his ear in an effort for her inquiry to be processed accurately, as her entire life basically depends upon him giving her the correct information to her question. However, probably as expected by every person in the world except for Joelle, the man mistakes her gesture for one that he interprets as her wanting to get her groove on with him—and his groove on, the gent immediately begins to try to get before Joelle can even finish asking her question.

"Uh, what the hell are you doing?" she asks as the man begins gyrating his hips against the army jacket she stole from the base after she destroyed it. Unfortunately, Joelle hasn't yet realized that there's a one question-per-oaf policy that's been in place in clubs everywhere since the invention of the turntable. Luckily, Reginald, who's much more familiar with proper clubbing decorum, intervenes to save Joelle before the headache that comes with learning this most useful knowledge.

"What's wrong?" she asks Reginald when he pulls her back by the wrist, much to the dismay of the perpetual-gyrating hipster who's tipsy grimace continues to alternate between shades of neon blue, yellow, pink and green, thanks to the frenetic light behavior intrinsic to most clubs that's currently shining on him.

Reginald answers Joelle's question with a simple head shake, one she is able to easily interpret as him rescuing her from a series of futile attempts of trying to pry information from that guy.

"Oh my god, I don't believe this," Reginald says when his wandering eyes catches something he didn't want to believe was possible.

"What is it?" an uninformed Joelle asks, as she looks in his direction. She turns once Reginald lifts his arm and points in the direction he's looking. It takes her a few seconds before she realizes what he finds so interesting.

"What? Is that him? Nerosion?" she asks, unable to distinguish any person from another, but assumes must be the case, considering Reginald's overall sentiment of the entire situation up until now. What she does see that may register as peculiar, is that there seems to be a shadow that's currently encircled by a group of women who all move in synch around it but without ever touching it, like a pack of coyotes encircling a wounded moose trying to get a feel to see if it's okay for them to start gnawing on it. Except the difference between this moose and the hypothetical one, is this one is far from wounded—at least physically. If anything, he's bringing a sense of vitality to the coyotes that wish to shred him to bits.

"Let's go," she orders.

No longer able to suspend his disbelief, Reginald follows her this time without saying a peep or any hesitation; apparently, this—he has got to see to believe. They waddle through the crowd and it appears as if Joelle's entire persona has turned more brash since transforming into the Mobile Statue, considering she does very little to avoid not bumping into anybody on her way to the moose and coyotes.

Once they're but a few paces from the man she seeks, the dancing coyotes seem to somehow sense her presence even though it's extremely difficult to see anyone in this club. The circling of the pack slowly comes to a standstill the closer she gets to Nerosion, he who continues to rebelliously sit on the top side of the sofa as opposed to the cushion area where one would normally sit.

Reginald nods his head to Joelle when she looks back at him as she checks with him to see if it's okay to approach the circle now that it has fully stopped moving. The coyotes take their eyes off of their wounded moose and all now stare at this new, unknown creature.

The elevated platform that the section that Nerosion stands atop of begins to descend once Joelle enters into its vicinity; it appears Nerosion wishes to greet her alone considering the coyotes have vacated the area by the time this happens.

"So, this is where Nerosion's been hiding for a whole week—in the back of some club. Ridiculous," Reginald vents.

"Is that really him?" she asks Reginald as she and half of the party-goers watch this magnanimous icon continue to descend from what was probably considered his throne.

"It appears to be. Well, he looks a lot skinnier in person and his outfit doesn't appear as refined as I thought it was. Then again, I've never seen him in person but yeah, I'm sold. You know, I always wanted to meet this guy ... never thought it'll be on a dance floor though. Yeah, I know," he says to Joelle when she looks back at him appearing to about to say something. "Stranger things."

The platform finally reaches the level where Joelle and the rest of the peons of this establishment dwell.

"So, you're Nerosion?" she asks him once they're officially at eye-level.

"So I've been told. It appears you've been looking for me."

"Do you know who I am?"

"No, but I'm pretty sure that's going to change after today. What can I do for you?"

"I was giving very specific instructions to seek you out so you can help me. I'm told you can help people ... help them learn to control themselves."

"I am grateful to learn that you weren't misled. What you have been told is correct."

"Then it is true. You can help me find Aleph Null! When does the training begin?"

"The training, my child—" he says to her. Suddenly a large cage begins to descend from the ceiling from above them. "Has already begun."

"What?" she says as she looks back towards Reginald hoping for some answers, the likes of which he can't provide as he's too busy across the room whispering sweet nothings into the ear of some girl. "What is this?"

"This ... is your first training session."

"What do I have to do?"

"Survive."

The cage drops and locks into the ground, leaving Joelle and Nerosion completely sequestered from the rest of the crowd. "Show me what you got, and I'll decide if I'll take you on as my disciple."

"You mean right here, in front of all these people?" she says, as the platform begins to ascend once again, looking to put these two at the center of everyone's attention.

"If you haven't learned how to perform in front of an audience then you've already disappointed me."

"Fine."

"Go!" Nerosion yells out. At that moment, the music instantly changes to a heavy bass rhythm and Nerosion immediately begins dancing and moving his body in a way that would win over any female counterpart, if part of attracting a female mate included human males having to compete in dancing routines akin to those perform by a variety of different bird species.

Mistaken his awkward movements for some sort of offensive attack stance, Joelle immediately transform into her hardened, shell mode and hits Nerosion through the cage. He lands somewhere behind the DJ booth and the club goes completely silent. She then leaps out back down onto the dance floor and all the lights in the club turns on, illuminating every single person, including their weird costumes and their jaw-dropping expressions. She looks around at everyone, as they appear to find the words to describe what they're currently looking at. If they ever saw a costume this real, chances are one of them would've already had it on.

"IT'S THE MOBILE STATUE! RUNN!"

These are the words that causes just about everyone in the club to start spilling over one another. However, thanks to the varying levels of alcohol currently present inside of the bloodstream of just about everyone in attendance, there are those who stay back and decide they are adequately equipped to take down the Mobile Statue, now that they finally have it in front of them. It isn't before long that the Mobile Statue is encircled not by coyotes this time, but instead, jackasses.

The group begins attacking her one by one—apparently they've reached the proverbial point of inebriation where confidence has overtaken rationale. Thankfully, Joelle quickly learns that the Nerosion she flicked out the cage a few moments ago was just some imposter dressed up as him, and has already regretted mistaking his dancing for attacking. As a result, she knows these people, as obnoxious as they are, poses no real threat to her. Reginald was right all along to be dubious about finding the real Nerosion in such a location. She lets out a small huff of regret while the men, who now all wince in pain from trying to punch her and more than likely breaking their hand in the process, all crawl and roll away from her holding their respective afflicted appendages.

Speaking of Reginald, she thinks to herself before she starts looking around the club to see if she can spot him. When her wandering eyes spy a man bent over near the bar where Reginald was last seen, she decides to make her way over to him and hopefully, if it is Reginald after all, have him explain everything that just happened in here.

"R-Reginald?" she leans over and calls out to the man crouching behind the bar. "Reginald, please come out, I can explain."

After a few seconds, Reginald slowly stands up, hoping that the same sweet pleasant voice that belonged to the woman he just finished traveling all over the city with, doesn't belong to the gray obelisk he just saw bending metallic cage bars like they were rubber, inner tubes.

"Jesus Christ ..." he almost cries out when he becomes courageous enough to turn and face what he feared most. "It's you, it's really you—you're the Mobile Statue."

"The *Mobile Statue?*" she repeats, never hearing of the term before the crowd screamed it a few moments ago.

"Pu-please, don't kill me. Please. I'm sorry for bothering you earlier, I didn't mean any harm by it, please don't hurt me."

"Reginald, I'm not going to hurt you, I still need your help finding —" she says before Reginald takes off, sprinting for the exit.

"Reginald, wait!" she yells out before she's forced to chase him out of the club and into the awaiting busy street.

"Help me, help me! It's going to kill me!" Reginald screams as he frantically runs down the street. At first, most of the people and cars who's stopped to notice this troubled man, has no clue as to what has him so mortified. It isn't until a few moments after Joelle emerges from the club, that every pedestrian and commuter in the area acknowledges why this man is screaming the way he is. And it isn't long until many others follow suit.

"AAAHHHHHHH!"

Across the street, at the nearby Sunglass Hut, a self-diagnosed oniomaniac, finally takes her eyes off of the mirror where she was examining her seventeeth pair of Tom Ford shades. "What was that?" Laharin asks Olpha, looking at her bored fiancé—who also now wants to know the answer to her question.

"I'm not sure," he says, as he gets up and walks towards the large glass windows near the door of the store, to get a better look at what's going on outside. When he goes to peer through the window, about twenty people all come dashing by him. Wanting to get a better sense of what's happening, he starts making his way towards the exit.

"Stay here," he instructs to Laharin before leaving the store, which is something he apparently didn't have to tell her since she has long since returned back to trying on different glasses in the mirror.

"I'll be here," she assures him.

"Imma borrow these," he says, before grabbing the pair of shades out of her hands and walking out.

"Reginald, wait!" Joelle screams to him as she watches him cut into a nearby side street perpendicular to the one she's currently on. She immediately begins running after him.

"DON'T MOVE!" a nearby officer yells out after he and his partner exit their cop car, hiding behind the car doors and fixing their weapons on her.

"No, how about *you* don't move," she says to herself.

Olpha watches as the Mobile Statue picks up a nearby, thankfully empty, food delivery truck and lifts it over its head. Before she chucks the truck at the severely ill-equipped officers, a pair of trendy Tom Ford sunglasses somehow lands perfectly on her eyes from out of nowhere, obscuring her vision and distracting her long enough for her aim to be a little off when she throws the vehicle at them. The truck instead lands in front of the officers, causing them to flee from the impending explosion. After getting rid of the truck, she snatches the sunglasses off of her face and crushes them in her hand.

"Reginald, please slow down!" Joelle yells as she follows Reginald into the alley that he tried to escape through.

"You've chased him far enough," Olpha says when he arrives into the alley after Joelle and Reginald. "I know you're not from here, so I can see why you might think he's just playing hard to get, but take it from me, when a grown man is running down the street screaming help, it usually means he's not interested."

"O-Dog!?" Reginald says when he looks up and notices he recognizes the man who stands in front of him.

"Reggie? Oh wow, where you been man—you quit or something?" Olpha responds back.

"Nah, I'm on vacation actually."

"*This* is how you spend your paid time off?"

"Sir, please move, this is none of your business. Besides, we are together, tell him Reginald," Joelle says.

"Oh, so you *can* talk. My wife owes me thirty dollars. Wait, Reggie, is that true?"

"No, I've never seen this thing in my life. I was just getting a drink inside Copen and this thing just started chasing me! Please call someone, man," Reginald pleads.

"*This thing!?"* Joelle growls inside her head.

"Reggie here says you are a liar. Wait, y'all just came from Copenhagen? Oh, well no wonder you ran out."

It's more of the fact that Reginald pretends he doesn't know her that upsets her, more than Olpha intervening into her affairs.

"Leave now. I won't tell you again," the Mobile Statue threatens to Olpha behind her. *"Reggie,* let's go. Now."

"Reggie, you should go. Enjoy the rest of your vacation brother, I'll keep this thing busy until the police show up." Olpha says to him before the confused Reginald gets up and sprints away in the opposite direction.

"I'm really getting sick of all you people getting into my business," she says as she turns and towers over Olpha.

"A statue with feelings—that's new," Olpha quips.

"Who the hell are you?"

"I guess you can say I'm the craziest guy alive. America's nightmare. Young, black, and don't give a—"

"You talk too much," she interjects, cutting him off.

"So I've been told. How about we have a little chat, and you can tell me all about who's been getting in your business lately."

"You can't talk if your jaw is broken."

Joelle, still in her fortified Shell mode begins throwing punches at Olpha, each one capable of crippling him if any were to connect. Assuming he's just a normal person like everyone else, she holds back tremendously, being extra careful not to accidentally break his bones with one of her jabs. Even one of her light punches contains enough power to put a dent in a brick wall, which she does, but when she tries to grab him, she fails.

"That's a lot of power you're throwing around over there. With a little training, you might actually be able to handle your own out here," he remarks after avoiding her attacks.

"I've been doing pretty fine all by myself. The only reason you're still able to talk is because I'm holding back."

"Oh, you too? Good, because I was beginning to think that this was the best you can do."

"You really want me to get serious? I'm sure you've heard what happened to that base, recently."

"Yeah, I heard. So, what? See, unlike Reggie there, I don't run from fights. I'll tell you what—if you can land a single hit on me, I'll let you go. How about it?"

"Unlike you or Reginald, neither of you can tell me where I can or can't go. And since you scared him off, I'm not going anywhere until you now tell me exactly what I want to know," she promises.

"Fine. OPD'll be here any second, so I better finish this quick." Olpha says as he starts casually walking directly towards her. When he gets close enough, Joelle throws another punch and much to her surprise, instead of completely dodging it, Olpha parries her attack, which should downright be impossible for someone of his strength compared to hers.

"How the—" she says, stunned. Olpha then delivers a roundhouse kick combo attack to her chest and face that knocks her back and almost makes her fall over backward. She catches her balance as she has trouble accepting what just happened. Again, Olpha starts walking towards her as if he just didn't almost knock over someone who an entire army couldn't even make flinch.

"It sounds like," Olpha says, while appearing to zero in and perhaps pick up the sound of a police siren from a few blocks away. "We have about a minute, if that, before we have company and trust me, you don't want the OPD asking you questions because the interrogation won't start until they put at least a couple of bullets in you."

"You think this is a game?" she yells. Suddenly Joelle starts unleashing a fury of punches that Olpha continues to dodge gracefully. Though he just about delivers a counter-punch between each of her attacks, they don't at all seem to faze her.

"I'll bring down this whole damn building if I have to!" she says after she realizes Olpha shows bouts of concern every time one of her punches knocks out a slab of bricks from the nearby walls of the buildings inside of the alley.

At this point, Joelle decides that if she can't destroy this man, then she's going to destroy something that isn't as nimble. As expected, she begins to. With astonishing power, the Mobile Statue begins pummeling away at the seventeen-story building next to her, causing untold amounts of damage and possibly injuries to the structure and people inside. Feeling helpless without his arsenal, Olpha looks around to see what he can find to subdue this fiend from leveling this complex.

After looking around while dodging falling debris, Olpha find his instrument for stopping this beast: a mangled, fire escape dangling from the side of one of the buildings in the alley. Olpha leaps three stories high and rips off the remaining of the dangling part and makes his way back towards the Mobile Statue. It isn't until Joelle gets a glimpse of his swift, acrobatic movements as he cartwheels up the side of the building, that she finally agrees that this man isn't like anyone else. As a result, she is now more on her guard than she's has been since their encounter.

Assuming the Mobile Statue is much too busy trying to level a building to notice him, Olpha lands and makes a daring dash at her, this time with a weapon in his hand to end this scuffle once and for all.

Anticipating that this man she's fighting, who's currently running at her holding a piece of fire escape, is looking to somehow put an end to her savagery through some inexplicable plan he must've muster up, Joelle patiently waits for the exact moment when Olpha makes a move on her to then swiftly counter his attack. If it were anybody else, her counter-attack would've more than likely sent them flying somewhere several dozen meters from the alley she is currently in. However, Olpha Chambers isn't just *anybody else*—in fact he just happens to be the third most dangerous man in the world according to the United States government *and* a disciple of the Hannibal Article—which basically grants him more than enough skill to counter the counter-punch of the half-ton obelisk and using its own attack to effectively tie its arms behind its own back, completely immobilizing it.

Olpha watches on as Joelle pointlessly struggles for a while, more shocked that she can't rip out of this metal hold like it was a mere paper ribbon, than she is that he was able to even subdue her like this.

"Well, it appears my jaw is still intact, so I might as well continue to use it. Oh, and you can struggle all you want, unless you can shrink, you're not getting out of that. So, now that I know you can talk, how about you tell me all about this thing you want to know so bad? Oh, and don't try anything funny like kicking, I would hate to tie up those cute little size nineteen feet also," he says pointing to her large feet.

"This was fun, but I've wasted enough time here. As surprisingly talented as you are, you aren't the man I'm looking for. But I had fun," she calmly says to him. The very next moment, the sophisticated arm lock that Olpha skillfully applied to the Mobile Statue with his metal bars of fire escape remnants, become undone and the metal bars hit the floor without Joelle even making a flinch.

"We'll have to do this again sometime," she says to him with her back turned to him. From this position, she is right to assume that his face is currently as it is—in total shock and disbelief. Whether it's because a five-foot-six young, fully nude, tattooed body is somehow now standing where the Mobile Statue just was, or because his infamous arm-lock was undone, is anyone's guess. "Take care."

Joelle begins to casually walk away as if she just didn't dupe a man who hasn't been duped by someone who wasn't at least a member of Chapter Five, in ever.

"Hey, wait!" Olpha screams as he rushes to grab Joelle by the shoulder. The shock factor of what he experienced just a few moments ago is paltry compared to the one he is currently experiencing, judging by the way he's trying his best to understand why the shirt around his arm has frozen in space and tightened to the point where it feels like it's going to rip his forearm off.

"What the hell is this?" his mind screams. His frantic thoughts are interrupted by the swift right hook a naked Joelle delivers across his jaw, knocking him down onto the ground. Confused and slightly frustrated, he tries to get up and when he leaps at her, his body freezes again, this time in mid-air. This time, Joelle uses all of her strength to deliver a punch to his gut that knocks him back down.

Holding his stomach and perhaps more shocked than hurt, Olpha looks up at the naked woman and for the first time in a long time, has no idea what his opponent is going to do next.

"What the hell is going on over there?" Laharin yells out from the entrance way of the alley that leads back to the street a several meters back. "Olpha, who is that woman?? Why is she standing over you like that! Boy, you better answer me now before I get down there. I don't care if you *are* Nerosion, Imma whip both of y'all's asses!"

"Nerosion?" Joelle says, astonished at what this woman just called this man she's been fighting.

"Dammit!" Olpha says to himself when he realizes Laharin just blurted out his secret identity. "Laharin, get out of here, I'm handling it!"

"Handling it! Handling what? Wait, what the hell ... is this bitch naked? Oh, hell no!" she yells.

"You're ... Nerosion?" Joelle asks the man on the floor next to her. "You're the one I'm looking for."

"Me?"

"Yes, I was told you can help me find a man called Aleph Null."

"Aleph Null?" Nerosion says, stunned to hear such a name from this ... thing.

"Yeahhh, that's right—y'all better whisper and get y'all excuses all together before I get there, because it's gone take the OPD, the National Guard, the Army, the Navy, the Air Force, Chapter Five, a Strawbitch, a space-wolf, a Mobile Statue, and a motherfucking UNSELF to stop me from beatin' yo ass!" she screams out boisterously as she continues to walk towards them.

"Damn, she's mad," Olpha says to Joelle.

"Who is that?"

"My fiancée."

"A *fiancée?* Is she as good a fighter as you?"

"Trust me, it won't be a fight once she gets here."

"Someone told me you can help me find Aleph Null. Can you?"

"Maybe. But we have to survive this first," he says as he continues to sit and watch as his woman approaches.

"Don't worry, I'll take care of this," Joelle says rather reassuringly.

"Wait, are you crazy!?" he says in response to her bold, yet foolish claim. Joelle begins walking towards Laharin, still completely nude.

"Yeahhhhh, that's what I'm talking about bitch! I've been waiting for this for sooooooo long! HAHAHA!" Laharin maniacally yells out as she starts taking her earrings off and rubbing blobs of Vaseline on her forehead and strangely only her forehead.

The moment the two finally get within punching range, Laharin swings, and before the punch can connect, it is caught by Olpha. He grabs his girl by the waist, picking her up off of her feet and holding her under his arm the way she holds her own clutches, while she flails wildly. He then carefully does the same to Joelle also before leaping up and high-stepping off of the sides of the buildings around them until they get to the roof. On the way up, Laharin throws a bunch of fury swipes at the naked woman under Olpha's right arm, trying her best to get a hit on her.

As soon as they land on the roof, Laharin tries to jump on top of Joelle. Olpha grabs her and she instead turns her fury onto him.

"How. The. Hell. Could. You. Put. Me. Through. This. Shit. After. All. The. Shit. I. Went. Through. For. You," she says as she delivers each word with a rhythmic yet accurate corresponding punch to his head. A naked Joelle looks on more confused than worried.

"Relax, Laharin. Relax!"

"Who is she, Olpha?"

"She's the Mobile Statue!"

"The Mobile Statue, really?" she says. She takes a brief pause, and everyone goes silent seeing if she's finally decided to take it easy. "This. Is. The. Shit. I. Be. Talkin'. Bout," she says as she resumes her attacks, all her words once again in impeccable sync with her pinpoint slaps across Olpha's head.

"Would you please stop hitting me! There're going to be OPD choppers everywhere in a few seconds. We have to get her out of here."

"No problem! She can go home. Ain't nobody stopping her. Byeeeee, Mobile Statue. It was nice meeting you, boo—I'm sure you know your way down from here, take care, love."

"Laharin, she's not safe here," Olpha reminds her.

"Why are you concerned about the safety of the thing that destroyed a whole military base?"

"Because Laharin, she asked about Aleph," he responds. It is these words that render Laharin completely quiet. "So, can you please give her your sweater, so she can cover up and we can safely get out of here? Please?"

"Okay," Laharin, suddenly expressing remorse, says back.

"Okay," Olpha repeats. "You ready?" he says to Joelle, to which she nods. Olpha stands up to look around. Laharin takes off of her cardigan and hands it to her. He then grabs each one of them again under each arm and bends his knees as if he's about to leap. Before he does, he turns towards Joelle.

"Please don't transform."

"Couldn't even if I wanted to," Joelle replies.

"Hang on."

Olpha leaps several meters at an amazing speed to the next rooftop, and does so again and again until they are multiple blocks from where they just were in seconds. After he's convinced that they are now far enough to not be seen, he lets them out of his grasp and they all exit the roof through the door to the building below.

Chapter Thirty-Three

ILLEGAL ALIEN

April 25th. 3:39 P.M. (EDT)

NOW BACK HOME, Olpha continues to do what he can to justify to Laharin why he feels the Mobile Statue ought to stay with them for a while until he figures things out.

"We were doing so fine, soooooo fineeeeeee, Olpha. Sooo fineeee. But you just had to bring this woman into our home from out of freaking nowhere. You know how I feel about having strangers in my house man—she from outer space too? We don't know what this woman got, she could be dragging all types of moon diseases in here, spreading her space germs all over the place. We don't have any kind of medicine for something like that," Laharin complains.

"Baby, please, just take it easy. Let's just all go into the living room and just talk to her, okay? Get to know her a little better, you'll see ... wait, where's Ori?"

Meanwhile in the living room, Ori is already on her forty-second question, looking to have all 317 of them answered before the day is over.

"So, this soldier that shot you with the tranquilizer—when you grabbed him, you said he started begging for his momma or grand-momma?" she asks with a tiny notepad in her hand and a giant purple crayon in the other.

"Grandmomma."

"Okay, Ori," Olpha says as he and Laharin enter into the living room. "That's enough. I'm sorry about my daughter, she can be very um, curious at times."

"It's fine—she reminds me of an old friend actually," Joelle responds.

"Considering everything that has occurred up until now, I want you to know that my family and I has decided to allow you to stay with us."

"Oh, Daddy, you're the best!" Ori joyfully exclaims.

"If you prefer, of course. I don't want you to think you have to stay here if you don't want to."

"Oh, please, please, please stay, Ms. Joelle," Ori pleads. "I promise you will love it here."

"You can just call me Joelle, and I can already tell I will," she says while smiling at her. "If it's to help me find Aleph Null, then I gladly accept your generous offer."

"Wonderful. So, Joelle?" Olpha begins." That's your name—it seems like such a ..."

"A boy's name?" she interjects.

"Oh, no, I was going to say ... human."

"It is. Where I'm from we don't really have names. It's a novel concept, one I happened to grow quite comfortable with. My earthly designation however, is pronounced Kayelimneusia in your language."

"Oh. Yeah, I think we're just gonna stick with Joelle then. So, you're not human?"

"No."

"But you look just like a woman."

"Where? You must've not been paying attention in that alley," Laharin sardonically shares.

"At least for the most part," Olpha continues as he side-eyes his fiancée.

"Yes, it turns out I'm an emissary from my star system, Vartiga, and I was on some sort of mission to protect this planet from being destroyed by a nearby star explosion. My people are known as Kun-Veil," she explains to him.

"Kun-Veil? And the UNSELF, is he Kun-Veil also?"

"Jumo. Considering I worked directly with him, it appears so."

"What kind of work?"

"I don't know the details, but it has something to do with a process our people are known to conduct known as the Harness—a system designed to absorb energy from exploding stars. But according to him, this is the first time we ever used it to protect a planet from being destroyed."

"That's interesting," Olpha remarks.

"To say the least. So, this Man in The Dirty Robes—do you know him?" Joelle asks.

"You mean Aleph Null—*The Man in The Dirty Robes,* that's hilarious. I do, but how do you?"

"A boy named Calvin Sonder told me he has the answers I'm looking for," she shares.

"Sonder huh? Never heard of him. No, I know him because he trained me. Or rather, I *knew* him."

"What do you mean?"

"The Man in The Dirty Robes is now resting in the dirty ground," Laharin tells her.

"What? How?"

"He was ambushed over five years ago in a covert military operation known as Final Chapter."

"Final Chapter?"

Olpha looks at his fiancée before he explains.

"It's the day the United States invaded a country called Gloria and destroyed a powerful organization known as Chapter Five."

"Were you apart of them? This Chapter Five?"

"I was," he admits.

"And Aleph Null?"

"In a sense—he's the founder."

"Then I'm certain he's still alive."

"What makes you say that?"

"Because you're alive and he trained you," she posits, which makes Olpha chuckle at her directness and makes him realize that she knows more than she makes apparent to him.

"Even if he is, finding him would be impossible."

"I found you, so I say that my odds are good."

"Odds. That's funny. That's exactly *why* you will never find him," he retorts.

"You know ever since I got here, all everyone has been telling me is how impossible things are. And you know what I've learned, you people have absolutely no idea what that word means."

"You don't understand. Aleph Null isn't your typical guy."

"And I'm not your typical girl."

"Are you even a girl?" Laharin asks, sneaking a jab in.

"If you're not going to help me find him, then at least train me to help me get to him. For some reason, I get the feeling that wherever he is, I'm going to need to fly through the air like you do in order to reach him. Also, he seems like the type of person that tends to fight people in order to get to know them, instead of just simply asking them their name," she says, which Olpha confirms with a corroborating chuckle. "And I figured, who better to teach me to properly introduce myself, than one of his own disciples."

"Ahem, well be that as it may, *Joelle*, whoever it was that told you to find Nerosion forgot to tell you that he's now retired," Laharin decides to share with her new roommate.

"But, aren't you Nerosion?" Joelle asks Olpha.

"No, he's *Olpha*. *Nerosion* is his-now retired alter-ego."

"Alter-ego? I don't understand."

"Hmm, how can I explain this?" Laharin says while scratching her head comically. "You see how on your planet you're some emissary named Kim Cauliflower or whatever, yet on Earth you go by Joelle? Inside this home, he's Olpha, and outside this home out there in Monachopsis, he's known, or rather, *was* known, as Nerosion. However, as of recent, he is now known only as Olpha ... Olpha Chambers—both *inside* and *outside* this house. And I'm Laharin Chambers. And that's Ori Lorraine Chambers. So, *Nerosion*—like *Kay-LMNOP*—is officially retired."

"Is that true?" Joelle says, directing her question at Olpha. Before he can respond, Laharin again speaks for him.

"As true as the sky is blue," Laharin says.

"But it's cloudy, Mommy," Ori says to her mom while pointing to the window.

"Eat your applesauce, honey," she says back to Ori.

"What's applesauce, Mommy?"

"I was told to find the one called Nerosion so that he can help me find Aleph Null. I just hope I'm not wasting my time with the wrong man," Joelle spats before excusing herself from the living room. "I assume the bathroom is this way."

"Yes, it's just down the hall to your left. Ori, can you please show Joelle where the bathroom is?" Olpha asks of his daughter.

"Okay!" Ori says as she leaps up and escorts Joelle to the bathroom as instructed.

"Um, all I want to know is what landlord she sleeping with to cover this rent, to think she can be talking like that in my house?" Laharin remarks.

"We don't pay rent. You know what Laharin, all that was uncalled for."

"What did I do?" she asks, her question lacking any substance of sincerity.

"You know what you are doing, Laharin. Come on, don't play these games."

"What did I do besides tell her the truth? Nerosion *is* retired right now. Or is he not?"

"Retired? You're being dramatic. We spoke about this, I'm laying low until my hearing."

"So, what, you on strike or something?" she asks him, which Olpha takes a second to think about.

"Yeah, I guess you can say that," he agrees before suddenly switching to a hushed tone. "Listen, you remember what I told you about the Prophecy, right?"

"Yes, I remember—wait a minute ... come on Olpha, you don't actually believe she—this ... thing? Are you crazy?"

"If she isn't, she sure as hell makes a good candidate."

"How? She's not even human!"

"Come on, look at everything that has happened up until now—just days after we blow up an asteroid that was supposed to hit us, suddenly a bunch of foreign creatures rise up and start running rampant across the country? And now we have a woman from outer space who can transform into a statue that can break buildings apart like they're Legos? You can't tell me something isn't up."

"You act like this is the first time you've seen strange things happen. Weird doesn't equal prophecy, Olpha. Odem alone is more unusual than anything you've just named."

"Odem is weird, true. But Odem is only a man."

"So, what does that mean? Didn't you tell me he thought that he was the Warrior of Prophecy for the longest time?"

"Yes. And as powerful as he is, it surprised us all when we learned he wasn't."

"But the prophecy never said anything about the warrior being some alien, it said the warrior was supposed to *protect us* from some aliennzzz," she reminds him.

"But it never said it *couldn't* be, either," he counters.

"Oh boy, see these conflicting interpretations is the reason why Odem is the nut job that he is today and been bugging since y'all dropped that bombshell on him. We even have Adaptists still claiming that their savior is going to come and bring peace when the Shee invade."

"Laharin, I'm beginning to think the invasion has already started," he says in a more serious tone.

"What are you talking about? Wait, you don't mean ..."

"Yup."

"But what if she's one of them?"

"Then who better to keep an eye on her than me? There's only one way to know for sure if she's the Warrior of Prophecy or not—and that's to take her to meet him. I don't know how she knows about Aleph Null, but at this point we don't have a choice but to honor her requests, and let this play out especially while we have her. Don't worry, if I'm wrong, then at least I can take her out before things get out of hand."

"How does she even know about him? She said a child name Calvin told her. Maybe she read about it in the Toska?"

"When was the last time you seen a copy of that ancient book? No, someone told her—and I think it was the UNSELF."

"You really think her and that Jumo guy are working together?"

"That's what I'm going to find out."

"But you told me Aleph Null was dead anyway."

"I also told you Surii was dead and we saw how that turned out."

"They probably are working together," she says after a brief pause.

"By the looks of it, it doesn't seem they get along very well. Don't worry, I'll train her. The Mahze Du Verses doesn't just focus on teaching you how to get your body to do whatever you want it to—it also applies to the manipulation of the mind; I'll train her to the point where she'll become powerful enough to get rid of the UNSELF herself. This way I won't ever have to worry about taking out the both of them."

"Manipulation of the mind, huh? From what I've learned, those scenarios never end well for the manipulator. You saw what she done to that facility."

"Then let us pray my hunch about her being the Warrior of Prophecy is correct."

Olpha and Laharin hears the bathroom door open, and Joelle walks back into the living room, this time wearing a new outfit straight out of Laharin's wardrobe.

"I've taken the liberty of changing my clothes, I hope you don't mind," Joelle says when she reenters the living room.

"No, it's fine," Olpha says, looking to do anything to appease his guest, leaving Laharin more stunned than she was when she saw this stranger walk into the living room wearing a pair of her leggings, her top and looking *surprisingly* good in them.

"So, when do we start?" Joelle asks him.

Chapter Thirty-Four

THE MAHZE DU VERSES

April 26th 1:35 A.M. (EDT)

DEEP on the southernmost side of Kenopsia, exists an area that has long since been abandoned by the people who used to spend time here finding solutions to the many developmental burdens that a city planner may have faced when tasked with trying to build facilities in a remote location, only to have to then transfer them somehow to somewhere else.

In most first-world regions around the world, it isn't normal to hear that the very people who worked on building structures also had to live in them while they did so. Just about every single individual who constructed buildings in Kenopsia also lived in the very places they built, as it was pretty well understood that the nearest "residential" area, which was over in Vesto Melvin, was off-limits, considering they were currently engaged in a citywide, violent dispute. Monachopsis would be the next best place for a person who's spent his whole day building the very places those in Monachopsis had the luxury to stay in to rest their head, except it would take about half of the average worker's yearly salary to even afford the security deposit to rent the average studio in the opulent city. In other words, if a worker needed a place to stay—he or she would have to build a place to stay.

Though it worked for a while, this notion soon lost its merit when Kenopsia eventually found itself unable to continue to fund the projects that generated most of the profits that kept the borough afloat. Once the Melvin Riots ended, Kenopsia found itself in a precarious position where it didn't know what lied in the future of the island. Because of this, and with no incentive to keep working, many of those who had essentially built a life around their projects had begun to abandon their homes at a substantial rate, leaving many of the buildings they were developing unfinished.

That is why Olpha has chosen Lagrange Point, the region in southern Kenopsia where many underdeveloped, abandoned buildings are now left to rot away, as the perfect place to train his new pupil in helping her control her abilities.

"You certainly took your time," Joelle says when Olpha finally arrives to the area he told her to meet him at over a half hour ago. "I was beginning to think you weren't going to show up."

"Besides the fact that I had to practically walk here after taking two trains, I also had to be sure," Olpha responds.

"Sure of what?"

"That you weren't being followed. I can't afford to be seen with someone the entire U.S. government is looking for."

"They've only seen me in my Shell form and the only footage that existed of me transforming was in that base I flattened."

"You know there's a video online of that also, right?" he informs her.

"I've seen it, I'll be okay. Besides, aren't you also on the run?"

"No, I'm on strike. There's a difference."

"I'm sure. That's why you're dressed and rode the train like a civilian too, right?" she says, referring to Olpha's otherwise plain looking short-sleeve T-shirt and trendy chino shorts.

"You may not be aware of this, but when you're on strike from your job, you don't walk around wearing your job uniform. Besides, the trains here are free. Can't beat that."

"That's unfortunate, I was looking forward to finally meeting this Nerosion character. What is this place, anyway?" Joelle says as she finally decides to inspect the surroundings of this unusual location.

"I told you before we left, this is Lagrange Point—what I didn't tell you is that it's also known as the Complex Cemetery."

"Cemetery? From what I've come to know about your burial process, that means there should be a bunch of gravestones around ... but I don't see any," Joelle says to him.

"Really? Because I see nothing but gravestones," Olpha says while looking at the old, gray, dilapidated buildings that almost was. Soon, Joelle catches on to what he means.

"Anyway, so what are we doing here? We're digging up dead bodies or something?"

"Edgy, but no. This is and shall remain the only place where we go to help you develop and control your unique abilities. Per your request."

"Okay. How are we going to do that?"

"The first lesson would be to educate you in the Verses of the Mahze Du Arts. Normally, to begin to even approach learning it, one must first study the Toska and its scriptures thoroughly—then, one must go through a trial of mental exercises, ones that are known to take years to master. From there it only gets more difficult. Considering that every day that passes is another day the government gets closer to finding you, it'll be wise to skip ahead a little and give you a direct crash course in the Third Verse of the Arts—the Art of Syndeton, or as you may have come to know it—Close Quarter Combat."

"You mean fighting? Actually, on the way here, I've been thinking and I decided we might as well skip that step, too—considering I know how to do that already. What I want is do is learn how you're able to fly through the air like that."

"That's harder than you think, and can't be learned in the length of time we're limited to. Besides, I've seen you fight and—"

"And?" Joelle emphatically repeats in an interrogatory way, to which Olpha shakes his head disparagingly. "Are you kidding! I knocked you on your ass. Twice!"

"Yeah, and we're going to get to that in a bit. Now, the truth is, there's no way you're going to be able to master Syndeton overnight, let alone the entire Mahze Du style in such a short amount of time. But it's a good thing, because you won't have to."

"What do you mean?"

"I mean this."

Suddenly Olpha tosses up six ball bearings and performs a series of kicks that smack each and every one of them directly at Joelle. Needless to say, Joelle is amazed at the speed and power at which he hit them.

Those balls traveled almost as fast as bullets, I couldn't even see what he was hitting, she thinks to herself. *I see why Arthur wanted me to find him.*

"That—that right there," he says while pointing at her. "That's what I mean. How are you doing *that?*"

"I-I don't know. It kind of just happens on its own," she responds as she tries to shake off the fact that he's more amazed by her Warp Zone than he is at his own special skills.

"I've never seen anything like it," he says, as he walks towards her to get an up-close view of the always, jaw-dropping spectacle. "After a certain speed, anything thrown at you instantly slows down the moment it comes near you, but," he says as he throws a punch just past her face fast enough to make the skin on her cheek wave slightly. "Anything organic doesn't slow down in the least. Also, its automatic."

How was he able to figure that out so soon? Arthur had to run a hundred tests to even come up with a hypothesis, and this man nails it in a few hours!

"It's called the Bouya Effect—the slowing down thing that you see," she tells him, deciding to switch the name of the strange effect to the name of the man who rightfully discovered it.

"I want to test something," Olpha says as he grabs his ball bearings out of the air. "Transform for me."

"Transform?"

"Yeah, turn into the Mobile Statue thing you do when you turn silver and start throwing things," he asks of her.

"It's called my Shell form."

"I like Mobile Statue better. I don't know, it just fits you. Some people call you the One-Up though, have you heard that one—"

Joelle shoots him a look that makes him completely aware that she's not a fan of either term. "Okay, sorry—turn into your Shell form.

Please. Please turn into your Shell form thing for me—please. Thanks. You. T-Thank you."

After obliging his request, Olpha backs up and waits for Joelle to transform but instead she continues to just stand there. After a few moments pass, he decides to talk to her, perhaps looking to ease her mind a bit.

"Take your time. I'll wait. Getting a little hungry, but no rush."

"I can't transform."

"What do you mean?"

"I don't know, it kind of just happens on its own."

"You mean like the Bouya Effect?"

"Yes, well, no, well, kinda. I don't know, it's similar but different. It happens on its own, too, but it seems to only occur when I'm going through something. I don't know."

PAMP!! Out of nowhere, Olpha delivers a knee strike that knocks Joelle onto the ground, scraping her forearm and causing her to bleed a little.

"URGH! WHAT THE HELL DID YOU DO THAT FOR!" she screams out in pain.

Purple blood? Olpha thinks to himself. While he analyzes the strange liquid leaking out of her arm, he's amazed by how quickly she heals as she starts to transform. "You can even heal yourself the instant you transform," he says, astounded.

"You're going to pay for that!" she beams as she starts walking towards him, growing taller and bigger with every step until she reaches a full height of eight and a half feet.

"So, that's how you were able to get out of my—whoa-whoawhoawhoawhoa, okay relax, relaxxxxx," Olpha says, holding his hands out and slowly backing away.

"Why did you kick me!?" she growls, her voice automatically switching to a different pitch, thanks to the transformation.

"I didn't kick you, I *kneed* you—a kick would've torn my foot off—wait, let me explain," he says as he continues to back up. "I think I know the trigger for your transformation—it's stress. You transform when you're stressed out or mad."

"You're damn right I'm mad!"

"Yes, but that's just an instinctual trigger, you don't need it to transform and if you let me, I can show you how to transform whenever you want without being mad pleasedonthitme!" he cries out while covering his face as Joelle lifts her large, solid fist.

"How?" she says, calming down thanks to Olpha's last statement.

"I told you—"

"The Art of Syndeton, I know," she says as she lowers her fist. "But you said that was only to learn how to fight."

"That's true. I also said we have to skip a few steps. You see, Close Quarter Combat, or CQC, is just the *application* of Syndeton, or other in words, as it exists in its most efficient form. The principle however, lies in your ability to master the control and connection with your body. And to apply the knowledge of control, you must first master the First Verse—Aposiopesis."

"This isn't sounding like a shortcut anymore," she admits.

"The truth is, the version of Syndeton I was going to teach you was going to be more of a crash-course version—like a *How to Fight for Dummies* almost. But, after understanding a little bit of how your transformation works, I think you might have the potential to go much, much further. Look, I never taught this stuff to anyone, okay? So, bear with me."

"Fine. And just how many of these Verses are there to master anyway, *teacher?*"

"Nine. And the proper term is *Ilisaiji.*"

"So I need to learn all of them, so I can fight like you?"

"Fight like me? Hehe, no, to fight like me, you would need to master at least eight of them. It's complicated, so I won't bore you with the details."

"Fine. Well, has anyone ever mastered all nine of these Verses?"

"In the eight hundred years they existed—only one."

"Aleph Null," she says.

"Nope. The former leader of Chapter Five—a global dictator named Odem."

"The former leader? Wouldn't that make you—"

"Yes, I am his former comrade."

"I was going to say *current* leader. So, there's more of you?"

"Yes."

"How many more?"

"There was a total of five of us. Not counting Aleph Null."

"Is he not one of y'all?"

"No, he's more like a ... mentor, than a teacher," Olpha clarifies.

"Five members in a group called Chapter Five? Seems kind of contrived if you ask me."

"You mean fake? Well, there *were* more of us," he tells her.

"What happened to them?"

"Some defected, most were killed."

"And now there's none of y'all?"

"Well, you can't have a chapter without any pages."

"Is that what y'all were referred to as?"

"Jesus woman, you ask a lot of questions. Yes, most of those who served in the Chapter were referred to by their Page handle, or Number."

"Only most?"

"The five of us that remain are known as the Hannibal Article. Let me ask *you* something now—why do you want to find Aleph Null so bad, anyway?"

"I was told that he's the one who can help me find my artifact."

"Hmm. This artifact wouldn't happen to be called a Seriff, would it?"

"It doesn't really have a name. Why, what is that?"

"You didn't have a name when you first got here, either. It's just an heirloom that's been passed down through the Chapters."

"How long has he had it?" she asks.

"Since the first Chapter."

"Wow, he's old. Did you think that this *Seriff* was the artifact from Apophis?"

"Not really. You said this thing you're looking for has immense power and the Seriff is nothing but a keepsake from an ancient time. Its value is more in its symbolism than anything—kind of like the Cross or the Holy Grail," he explains.

"The what?" she asks, never hearing of either term.

"Nothing. Let's continue."

"Okay, what do I do now?"

"Now—you be still," he tells her unambiguously.

"Be *still?"* she repeats, slightly flummoxed.

"Yep."

"Okay—I'm still, now what?"

"I said be still."

"Okay? For how long?"

"Until you learn how to move," he responds.

"This is stupid."

"Well, once you learn how to be *still* you can then learn how to *move*, which will enable you to *leave*, which is the only way we can move on to the next lesson," he explains.

"What are you talking about? This doesn't make sense."

"Of course it does. Before we learn to move, we first master being still, don't we? We're not born walking even though we eventually learn how to—first we're still, then we, I don't know, stand I guess. After you master that, you then learn to walk."

"I guess? And what about you, what are you going to do?"

"Me? Oh, I'm going home. You can meet me there when you're done."

"This is a waste of time, how is this helping me?"

"Well, you eventually want to get out of here, right? I mean look around you, nobody wants to be *here.* If you can learn how to walk, then you can walk out of here and we can move on the next lesson."

"That's it? Just *walk* out of here? This is a joke, right? I walked *into* this place," she says as she goes to take her first step away from what she's slowly starting to realize is a grievous, not to mention senseless, waste of her time. "I'm outta here. Thanks for nothing."

"Uh, I wouldn't do that if I were you," Olpha says after she takes her first step. Remember, you walked into this place as *Joelle*—the *presumably*, young, enigmatic visitor from deep space. But right now however, you're the Mobile Statue—a half-ton monolith of destruction. And I mean that in the nicest way possible."

"You really think this place can hold me? I'll punch through every building in this graveyard until I get out," she asserts.

"Yeah, I guess you can do that—to be perfectly honest, a collapsing building is the least of your worries, but—"

"Have you seen what I'm capable of? I'm hardly worried about being hurt by such a thing."

"Oh, I'm well aware on how much that shell of yours can tank. Again, a building falling is the least of your worries because if you're careful, there's a great chance of that *not* happening. However —" Olpha lifts his leg straight up into the air and delivers a notable heel-kick to the ground a foot in front of him. This humble yet stern strikes causes the ground between him and Joelle to collapse, creating a large, gaping hole about five feet in diameter. "I'm just not too sure how much the ground beneath you can tank. That kick just now generated only about four thousand newtons, or just under a half a ton of force—that's about a little less than what you can create with one simple step. I haven't been here in a while, so I'm not too positive if it's gotten worse, but the last time I was here the ground around us caved in on me a good dozen times or so, and I only clock in at a measly one-hundred ninety-three pounds. I would hate to imagine what this place would do to a tank hopping around punching things. Besides, I'm not too sure how far down these sinkholes go," he says as he peers into the one he just created. "It's a good thing that you weigh only about what — one-thirty? One-thirty-five?"

"Why would you do this to me?" she laments.

"Do what? You can get out of here with no problem. Just transform," he says reassuringly.

"I told you already, I don't know how to transform at will!"

"Really? You seemed to do it with no problem when you wanted to get out of my little trap yesterday."

"You lied to me," she says to him, her voice beginning to fill with first despair and then anger. "I came here believing you were going to help me."

"Just think about what I said: learn to be still, so you can learn to stand and then walk. Also, just try to look at this as just another one of my traps—only bigger," he says as he starts walking away.

"Wait!" she screams out to him as he walks off. She takes a step forward and more of the ground gives way beneath her.

"Oh, that's the other reason they call this place a cemetery—most of the families of the people who fell down there decided it doesn't make sense to dig up a person who's already buried underground. I'll see you at home," he says before leaping away.

Maybe it's the simple act of her knowing just how decrepit her environment is, that causes her to suddenly start hearing the cracking and cackling of the floor beneath her and the semi-developed buildings around her. However, she is unable to determine if she's just simply imagining this or not.

Chapter Thirty-Five

POTUS FLOWER BOMB

April 30th. 2:39 P.M. (EDT)

"HEEEEEEEYYYYYYYYY! LOOK WHO IT IS!" Olpha screams when Joelle finally enters the house after Ori lets her in. "That was quicker than I expected."

"Quicker than you *expected?* I was out there for three days. I could've starved!" she says after glaring at him.

"I knew you'd be fine. And now that you're here, we can continue the training."

"You must be insane if you think I'm going to let you put me through that again."

"I was under the impression that you wanted to meet Aleph Null—now isn't the best time to lose sight of what's important," he imparts onto her. "I see you've learned to control your transformation."

After some convincing, Olpha and Joelle head out and return to Lagrange Point. Olpha decided it was best they went by car together this time.

"What the hell happened to this place? I was led to believe you walked out of here without any problem," he says once he takes a look at the tremendous damage that occurred over the past three days.

"Can you transform?" she bluntly asks Olpha after his insensitive statement.

"What?"

"Can *you* transform?"

"Well, I'm not really—"

"Okay, so shut up and let's continue," she snaps.

"You know what—that's fair. Okay, now that you have a better grasp as to how to be still, something that I honestly didn't think you would be able to achieve, I think it might be in our mutual best interest to teach you how to properly move."

"I agree."

"This next Verse I'm going to teach you is known as Palindrome. This Art can be mastered, however there's a catch ..."

"A catch?"

"Yes. Can you go into your Shell form for me?" he politely asks her. Joelle replies by turning into the Mobile Statue at will.

"Amazing! Very good, very good. Now, you're going to have to unlearn everything you've just learned about transforming."

"Say what?"

"The Mobile Statue—forget it exists. From now on, I don't want you to ever transform again."

"I just spent three days learning how to transform, now you're telling me you don't want me to?"

Olpha can feel her anger starting to rise again. So he hurries and starts speaking, hopefully to tame the beast that she just spent three days trying to control.

"Let me finish. I don't want you transforming for the simple purpose of fighting. Now that you know how to access your Shell form at will, in order to learn how to effectively perform Palindrome and eventually Syndeton, you have to completely abandon relying on it."

"Then why did you even waste time teaching me how to control it if I'm not going to use it?" she appropriately asks him.

"To achieve Palindrome, one must master how to control the intrinsic energy in their body; being able to transform at will is just the result of mastering how to be still."

"That still doesn't explain why I should no longer transform."

"Your Shell form requires you to access the hormones in your body responsible for releasing adrenaline. This puts a stress on your body and mind and causes the energy within you to become disturbed. There is no greater hindrance to mastering Palindrome—which you can only achieve when you have direct control of this energy."

"Wait, are you saying I'm too *fat* to fly in my Shell form??" she asks him, threateningly.

"Is that what you got from all that? No. What I'm saying is if you are really interested in defeating Jumo, you need to stop looking at the Mobile Statue simply as a transformation and start looking at it as another entity that lives inside of you. Because you'll never stop him if you don't stop that thing first."

"Transforming isn't a problem anymore, now that I can control it at will."

"I don't think you need me to tell you what happens to someone who breaks free from someone's control, do I?" he tells her.

"You speak as if this thing is really a person."

"As should you."

"Let's just get on with the next lesson."

"Let's."

"Before that, I have one question—if I'm able to learn to control my transformation ... does that mean I can also eventually learn to control the Bouya Effect?"

Joelle's question sends goosebumps down Olpha's arm.

"I can only hope. So! Now that you've gotten pretty good at being still, I can now begin to help you understand how to start moving."

"Understand? Look Olpha, I think I *understand* that quite well. What I need you to do is *teach* me, okay?"

"Unfortunately, Palindrome cannot be taught—not in the traditional sense. I know it sounds like made-up drivel, but it's the truth. Thankfully, once it's understood, you'll begin to learn it on your own."

"Great, more of your cryptic nonsense. Fine. Help me *understand* how to move then," she says after shaking her head.

"Okay, as I told you before one must master being still before one can begin to move. Now by conventional standards, people move when a signal in their brain tells them which muscle or set of muscles to utilize in their bodies to perform a particular action. The body can only move if there's enough energy present to execute these set of instructions. What I want you to understand is that there are more than one type of energy source within us. In additional to chemical energy, which is the energy we use from food to power our bodies, there is also electrical and even atomic energy. Now, there are two types of movements that I am going to refer to from now on: General Motion, and Reflex or Reflexive Motion. The type we are going to focus on first is General. This is the movement I usually perform by using the intrinsic energy found inside of the atoms in my body to enhance my general motor functions. Things like running, jumping, swimming, etc—basically, anything that requires you to use your whole body to perform, more or less. Now, I want you to jump up, but before you do, try to first be 'still' like you are when you transform. In other words, achieve the same state you achieve when you want to transform back to normal."

"Uh, okay. So don't move using my muscles ... I don't even know if I have muscles!" she exclaims.

"Good, then this should be a cake walk. Now, follow me," he tells her before they walk to another area of the lot.

"Now, transform into your Shell form again for me," he again asks of her.

"Why would I need to do that?"

"It'll help you get to the place you need to be to successfully access the explosive atomic energy dwelling within you."

"But you told me to forget about transforming."

"Forget about using it as a weapon. However, don't forget about its principles."

"I see. So, Shell form first; then Verse One; then Verse Two."

"Exactly."

Joelle focuses for a moment, then goes into her Shell form. Immediately, the floor beneath her collapses.

"Noooooooo!" she screams as she plummets six stories down into an abyss. "You lied to me, again!"

"I can't get over how quickly you can switch like that. This is off to a great start. While you're down there try to remember, it's more than the action ... it's the feeling—movement is just the ultimate achievement of mastering Palindrome. You have to first understand that, then *apply* that understanding," he yells down to her in the hole. "If anything, you'll learn that its execution, in fact, requires very little movement!"

"You better not leave me down here!" she yells back up.

"You don't expect me to hang around here until you figure this out do you? You spent three days learning how to be still, so it's going to take you at least double that to learn how to move. The truth is you won't be getting out of there anytime soon and I promised Laharin I'll take her to her doctor's appointment," he explains to her.

"Olpha, I swear I will level this entire island if you don't get me out of here right now!" she screams out.

"And drag in all that nasty water from the Krauss River? Can the Mobile Statue even swim?" he quips.

Joelle delivers a powerful punch to the inside wall of the hole she is currently entrapped in, causing the ground Olpha is standing on to rattle violently.

"You better pray I never get out!" she threatens. Olpha leaps away and heads back home. He arrives home about twenty minutes later.

"Babe, you ready?"

"Where's Joelle, Daddy?" Ori asks, mildly concerned.

"Joelle won't be here for a good while, sweetheart. You can breathe a little this time Laharin, she's on the second Verse now—it took me eight months to learn to perfect Palindrome. The fact that she's even got the first Verse down pat that quick is nothing short of a miracle. I swear, if that woman isn't the Warrior of Prophecy then that negro just doesn't exist. I saw Leander downstairs by the way, he brought the car around."

Ding-dong! The doorbell rings, indicating Leander is ready to take off.

"Oh, that must be him now," Olpha says as he goes to answer the door to let him into the house.

OOOOOHHHFFFF! Olpha answers the door, only to get hit in the chest with a hard punch that sends him back into his house, making him roll at least once on the floor before his tumbling body is eventually stopped when he hits the side of the kitchen counter. Standing in the doorway is Joelle with her fist extended as she slowly reverts back to her normal form.

"Hello, *Ilisaiji*. I learned how to move—so what's the next lesson?" she says to her fallen sensei.

Back at Lagrange Point, Olpha and Joelle prepares for the final lesson —Syndeton.

"I owe you an apology," he remorsefully tells his prodigious student. "It's extremely rare for someone who doesn't have a proclivity for the Verses to learn them so quickly. I severely underestimated your ability to learn these techniques, and never in a million years expected you to grasp the principles behind them. So for that, I'm sorry."

"Don't mention it. Heck, even I'm surprised at my progress. I must say, learning this second Verse wasn't nearly as difficult as the first one," she admits.

"But answer me this, now that you've gotten some understanding of Palindrome, what have you come to gain from such knowledge?"

"Well, I can do this now."

In that instant, Joelle leaps up high into the air and begins leaping around the many buildings located in Lagrange Point very similar to the way Olpha himself can, though not as coordinated. After bouncing around for a bit, she lands back in the spot she first leapt from.

"This new movement, combined with my Bouya Effect, makes me more powerful than I could've ever dreamed," she happily shares.

"I see."

"After you teach me the Third Verse, any kidnapper, cop or soldier that stands in my way again, will forever live to regret it. At this rate, don't be surprised if I even surpass you," she confidently boasts.

"I was foolish to doubt you once, luckily, I am wise enough to know when I am wrong. Before we move on to the Third Verse, there is something I first need to know—what do you plan on doing once you find Jumo?"

"Well, the plan is once I'm done with your training, I'll be strong enough to take him out."

"You mean kill him?" Olpha asks.

"I-uh—I haven't really thought about that."

"You told me Jumo was a former friend. Are you sure you are even capable of doing that?"

"Exactly. *Was.* Jumo stopped having a relevance in my life the moment he left me to die on Apophis. Whatever problems he has coming to him was fostered by his own will," she says after shaking off her moment of doubt.

"I see."

"This Syndeton thing must be something special for you to ask that right now."

"As always, it's the principles of the Verses, and not the execution of them, that I implore you to appreciate. Even in the hands of a master, if one loses sight of its virtues, they can be easily overtaken," he forthrightly tells her.

"I guess. I don't see how learning how to fight can possibly put me at a disadvantage."

"It can. I just hope the day never comes when someone shows you how. Now, you seem to have some grip on the first two Verses—this is necessary if we are to begin learning the third."

"Let me guess, you want me to forget everything I've learn so far."

"Actually, I want you to *use* everything you've learned so far. Now that you know how to be still and know how to move, it's time you learn how to move with purpose. This requires learning how to control a different source of energy inside of your body—namely, your bio-electricity."

"You're talking about the stuff that sends signals through your body —but isn't that what we use to control our muscles? The very thing you told me to forget?"

"I am, and yes, it is. Think of it like diving—though normally we need to breathe to stay alive, when we dive under water to swim, we must forget to breathe or rather, we must stop breathing in order to continue to live. I told you to forget how to move using your muscles, so you can eventually learn how to move using your energy. Now to move with purpose, you must remember how to use your muscles."

"Great. More cryptic bullshit."

"Moreover, the art of Syndeton has many, many applications—fighting is just one of them. Biokinesis is another."

"Biokinesis?"

"Once you can control both the atomic and electrical energy present within you, you'll be able to do things like this," Olpha leaps up to a building and stands on it with his feet firmly planted on the side of the wall as if he were a fly.

"Whoa. So learning to fight can somehow teach me to stick to walls?" she says, not really understanding the connection between the two.

"Well, you tell me. Though you can move, you don't know for what purpose. Once you do, such a feat will be simple to perform," he says when he leaps back and lands next to her. "Now, I want you to try to hit me. But instead of only using your muscles, apply the lessons of the first two Verses and guide them into the third to execute the punch."

"Okay."

Joelle throws a punch that insults Olpha. With a simple movement of his head, he dodges it. Joelle picks up on his sheer disappointment from her attack and decides to get more serious.

"I don't know what it is, but whenever you're in your normal form, you seem to lose that passion you have for fighting while you're transformed. Why is that? It's like you're holding back for some reason," he notices.

"Whenever I get involved in aggressive situations when I'm like this, people get hurt, accidentally. But, when I'm the Mobile Statue—I can't explain it. It's like ... I *want* to hurt people—purposely."

"Go on, try again."

She plants her feet firmly into the ground, and starts swinging at Olpha with what she considers to be combo attacks.

"You're never going to get better if you don't let go of whatever it is that you're afraid of," he says as he weaves her pathetic fury of strikes.

"I'm not afraid for me, I'm afraid for whoever is around me."

After weaving about seven more of her attacks without so much of looking in her direction, let alone paying attention to her, Olpha stops one of her punches with his finger and decides to make a suggestion.

"Stop. You think just because things have trouble hitting you that you owe it to someone to restrain yourself. So, I tell you what, now *I'm* going to start hitting you. And the only way I'm going to stop is if you learn to stop holding back."

"You saw what happened last time you tried to attack me."

"Oh, I know," Olpha says as he begins taking off his shirt and SHED band, revealing nothing but a sleeveless tank-top. "That's why I'm changing my tactics around this time. It's time I got serious. If you want to stop me, you might want to—"

Unexpectedly, Olpha's SHED band begins to vibrate right before he throws it on the ground. However, this isn't what stops him from finishing his last sentence. It's the sentence that scrolls across his band that has completely frozen him and sent a rare, cold chill down his spine; the accompanying expression he now wears is enough to even cause Joelle to become slightly worried.

"What is it?" she asks him, hoping whatever it is he tells her isn't some more philosophical humdrum on how to achieve a new skill. "Olpha, what's wrong?"

He looks up at her. "It's the president of the United States—he's dead."

Chapter Thirty-Six

DIVIDED STATES OF AMERICA

April 30th. 6:39 P.M. (EDT)

JOELLE AND OLPHA'S integral training session is interrupted by the news of the president of The United States being murdered. Immediately, the two head back home. Olpha quickly begins to realize exactly what this may mean for him and his family. Considering that President Lamarch was the one who created the Nerosion Pact and frankly was the strongest and by large, the only proponent of it, the direction of the country and ultimately the fate of Nerosion now rests in the hands of his biggest opposition—Vice President Reed Wise.

"Slow down, would you!" Joelle screams out to Olpha as they make their way back to his apartment. Though Joelle is now fully capable of leaping dozens of meters across the thousands of rooftops dotted throughout Monachopsis just as Olpha is, even she is unable to keep up with how fast her sparring partner is currently skipping across them. "The president was assassinated—what's the big deal, anyway? I know he's important, but aren't they just going to replace him with someone else?"

This absent-minded line of thought finally evokes a response from Olpha, who, for the past fifteen minutes, has been awfully quiet during their trip back home.

"That's exactly what they are going to do. And that's why we have to hurry."

"What, is this next guy a jerk or something? I haven't known you long, but I can say I never thought I'd see you like this," she admits.

"Stay close, we're almost there."

Olpha finally reaches his apartment building and he tells Joelle to wait on top of a nearby rooftop before he gives her the okay to fly in through the window. He looks around and like he's done over a thousand times, then flies inside of the window that's always left open for him faster than anyone who happened to be looking at him can notice.

After landing inside successfully, he turns and looks for Joelle to let her know it's cool for her to now enter the same way he did. After waiting for a moment, Joelle sees his signal and prepares herself for the final leap home. She readies herself and begins sprinting towards the edge of the roof.

KRACK! Unexpectedly, her foot nicks the bricked edge of the rooftop, causing her to slip and begin plunging thirty-two stories towards the busy streets below.

"AHHHHHHH!" she yells out as she approaches terminal velocity. Suddenly, several nano-carbon, reinforced-tensile wires fall beside her before gently wrapping themselves around her body several times, safely catching her. The staff slowly reels her back upward towards the apartment, away from dozens of cars below that she was so anxious to hug and kiss. Olpha removes the wire from around her body while she hyperventilates on some of the air she most likely doesn't ever need to breathe.

"Thanks to that annoying Bouya Effect of yours, I almost didn't catch you. You okay?" he asks once she's safely panting inside of the apartment.

"I don't know what happened. I just got dizzy and ... slipped," she says to him while sitting on the floor, hardly able to believe it herself.

"It happens. Don't worry about it. It takes a while before your body gets used to traveling at those speeds. Come on," he says as he extends his hand towards her and she takes it to help herself up off of the floor.

The two make their way to the living room and Laharin and Ori are already watching the news anchor give descriptive details about today's unfortunate events. When she sees Olpha enter, she immediately gets up to hug him.

"Oh my god, Olpha!"

"Are you okay?" he says as he hugs her back and grabs his princess as she runs towards her father.

"We're fine," Laharin tells him. "Have you heard?"

"I have, I have," he says to her before turning his head towards the T.V. "What are they saying?"

"They're saying his motorcade was ambushed. The whole convoy was destroyed."

"Goddamn it. I don't believe this. Why is this happening? Why now?" Olpha asks aloud, now completely vexed.

"What is going on? Did y'all know this guy personally or something? Was he a family member? Why are you so torn up about this?" Joelle inquires, still unable to wrap her head around why a man of Olpha's skill is worried about some weak man in a suit who only happens to run a nation of 350 million people.

"Breaking News. We are now being told that we do have footage of the unfortunate event. Viewer discretion is strongly advised," the news anchor on the T.V. says to her viewers. Without being told to, Laharin turns up the volume from her SHED band and Joelle watches the Chambers' faces intently before turning her head and gluing her eyes to the program just like the rest of them.

On the television, footage from a camera located on the dashboard inside of the president's car shows an ordinary drive through the roads that were taking him to the Ubiquitous Union located in downtown Monachopsis—the place where he planned on speaking at a convention addressing strategic initiatives on apprehending the UNSELF.

As the motorcade continues down the road, there is some indistinct radio chatter in the background, much of which is censored out. The president's voice is also muffled in the video, but the cadence of his tone doesn't imply anything other than normal banter going on between him and whoever else is in the backseat.

Not too much longer after, the motorcade begins to slow down. There's silence for a few seconds, then the distinct engine sound of a motorcycle approaching in the distance. The camera switches to an outside view of the motorcade, displayed from a camera located on top of the president's limousine. One of the officers in the video is heard saying: "It's just a bike. Confirm, it's just a—", and the video ends after a large explosion is seen and heard a second before it's cut off.

"Whoa," Joelle says, once the video cuts off. A word that Ori repeats after watching the same thing. Joelle looks over to Olpha and sees that his expression has changed. Maybe it's because she doesn't possess the descriptive powers to describe what she sees, but Olpha's expression does at the very least cause her to feel something—something different from him she hasn't felt since she met him. Laharin turns to Olpha, knowing full well what the implications of the same motorcycle sound everyone in the country heard, but only these two in the room can identify, must mean for her fiancé.

"You don't think—" she looks up and say to him before he bellows out his own version of what he just saw.

"Why would he do this? *Why?*" Olpha says, almost growling. "He's DEAD!"

Olpha immediately heads to the closet where he keeps his costume.

"Honey, wait!" Laharin calls out to him.

"Who's dead? What is going on?" Joelle yells as she forfeits her position of trying to organically learn about the situation at hand, instead of forcibly asking questions. Tired of her incessant questioning, Laharin finally turns to her to shed some light on the entire ordeal.

"The President of the United States was just assassinated. That's what you saw just now. That, in of itself, is perhaps more devastating than Apophis crashing into the planet and killing half the people in this country. It's what you *didn't* see that has my fiancé in there freaking out right now."

"What is it?"

"You have a best friend, Joelle?" Laharin asks the curious alien.

"I ... used to," she says after thinking about Calvin and Arthur.

"What if you found out he or she just did something so horrible, that it put you or your family's life in mortal danger?" she asks her. The existential relation Joelle has with Laharin's statement is enough to make her physically shiver a bit.

"So, the president *is* related to you then?" Joelle surmises.

"No, but he might as well be. President Lamarch was the only thing protecting this family. Without him, it's only a matter of time before the Nerosion Pact is dissolved."

"What is that?"

"It's a contract that allows Olpha to continue to protect this city while protecting his identity. Without it, they can arrest him—and his "best friend" just set that contract on fire."

"How? As I've come to understand, there are laws in place on this planet that have existed for hundreds of years. Some, even thousands. Why is this any different?"

"Because certain laws can be changed if the person currently in power doesn't like them. And the person who's now in power has made it very clear since we got here that he doesn't agree with the Pact," Laharin explains.

"Why wouldn't he? Did Olpha do something wrong?"

"Olpha? No. But Nero has."

"You mean Nerosion."

"No—I mean *Nero.* The man who helped destroy a United States military base in New Mexico nine years ago. The man who rescued me from that same military base. The same military base I was supposed to kill him in."

"Helped? You mean Chapter Five? You betrayed your country—so you're on the run, too."

"Today, Chapter Five is only known to the world as a terrorist organization—which would make Olpha ..." she says before stopping herself, not sure how she feels about calling her fiancé ...

"A terrorist," Joelle says in her place.

"Yes. And he saved me—and for that I had his baby. Smart, right?" she says, forcing a chummy chuckle.

"I'm just a baby terrorist, Joelle," Ori smiles and says out loud.

"When President Lamarch made the decision to sign the Nerosion Pact, Olpha never been happier. It made him feel like he can finally have a normal life—something I now realize he didn't know he wanted until I taught him what it was. Before that, it was only about the Chapter. That night, he proposed to me—and I never been happier. I've been his fiancée ever since," she shares before unconsciously brushing Ori's short hair with her hand. "Now, it appears Surii has destroyed all that we've worked for."

"Surii is his best friend?"

"He *was* his brother. Best friend is what it devolved to when they attacked my base. The day after that and since, they've been sworn enemies."

"Why did they attack your base? Were they at war with this country or something?"

"Some people will say yes, others will say no. At the very least, Chapter Five and the United States weren't on speaking terms. It wasn't the first time, either. But it was the first time the United States stole something from them."

"What did they steal? The Seriff?"

"Hehe, I wish. Believe it or not, it was actually something even *more* valuable. What they stole was Odem's little sister—Seren. And let's just say her brother wasn't happy about it. Since then, the group was classified as a terrorist organization led by the world's most dangerous dictator. After saving me, Nero decided he didn't want to go back to Chapter Five, and I know I didn't want to serve in the military any longer. So we went into hiding—together. During that time, Nero used his talents to turn any area we happened to stay at during our escape across the country, into a safer environment for the law-abiding citizens that lived there, by ridding whatever town we were in of any crime. It wasn't long before he made headlines across the country, and even a shorter time before our acceptive president wanted him on his team. So, he asked Nero if he would like to perhaps do what he was already doing, except legally and be payed to do so. Nero agreed under the terms that he gets to change his name and that his family is protected, also."

"I'm guessing this Reed Wise wasn't a fan of the decision."

"Reed Wise was there during Final Chapter. And he knows I helped Olpha escape. Not happy? I wouldn't be surprised if he paid Surii himself to assassinate Lamarch if it meant he can destroy the Pact."

At this moment, Olpha comes back into the living room, this time fully dressed in his trademark Nerosion gear.

"So, you're really bent on going through with this, huh?" Laharin says as she shakes her head.

"Surii has gone too far," he coldly remarks.

"And what are you going to do, Olpha? How are you even going to find him? You have no idea where he is."

"I know where he is," a hidden voice calls out from the hallway which makes everyone in the house look in that direction.

"Uncle Roger!" Ori joyfully shouts as the voice from the shadows reveals itself.

"You really need to learn to keep your windows closed," Boluscant says to Olpha as he walks into the living room.

"Hello, Roger," Laharin softly says. Surprised, but not at all startled.

"You're one of the last people I expected to see right now. Welcome back," Olpha responds to him.

"I'm going to go ahead and assume that Surii *would be* the last you expect then," Boluscant says back to him.

"I plan on changing that. Why, you know something I don't?"

"No, not really. But I *have* something you don't," Boluscant says as he removes his arms from behind his back. His arms a covered in a black, shiny sheath of armor.

"Heh. I don't even want to know what you went through to get that. You didn't kill—"

"No, he's breathing. But I can't say the same for their employer—who I'm on my way to go see now. I can drop you off if you need a lift."

"You know what, I actually do," Olpha replies.

"Olpha, are you kidding me right now?" Laharin whines, distraught.

"Laharin, Allen was our friend. I owe it him to find Surii and bring him in. This is the only way the Pact can stay in effect."

"I'm your fiancée, Olpha! She's your daughter. Your duty is to protect us first. And you're just going to leave us in the middle of all this? What if the Pact dissolves while you're gone?"

"Even if the vice president wanted to do that, it's going to take weeks before he can. The Pact may be compromised, but the order must stand until it's fully repealed. That won't happen for a while," Boluscant informs them.

"Olpha. I didn't tell this before but ... when those Strawmen attacked at Ori's school ... one of them ... one of them said my name ..."

"What?"

"One of them knew me, Olpha. She called out my name after I hit her. I wasn't just another innocent civilian that day. I was a target. Whoever created those things, whether it's Surii or Odem—they were trying to kill me," Laharin shares.

"I ... had no idea," he says mortified. "Why didn't you tell me?"

"With everything going on, I didn't want to add to your grief."

"Okay ... I'll stay," he says, submissively.

"I'll protect you," Joelle suddenly says after not speaking for a while, shocking everyone in the room.

"Who's she?" Boluscant asks the people he does know about the person he doesn't.

"That's Joelle—The Mobile Statue, uncle Roger," Ori happily shares with her father's ex-comrade. Boluscant looks at her confused and amazed at the same time.

"Go. Don't worry about your family—I'll look after them," Joelle says.

"What?" Olpha says, not expecting Joelle, of all people, to say what she just did.

"I owe it to you all for the way you've treated me these past few days. You didn't have to take me in the way you did, or teach me the things you did. Even after learning who I was, you still fought to protect me and help me in my journey. Now I see why this president of yours fought so hard to keep you around. Since my time here on this planet, I have come to accept your species as a vile, unappreciative race who has no interest in supporting one another if it means any of them can get ahead. You are the first to show me what it means to fight for something other than yourself. Thanks to you, I now have the ability to do the same, and I want to honor that by fighting for you and your family's right to exist, as you did not only for mine, but the countless others who can say the same because of you," she tells him before turning and looking at Laharin. "I know you have your feelings about me—which I've come to understand is how you're really supposed to feel about someone like me. That's what makes this family that much more special. Before, I thought people were naturally cruel, but I see it's in your nature to be that way towards things you're not familiar with. So, the fact that I can sit here and even have this conversation with you lets me know that you've been going against your natural feelings, just to make me feel more welcomed. Laharin, you asked me if I had a best friend or family. A friend, yes, I did once—but now that he's gone ... I wanted to ask you if it would be okay if I can now have a *family*—yours."

Laharin begins to tear up, then looks down at her daughter.

"You said you always wish you had a sister, Mommy. Now you can have one, and you don't even have to give me one, either!"

Laharin can't help but to laugh at her daughter's innocent banter, even as the tears well up in her eyes. She closes her eyes and begins to nod.

"That's true. Yes, sister, of course you can protect us," she says before making a move to hug Joelle, one Joelle happily returns back, which causes her to have a mini-seizure—the best one she's had yet. "Please turn into your Mobile Statue if you see any of those junkies or creatures coming, I give you allllll the permission, girl!" Laharin remarks while continuing to embrace her sister.

"Can I just hold them down while you punch them??" Joelle jokes back.

"Ready?" Boluscant asks Olpha. Olpha looks at him without answering then walks to his fiancée and daughter and lifts up his mask.

"I'm only doing this because your lips give me strength, not because of some corny, goodbye kiss or anything," he says to Laharin.

"Just shut up and kiss me, before I decide to change my mind," Laharin sensually snaps back. The two lovebirds then share a passionate kiss. Olpha then bends down and faces his daughter.

"Are you going after the Bee-Killer, Daddy?" Ori asks her father when he knees down in front of her.

"I am, baby."

"But isn't he your friend?"

"What makes you say that?"

"Because he protected me and Mommy from those bad guys in the Borick Valley."

"He did, huh?" Nerosion says before taking in and releasing a deep breath. "Well, he just put me, you, and Mommy in a position for everyone in this city to come after us. So, I have to go ask him why would he do something so horrible if he's really my friend."

"Well, maybe if you two stay friends, nobody in this city will ever be able to touch any of us," she responds which causes Olpha to choke up a little bit.

"Why are you so wise, huh? Ori, I want you to know that I live to make the world a better place so when you grow up, you can make the world a place to be better."

"I understand, Daddy."

"I know you do. Where's my hug?" he says with a smile. She runs to him and the moment she's in his arms he starts to excessively tickle her. As usual, she becomes hysteric.

"I love you," he says to her after she begs him to stop, before standing back up and facing Joelle.

"I'm sorry our training got interrupted—I know how important it is for you to meet Aleph Null, but I now believe everything I used to live and train for, was so one day I would be able to teach it to you. Please, protect my family, Joelle. When I get back, there are many more things I want to show you. I don't know if the things I know are going to make sense to you, but I believe the only reason I know them is because of you. I put all my faith in you, Joelle—not in what you can do, because what you can do—"

"— is just the application," she says, finishing his statement. Olpha smiles, the same smile one smiles when two people understand each other. He knows they do because she is currently flashing him the same smile.

"I'm ready," he says to Boluscant.

"You sure? I was about to start recording you, sheesh," Boluscant snaps back.

Olpha puts his mask back on, and the two head for the room that they both entered through, and disappear out the window in a flash.

Chapter Thirty-Seven

MISSILE LOCK

April 30th. 6:59 P.M. (EDT)

"I KNOW a part of me should be surprised—but I'm not," Paula suddenly says as she catches Roger re-emerging from the Artisan well that, despite the egregious attack on 7308 Yelloho Road, somehow still remains fully intact and unscathed.

Not at all ever anticipating her following him back to their own home, Roger gets nervous for the first time, since he's been off of a battlefield in years.

"Paula—" Roger stammers.

"If anything, a part of me kind of figured this was the case," she continues.

"Paula, I can explain."

"Why would you want to? Only an idiot would need you to explain what's happening right now. I just want you to know that whatever you're planning isn't going to work," she says to him, perhaps looking to break his morale and dissuade him from carrying on, or maybe because she truly feels that way and is trying to save his life. "Damn it, Roger, I begged you. When you were in the hospital, I begged you. Just ... just talk to me, let me in—that's all I asked. How come that was so difficult for you?" she asks him, but never receives a response. "Was there something missing? With me? Something you wanted that I couldn't give to you? If so, what? I would much rather know where it was I went wrong, then to know why is it you have a truck full of guns in our driveway."

Roger looks over at his truck and realizes Paula's been here for well over an hour.

"There's nothing missing. But there's something I have to do," he says with a hint of remorse in his voice.

"Then that means there is something missing. What is it?" Paula calmly asks him. Roger then looks at the charred home that he thought he and his family once had a future in.

"I did that, Paula. I broke that," he says pointing to their destroyed house.

"So what? You also built that, Roger. We both did, together," she acutely responds to his lamenting.

"I know. But now I have to fix it."

"Then let me help you."

"You can't."

"Why? I'm your wife."

"Because I broke that before I met you, Paula. And I can only fix it without you."

"You're really going to do this to me again?"

"The man responsible for who I am doesn't believe I deserve a life without him in it. And I'm scared that he may be correct. As long as he is alive, I can never be happy—we can never be happy. So, I have to get rid of him, so we can be."

"Who is he?" she asks him.

Roger remains silent for a reason that she's much too exhausted to continue to harp on.

"Better yet, don't even answer that. Instead, I want you to ask yourself ... who are you?"

"I'm just—" he begins.

"No. Don't tell me," she interrupts. "Because you don't know the answer. But when you figure it out—I want you to honor that. I want you to embrace it. I want you to remember what it took for you to figure that out. I want you to remember this life—where you had someone desperate enough to help you discover what your real purpose in it was. And I want you to remember that it was your woman and not some man that was there to ease your pain. I tried my best to give us an identity, even when everyone was telling me to give up on us, I went against their words, their insults, my thoughts and even my instincts—all to give us a purpose. A life. I even took in Jasmine like she was my own daughter, without a single fuss or regret. Not because I wanted to, but because it's what was expected of me, to show those who didn't want us to win, that they didn't

have a choice in the matter. And all this time, you were giving them one. We were going to prove them wrong, Roger—but all you did was prove me wrong. Here," she says as she tosses him his old dog-tags. "You're going to need them ..."

"Hey Boluscant, you heard what I said?" Nerosion says to Boluscant as they continue to leap from rooftop to rooftop on their way to Kenopsia. "I asked you if Paula knew what you were planning?"

"... because when they find your body, I won't be there to identify it."

"She's aware," he replies when he snaps back to reality after dwelling on the conversation he just had with his wife before he made the choice to pick up his ex-comrade. "Hey, I got a question for *you* now."

"Shoot."

"Why haven't you made that woman your wife yet?"

Nerosion takes a few moments before he answers. "I will. There's no rush."

"You sure about that? She seems to think there is. The night before Apophis hit, when Laharin and Ori stayed with us in the bunker, Paula told me Laharin was convinced you had completely forgotten that there's another step after becoming engaged. How long it's been since you popped the question?"

"Next month makes five years."

Boluscant lets out a long whistle. "You do realize an engagement is only a placeholder for an eventual marriage, don't you?"

"I'm aware. You do realize that Opia is far from cleaned-up, don't you?"

"What does that have to do with making that woman your bride?"

"Everything. The Nerosion Pact is about more than just keeping me and Laharin from facing a jury. I've been hired to do a job. And I can't just abandon that to appease someone—even if it's her. The only thing that can come from that kind of forced shortcut is a sample version of a life that I truly want for my family. I'm not going to shortchange myself like that just because I can't be patient. Once I take care of Surii first, I can then take care of Laharin next."

"Those are some priorities, man. You're worried about being a prisoner in a cell, and can't even see how much of a prisoner you already are to the Chapter," Boluscant remarks.

"Surii and the Nerosion Pact are undifferentiated—in fact, they're one in the same."

"You really think there's going to come a day where you or your family are truly going to be free?"

"Once I capture Surii, it won't be up for debate," Nerosion replies.

"Take a good look at me. I've been down your road—and what you see before you is the result of someone who used to believe he can balance the Chapter with having a normal life. Once we became one of the Article, our lives no longer belonged to us. You know what I am? All I am is you arriving at your final destination—the only difference is that I'm just a couple hours early."

"I thought you didn't believe in fate."

"I don't. But I had to remember that I don't. Which is why I'm exercising my free will by heading to Odem to prove that there's no such thing. I've come to realize that my purpose here is to prove that nothing is this world is preordained—nothing except God's Will. Even if we were made to believe that there is no life outside of the Article, I'm here to prove that that's just not true. You see, I believe in sacrifice. Like how I had to just sacrifice Paula and my children just so I can show her that what I'm doing is necessary, so that maybe she and I can one day truly live a life without having to look over our shoulders. I can already tell that you think that alien in your house is the Warrior of Prophecy. Hell, I'll be a fool not to believe the same. But not everyone believes what we believe. And nor should they have to. Laharin doesn't care about your plans to fix things just so that you two can live a better life in some unseen future. Her beliefs are different. She understands better than anybody that it's okay if this is only as good as her life is going to get—just as long as it's spent with you, now —in the present."

"Then shouldn't you be with your family right now?"

"If I believed in fate, of course. If I wasn't an advocate of free will, then I would just roll over and say my destiny is tied to living a life where the Chapter will always be involved in it no matter what. But the Lord has better plans for me, for all of us. What I'm trying to tell you is that, you don't have to go down the same road I'm going down just to prove something to someone. That's my choice. You can walk a different path, and sacrifice it all, to prove to those who matter that there is a life outside of the Chapter. And it starts by showing that woman how much she means to you, today."

"Now I feel like it's my turn to start recording. My faith is in the Prophecy. As a Child of the Seriff, you should understand that I owe it to myself to do what I can to help the Prophecy be fulfilled. What you call free will, I see is simply you upholding and living by the scriptures of the Toska—which is what we were born to do. If the alien truly is the Warrior, then there won't be any need to worry about any pact, Odem, the Article, or Chapter Five—and I can give Laharin the life that she truly deserves," Nerosion tells his former comrade.

"Boy, you're just as stubborn as when I first met you twenty-years ago, hehe," Boluscant chuckles.

"I guess we're both delusional in our own way. Where are we headed anyway?"

"The Hit Factory. Your favorite government agent left me a parting gift in the form of an aircraft."

"Two toys? I figured a retired war general shouldn't have to beat up PHADSYN's director just to get access to a jet."

"*Former* Director. And does *that* look like an ordinary jet to you?" Boluscant says, as he points to the lone aircraft that sits on top of the heliport on the roof near PHADSYN's headquarters.

"So, Serota got the ax. I can't even imagine who they got to replace him," Nerosion says out loud, but mostly to himself.

"Oh, you haven't heard?"

"You're going to tell me something else I don't know?"

"Would you believe me if I told you that there's somebody going around saying they're the new Obelisk?" Boluscant says to him.

"I don't want to believe you, but it's looking like I don't have much of a choice."

"He calls himself Bobandy. And get this ... he's my clone—only far younger and apparently, far more skilled."

“That second part I’m going to have trouble believing. The younger thing though, yeah—that’s easy to believe,” Nerosion quips.

“Funny,” Roger scoffs as they land on the heliport and begin climbing inside of the compact aircraft.

“So, that’s why you have those things on your arms. In case you bump into him,” Nerosion acknowledges.

“My beef isn’t with some Hannibal Article knock-off. I call these babies the Fate Changers for a reason. And they’re specially made to only rip apart the man who tried to rip apart my family.”

“The last guy I saw with those on was fried out of his mind on Exile. You sure you’re okay to fly?”

“If he was fighting you, I can see why he would've needed to be. I’ve operated every type of vehicle in the U.S. military known to man. There’s nothing I *can’t* fly,” Boluscant remarks.

“Aye, aye, Captain.”

“Where am I taking you by the way?”

“Hmmm. If you were Surii and you needed to execute a plan that included distributing a new experimental drug into a city, where would your base of operations be?” Nerosion asks.

“If I was Surii, I would be dead because I would've killed me.”

“You sure? You didn’t seem to feel that way in the hospital.”

“It makes me want to puke when I say this but ... Surii saved me from PHADSYN.”

Hearing this does something to Nerosion’s expression under his mask that will continue to be a secret to everyone but him. Whatever it did caused him to become speechless.

“Don’t be mistaken,” Boluscant continues. “He only did so because he’s convinced the Article must remain intact. Also, he knows what I have planned for Odem. And if I know him, he’s going to do everything in his power to stop me from getting near him, just like at White Sands.”

“It looks like we’re both going to the Almagest then,” Nerosion tells Boluscant, he who now sits behind him in the two-seater commuter jet as he waits for him to finish running a system check and initializing the ignition process. After flicking a series of switches, the craft begins to hum, and not too long after, begins to levitate in place.

From there, the craft continues to ascend from its original spot, higher and higher up into the air. When it reaches about 2,500 feet, the craft tilts back and points its nose seemingly at the now-known location of Almagest's position. Ionic thrusters silently ignite from the back of the craft and the two take off, heading straight for the Almagest.

After about thirty-five seconds, the craft reaches about 25,000 feet. Boluscant continues to gradually accelerate the aircraft faster and faster, impressed that it is capable of doing so, even as they continue to ascend at the angle they do.

"Newform Industries surely knows how to develop some impressive tech. I've never flown anything like this in the Marines."

"Looks like your fancy torture methods paid off. Good job," Nerosion remarks.

"Actually, it looks like they didn't," Boluscant says as he notices a blip on his radar indicating that he isn't the only one trying to get to the Almagest.

"What is it?"

"I didn't get the last laugh after all. Take a look at the monitor in front of you," Boluscant says.

Nerosion activates the video feed in front of him and notices an exact replica of the craft he currently sits inside of is now tailing them.

"Who is that?"

"Take a guess."

"Surii."

"Well, at least you won't have to wait til you get on board to handcuff him. Son of a bitch! Alright, hang on, if there's one thing I can do better than all of y'all, it's cook and fly."

Not a second after he says that, does an alarm go off inside of their craft, indicating that the aircraft behind them is trying to get a lock on them so it can fire a missile.

"Uh, what's that noise?" Nerosion asks, now getting worried.

"He's trying to get a lock on us."

Boluscant begins performing aerial maneuvers the likes of which make the aircraft appear as if it's moving like an erratic moth.

"What the hell was that?" Nerosion shouts in response to the fancy, evasive flight maneuvers Boluscant just performed.

"The beeping stopped didn't it?"

And for a second it did. But it doesn't take long for Surii to catch up to them and attempt another lock.

"Shit."

"Are you sure that's Sur—WHOA!!"

Suddenly a missile flies right by Nerosion's window.

"I didn't hear any beeping; how did he get a lock!"

"He didn't. That son of a bitch is dumb-firing."

"That did not look like a dumb fire. It actually looked smarter than anything he's tried to do yet," Nerosion responds.

"No, he's strategically using gunfire to get us into the position he wants so we can collide with a blind missile that he fires without locking on to us. At this rate, it's only a matter of time before we get hit. This man is something else—I see why this country wants him dead."

"Boluscant, open the top. I'll put an end to this."

"Are you kidding? Even you won't survive a fall from this high up."

"It's a good thing I don't plan on falling."

"We're flying at about Mach 2 right now. You open that canopy and the wind blast will not only tear your little mask off but your face along with it," Boluscant warns him.

"Well, sitting inside of this thing running away isn't helping either."

"Hold on, I have an idea. I was hoping to save this as a last resort, but it looks like we don't have that kind of luxury."

Boluscant closes his eyes, lifts his forearm and begins to concentrate. After several seconds of silence, Nerosion grows a little more worried, considering Boluscant seems to have fallen asleep at the wheel and the alarm that telegraphs that a missile lock has been achieved is now blaring all throughout the canopy.

Inside of Surii's craft, the controls that he's quickly grown accustomed to are now beginning to shake and malfunction. It isn't long before the entire craft itself starts rattling uncontrollably. During this time, Surii has figured out that this isn't due to any turbulence of any kind—someone is purposely trying to sabotage his aircraft.

He does what he can to regain control of the plane, but it's almost as if there's a force more powerful at work within the machine. It doesn't take long for Surii to learn that this force is powerful enough to completely destroy his aircraft and knock it out of the sky, ending his pursuit—so he, wasting no time, uses what little control he has left of it to fire a missile, this one successfully achieving a lock. The missile leaves the aircraft before Surii loses total control and begins spinning back towards the ground from 75,000 feet in the air.

A different type of alarm begins to go off inside of Bolsucant and Nerosion's aircraft—a telltale sign that a heat-seeking missile is now on its way to destroy them. The sounds of the alarm break Boluscant's concentration and he relinquishes his grip on Surii's craft and focuses it on the rocket in flight.

For reasons unclear, Bolsucant is having much more trouble trying to get a hold on the missile in flight towards him—this may be due to the speed the missile travels or due to Boluscant being unable to focus hard enough to control it.

"Hey Bo, I think this rocket has a bead on us. Do something!" Nerosion cries out.

"I'm trying!"

"There it is! I see the Almagest—that thing is gargantuan," Nerosion says when he catches his first glimpse of the titanic airship.

Not too far from them now is the floating fortress that perhaps no one in human existence has ever seen in flight this high up, besides these two individuals. The size of the craft dwarfs anything on Earth that can currently fly in the air, or even sail in the ocean.

"It's like something out of a movie. That thing has to be half a mile long," Nerosion says to himself, before looking at Boluscant and realizing he's still doing his best to destroy the missile that seeks to destroy them. Nerosion looks back and sees that whatever he's doing is actually working as the missile seems to be losing power and control.

"Yes, Bo! You almost got it!"

Suddenly Surii ejects from his spiraling aircraft, spinning out of it uncontrollably, it appears. However, one would be fooled to think any move Surii commits is one that isn't fully capitalized upon.

The missile that took of all Boluscant's concentration to veer off course finally explodes behind them, allowing the aircraft they're on to continue flying without any severe damage.

"YESSSSSssss—oh ..."

Nerosion stops his premature celebration the moment he notices Surii's U.R.O. cut through the cloud of smoke the missile left when it blew up. Like a saw blade traveling twice as fast as the missile was, the U.R.O. makes its way from 8,000 feet below them, to their position in all but a second.

Surii looks on while he falls from the sky, as his unique blade makes its way to the aircraft he couldn't shoot down by any conventional means, and watches as the blade slices through the craft, causing the entire airplane to explode into a thousand pieces.

Chapter Thirty-Eight

TERMINAL VELOCITY

April 30th. 7:57 P.M. (EDT)

IT'S hard to determine just from looking at Surii's blank expression, while he continues to fall out of the sky, how he currently feels about just killing two of the closest people he ever had to calling a brother and a pastor. Maybe it's when he notices that one of the pieces of debris that exploded from the aircraft he just blew up is floating towards the Almagest, that it's easy to get a better understanding of how he feels about everything he just had a hand in causing. Or perhaps, it's because after a few seconds, he notices that that piece of debris floating towards the Almagest is actually one of the two people that he thought he had just turned into buzzard brunch.

It's when he takes his headphones out of his ears that Surii somehow gets a better look at Boluscant using the Entropy to navigate his way towards the floating fortress some 80,000 feet above the Earth, similar to how he usually turns down his music for some inexplicable reason every time he needs to park his bike—as if sound somehow makes his vision better or something.

"How are you doing that, Bo?" he asks his former comrade, even though with their amazing ability to hear things from far away distances, there's absolutely no way Boluscant can possibly hear his question from where he currently is.

Surprisingly enough, Nerosion himself is able to hear Surii's forlorn question, because he makes the choice to answer him before he tries to strike him with his trusty, never rusty, Mauerbauertraurigkeit as he descends from the sky like a meteor aiming directly for Surii's head.

"It's called the Entropy!" Nerosion shouts. It's only because the U.R.O. decided it finally wanted to boomerang its way back into Surii's palm at this exact moment, that Surii is able to defend himself from getting cracked over the skull by Nerosion's nano-graphite staff. "My guess is he's using it to lock on to the Almagest's center of mass and pulling himself towards it somehow."

Surii tries to counter Nerosion's attack by delivering one of his own after his split-second block—a twisting, back-flipping kick that misses but at the very least puts some distance between him and his arch-nemesis.

Nerosion puts his staff away and starts to stretch his muscles and Surii puts away his U.R.O. and starts wrapping his pink headphones around his iPod before tucking it away into his dingy jacket. Even as the two continue to plunge towards the ground at a speedy 122 miles per hour, they continue to conduct the rest of their conversation as if they were simply having coffee in some random deli.

Meanwhile, just as Surii surmised, Boluscant is indeed flying towards the Almagest at a speed close to the one he was traveling while in the aircraft. As Nerosion explained, the Entropy Boluscant wields on his arms, was close enough to the Almagest where it was able to use the ship's huge mass to pull itself towards it, like Jupiter did to the Shoemaker-Levy 9 asteroid back in 1994. Soon he disappears from Surii's sight, and anything that's left to be known about him from henceforth is only witnessed by those unlucky enough to occupy the Almagest at this time.

"You know I was trying to save him, right? Bo? Yeah, I was trying to save his life," Surii says to the man who falls from the sky with him with his arms folded.

"Yeah, just like you saved him from PHADSYN, right?" Nerosion responds.

"Odem is going to kill him. I was trying to prevent that. It doesn't matter if he now has some toy that can make him float, his blood and the death of the Article will now be on your hands," Surii grimly, yet calmly explains.

"Like the president's is on yours?" Nerosion fires back.

"Why did you let him go, Nero? What is wrong with you?"

"Why did you kill the president? And sentence my family to death? I thought you wanted to help me, Surii. Why would you do this to me? All differences aside, Laharin told me you helped her. So, why would you suddenly betray us like this? Why are you so evil?"

"I see you're going to keep switching the subject, fine. I did it because I had to. You had more than enough time to fix Opia. Five years. That city should've been cleansed in less than three with you there. Your job was to get in, clear your name, then get out. But you started slacking. You got lazy. Then you had a baby—and you got comfortable. You was never going to fix Opia. Look at you—you need a suit now to help you fight because of how badly you fell off. You're a disgrace, Nero. So I took the initiative to hurry and get things in order since you wasn't up for it. With your little bodyguard now gone, we can now begin to bring Gloria back to life."

"You said you weren't working for Odem."

"This isn't about Odem—this is about you fulfilling your role. Get your insolent head out of your ass and read your Toska for once, Nero. Nothing I'm doing should be surprising to you."

"But whoever said I wanted her brought back?" Nerosion responds, a statement Surii finds downright hubristic.

"Whoever said you had a choice? This is what I'm talking about. You've been acting so brand new ever since you got a new outfit. Fine. I'm done trying to help you. As a Child of the Seriff, I can't allow you to compromise it like this any longer," Surii says to Nerosion as they continue to free fall. "Forgive yourself."

"Surii, I came all the way out here because I realized you are much too dangerous to be left alone. I can no longer allow you to continue to roam freely as you please," Nerosion says to Surii. "And I won't let you destroy my family."

"Nero, you destroyed your family the day you met them."

Exactly at 48,000 feet, both combatants draw their signature weapons again—though death at this point seems inevitable for both of them, either of them would much rather be done in by one another, then granting the pavement below the honor of taking their life.

Nerosion, uncharacteristically, is the first to attack, almost throwing Surii off. He initiates a punch combo that includes him letting go of his staff and letting it free fall beside him while he attacks Surii.

Surii continues to block and dodge the onslaught of blows, but making sure not to take his eyes off Nerosion's staff. In fact, if he's come to learn anything about his sparring buddy, it's that he's a master at using feint attacks to set up a finishing blow. Surii decides to see if the Nerosion that's in front of him is still the same one he used to respect as a formidable duelist, so he finally stops blocking and throws a punch of his own to put his theory to test.

The moment he does, Nerosion counters it by using the staff that continues to free fall next to him to try to hit Surii, which would've been successful on anyone else besides him. The attack barely misses him, but the fact that he predicted Nerosion's amateur attack disappoints him and makes him grow substantially more upset, which he uses to deliver a powerful kick to Nerosion's abdomen.

"Still using those same lame set-ups? You disappoint me, Nero!" he shouts, as Nerosion reorients himself from the stiff attack.

Nerosion realizes that his opponent is not only not your everyday criminal, but is known as the second most dangerous man in the world. He was silly to even suspect such attacks would work on him.

Realizing that at the speed they're falling, it's only about four minutes left before they smack into the ground, Surii decides to go on the offensive to end this battle quickly, so he can perhaps take a couple of minutes to come up with a way to survive this plunge.

"What kind of plane doesn't come with a parachute?" he mutters to himself. "Hey, did your craft come with a parachute?" he asks Nerosion after he catches him with a stiff jab.

"UNF!" Nerosion grunts. He shakes off the effect from the punch before answering him. "I'm starting to think Serota played us both."

"Who?" Surii asks as he starts trying to slice Nerosion in two with his U.R.O.

"Really? You don't even know who it was you got your plane from?

I thought y'all were working together if anything," Nerosion replies while dodging.

"Nah, bruh. I stole that thing from the same factory you and ol' Bo took off from."

"What? Wait, so you're not working with PHADSYN?"

"With who?"

"Odem's bodyguards."

"You mean those guys who tried to kidnap Ol' Bo? Hell no! They tried to 'nap my mans up, I don't switch sides like that. It's Hannibal Article til the death of me!"

"You sure you and Odem aren't working together ... because you're starting to talk just like him. So, you're telling me you're not the one moving Exile through Opia?"

"Working with Odem? How the hell can I work with a man who lives in the sky? Listen, Odem is a weirdo man, I keep my distance from that dude at all times. And what the hell is an Exile?"

Surii continues to tag Nerosion with every third or fourth punch or kick, whichever he happens to deliver at that time. Up until now, Nerosion has done a great job at avoiding most of them, especially his blade attacks, which he's been successful at countering with his own staff. However, everything he has tried to throw at him, from his ball bearings to trying to ensnare him in his wires—none of it has been successful. He realizes there is nothing in his arsenal that will disable Surii before they hit the ground—all except one thing.

"There's about 11,000 feet left before we become fertilizer," Nerosion says, updating his opponent.

"Then you better hurry up and handcuff me and take me in so I can answer for my crimes. That *is* your plan, right?" Surii asks.

Instead of answering, Nerosion removes his mask.

"What are you do ... what the hell happened to your face?"

"Same thing that happened to your jacket. You know ... you're right Surii, this suit *has* been holding me back," he says as he starts taking off of his costume.

"Bro, I know you're not about to ... bro ... I know you're not about to strip in the middle of the air right now while we're fighting."

Nerosion continues to undress.

"Nero, Nero okay, all jokes aside. Stop, you're freaking me out now. Okay, I'm sorry for killing the president, but please, enough—you win, you win! Look," Surii puts his U.R.O. away and puts his hands up. "I give up."

"But I don't," Nerosion says back.

In that instant, Nerosion throws the armored vest he uses to protect his torso directly at Surii, which Surii immediately tries to slice in half. Nerosion anticipates this move, and uses his staff to knock Surii's U.R.O. out of his hand.

"ARGHH!" Surii screams. Nerosion successfully disarms the blade from his hand, and the moment Surii grunts, Nerosion wraps Surii completely inside of a roll of his staff's cables, encasing him in a tight bind that he can't escape from.

With seconds left before they smack into the pavement, Nerosion quickly pulls the ball of cables towards him, and uses a great deal of his strength to kick himself off of Surii in an effort to break both of their falls.

The two fighters smack hard into the ground at the same time opposite of one another, and neither of them show any signs of moving.

Boluscant now strays only a couple thousand feet from the super-fast Almagest. With every meter he gets closer, the stronger his resolve becomes for his mission.

"Burt? Burt Bondi?? Hey, long time no see! Wait a minute, you can fly now? Since when??" Odem says to Boluscant as he appears out of nowhere and starts flying next to him. "Wait, are you on your way to the Almagest, also?"

In less than a fraction of a second, Boluscant swings a powerful punch at the man he just was on his way to see. Unfortunately, all he manages to hit is the millions of air molecules that he continues to fly by, since Odem seems to have vanished just as fast as he appeared. And only millions of molecules, considering the oxygen at this extreme altitude is growing considerably thin.

Boluscant grows infuriated at the fact that he missed ripping apart the man who he's currently on his way to go rip apart. What only intensifies his rage, is that he notices that a small Post-It note is now pasted on the back of his hand.

Dear Burt,

Sorry, I didn't mean to bail on you like that, but I really got to take a shit. Text me when you get

inside so I know you got in safely. - Love, Odem

Boluscant immediately snatches the sticky note off of his hand and crushes it before tossing it to the wind.

"Unh ..." Nerosion whimpers, after a minute of lying unconscious. He rolls over to his side and attempts to stand up—this too taking a whole minute to perform. After finding his balance, he weakly looks over to see that the ball of wire he encased his formidable foe in has yet to move since he's regain consciousness.

He starts walking, or rather, starts limping, towards Surii, who's condition still remains unknown. As Nerosion begins slowly uncoiling the cocoon, he begins to consider if he should've just stopped Boluscant from heading to Odem. He chooses not to spend too much time dwelling on this, considering the man he's unwrapping has survived things much worse than this, so all of his focus should be on anticipating a surprise attack.

He finally goes to uncoil the final wire that'll allow him a look at Surii's face, and he lifts his fist, preparing a punch that he's ready to use if his opponent tries to attack him first. He pulls the wire back at first very carefully, the unwraps it as quickly as he can and goes to make the first strike.

When he looks down, all he sees is his ex-brother bloodied and laid out, showing nothing resembling a threat; at the very least, Nerosion can tell that he's breathing.

"You're wrong, Surii. A member of the Article can have a life and still be a Child of the Seriff. You tried to destroy my family. But it's not too late to save them. When I bring you in, all you've done will be made right."

Nerosion picks up Surii and starts carrying him in his arms. After walking for a few minutes, he makes his way to a nearby gas station. He places him down, some of his body still coiled up in his wired cage, and walks inside to purchase something to drink for the long hike back home.

The gas station clerk, wanting nothing to do with a dirty man carrying an unconscious body and dropping it off directly outside his store, does everything he can not to raise any alarms, and simply rings up Nerosion's bottles of water as he would if he were just any other person. The entire transaction could've not have gone smoother for Nerosion. The only thing that stops him from exiting the store is the current news report that comes in over the gas station's television. Because every station in the world is more than likely reporting on the assassination of President Lamarch, it's a wonder Nerosion even stops to pay attention to what's on the television at all, considering he more so than anyone has a much more important task to handle right now. The only logical explanation is that whatever it is that stopped him in his tracks is perhaps slightly more important than delivering Surii's body to the nearest police station.

Inside the White House, Vice President Reed Wise takes the podium for the first time since he's become Lamarch's running mate. His first words as acting president, at this point, hold the attention of the American people more so than his words ever had in his entire life. Now at the podium, he takes a few moments to collect himself, then he begins to speak:

"My fellow Americans. Today, we have experienced a tragedy the likes of which hasn't occurred in this country in over sixty years. Many of you here weren't even alive at the time when this nation had to deal with such a national

tragedy. As you all know, President Allen Owen Lamarch, my best friend and confidant, was killed when a group of terrorists plotted a scheme to intercept his motorcade and blow it up. The attack took the life of every single officer and diplomat riding with the president at the time, leaving no survivors.

But I'm not here to remind you of what millions of you already know by now. No, I'm here today to share with you, in light of the grim turn our day took, some information that I believe will begin helping us heal from this depressing tragedy. I'm here to tell you that we have identified the men responsible for this attack. Many of you have heard of them but almost none of you know who they are. This wretched terrorist cell responsible for taking our president's life is known as Chapter Five—the extremist regime that operated out of the now failed-state, Gloria, from 1977 until 2020.

Though the United States was successful in defeating and destroying the terrorists' state, it appears we were regrettably unable to successfully capture and defeat every single one of Chapter Five's members. In the midst of this unparalleled tragedy that's befallen the people of this nation, it's with a vacillating heart I share with you all today that through this deplorable act of terrorism, we were lucky enough to obtain the identities of the members of this evil organization.

In addition, we've learned that since the collapse of Gloria, these terrorists have sojourned themselves within our very own borders, and have been hiding in plain sight every day since. Of the four members who make up the remnants of this band of miscreants, the first one we've identified is one that many of you have come to love and grow to respect since his inception and inclusion into one of our greatest cities back in 2024. His name is Olpha Chambers, and he is known to many of you around the country as the superhero, Nerosion. As we speak, every government agency available is on their way to his home in Monachopsis to apprehend him and anyone that has been aiding in keeping his elaborate, sinister plans a secret from us.

The next is..."

Nerosion drops his bottle of water and begins to feel light-headed. The clerk looks up at the picture of the man they show and realizes that it's the same man who just left a dead body right outside his store—only more bloodied and dirty.

They stare at each other for a while, neither of them making a move. Nerosion turns and limps out of the store, as the man remains frozen in place, unsure of what to do or even what to think.

Upon exiting, Nerosion gathers what little energy he has left, and takes the biggest leap his body probably has ever taken in his life, propelling him close to a mile towards the direction of Opia—leaving the fate of his unconscious prisoner, who remains tied up and slumped over on the ground, at the mercy of Terry, the On-The-Run cashier.

Chapter Thirty-Nine

THE MONSTER BEHIND THE MASK

April 30th. 11: 47 P.M. (EDT)

IT TAKES ALMOST four hours for Nerosion to make it back to Opia—a trip that may have been cut in half if he wasn't as injured as he currently is. The only thing that may have been moving faster than his body was his thoughts, the likes of which ran through every scenario, mood, and emotion that one man can experience in the length of four hours.

When he enters Monachopsis, he's relieved to see that the streets and buildings aren't on fire. With the entire world tuning in to President Wise's speech, it wasn't all that unbelievable to think that such a thing wouldn't be the case. That being the case, it doesn't necessarily mean that his particular apartment that sits at 410 Heimer Plaza—the one he's called a home for the past five years, isn't itself in flames. It's no wonder he lets out of a far-too-long held breath when he sees apartment 32D still fully intact from the outside. He gives his thanks to Joelle, and thinks about all the things he owes her for keeping his family safe in these trying times. He may even teach her the rest of the Verses after all.

But all luxuries will have to wait until he gets her and his family out of the city and back to Boluscant's hidden base that doubles as a bunker—the same one he told his family to stay in the night Apophis was supposed to crash into the planet.

As usual, the window that Laharin leaves open for him when he's out, is, as expected, open when he arrives to his building. Maybe it wasn't as easy for people to find his place of residence as he expected it to be. Which isn't too much of a leap to take, considering that there is probably no more than ten people in the city that know who Olpha Chambers is.

Nerosion leaps in through the window, though not as elegantly as he's known to, and hurries to the living room, so he and his family can begin making their escape.

He rushes into the living room and is surprised to see no one there. No Joelle, no Laharin, no Ori. Good, he's taught them well. If an event such as this were to ever occur, the family has spent dozens of hours practicing hiding in secret locations built inside of the apartment.

He heads for the first location that Laharin and Ori have made their own, which is inside of their bedroom closet. The hidden area is behind a wall that's inside of the closet—a space most people won't ever think to check.

Now inside the bedroom, Nerosion opens the closest door and begins rapping on the wall inside of the closet, in the codified way they practiced if they ever had to identify one another in such a circumstance. He does this a few times and is puzzled that he doesn't get a response. Frustration begins to set in, and he starts to call out their name.

"Laharin? Laharin? It's Olpha, you can come out now. Laharin! Ori? Shit!"

He leaves the room and heads to the second hidden location, the one that would've been reserved for him—the one that's perfect for a stealthy ninja such as himself to use to incapacitate anyone that may have been trying to sneak into their home. This one is located inside of the wall of the tub in the bathroom. Again, he calls out their name.

"Laharin? Ori?" he says as he continues to perform the unique knock that only the three of them would know. After spending a minute or two doing this, he begins to panic a bit and rushes back into the living room to see if they left a clue as to where they could be.

Because there seems to be no signs of a break-in, he doesn't allow himself to imagine the worst. More than likely, they headed back to Boluscant's bunker with Leander, as they've been taught to do if hiding in the secret spots weren't an option.

Assuming they did head out to the bunker, the first thing Nerosion checks is to see if Laharin took her medicine with her. So, he heads back into the bathroom and checks the medicine cabinet.

Even though leaving a clue to tell him that they were heading for the bunker was something that the Chambers family never really practiced or agreed upon, he feels exceptionally good knowing that his better half went out of her way to do that very thing for him anyway. As a result, a clue she made sure he got, in the form of a letter, is left for him in the compartment area of the cabinet where she keeps her medicine.

A brilliant physicist who once went by the name Dr. Arthur Bouya, was the one who suggested that I seek you out. He told me in his last words that you can help me more than anyone else. Until this day, I'm not sure what made him believe that you were the one I was supposed to find, but what I do now know for certain is that he was completely wrong. He gave up his life for me, because he believed that whatever it is you were supposed to do for me was more important than him seeing another day. But I disagree. I believe his life was more important than either of ours. When you first brought me to your home, I genuinely thought that you really had my best interest at heart. But like I've come to learn about everything that calls itself a human being—you lied to me. Your true interests were made clear the day you told Laharin how you really feel about who I am—and I heard what you plan to do to me if you were wrong. The only reason you continued to help me is so you can rid yourself of having to deal with my associate, before you would, unbeknownst to me, eventually take me out also. Every single one of you despicable creatures are nothing but self-serving, pretentious liars. It is the one element you all have mastered in order to continue to sustain yourself within your individual, pitiful existences. Don't believe me? Well, you don't have to look far for the evidence: just take a look at your family—you lie about making Laharin your wife. Laharin lies to herself thinking that someone wants to marry someone who's disabled, and Ori lives a lie day after day pretending that she's okay with everything going on between her parents.

But all isn't bad. My time on this planet has been so, so very enlightening. Over the weeks, I've learn how to adapt to your kind, learned how to blend in—and as a result, I, too, have mastered your species' greatest skill. By telling the greatest lie, I've convinced you that I actually care about any of you. This is how I was able to take your girlfriend and child, and now they will serve as the subjects for what you can consider is a hypothesis I'm testing. You see, what I learned about liars is it's hard to serve only yourself when you choose to associate yourself with other self-servers ... which is basically what everyone on this planet does. Now if everyone who was being deceptive would just stop being dishonest about their dishonesty, then perhaps your people wouldn't have the inordinate amount of problems that continue to plague them. It's only because your species is incapable of being open about their duplicity, that your self-serving world continues to burn slow like the wood on an open campfire—that which appears to aid those in need but ultimately only serves to sustain its own glow.

For a while, I begun to think that my purpose here was to learn the ways of man and maybe through them, learn and ultimately create a new way on how to prevent anymore discord amongst them. I truly believed this. But your kind is one that isn't meant to be united. Not by peaceful means, anyway. Even without suffering at the hands of them, all I had to do was take a look at your history, and there it was. And it isn't all of you, there are exceptions. And each single exception who tried to embrace change by eliminating selfishness, was killed by a self-server. I learned that the change that's needed to save you, is one that cannot be created by you. So, it's time I stop lying to myself as if I'm one of you, and start embracing who I really am. I am the Warrior of Prophecy, you were right—but I'm not here to protect you from any invasion...I ***am*** *the invasion. I'm here to protect you from yourselves, but to do that I have to take the power back from those who consider themselves the rulers of man—starting with you. Your family will serve as the first example of the approach necessary to begin the inception of true change and it will continue until I rid this entire planet of every single entity that considers themselves a ruling power, where then I will lead all solely under one—myself. It's funny, all the skill you taught me to help protect your family will now serve as the method I use to kill them. The invasion has begun.*

- *Mobile Statue*

May 1st. 12:00 A.M. (EDT)

Utter despair replaces the oxygen in the apartment. Nerosion can't seem to breathe, so he takes his mask off. The only other thing that seems to have been replaced in the apartment is the silence that is substituted by the loud cocking of multiple machine guns that now echo directly behind Nerosion's ears. There isn't a single space left inside of his bathroom that doesn't have an FBI agent pointing a machine gun at his skull.

Nerosion looks up at the mirror in front of him, mask-less, and sees for the first time the face of the monster known as the Tyrant.

End Of Volume One

AFTERWORD

Names of Characters: (in order of appearance/mention)

Surii: (SU – REE)

Seren: (Sear -- RIN)

Serota: (SA – ROE – TA)

Jumopikwaris: (JUME – O – PEE – KWAR – ES)

Olpha: (OHL – FA)

Laharin: (La – HEAR – EN)

Boluscant: (BOE – LU –SKANT)

Nerosion: (NUR -- ROE'ZHEN)

Kayelimneusia: (KAY – EL – LA – MEH – NEW – SHA)

Minutia: (MEH – NEW – SHA)

Leander: (LEE - AN - DUR)

Author's note: *The alien beasts the world has to come to know as the 'UNSELF's creatures', are soon given the name 'Unself.' They are named by none other than their creator Jumopikwaris, after he learns that people have come to know him by his earthly designation. No longer interested in being referred to as the UNSELF, he decides to call his creatures that name instead. This, and many other significant events that explain many of the characters' backstories, occurs in the Extended Edition of Tactile Therapy Volume One, set to release very soon in the near future.

ABOUT THE AUTHOR

Born in the heart of New York City—Harlem, Durell Arrington has spent the second half of his lifetime exploring the visual arts through a multitude of mediums. From Illustrating to Acting, each of these avenues always seem to have brought him back to a place of writing. It wasn't until fifteen years after he first conceptualized *Tactile Therapy,* that he realized the expansive story could best be told through a series of novels. Today, he continues to develop and expand the *Tactile Therapy* series while juggling life as an educator for inner-city youth in the Bronx.

Find Tactile Therapy on Facebook
Follow Tactile Therapy on Instagram

79723330R00235

Made in the USA
Lexington, KY
26 January 2018